ABOVE

ALL

THINGS

ABOVE
ALL
THINGS

———————

Tanis Rideout

AMY EINHORN BOOKS
Published by G. P. Putnam's Sons
a member of Penguin Group (USA) Inc.
New York

æ

AMY EINHORN BOOKS
Published by G. P. Putnam's Sons
Publishers Since 1838
Published by the Penguin Group
Penguin Group (USA) Inc., 375 Hudson Street, New York, New York 10014, USA •
Penguin Group (Canada), 90 Eglinton Avenue East, Suite 700, Toronto, Ontario M4P 2Y3, Canada
(a division of Pearson Penguin Canada Inc.) • Penguin Books Ltd, 80 Strand, London WC2R 0RL,
England • Penguin Ireland, 25 St Stephen's Green, Dublin 2, Ireland (a division of Penguin Books
Ltd) • Penguin Group (Australia), 707 Collins Street, Melbourne, Victoria 3008, Australia
(a division of Pearson Australia Group Pty Ltd) • Penguin Books India Pvt Ltd, 11 Community
Centre, Panchsheel Park, New Delhi–110 017, India • Penguin Group (NZ), 67 Apollo Drive,
Rosedale, Auckland 0632, New Zealand (a division of Pearson New Zealand Ltd) • Penguin Books, (South Africa),
Rosebank Office Park, 181 Jan Smuts Avenue, Parktown North 2193, South Africa • Penguin China, B7 Jiaming
Center, 27 East Third Ring Road North, Chaoyang District, Beijing 100020, China

Penguin Books Ltd, Registered Offices: 80 Strand, London WC2R 0RL, England

Copyright © 2012 by Tanis Rideout
Previously published in Canada by Emblem Editions, McClelland & Stewart, June 2012
First American edition published by Amy Einhorn Books/G. P. Putnam's Sons 2013

Library of Congress Cataloging-in-Publication Data

Rideout, Tanis.
Above all things / Tanis Rideout.
p.   cm.
ISBN 978-0-399-16058-5
1. Mallory, George, 1886–1924—Fiction.   2. Mount Everest Expedition (1924)—Fiction.
3. Mountaineers—Fiction.   4. Marriage—England—Fiction.   5. Everest, Mount
(China and Nepal)—Fiction.   I. Title.
PR9199.4.R5373A65   2013   2012028012
813'.6—dc23

Printed in the United States of America
1   3   5   7   9   10   8   6   4   2

Book design by Meighan Cavanaugh

While the author has made every effort to provide accurate telephone numbers, Internet addresses, and
other contact information at the time of publication, neither the publisher nor the author assumes any
responsibility for errors, or for changes that occur after publication. Further, the publisher does not have
any control over and does not assume any responsibility for author or third-party websites or their content.

For Simon,

who knows there will always be mountains

There have been joys too great to be described in words, and there have been griefs upon which I have not dared to dwell; and with these in mind I say, Climb if you will, but remember that courage and strength are nought without prudence, and that a momentary negligence may destroy the happiness of a lifetime. Do nothing in haste; look well with each step; and from the beginning think what may be the end.

—EDWARD WHYMPER

Upward I looked, and beheld its shoulders,
Vested already with that planet's rays
Which leadeth others right by every road.

Then was my fear a little quieted.

—DANTE, *The Inferno*, CANTO I

ABOVE

ALL

THINGS

1920

Tell me the story of Everest," she said, a fervent smile sweeping across her face, creasing the corners of her eyes. "Tell me about this mountain that's stealing you away from me."

George and Ruth sat on the drawing room floor, laughing and tipsy, dinner growing cold on the table in the next room. Ruth was cross-legged opposite him, her gray skirt pulled tight across her knees. She picked up the single sheet of thick ivory paper from her lap and reread the invitation from the newly formed Mount Everest Committee again. "My husband, the world-famous explorer." Ruth held up her glass of wine and he reached out with his own, the crystal ringing in the lamplit room. She was fairly bursting with happiness.

"I like the sound of that," George said, and let himself imagine what it would be like to have people thinking about him, talking about him. The opportunities that success on Everest would bring. "I might be able to leave teaching, maybe even write full time. We could travel," he said. "Have our own adventures."

Handing him the invitation, Ruth rose unsteadily to her feet and gulped at her wine. He scanned the words again—*hope that you'll join the Everest reconnaissance, pursuit of the final Pole, for the honour of King and Country*—as she crossed the room to the bookcase. Stretching up on her bare feet, she reached for the atlas on the top shelf before turning to pad back to him. "Show me," she said, sitting back down beside him. Her hair had come loose from where it had been pinned up and haloed her in the dim light. She pushed it off her brow with the back of her hand.

He laid out *The Times Atlas of the World* on the floor, on the blue Turkish rug with its woven colors of water and sky, ice and snow. When he found the proper map, George took Ruth's hand and with her finger drew a line around Europe, the path of a ship past France, around capes and narrow islands and the ruins of the Greeks. Through the canal that split the desert in two and past the land of Lawrence's Arabs. Their hands described reckless adventure, sailing over longitudes and latitudes, past *Here there be monsters* and the arched backs of sea serpents painted on the blue of the Indian Ocean, and into the port of Bombay. George drew lines across the plains of India, around bazaars and villages, landscapes of tea and Hindu cows, into the curved spine of the Himalaya with its foothills and plateaus.

"It's blank," Ruth exclaimed when their hands reached the spot where Everest should be; there was only a series of names—no relief, no lines of ridges or elevations. Just words floating in an empty space, waiting to be claimed by him.

"No one has mapped her yet. That's what we're going to do, Ruth—reconnoiter her, bring back the shape of her." He stroked his fingers across the map, as if he could explore the range through the pages, feeling for the relief of peaks. "These are the highest mountains on earth." There was an awe in his voice that he wanted her to share. He recited names and caressed the page before moving from the map to navigate her skin beneath the folds of her skirt. "West to east—imagine them. Cho Uyo, Gyanchungkang, Everest, Makalu, Kangchenjunga." They were like spices on his tongue, on hers, tingling.

In a cloud of lavender soap and cloves for the toothache she had complained of earlier, Ruth pressed against him, promised curries for dinner. "You'll have to write me about everything. Every detail so it will be almost like I am with you." There was a thread unraveling at her collar, marking a line on her pale throat.

"You *will* be with me," he said. "Every step of the way."

"Everest," she said, "sounds like a foreigner."

He took her hands again and traced the lines of her palms, like horizons. "She was named for George Everest. He was the surveyor general of India, but he died before he ever saw her. From malaria, after blindness, paralysis, and wild bouts of insanity. He was a bully apparently—drove his men mad. He set out to force some order on the world with his maps. He started at the bottom and swept his survey up the whole arc of India."

He whispered words like "trigonometrical" and "triangulation" against her throat, at the pulse below her ear. With the back of his fingers he skimmed the long declension of her throat, traced the line of her collarbone where it slipped beneath her blouse.

"Everest was measured from a horizon away." He traced the curvature of the earth along the concave of her stomach. Pushed her back onto the blue carpet, unearthed her.

"They crept from hill to hill, building towers and measuring the angle of peaks on the horizon. A fraction of a degree could make all the difference." He pressed on top of her, tilted her hips, and pulled her to him.

The atlas ripped under her, the paper stuck to her wet skin.

After a few minutes, Ruth rolled onto her side, curved her body around his, and tucked her head under his chin. She could smell herself on him.

"There were three problems with the measurements. Corrections to be made, all by mathematics. The curvature of the earth, the refraction of the light through the thinner air and colder temperatures. And the weight of the mountain."

The air was cooling now on her naked skin. After a moment, Ruth began to shiver despite still being slick with sweat. She pulled herself up, sat facing him, hugged her knees to her chest. She couldn't believe how happy she felt, how proud, that George had been chosen. The scent of him rose off her skin. "The weight of the mountain?" she asked.

The light was thinning in the room, etching the two of them in dusk-blue lines. George stood, strode to the window, and gazed out toward the towers of Charterhouse while Ruth shrugged into the jacket he had thrown aside. He shut the window tight and came back, kneeled in front of her. He tugged at the lapels of his jacket, drawing it tight around her shoulders.

"It's so massive it affects the gravity around it. They used theodolites to survey her, but the pull of the mountain threw the measurements off. Can you imagine anything so powerful, Ruth? This mountain has a presence. Everest knew it when he planned to measure her—and he didn't even go near her, never even saw her." Closing her eyes, Ruth leaned against his shoulder and pictured the jagged skyline of the mountain.

"Twenty-nine thousand feet." A whispered invocation. A prayer.

She imagined his letters arriving from the Himalaya, herself curled up by the fire to read them. She thought about his returning home to her, victorious. Her face split into another smile, her cheeks aching from it. She couldn't help it. The happiness she felt for him swept through her. She tried not to think that being apart only seemed romantic when you were together.

"How do they know?" she asked. "How do they know how tall it is if no one's been there?"

He reached out again and Ruth stretched out her hand to meet his. She would take his hand, pull him to his feet, lead him up the stairs to their bedroom. But he brushed past her to touch the waiting emptiness of the map.

A little while longer, then, she thought. She would wait while he planned for and dreamed about the mountain, the future. "How do they know?" she asked again. "Maybe it isn't even the tallest."

"It has to be," he said, his fingers lingering on the map. "It has to be."

THE VOYAGE OUT

Sea Level

1924

He still remembered the first time he saw her. He felt the pull of her, even then.

In 1921 the members of the expedition had planned the sighting, knew roughly where they would get their first glimpse of her. But when the group arrived at the predetermined Himalayan pass, they saw nothing but banks of clouds pierced by the nearer ridges. Still, they set up camp and over the course of the afternoon and evening Everest slowly unveiled herself. They watched her stripping away clouds and light.

"There!" someone had called out when the summit finally appeared—a great fang thrust into the expanse of sky. She towered head and shoulders over all the other peaks nearby.

They camped at the apex of the pass overnight and watched her reappear in the morning, noting the play of light and weather on her. The way the clouds rushed up to veil her again in the afternoon. They had already come closer than anyone else had ever been.

The first time, George thought, he'd been successful before he even left.

By the time he returned to England from the second Everest expedition a year later, success was impossible to claim. *The Times* was already blaming him for the disaster that had put an abrupt end to the 1922 attempt. It wasn't fair, but for good or ill it was his name that had become synonymous with Everest.

When he met Ruth in Paris on his return, he was certain he was done with the mountain. In the hotel room, he swore to her he would never go back: "I promise I'm done with it. I don't need it. I need to be with you." He believed it at the time. Continued to believe it the next year, even after Arthur Hinks, the chairman of the Mount Everest Committee, asked him to consider returning a third time, in 1924, even as other names were put forward and a team began to form without him.

He tried to push Everest out of his mind, but it remained—his first thought on waking, his last at night. She was there as he read the newspaper articles about who from the previous expedition was returning for the new attempt: Colonel Edward "Teddy" Norton, Dr. Howard Somervell. As he imagined that they might summit his mountain.

Then one day Ruth said, "You're thinking of going back." It wasn't a question. She looked past him to the rain-pocked window. He could hear the spatter of water against the glass, the gush in the downspouts. He should have denied it—he shouldn't have said anything—but it was too late for that.

"Perhaps we should at least think about it. They need my experience. No one has been to Everest more often than I have. If they succeed this time and I'm not with them . . . Do you remember everything we dreamed about when they first asked me?"

"Teddy's been to the mountain," Ruth countered. "And Dr. Somervell too. You only have one more season than them, George. They're not your responsibility. You have responsibilities here. There's your new teaching position at Cambridge. And I don't think the children could bear for you to go away again."

He tried not to remember how John had shied away from him when he came home in '22. But John had been only a baby then. Now he'd had time with his father, knew him. This time would be different.

"You said you were done with it. You promised." Her voice sounded tight. She breathed in deeply. "I know you, George. What you want is for me to give you leave to go."

"No," he started to protest, but she was right. They both knew it.

Eventually, Ruth agreed they should think about it, and he promised they'd make the decision together. But when Hinks's final invitation came, George accepted without discussing it with her. He couldn't help himself. For days after, he waited for the right moment to tell her what he'd done.

He returned from a meeting at the college determined to tell her. She was in the dining room—a perfect silhouette in the evening gloom, her features outlined by the dusk glow of the window behind her. Stepping into the room, he wanted to kiss her, to scoop her up, but something about how still she was, the sad line of her mouth, stopped him.

"I knew you'd never let anyone else climb it," she said, not even looking at him. Her backlit profile was a cameo he wanted to carry with him. "As soon as the Committee decided they were going back, I knew you'd be going, despite all the protestations, all the promises. You should have just told me."

She was right. He hadn't meant her to find out this way. The telegram on the table in front of her was luminescent on the dark wood. He knew what it must say—*Glad to have you aboard again.* Damn Hinks.

"I'm sorry, Ruth," he said. "But I have to do this. I have to. It's my mountain. You have to understand." She shook her head as if to say she didn't, she wouldn't. "This will be the last time. It has to be."

"You've said that before, George. And I believed you. I'm not sure I can this time."

"Ruth—"

"Don't." She stood, and the movement sent the telegram wafting to the floor. When he looked up from where it had landed, she was staring at him, her eyes shrouded by the dim light. Her hands fluttered near her mouth, her throat. "You'll have to find a way to tell the children. Clare will be so disappointed," she said as she stepped around him, moving toward the door. *Disappointed.* The word stung. He knew that's what she felt more than anything. Disappointed, betrayed. He winced, tried to banish the word from his mind.

"When do you leave?" She stood in the doorway, her back to him.

"Ruth, you'll see. It will all be all right. I'll do it this time and then I'll never have to leave again."

"When do you leave?" she asked again.

The months that followed were difficult. Ruth was quiet, withdrawn, her words always politely supportive. He found himself missing her before he'd even left.

The night before his departure, they made love in the unfamiliar hotel room and she clung to him desperately, like the wind on the mountain, bucking against him until he was gasping, drained. They were both different when he was leaving; the imminent separation had changed them, made them bolder.

The next morning, on board the SS *California,* she kissed him good-bye, nodded emphatically, and then turned to walk down the gangplank, her hips switching under her long skirt. God. How could she not believe him when he said she was beautiful? She'd shake her head and cover her mouth with her hands—even more beautiful for her denial. There was the hot prick of tears in his eyes, a dull ache in his throat. He swallowed and watched her go. He counted in his head. It would be six months, maybe more, before he saw her again.

That was weeks ago. Now, standing on the deck of the *California*, George cast his gaze back across the Indian Ocean to where he imagined the horizon must be, where it had disappeared when the sun set an hour before. There was no way to make things right between them except to do what he'd been promising Ruth for years: succeed and put Everest behind him once and for all. He had tried to explain again, in the letter he'd started earlier, just why he had to go—how it had nothing to do with his love for her—but the right words never ended up on the page. *My Dearest Ruth, I know this has been hard for you, but you must know how very much you mean to me, how much knowing you are waiting for my success and return drives me forward so that every day farther away is also a day closer to my returning to you again.*

The ship rolled slightly under him, raising a chorus of metallic clangs and creaks from nearby lifeboats and chains. Ignoring the clamor, he pulled out his diary from the pocket of his dinner jacket. The bold dates at the tops of the pages were barely visible in the gathering darkness. He leaned farther over the railing to catch some of the light reflecting off the water. He counted down the days. Two more nights. Then the Indian subcontinent, the baked heat of it, the blaze of exotic chaos before they disappeared off the map. He wanted it to burn the salt, the smell of fish and algae, from his nostrils. The ocean air was too thick and heavy. It clung to him, clogged up his lungs.

"Am I interrupting?"

George glanced up. "Not at all," he said as Sandy Irvine stepped to the railing beside him. George closed up his diary, trying to remember what he had written about Sandy in his letter to Ruth. Probably some remark about the boy's bulk, the sheer size of him. *Our attempt at a superman,* he remembered. He slipped the diary back into his pocket, removed his cigarettes, and offered one to Sandy, who shook his head and leaned forward against the rail. Behind them, the dining room was ablaze with light as waiters cleared tables and joked with one another, louder than when there were diners present.

"Missed you at the shuffleboard contest this afternoon," Sandy said.

"Not really my game."

"I won."

Of course you did, George thought as Sandy described the closeness of the match. He suspected physical challenges came easily to the boy. Sandy was the largest member of the entire team—not the tallest, but he seemed stronger than any of the other climbers.

"Sandy's the Committee's attempt to inject some young blood into the expedition," Teddy Norton, the expedition leader, had explained months ago when George questioned the boy's inclusion. "To balance out our, shall we say, *experience.*" Teddy had raised an eyebrow as he said the word.

"They think brute strength is the way to go, then?" George had responded. "You and I both know it takes more than muscle to get to the summit. And he doesn't look like much of a climber. He's too big. With too much weight to carry up an incline."

"You imagined someone more like you, I suspect," Teddy had teased.

But the best climbers *were* built like him. And Teddy, George thought. Long and thin, with a good reach.

Now, next to Sandy on the deck, George pulled himself up to his full height and ran a hand through his hair, stretched out the muscles in his back. Still, if the boy could continue to sharpen his skills, he might be of some use higher up on the mountain.

"Have you been practicing the knots I showed you?" he asked now.

"I know those knots already."

"You'll want the practice, believe me. When your fingers are frozen and your brain is fizzing away and suffocating, you'll pray your body remembers what it needs to all on its own. Practice."

"I have climbed before. In Spitsbergen with Odell. I wasn't bad at it. Quite good, even."

Of course he was. "Sandy, this won't be like anything you've ever done before. God, we could all die a dozen times before we even get to the mountain—malaria, wild animals, a fall down a cliff face. And then there's the mountain itself." He sounded as if he were back in front of the classroom at Charterhouse, the bored faces of his students glaring up at him.

He inhaled and tried again. "There's just no way to know how you'll respond. Not at those altitudes. Twenty-nine thousand feet. That's much higher than even the Camels fly. And those pilots, they'd pass out without their oxygen masks. My brother, Trafford, was a pilot. He loved flying. But he told me he thought he was going to die the first few times he went up. From the vertigo and nausea.

That's what it's like on Everest all the time. Like the most terrible influenza you've ever had. Like something horrible is sitting on your chest, ripping at it. Everything just hurts. Your joints, your bones, your skin, even. And the only way to end it is to climb the bloody mountain."

"So." Sandy turned to stare at him dead in the eye. His were striking, a flat blue color. Almost too pale, like light reflecting off stagnant water. "Tell me again why we're going." He reached over and punched George lightly in the shoulder, more a push than a punch. Then he smiled and his face opened with it and his eyes weren't flat anymore; they deepened, the color shifting. "Just joking," he said. "I wouldn't be anywhere else." He turned back to the expanse of water before them.

Behind them, through the open window of the captain's salon, George could hear the clink of glasses, the laughter and chatter of their other teammates—the expedition leader, Teddy Norton, along with the team doctor, Howard Somervell, and the naturalist Noel Odell. The three of them, along with George and Sandy, would make up the climbing team. There were two more men awaiting them in Bombay: Edward Shebbeare and John de Vere Hazard, soldiers attached to the local Gurkha regiments who knew the Tibetan languages and customs (more so even than Teddy) and would serve as their translators and guides.

Every so often, the pop and flash of John Noel's camera strobed across the deck, punctuating the distant murmur of conversation. George couldn't make out any of the words but he could imagine easily enough what was being said. He was already tired of the same old conversations—provisions, oxygen, strategy. And Teddy's waffling. Somervell's condescension. Odell's insistence that he knew what was best.

"Look at that," Sandy said, pointing to the black water roiling in the wake. A green phosphorescence bloomed just beneath the surface of the water where the *California* had passed.

"It's algae," George said, watching the glowing trail stretch out behind the ship.

"Incredible." Sandy's voice, hushed now, slipped in with the murmur of the engines deep inside the ship. "Odell told me about this green glow once, on the way to Spitsbergen. We went out on deck every night, but I never saw anything. So strange. Reminds me of the Northern Lights we saw once we arrived in Greenland."

"Mmmm." George leaned over the railing to get a closer look. Cool air rose up from the ocean eighty feet below. He'd never seen the Northern Lights, but this color was too heavy, too viscous, to be thought of as light. It reminded him of the seeping gases in the trenches, in the shell holes of no-man's-land. It moved the same way, wet and congealing as it rolled and gathered in pockets, thicker, heavier than the medium it traveled in. He remembered how the gas crept toward you, as if it knew where you were. Stalked you. His throat tightened; he could smell the rubber of the gas masks. George straightened up and inhaled deeply into his lungs: salt, oil, the tobacco burning in his hand.

He shook his head free of the memory and took another drag from his cigarette. Sandy would be too young to remember much of the war. "How old did you say you were, Sandy?"

Sandy bristled next to him. "Twenty-one. I know what you're thinking, but I'm ready for this. Maybe, as you've said, Everest is different, but Spitsbergen wasn't easy. God, the cold there. The snow would melt inside our boots, down our collars, so it was impossible to stay dry. It was the hardest thing I've ever done. But it was incredible—to feel like what I was doing mattered, that people were counting on it. Like this does. Don't you feel that too? We have to succeed. We have to. Everyone's counting on us."

There was a sharp laugh from down the deck. A woman, her laugh too forced. Clearly her companion wasn't the least bit funny, though she wanted him to think he was. George flicked his cigarette out to sea.

"That's what my mum thinks too," Sandy went on. "That I'm too young. She's worried I'm going to get myself killed. 'Haven't enough boys already died?' she said. I told her I'd be fine. But she stopped speaking to me before I left. She hugged me good-bye but wouldn't say anything to me." Sandy grasped at the railing, then shoved himself away, as if willing the ship to hurry up. As if he could will the outcome of the expedition from there. "But when we succeed," Sandy continued, "when we climb Everest, then she'll understand why it had to be done."

George glanced over at Sandy. The boy really believed they couldn't fail.

"They grow out of it," George said. "Mothers." He stuffed his hands in his pockets. "Mine doesn't worry much anymore. 'But I do wonder about you,' she says, and I like the idea of her wondering." His father, though. He would have preferred Sandy's mother's silence to his own father's overloud opinions.

The two men grew quiet as a couple leaning close together, voices low and intimate, passed by them. Sandy watched after them and didn't speak again until the sound of their footsteps had faded. "I suppose one gets used to it eventually. Being so far away?"

How to answer that? Clearly Sandy was looking for some kind of reassurance, but George wasn't sure he could give it. "No, you don't," he said finally. "Or at least I never have." Even now he felt torn. Part of him hated being separated from Ruth and the children. And another part hated himself for being so damn sentimental. It was weak. Still, there was the luxury of freedom this far from home. He felt different away from Ruth, away from everyday life, and he was never quite sure which person he was, which he wanted to be.

Somewhere down the deck a door opened and closed, releasing strains of music. Beside him, Sandy picked up the tune, humming a moment before trailing off, as if he hadn't noticed he was doing it.

Ruth did that, hummed fragments of songs or tunes she made up without realizing. She laughed when he pointed it out to her. "I wasn't humming," she'd tease. "You're hearing things." Dear God, but he missed her.

"Still, I'm glad to be here." Sandy seemed to rush his words, as if his concern over his family might have been misunderstood. "I mean, I'm glad you picked me for the expedition."

"It wasn't really my decision," he said, and felt Sandy retreat somewhat beside him. He hadn't meant it like that. "Odell's a good man. Proved himself before on big mountains, and he's a first-rate naturalist too. He's brought home at least a dozen new species of plants. This time it seems he's hoping for fossils. His recommendation would have been taken very seriously. Obviously it was." He went on. "Odell wants to prove that Everest was once at the bottom of the ocean. Imagine that." George stared out over the rolling water moving away and away. Tried to imagine the depth of it. As deep as Everest was high. "Ridiculous, really."

"What does it matter?"

"Exactly."

"All that matters is that it's there."

He looked sidelong at Sandy, who smiled, teasing him with his own flippant quotation. "I haven't heard that one before," George said.

"Couldn't resist." Sandy stared up at the night sky, the shapes of foreign constellations. The damp air settled on him, and the faintest dusting of salt water coated his lapels. Backlit by the night sky, Sandy made a handsome shadow. A fresh burst of talk came from behind them, followed by staccato laughter. It sounded like Somervell. Sandy turned toward the sound now. "Shall we rejoin them?"

"You go ahead. I have some letters I'd like to get written. Besides, it'll just be the same old conversations."

"If you're sure." Before he moved away, Sandy peered over the railing again. "It's gone." There was disappointment in his voice.

For a moment, George wasn't sure what Sandy meant, then he noticed a fresh darkness in the water, deeper than it had been a few minutes ago. The algae had disappeared, the green behind them had faded away; all that was left was the black boil of the ocean.

"I'll let you know what you missed." Sandy paused a moment, as if expecting something, before walking toward the salon.

George knew that Sandy had been watching him, measuring him. What did he see? An old man? Thirty-seven wasn't so old. He was strong, in good shape. *A perfect specimen for the expedition,* his medical report had read. Sure, the others were fit. They had to be. None of them were slouches. Though Odell was much too weedy. There wasn't much there for the mountain to rip off him. But Sandy . . . Sandy looked stronger than any of them.

George turned back to face the ocean and watched the waves, peak after peak, as far as he could see.

✦   ✦   ✦

THE PORT AT BOMBAY was overwhelming. George had tried to describe the chaos of it to him, but still it was more than Sandy could have expected.

It didn't help that he'd slept only fitfully as they waited for land-fall. Between his nerves and the wash of sounds that came from the city, he'd woken up again and again. *It's almost like Christmas morning,* he'd written to Marjory in the middle of the night, using his torch, until Odell in the bunk below had thudded on the underside of Sandy's bed and muttered at him to go the hell to sleep.

When dawn finally arrived, it was a relief. Now Sandy stood on the deck, stunned to silence by the port. After the long days at sea, even the air was different, no longer scoured clean by ocean winds. Here the air was thick in his nose and lungs. He could taste it: diesel and something frying, rotten fish and the stinking detritus of the harbor. From high above he watched the scurry and swirl of men in white suits and kurtas, their heads covered in reddish turbans or tan pith helmets. Scattered among them were women in jewel-colored saris—greens and pinks no Englishwoman would wear. A sea of people all blurred by the heat.

A thump on his back pulled him back from his thoughts. "You should probably be about something," George said as he strode down the gangplank into the commotion below. He was right, but Sandy couldn't tear himself away. Even if he returned to Bombay over and over, the way George had, he knew he would never see it like this first time ever again. Ahead of him was the great Gateway of India, and behind that the Taj Mahal Palace Hotel with its min-arets and turrets. That's where they were staying. Just for the one night. One last glimpse of luxury, Odell had said, before they pushed out across the countryside and through the provinces, sleeping in train cars and tents.

As Sandy made his way down into the crowd, he spotted Odell bent over a large crate, wiping at the sweat on his brow and swatting away a skinny child who had approached him, hands out. He couldn't bring himself to ask Odell for an assignment. True, he wouldn't be here without Odell's recommendation, but he didn't want to always be associated with the naturalist. And he didn't need taking care of. If he stood a chance at the summit, it wouldn't be with Odell. George would never pair them together—they were the wrong combination of strength and experience. Or lack thereof.

Colonel Norton was coming down the gangway with the purser. *I like Norton,* Sandy had written to Marjory the previous night. *Teddy, as the others call him. He's the expedition leader. He's been in the military all his life—spent more time abroad than in England. Apparently he hosts a mean pig-sticking competition out here in the colonies. Though he seems too civilized—too neat—for something that barbaric. Norton seems calm in a way that George (who's the climbing leader) doesn't. George is always moving, fidgeting, even when he's just sitting at his desk. He's forever picking things up, putting them down. Norton, though, moves more slowly, talks more slowly. He says something once and he says it right.*

Sandy made to intercept Norton, dodging around a group of small Indian men, but he was stopped by a petite figure stepping in front of him. "You'd best keep an eye on anyone getting too close," Norton had warned before they disembarked. "Especially the children. They'll beg with one hand and slip the other into your pocket." Sandy stuffed his own hands into his pockets and stepped aside, shaking his head, trying to remember the Hindi word for no. But the figure continued to block him, and when he looked down he was surprised to find instead of a child a young woman. She was tiny, strangely so, as if cast in miniature, and dressed in white, her head draped with cloth. He wondered if she was a distraction, if someone else might try to pick his pocket now, but she appeared to be alone. She smelled sweet—not of perfume, but of some scent he didn't recognize. She waved him down and he bent toward her, inhaling

her deeply. She reached up and touched the spot betwee
brows but didn't meet his eye. Instead she looked at hi
angle of bone below his ear. She pressed yellowed palms together
and bowed to him.

He bowed back, still towering over her. She held out her hands.
He dug in his pockets now for coins, but all he had was English
money. He pressed a shilling into her hand and the yellow came off
like pollen on his fingers. She smiled up at him and bowed again
before she moved off to stop another disembarking passenger, who
waved her away. Sandy's fingers found the spot where she had touched
him. Amazing. It was all amazing.

"Sandy?" Odell was waving to him from where he struggled with
a few of the larger crates. Beside him were Shebbeare and Hazard,
neat in their tropical khakis. The last two members of the expedition had met the *California* when she docked and come on board
armed with customs documents and contracts, details of what train
they were to board and when. "Give us a hand?"

Sandy leaned over the crate and with a grunt he and Hazard
hoisted it onto the truck. "We'll take care of this," Sandy told Odell
as he and Shebbeare bent for the next one.

"Just think," Shebbeare said smiling, "not long now and we'll be
carrying these up a mountain."

Sandy was breathing hard and sweating as he turned the corner to
sprint the last quarter-mile to the hotel. Each step jolted his knees,
his shins. It wasn't a long run, but he did try to go all out, even
against the stitch in his side, the shortness of breath. "Push yourself
like you're rowing your last eight," Somervell had told him. "Come
back good and spent."

Even with the stiffness in his legs, he felt strong as he ran through the lobby and toward the lush courtyard where Somervell was waiting for him. And it did feel good to exert himself, to feel his body respond. The four weeks spent on the ship, even using the gymnasium and running the decks, had left him sluggish. That melted away now as his muscles burned back to life.

He pulled up as he reached Somervell, who put down his pipe and newspaper and picked up his stethoscope. Sandy bent at the waist; his lungs heaved and sweat dripped from him onto the marble floor. The air was filled with the scent of the woman who had blessed him earlier, but now the smell was coming from him. He licked at the salt on his lips.

"You really didn't need to overdo it." Somervell checked his watch as he pressed the stethoscope against Sandy's chest.

"You said. Run. Like it was. My last. Eight."

"All right, well, stand up straight. Breathe normally. I need a base reading. Sea level. Low stress."

Pressing against the stitch under his ribs, Sandy stood upright and tried to steady his breath, his pulse. Somervell listened and measured. Most of the tables in the courtyard were empty except for a few men who sat drinking from highball glasses, ice cubes tinkling. Bright flowers overflowed from pots on the walls, releasing their evening perfume into the air. He'd never stayed in any place this luxurious, even with Marjory, who liked to splash out and meet him in fancy hotels in London.

"Enjoy it now," George had told him when they'd registered. "It's all downhill from here."

"Isn't it uphill?" he responded, and smiled at his own joke. George had just nodded.

His pulse was dropping quickly. That was good. He'd known

these tests were coming. "We want to see what happens to the body at altitude," Somervell had explained one afternoon on board the *California*. "We'll test all the way there, all the way back, track the changes. Physical, mental, emotional. All of us."

"Looks good," Somervell said now as he pulled the stethoscope away from his ears and jotted something in a notebook. "Good resting rate, good under duress. Mind you, I'd be surprised to see anything different. Keep it up. But now to the real stuff—mental acuity." Somervell pulled a sheet of paper from a leather portfolio on the table and handed it to him. "You've got three minutes." Somervell hit his stopwatch, sat down, and picked up his newspaper and drink again.

The problems weren't difficult. Sandy finished them easily, even with the distracting sound of ice clinking in Somervell's glass and a bird flitting about somewhere, unseen, in the courtyard. "You'll have to make them tougher, Somes," he joked, handing the sheet back to Somervell.

"You say that now." Somervell didn't look at the answers but set the sheet aside. "And now? The Bible passage I asked you to learn?"

Sandy recited the passage without fumbling once.

"Right. Thank you, Mr. Irvine." Somes nodded formally. "That concludes our first round of testing. Congratulations."

"And? How did I do?"

"It looks like you did just fine. Of course, I'll have a better idea when I collate all of this data, but you've nothing to worry about. As a doctor, I'd say you're fit for service."

"Well, not to be too boastful, but I did just come off a good rowing season. And Spitsbergen was a good test."

"I've no doubt it was. You're a solid specimen."

"But how'd I do compared to, say, George?"

"Ah. Sorry, Sandy. Doctor-patient confidentiality. Besides, even we old men are in pretty good shape here. But . . ."

"Yes?"

"Well, your working pulse rate is the lowest. That's a good sign, I think. Still, it's damn near impossible to tell how any individual will respond at altitude. Fitness doesn't seem to have much to do with success up there." Somervell handed him another sheet of paper, another Bible passage. "Learn this one. I'll test you again when we get to Darjeeling."

Later, in his room, damp from the cool bath, the humid air, Sandy sat at the desk and took a break from his letter to Marjory to gaze out over the city. The air was heady with the heavy smell of the city, spiced with strange foods and night-blooming flowers. There was music coming from somewhere down on the docks, a clanging riot that he couldn't find the rhythm in. For a moment he imagined Marjory had come with him, pictured her naked on the linen bedcover, her eyes closed so her other senses could take over. He almost wished she could have come, just to see her lying there, her skin freckled from the sun, the coverlet damp with her sweat.

She'd joined him on the ship to Spitsbergen, paid her own fare, had her own cabin that he'd sneak into at night. "I want to see you off," she'd said when he was packing for Spitsbergen. "Properly." She was so happy and proud of him. "You're not like my husband at all," she said, lying on top of him, her small breasts solid against him. "He never tries anything. You—you'll try anything." And she gave him that look she had, the small twist of her mouth, the raising of her left eyebrow just a fraction. On anyone else it would look vulgar—or, worse, ridiculous—but it suited her. *She* was the one who would try anything.

It's nice to have a familiar face in Odell. His role on this expedition is different than when I went with him to Spitsbergen. There, he seemed to have more input on leadership. But here, it's George and Norton I need to impress. As the climbing and expedition leaders, they'll decide who gets to take a shot at the prize, who gets left behind. I'm not their first choice, that much is certain, but I do want a shot. I know I could do it. I just need a chance to show them.

All in all, things seem more ambitious too. Spitsbergen was surveying—this is a different end altogether. Conquering. Norton talks constantly about plans, about schedules. George writes things down. I wonder if he writes about me. But my tests are good, Somervell says. And I'm ready. You wouldn't believe this city. Someday we'll come here. You and me. I'll show you this place.

Did he mean that? He wasn't sure. But the words were already written and there was no way to cross them out unless he started again, and he just wanted to be done with the letter and lie in the dark, listening to the city. Already the sounds had shifted—the whine of motorcars had tapered off somewhat and the music of insects and night birds had added a chorus to it. He scanned the words again and stared back out the open window. What could it hurt? She would feel loved and that was important.

The whole thing with Marjory had started out as a lark, but recently she had begun to talk about the future—while he hadn't thought of much beyond her bed. He'd leave it for now and sort it out when he got home. When he got home everything would be different.

Tomorrow we head out for Darjeeling, on the other side of the country, almost a week from here by train. It feels like this is where it all begins. I've been on ships before. But now there is all of India to cross. I hope I'll do you proud.

He didn't sign it with *love*, just his name. He turned off the desk lamp, and then the room was blacker than the world outside. He watched the small skiffs flicker in the harbor and then lay on his bed, drifting to the distant music that echoed across the water.

✦   ✦   ✦

IT HAD BEEN TEN DAYS since they made landfall at Bombay, and now, on the day they were to leave Darjeeling, heading northward through the Mahabharat Range and into Tibet, George woke with a hangover. Hoping to burn off the worst of the headache, he forced himself out into the misty morning to run along the Teesta, the slow, wide river that edged the hamlet and its terraced tea plantations.

His head throbbed with each step, and he gritted his teeth against it. This was how it would feel to work at altitude—this painful and foggy. The muddy riverbank sucked at his feet, and his legs burned as he dragged them free. His body was loose and lazy, but eventually he found his stride, gulping at the clean, wet air. Musty and rich.

The journey here had been a slow drift through the seasons—he could barely remember the damp, February weight of Cambridge, of London. Then they had slipped past the coast of France and into the humid spring of the Mediterranean. Now they were leaving the dry summer blaze of India and would soon enter the high Himalayan winter. There everything would be gray and white, the color stripped from the landscape, tinted only by the rising or setting sun. For the moment he basked in the lush green of the tea plantations. He would miss the first burst of spring green back home. It would be late summer before he returned.

Feeling the familiar twinge in his ankle, George lengthened his stride. His mouth was dry and pasty. If he'd been at home in Cambridge, there would have been a cool glass of water waiting for him when he finished his run. Ruth would leave it at the top of the stoop and it always seemed freshly run, droplets clinging to the inside of the glass. What was Ruth doing right now? He tried to calculate the time difference. She'd likely just be turning in, climbing alone into their bed.

Don't think it cruel, darling, he'd written her before dinner the previous night, *but I think of you most as I climb into bed. I am so used to your presence beside me that its absence is a palpable discomfort that makes sleep feel as far away as you are.*

He needed to finish the letter so he could get it in the post before they left Darjeeling. The letters he'd send from this point on—from remote settlements such as Kyishong or Khamba Dzong, even Everest itself—would take much longer to reach home. *From here our letters will travel more slowly. But they are coming, I promise. Watch for them.* He still wanted to describe for Ruth the tiny toy train they had taken from Rangtong—*like something we'd see at the Brighton Pier*— and the endless bickering with Teddy about plans and oxygen. It was almost impossible to remember every thought and sight he wanted to share. He had written his way to the Himalayan foothills—first across the ocean, then the Indian subcontinent, its cities opening out into yellow plains, turning first to forest, then to lush jungles, and finally to the dark, heavy green of these foothills.

On their arrival in Darjeeling, they'd been welcomed by Richards, the local consul, who had insisted, as the last bastion of the Empire before the great wilds, on sending them off in style. "I don't get much cause for hosting the Empire's celebrities," Richards said. "Not out here. I need to splash out where I can. The locals expect it. They want to be awed by English pomp." And so each time they passed through Darjeeling, either on the way to or from Everest, Richards threw a dinner party in his perfectly manicured English gardens. They always ate and drank to excess. Last night had been no exception.

His legs were warming up now, and the sweat was beginning to spring up along his hairline, down his spine. He could smell the alcohol evaporating off his body. He shouldn't have drunk so much last night. Though he wasn't the only one. They'd all gone a little overboard.

As the meal started, Richards had turned to Teddy, the great length of him stretched out in his chair, and gestured in George's direction. "George Mallory! I can't believe you convinced him to come back, Teddy. I thought I'd seen the last of him."

Teddy laughed. "Did you? Really? I knew George would never let anyone else climb her. He thinks it's his mountain. I always knew he wouldn't abandon us."

George panted into his second mile. The rest of the evening hadn't been so good-natured. As the dinner had ground on and the drinks became stronger, the expedition members had grown louder, more aggressive; the weeks of close contact on the ship and on the train edged their conversation.

"Sandy," Somervell had smirked at one point, "you won't believe it, but last time do you remember, Teddy? Last time George put the film in his camera wrong. What was it, George? A week's worth of shooting that we lost? Poor Noel. I thought he might murder you."

"It wasn't a week. It was one roll of film." Everyone else laughed. The gin had slipped into his brain and fizzled there. He tried to laugh with them but couldn't. "Besides, Noel took enough photos for all of us," George said, glancing over to where the photographer sat with his camera on the table in front of him.

Somervell ignored him and turned to Sandy, Hazard, and Shebbeare—the three novices. "That's why you always have to follow up on George. He's forever losing things, forgetting them. His mind gets ahead of him. He's always a little farther up the mountain than the rest of us."

As usual Teddy, calm as new snow, had interjected, smoothing things over before George even had a chance to respond. "But the man can climb."

Today they would leave their dinner jackets behind, shedding them along with all the other niceties of civilized society for the three-week trek to the Everest base camp. Their dinner jackets would be cleaned and pressed, waiting for their return. With luck, they'd need them for celebratory dinners on the way home. By then the suits would hang loose on their thinned frames. But for now they all appeared healthy, ambitious, strong.

As George rounded a long bend in the river, he slowed, and the churning froth of water spread out in front of him, a dreamscape in the weak, wavering light. Above the surface, mist and smoke clung to the current, dragged along as the river coursed south. His pulse pounded at his temples, heat radiated from his face, but at least his hangover was finally easing away. To hell with Somervell, he thought as he looked across the river and let the air slip out of his lungs.

On the far bank, pale flames flickered through the mist on built-up platforms, the flames stretching out in either direction to where the river bent away in the haze. Some of the platforms burned brightly; others were only smoldering ashes that scattered in the bare breeze. White shapes hovered above a few of the flames. Spirits, it seemed. No. Men. Stained white with the ash. They fanned the fires that were still burning or swept dying embers into the rivers. A keening, ceremonial chanting filled the air.

They were burning bodies.

Bile rose at the back of his throat. He bent and vomited the small contents of his stomach, then spat, and watched the smoke rising, the sputter of flames. Flesh burning, incense, the acrid smell of it thick in his nostrils. It was repulsive, savage. But the ritual was consoling, somehow, too. A release—of the body, the spirit—into the river, the air.

After his brother, Trafford, had been shot down during the war, their father had performed the funeral rites at their church at Mobberley. His father, the reverend at the altar, surrounded by the caskets of the three fallen soldiers and airmen. All of them empty. George knew what happened to bodies in the war, had seen the bloody pulp of them outside the trenches, the white gleam of skulls and bones in the moonlight when they were plowed back up, over and over again, by shelling and rain. Rarely were bodies ever sent home. But the families wanted—needed—something to mourn over. The coffins wouldn't be buried. They'd be used again and again, standing in for the bodies of other dead men.

His father had insisted on eulogizing all of the fallen together.

Fallen. Even the word glossed over the bloodiness and the unfairness of it.

"Trafford deserves his own service," George protested. "It's not right. And not fair to Mum. She deserves to mourn her son properly."

"And the others don't?" his father had shot back.

"That's not what I mean. Of course that's not what I mean. But Trafford—"

"He died the same way those other boys did. For his country. Do you think our loss is any greater than anyone else's?"

"No. It's just—"

His father cut him off. "Don't you see what it means to the Barkers? The Clarkes? To know we share their grief? We're all in this together and this is our sacrifice to make. Mine, your mother's, your sister's, yours." His father sat down, opened his Bible in front of him. "Your brother would have understood that."

"My brother? You won't even say his name. You can't. As long as it's not Trafford, as long as he's unnamed, you can bury him like everyone else. Say it." His father wouldn't look up at him. "Say his name. Please."

"They all died bravely."

"You don't know that. You have no idea what it's like over there. In those trenches, those skies. Your god isn't there."

"Stop it," his father said, "you sound like a whinging child."

"None of them died bravely. Not if bravery means not screaming, or crying, or pissing themselves." Even as he said it he tried not to think of how painful Trafford's death must have been. Tried not to think of him screaming, crying. Tried not to think of the rest of his friends, his students, still in France. Still cold and wet and frightened, waiting for gas attacks and for the whistle of shells, the snipe of bullets. He couldn't think of them while he was home in a warm bed with Ruth, waking up to his baby girl. Safe. Invalided out because of an old climbing injury.

He'd wanted to go back. Had to. He would have settled for Le Havre if he couldn't go all the way back to Armentières. But his blasted ankle was too much trouble, the doctors said. You can help in other ways, they told him. So he'd written pamphlets on how to conserve food, fuel, and electricity, instruction manuals for children on how they could help defeat the Hun. While Jack Sanders, Gilbert Bell, and Rupert Brooke had been killed.

His brother's name was on his lips. In time to the keening, George chanted his brother's name.

His father had never cried for Trafford. He never cried for any of the men he buried, just sat in his rectory and praised God and quietly went on doing His bidding. George hated his father for that, for his calm faith that the war was right and just.

Did his father think Everest was worth dying for? Did he even? Already it had cost them so much. Eleven dead so far. Seven in the avalanche. Others to frostbite and malaria, mountain sickness. Maybe there wasn't any way to measure the value of a life. But wasn't it important to risk something if you believed in the end goal?

The fires burned lower, bluer, devouring the heavy insides, the bones.

This was all there was. Maybe nothing was worth dying for. It was all foolishness, vain quests, and ambitions of glory—for themselves, for King and Country. But if there was nothing worth dying for, neither could there be anything worth living for.

He recited their names. All of his loved ones. He could go on with the losses.

Except for this, his mind was empty. For once there was no thought of success or failure. Or endings.

He watched until the last fire smoldered out.

He recited Everest.

◆　　◆　　◆

HIS PONY WAS a ruddy terror, liable to take off without warning and stop just the same. Sandy kept the reins tight now as he navigated a narrow switchback leading up to the next pass. When the animal veered close to the edge, he squeezed his legs tight against the pony's round stomach. It skittered forward a few steps, jolting him, before Sandy leaned back hard on the reins again, bringing the beast to a stop. He'd been riding the animal for almost three weeks, but every time it stumbled, his bones shuddered.

Already they had come so far. They had crossed rivers by fords or narrow rope bridges made from twisted vines and branches. Moved up and up onto the windswept Tibetan plateau, past settlements sculpted out of rock faces and the terraced balconies of impenetrable fortresses reaching up, their back walls buried deep within the granite of the mountains. Tomorrow they'd cover the last leg, journeying down through the valley, past Rongbuk Monastery—the last human outpost—and then onto the flanks of Everest herself.

Only a week ago, he'd seen her for the first time. He'd known the sighting would be coming soon; they'd talked about it the evening before at Shekar Dzong, where they'd hired their team of high-altitude porters. But he hadn't known what to expect when George had challenged him to race up one of the passes.

"I'll even give you a head start," George had said as they climbed off their mounts. "I'll turn the ponies over to Virgil and then catch you up."

It had taken almost everything Sandy had to beat George, but he'd managed it, reaching the pass in the lead, his lungs aching. If he was this out of breath now, Sandy thought, how would he be once he got on the mountain? Somes was right: the altitude was punishing. But his legs felt strong, fresh. That at least was something.

Still, he didn't let himself rest. Climbing would only become more difficult the higher they went on Everest. Sandy gave himself a test, as Somervell would; if he could carry the largest stone he could lift to the cairn at the apex of the pass without putting it down, then surely he'd do well on the mountain. The cairn was only twenty feet away. Not far. But in a boat race, twenty feet could mean a vast lead. Here it could mean the difference between the summit or not.

He bent down and heaved a stone to his chest. It was heavier than he expected. He stepped toward the cairn. George would be able to do this. Norton too. And they were practically old men. The rock was what, two stone? Stones suddenly made sense to him. The whole world should be measured in stones. At sea level he would have found the task effortless, but up here it had taken him almost five minutes to move the bloody thing. Still, he'd done it. Gasping, he slumped to the base of the cairn and tried to even out his breath.

"Feeling all right?" George was coming up the pass, breathing easily. "George is good at altitude," Somes had told him during the last round of tests. "He's part mountain goat. You'll have to work hard to beat his numbers."

"Yes. Fine." His voice wavered more than Sandy would have liked. He cleared his throat, spat. "Fine," he said again, louder.

"Did you see her?"

"What?"

"Come here." George led him to the far edge of the pass, where the trail sloped back down the other side. "There," he said, with a kind of ownership in his voice. "Just to the left. The highest one. That's it. That's where we're going."

The peak towered over its nearest neighbors. Sandy smiled, his lips cracking where they were dry from the wind and sun. He didn't care. Why should he? He was going to the highest place on earth. "It looks like a brute, even from here," he said.

"It is."

"We'll make it up there. This time. Don't you think?"

He expected George to agree, but instead after a slight pause he said, "My friend Geoffrey taught me to climb, a long time ago." George laughed slightly, incredulous, as though he was counting the years. "He liked to take me out the day before a climb to study the route. He said it helped to see a mountain from a distance; then you might know where you were if something went wrong, if you got stuck."

"Sounds like good advice."

"He's a smart man, Geoffrey. Almost like a father to me." A pause. "Though he'd hate to hear me say that. It would make him feel old."

"He's a good climber then?"

"He was. Probably the best of his generation. If Geoffrey had been able to come to Everest in 'twenty-two, it would have been climbed already. We wouldn't even be standing here."

"Why didn't he?"

"He can't climb anymore. He lost his leg in the war, has a wooden one now. Gets about with a cane."

"I'm sorry."

George was silent a moment, gazing out toward Everest. "He still comes with me to Wales, and we go out the day before a climb and spot the route together. It's a good practice."

"So, which way do we go, then?" Sandy asked, his eyes searching the flanks of the mountain, trying to choose a path.

George reached out to trace a route in the air. "We'll follow that valley to Base Camp—it sits in a shallow bay, surrounded by mountains. From there it's the longest single stretch. Fourteen miles up shattered slate, crumpled rocks, easy to break an ankle, a limb. And then on to the glacier, the Icefall. We'll make an interim camp somewhere there—just a depot, an emergency stop-off with a bed, a cookstove, not much. We'll try not to stay there. Then Advanced Base Camp, more home than Base Camp will be. That's where we'll live. Then up and down, up and down, to establish the other camps, six in all."

George stepped behind him, pointing over Sandy's shoulder so he could follow his finger. "Camp Six, if we could see it, would be just behind that peak there. Just on the lee of the ridge. Almost a day to the summit and back from there. The others will be spread out below. We won't see them until we get there. Without them in place, we don't stand a chance.

"It looks a clear run along the ridge," George continued. "That's the way we'll likely go."

Sandy hoped he was part of the "we" George was talking about. "Six camps. Three above the Col, three below?"

"Exactly. The Col. That's the key." George was quiet a moment. "Six camps. It'll take us almost a month to establish them all, to get everything in place. After that, they'll be a day apart. And then the summit."

Now they were almost at Base Camp. Tomorrow, after more than two months of travel, they would finally arrive at Everest.

At the edge of the trail, Sandy pulled an altimeter from his pocket and then turned in his saddle to look over his shoulder. From there he could see the whole expedition train below him. It was staggering.

The train of Sherpas, yaks, and ponies stretched for almost five miles behind him. Eight Englishmen and nearly two thousand crates of supplies. The manifest was a ridiculous testament: 44 tins of quail in foie gras; 120 tins of bully beef; dozens of wrapped squares of flaky chocolate; 9 tins of tobacco; 7 tubes apiece of petroleum jelly, to be smeared on chapped faces, to deflect the sun; 63 working oxygen canisters; 26 tents of varying sizes; a crate of cutlery and tin plates; one case of Montebello champagne; 17 bottles of Macallan whiskey, not less than fifteen years old. Miles and miles of rope, camp beds, tents, tools, and cooking pots.

The Englishmen: Teddy Norton in command. Somervell, who checked the men daily, deemed them medically fit to continue. Odell, obsessed with stones, always staring at his feet, searching for fossils, or distracted by the chirping clicks of hidden insects. Noel and his armory of cameras. Hazard with his lists and tables. Shebbeare, who could translate everything into Hindi and Tibetan, an Englishman who'd never been to England and laughed at everything that was said. George, who was always looking south and west for the mountain. Himself.

A hundred porters, including George's personal porter, Virgil, and the others who would climb high on the mountain—men and women with children strapped to their breasts, loads to their backs, sure the English were fools.

It was all but insane.

George pulled his own pony around the bend, reined her in next to Sandy.

"Sixteen thousand feet," Sandy said, handing George his altimeter.

"That's higher than Mont Blanc, Sandy. Higher than the tallest mountain in bloody Europe. Most climbers never get this high. And we've only another thirteen thousand feet to go."

"Child's play."

"Race you," George said, launching his pony down the steep slope at a mad gallop. Sandy stared after him, at the dust rising in a cloud that drifted upward, was caught by the wind, and swept out over the vast plateau. He dug his heels in, let out a whoop, and followed.

DAWN

———————

Five O'Clock

There are footsteps climbing the stone stairs outside the door. The shadow of a man through the colored panes of glass. A pause. Waiting in the gloomy entryway, I hold my breath and the shadow freezes, bent slightly at the waist as if he's heard me, knows that I'm here. Then he bends out of sight and there's the clink of glass against glass. Not the post, then. Of course not. It's too early for the post. I haven't let myself glance at any of the clocks yet, but now I know. Only five in the morning. The milk delivered like clockwork. If only the postman were as reliable.

The shadow retreats, taking his footsteps with him, down the stairs and the walk, into the road, and I retreat, too, back into the house.

How I'd like to hurry this day along. Scoop it up like a poky, whinging child the way I used to do with Clare—drop her in her bed and close the door until she cried herself out. Though bed isn't much comfort to me. A place to toss and turn and be reminded of how far away sleep is. How far away George is. Though not much longer now. He'll be home in two months if he turns around today. Perhaps a little more, a little less.

In the study I sit behind his desk. Even though it's June the air is cool in here, dressed as I am in only the thin cotton of my night-dress. I keep to the same ritual every night as I do when he is here—washing, undressing, peeling back the bedclothes, folding the heavy quilt down to the foot of the bed, saying good night—but sleep doesn't come. I force myself to lie there in that empty room until I lose count of the strikes of the clock in the hall downstairs and then I let myself get up.

Through the hours before dawn, I keep myself busy. There is enough to do. Boxes are still stacked up throughout the house where they were deposited when they first arrived from Godalming, waiting to be unpacked some seven months later. You'd think there would be a place for everything. This house is larger than the Holt was, and yet whenever I put something in what should be its place, it looks strange there, the object becoming unfamiliar in its new surroundings.

But it has to be done. Before George comes home everything must have its place. I spread my arms out and place my palms on the surface of his desk. No doubt he'll rearrange everything to his liking when he returns, but I am trying to do my best. The oak weight of the desk is turned so that he can sit here and see past the tiny front garden, over the hedge, and into the street. If I lean forward now, I can make out a glint of light in the window across the way. Someone else up early. Someone else unable to sleep.

There is nothing on the desk except the pile of letters that has come for George since he left almost five months ago. So much has accumulated that it's starting to cascade away from itself, and I try to tidy it. I sort through it as it arrives, opening the envelopes that look like bills, that look as though they need responses. The others, despite my curiosity, I set here, for him to attend to when he returns. I like the blank space the desk makes in the room. It calms me.

What I don't like is the loud tick of the mantel clock, demanding attention. I hear its insistent beat only if I'm still. I get up and move to the pile of boxes by the door, haul one down with a resounding thud, and freeze a moment. Nothing. No sound from up the stairs. The children, at least, should be allowed to sleep, even if I can't.

I sit cross-legged on the wood floor and pull the box to me, opening it, and lean in to begin pulling out books. Unpacking the books is easy, sorting them is taking some time. There are towers of them around me, arranged by topic, then by author. I sort and re-sort them.

"Why don't you hire someone to do it?" Millie asked me when she visited and found me with my hair tucked under a kerchief, looking for all the world, she said, like a kitchen maid.

"You don't say that when I'm painting," I told her.

"Well, no. But that's because painting is a sensible preoccupation for someone like you. This isn't. This is hired-help work." She waved her hand around and brushed dust motes hanging in the air, sending them scurrying. If she'd noticed the dust, there would no doubt have been a lecture about Vi and Edith not fulfilling their duties. A lecture about my not demanding it of them.

"I want to do it," I said. "It's comforting, rediscovering the things you packed away weeks ago, months. Like meeting old friends."

I couldn't tell her that with George away on expedition again we really couldn't afford to pay someone to do the unpacking, even if I wanted to.

There are traps in these boxes, too, though, to be avoided. The books are safe, but sometimes there are other things packed inside—photographs, letters, mementos from places we've been—that sneak up on me. Just yesterday I found the picture I painted in Venice. I was shocked to see it. I thought it had been lost long ago.

Yet there it was, pressed between two leather-bound tomes: the muddy view of the canal in murky colors that seemed sullen and moody from my third-floor window. Not how I remember it now, but then it was painted in the days before George joined us on our family holiday and that changed my view of almost everything.

My father collected young, talented men, inviting them to join us, particularly if they were away from their families at the holidays, as George was that Easter in 1914, just before the start of the war. These men showed up at our dinner tables at home and all over Europe and Father would shake his head and say, "I thought for sure I'd mentioned it." Helen would set another spot for dinner, and Millie and Marby and I would roll our eyes at one another.

But not when George walked in.

As usual, Marby was criticizing as I was painting in the parlor. "Your hand is too heavy, Ruth. All your light looks like dirty water, like you haven't cleaned your brush in weeks. It's too impetuous. You need more control."

And then he was behind me, with Father close at hand. "I think it looks marvelous."

"Mr. Mallory, these are my three daughters, Marby, Millie, and Ruth."

Millie and I nodded politely. "Do you know art, Mr. Mallory?" Marby asked.

George was stunning. I'd never thought a man beautiful before, but he was. His features were sharp and specific, as though each bone had been deliberately chiseled to showcase an ideal. His eyes were a blue-gray mist flecked with dark spots, tiny whirlpools of shadow. He gave off a sense of cold precision. Until he turned to me.

"I know what moves me," he said, and smiled, squinting his eyes as if it were a private joke just between the two of us. As if he didn't quite believe the painting was as good as he said, but he wanted us to be allies.

He reached for Marby's hand first, then Millie's, saving mine for last. He held my hand longer than he held my sisters', or at least I told myself he did.

"Ruth," he said, and it was a savoring pause. I imagined his breath against my cheek, his lips against my ear, and the feeling ricocheted all the way through my body—knocking against my ribs, swirling in my stomach, and settling finally between my legs. My father had entertained men before; I was used to them, liked them, even flirted with them, but this was wholly different and suddenly I was petrified.

George's hands were calloused on the palms and his hair was long for a man, curled down over his collar, hung over his forehead.

"We've met before," he said.

"I don't think so."

"Of course we have. At the Byrnes' New Year's supper."

"I'm sure we haven't," I insisted. "I would remember."

"But you don't and we did."

I couldn't remember, not for the life of me. I had gone to the supper, but there had been dozens of people there. There'd even been a pantomime and I'd played a lady's maid. "You wore a red dress," he said. But I hadn't.

Later, George told me I was the reason he'd accepted my father's invitation. "One wonders things, you know, when an ardent naturist invites you along on holiday. But I'd thought of you since that party. Your red dress and how you spat out the pips of grapes into an empty champagne flute."

I wanted to ask more about that supper, about who he might have thought I was—he was right about the pips—but my father was already leading him from the room. George considered the three of us lined up like *matryoshka* dolls and I pulled myself away from my sisters slightly.

"I'll see you at dinner, then?" he asked.

One of them answered for me. When he left, I took the painting back to my room and set it up on the easel. Marby was right, the painting was impetuous. But that was what made it come alive, I thought, made it move. I felt proud of it now, tried to see it through George's eyes.

Two weeks later, before he left to meet his climbing partners, I presented it to him. "Please, I want you to have it. It's small, will fit easily enough in your pack," I insisted, removing any objection he might have to carrying it.

"I'll treasure it," he said, and bent to tuck it along the inside of his pack.

I'd wondered about it, but never asked. And now here it was a decade later amongst the belongings he'd moved. The paint had cracked somewhat on the board. I leaned it against the back of the bookshelf, across from the desk, where he would see it.

Today reveals no such treasures, just piles of dusty books, some left from the days when George attended Magdalene College here in Cambridge. For him they might hold all sorts of memories, but for me, it is all dust and mold. My nose begins to run and I scratch at my eyes.

Glancing to the window, I notice that the room is beginning to lighten and I let myself check the clock ticking away on the mantel. Six-thirty. The morning will start properly soon. Already, I can feel the house warming around me, waking. The post should be here in another hour. Two at the most.

Silly to wait for it, really.

But word should be arriving soon. According to the telegram I received yesterday from Arthur Hinks, the monsoon arrived on the continent a week ago. Which means George is running out of time. He says they count on the burst of good weather that comes before the monsoon brings the heavy snows. But then the expedition will soon have to retreat and George will have to return. Soon another telegram will arrive, confirming he's on his way home, but still I wait for the sound of the post, to flip through the bills and invitations and inquiries to find a word from him. Any word. I prefer letters.

It was by telegram that I found out he was leaving again.

There'd been a knock at the door and I had answered it. The house was empty—everyone gone about their business, even the children.

"Telegram for Mr. Mallory?"

"I'm Mrs. Mallory." He tipped his hat and handed the paper to me. If the news had come by letter I wouldn't have known until George told me, but there were the words of congratulations from Arthur Hinks and the Mount Everest Committee.

I had thought we were talking it over. I thought we would come to some kind of agreement together.

I close the door on the memory now and stand in the hallway, trying to think of what to do next. The hours stretch ahead of me, like a line on a map. I will get dressed and rouse the children. By then it will be close to seven, a respectable hour, the rest of the world awake.

I climb the stairs to the first floor, past the empty walls in need of photographs, paintings. I'll add that to the list of things that need doing. Today, maybe. Or tomorrow. Perhaps I can find something in town. This place is not a home. Not yet.

The day after the telegram for George arrived I cried in the garden, dirt wet on my dress where I kneeled over the bulbs. We'd stood

in the garden together when we bought the house and decided what
to plant. George walked the perimeter of it, drawn to the small
stream at the end, and promised me a fishpond.

"We'll plant it all together. It'll be perfect. And then we'll sit here
and drink gin every evening until we're tight. Or the frost comes.
Whichever comes last."

The crocuses, I knew, would bloom and fade before he came
home. Already I was counting, measuring time and distance. He
stood over me but I didn't turn.

"Six months," he said. "But then it will be done."

There was heat from his hand where he touched the air above my
shoulder.

"And when do you leave?"

"It will be the last time."

He kept saying that. For months. Over and over.

"This time is the last time. I owe it to myself. To you. That's what
Will says. Geoffrey too. They're right. I need to try. One last time.
Will you understand that? You have to understand that."

I didn't. Nor did I know who he was trying to convince, me or
himself. The garden air was damp on my face and I wouldn't look at
him. I'd decided that I wouldn't let him see me cry.

Now as I enter the bedroom, I catch sight of myself in the mirror
above the dressing table. I am old, I think, a long way from the girl
who painted that scene at Casa Biondetti, though that is partially
the morning light, the swelling around my eyes from lack of sleep. I
poke my tongue out at the woman in the glass and go to the wardrobe to dress. I don't want a repeat of yesterday.

Yesterday the children found me still in my nightdress, returned
to bed after my morning wanderings. I woke to hear them tramping
down the stairs, then along the bare hallway, before they pushed

open the bedroom door. Clare first, followed by Berry leading John by the hand. The wooden floor under their feet, like tiny cat paws, didn't so much as creak from their fragile weight. They stopped at the edge of the bed.

Outside the door was a heavier footstep. Vi, following the children. She paused and listened at the door before moving on down the hallway and then the stairs. I waited for the sound of running water, the clank of the kettle against the tap.

Jumping up, I grabbed John and pulled him on top of me with a squeal. The room was so bright, the light reflected off his face, the vest pulled over his bulging tummy. My fingers moved automatically to his armpits to tickle him and I pressed my face to the sleepy, milky smell of his body, nuzzling him.

"Why are you still in bed, Mummy?" Clare wanted to know. "Are you ill?"

There was a note of hope in her voice. Poor Clare, always wanting to make things better. If I was ill she could be in charge, could bring me weak tea and toast in bed. She could lord over her brother and sister, chastise them for playing too loudly, not playing what she wanted. Illness she could do something about.

"No, pet, I'm fine." I reached toward her and she backed away. "Mummy's just a bit tired is all."

She looked at me darkly. *You won't believe how much she looks like you,* I had written to George when he was in France and she had just turned two. *She draws her eyebrows together and her face clouds and you are all I see. It makes me want to laugh and cry all at once. She is certainly your child.*

How is Clare? George wrote from the *Sardinia* the first time he left for Everest. *She is brave for her siblings,* I answered. What I didn't add was that she shouldn't have to be. She should only have to be a child with her parents there to protect her.

I grabbed her then and pulled her to the bed, too, even while she tried to resist. She thinks she is too big for roughhousing. Berry clambered up after her and I wrestled the three of them until we were piled, gasping, lungs heaving. Their weight pinned me down, stilling the jittery nerves that seem to run through my body all the time now, making sounds seem too loud, the light too bright.

Then Vi was back outside the door, come to claim them. Her weight shifted back and forth, back and forth. Like a cow, swaying slightly as it chews. Patient—always patient.

"Come in, Vi."

"Good morning, Mrs. Mallory."

"They're ready for breakfast now. Can you take these rascals? Get them fed and watered?"

John and Berry collapsed in giggles again at being called rascals, and I crossed my eyes at them. Clare climbed down, her back straight, and went to stand at the door. "Come on, you two," she ordered. She wouldn't look at me.

This morning I won't let that happen. I'll wake them instead.

I finish dressing, examine myself in the mirror. Better now. I brush my long hair back, wrap it into a loose braid. Then dig in the wardrobe again. I need something to wear this evening. For the dinner party. I pull out the black cotton and hear George's voice in my head—*too funereal*—and reach instead for the blue silk, hang it on the back of the door, and remind myself to tell Edith it is there and will need to be pressed. Carefully.

I check myself once more in the mirror. I look calm; my face is pale, my hands steady. I wipe them on the skirt of my dress to get rid of the sweat on my palms. Another day closer, I think, and nod to my reflection. It's just past seven now. Time to wake the children.

BASE CAMP

17,000 Feet

Virgil, this isn't my footlocker. Where's my locker?" George kicked at the small crate on the broken ground outside his half-erected tent and stared expectantly at his porter.

The wiry Tibetan man stepped from behind the sagging canvas to look at the box at George's feet. "Sahib Sandy say," he offered, nodding, then crouched down again to tie the tent's guyline around a small boulder.

"Well, it isn't mine. Take it back and find mine. I need my crampons so I can have a look at the glacier."

It had been two years since George was last at Base Camp, and so much had changed. He'd already noticed new boulders at the edge of the moraine, how the snow lines on the nearby mountains looked different. The glacier would be different too. He had been brooding about the Icefall for the past week. Everest might seem solid, unchanging, but it wasn't. The glacier churned down the mountain, shifting boulders, scraping out the terrain. He couldn't wait to examine the ice beyond the treacherous tumble of jagged rocks that made up their camp.

"First tent," Virgil said, continuing to tug at the line in his hands.

"Anyone can set up a damn tent. I need to get us through the Icefall and up the bloody mountain." George waited impatiently for Virgil to do as he asked, but the man kept at the tent. "Fine, Virgil." He bent to grab one of the guy ropes and pulled the peak of the tent taut.

"I send boy for locker," Virgil said.

"Boy? What boy?"

Virgil pointed past him to a small figure coming toward them. What on earth was he doing here? The boy looked five, maybe six. Close to Berry's age. It wasn't unusual for some of the female coolies to bring their nursing infants with them, but they never brought children.

Picking his way easily over the broken moraine, the boy hurried toward Virgil, a wide grin on his face. Virgil didn't speak to the boy but instead pointed at the box and then to where Sandy and the two new team members, Shebbeare and Hazard, were directing crates and bundles in various directions around Base Camp. Virgil mimed picking up the crate and walking with it. The boy's mouth moved soundlessly as he nodded, picked up the box, and moved off. Stopping every few steps, he set down the heavy weight of the box to glance over his shoulder at Virgil before continuing toward the center of camp.

"What's wrong with him?"

"He not . . ." Virgil pointed at his ear.

"He can't hear?"

"Yes." Virgil nodded. "He can't hear."

"Not sure this is the best place for him, then. Finish this?" George gestured to the tent and strode off. "Never mind," he said, taking the box back from the boy, who smiled at him, lopsided and vague, then tagged after him as he walked to Sandy with the footlocker. Odell's name was clearly stenciled on the sides of it.

"Sandy, where's my footlocker?" He dropped Odell's to the ground and the boy went to pick it up. Shaking his head no, he grasped the child's small shoulders and pointed him off toward a group of coolies, who all reached out to him, touching him, their hands on his head or his small shoulders. It was impossible to tell which one he belonged to.

"What?" Sandy continued to check off items on the manifest in his hand while delivering a final instruction to Shebbeare and Hazard, who went in the direction of the mess tent. It was Sandy's responsibility to make sure everything ended up where it was supposed to.

"My footlocker. This is obviously Odell's."

"Then he probably has yours. The porters must have mixed them up." Sandy glanced back and forth from the manifest to a large crate in front of him. The word FRAGILE was stamped on the wood above its equivalent in a squiggle of Hindi script. "I can't figure out what in the hell is in this one. I've checked everything off."

It was a strange crate, larger than most of them. "We should take a look, then."

"Shouldn't we check first?"

"Why? We're all in this racket together, Sandy. No secrets here." He picked up the crowbar at Sandy's feet. "Besides, *we* carted the bloody thing all the way here." He wrenched open the top of it and there was a spill of straw, the smell of splintered wood.

"Ha!" George laughed out loud. He pulled the crate apart, stripping down the straw packing, which was picked up and scattered by the wind. Mahogany wood gleamed warm and rich against the gray, cold desertscape of Base Camp.

"What on earth? It's a Victrola." Sandy's confusion was clear.

"Ah! There it is! Is it in one piece?" Teddy was striding toward them, carrying another footlocker. "George, I believe this is yours. Seems it ended up in the wrong place. You'll need to pay closer attention, Mr. Irvine," said the expedition leader. "These mistakes can't happen higher up."

"Right, sir." Sandy's faced reddened.

George turned his attention back to the Victrola and ran his fingers across the small plaque on the side of it—*In memory of those who fell*. It was the one from the Alpine Club.

"It doesn't look like it belongs here," Sandy said.

It did look foreign, George thought. Too delicate, its turned legs unsteady on the rough terrain. "None of us belong here, Sandy."

"I brought it for you, George," Teddy said, putting his arm around him. "I thought you might like it. There's another crate around here too."

"Of course, Teddy, for me. Seems to me last time you were the one missing music." He turned to Sandy. "He would sing. All the time. What was it, Teddy?"

The team leader burst into song. *"I'm forever blowing bubbles, pretty bubbles—"*

"Exactly. Let's not have a repeat of that. We should find the records."

While Teddy hummed, they found the crate filled with now mostly broken shellac records. "At least a couple survived," Teddy said, handing one over. "Let's give it a go." Sandy wiped the dust and straw off the record and placed it delicately on the turntable, then cranked the machine.

A fast tumble of notes from a high wailing trumpet filled the air. Jazz. The sound took George straight back to the speakeasies of New York. It was his record, the one Stella had bought for him. He had kept it at the Alpine Club, worried what Ruth would hear in its cascading notes, wild and abandoned. No, it had been better to put the record, and Stella, away, he thought. Another mistake, best forgotten.

He inhaled the music wafting on the wind.

Later, as the sun set behind the peak of Pumori, they gathered around the Victrola. The coolies, the climbers, all of them crowded together, sitting on camp chairs and boulders—the English in Burberry tweeds and sweaters, the coolies in red and yellow yak-wool coats, dusted with black soot. The deaf boy careered among the coolies, who put their palms to his cheeks and forced him to look them in the eyes. He calmed briefly before he tore away again.

John was like that, never sitting still. Really, all three of the children were, but George expected it more from John. That's what boys were like.

The night before he left, he'd gone to visit his son in the nursery. "John," he whispered, "there are things you should know." He had stood over his son's small bed and tried to think of something to say to him. Across the room, Clare and Berry slept as soundly as their brother. The girls had confounded him at first. *She seems so superfluous,* he'd written to Geoffrey when Clare was born during the height of the war, *in light of all the men that have gone and need replacing.* Now he cringed at the thought that he'd ever called Clare or Berry superfluous. The girls had taken time, a getting-to-know-you period, but they'd grown into his little imps and he loved them. Clare was braver than he could ever have hoped—a bold tomboy.

But John he understood from the first. He'd missed his birth, but that hadn't mattered at all. It was as if he already knew John. "I'll take him climbing," he told Ruth, sweeping John up in the crook of one arm, drawing vistas with the other.

"George, he can't even hold his head up yet." Ruth laughed from her bed. "He doesn't have teeth."

"First the Lake District and then the Alps. Maybe someday a faraway adventure. That village—in the Andes."

"Machu Picchu?"

"Yes! We'll go there and bring back gold."

"But not yet." Ruth took John back, cradled him against her. "Don't take him away just yet."

John would take to climbing. The boy already tried to climb everything in sight. His crib, the tables, the back wall of the garden. George knew he should rebuke him for it, but couldn't. He wanted his boy to be fearless.

"Don't let them get you down, John," he whispered above the bed, stroking his son's wispy hair. So blond, not like either him or Ruth. "You show them who you are. Don't wait for them to tell you."

"Gentlemen." As Teddy stood, Sandy reached for the Victrola, lifting the needle with a long scratch. George sipped at his enamel mug of champagne. Behind him, Shebbeare murmured, translating for the coolies, who sat empty-handed. "Sip slowly," Teddy said, holding up his mug. "There will be no more of this until we've finished this show. Then we'll be celebrating." Around him the men laughed a little, indulgently. "We've made it this far in one piece. And God knows it's a long way already. But there is still a long way to go." Teddy pointed dramatically over George's shoulder to the pyramid summit of Everest, its white peak glowing against the night sky. George didn't turn to follow Teddy's hand. He didn't need to. He could feel her looming behind him.

"Tomorrow," Teddy continued, "George will break the route up the moraine and onto the Icefall. And then, well, then we climb this bloody mountain."

If only it were that simple. George pictured it in his head: the push up the moraine, uneven but easy. He'd make an interim camp on the glacier's shoreline, a scant Camp I that he and Virgil would inhabit during the week they'd spend searching for a route through the Icefall. Next would be traversing the Western Cwm—the long bowl-shaped valley that ran up to the base of the North Col. George had named the Cwm when he first saw it, after the Welsh word for *valley*, as if to conjure something green this far above the treeline. After that they'd scale the ice cliff of the Col, and then—then he'd be within striking distance. Then he could climb the bloody thing. With perseverance. With good weather. With a willingness to suffer through whatever obstacles she threw in their way.

"That's the job," Teddy said, wavering unsteadily on his feet. "Get up and back down." He was drunk—not surprising in the thin air. George's own head buzzed slightly.

"Gentlemen," Teddy continued, planting his feet wide to keep his balance, "we are the best that have ever been assembled. We were handpicked to come here together. Some might even call it destiny. That's it up there. To Everest," Teddy declared, lifting his mug.

"To the King," the Englishmen replied, and raised their own glasses. Sandy was rapt, staring at Teddy, his face flushed with excitement and champagne.

"Virgil," Somervell slurred slightly as Teddy lowered himself back into his camp chair. "Tell us the story again. Of the mountain."

Virgil stood behind Sandy, halfway between the English and the coolies, before making his way to the Victrola in the center of the gathering. Virgil had been with George on the previous expeditions, where he'd proved himself brave, strong, and competent at altitude. George wouldn't have blamed Virgil if he hadn't come back this time, and he had been surprised by his relief at seeing Virgil in the lineup of porters Teddy had hired at Tingri. At least Virgil didn't seem to hold him responsible for what had happened the last time.

His presence gave George a new swell of confidence. If the mountain belonged to anyone, it belonged to him and Virgil. They'd seen Everest at her best and worst. They knew what the mountain could do. And still Virgil had come back a third time, like him, to try again. Virgil wanted it too.

"Chomolungma," Virgil said. "Mother Goddess of the Earth."

George shaped the name in his mouth. It was heavy on his English tongue, with too many syllables, too many consonants. But it was the right name for the mountain. She demanded something complicated.

"She not live here. She *is* here. She here now, but someday she go. Like everything. Not even gods stay always." Virgil laughed, long and bubbling, like water. George loved Virgil's broken English. Was proud of it every time, imagined it was better because of him.

"This her lap we sit on, we sleep on. Higher up, on her shoulders— demons. We hear them. In wind. The howling. You must go careful. Respectful—"

George cut him off. "Thank you, Virgil." He wished Somes hadn't asked for this. None of them needed their heads filled with this nonsense. There would be enough demons up there.

"Yes," Teddy chimed in. "A ghost story. Always good for a campfire."

But Virgil continued. "You must honor her on her flanks. Be clean. No drink. No lie together." Virgil turned his gaze to the deaf boy. Was that what Virgil had been getting at? Had the boy been conceived at the base of the mountain? Maybe by one of them, even? He'd never had relationships with the women here, but he knew others had. He eyed the boy again.

Virgil turned to George now. "We must do *puja* in the morning. Before we go. Show respect."

"Yes," Teddy said, standing again. "We'll do the *puja* first thing. Noel can film the blessing." Teddy raised his glass and restarted the Victrola.

The music beat against the mountain.

For hours their voices bounced around the camp, echoing across the glacier and the face of the mountains all around them. Louis Armstrong's trumpet piercing was amplified and repeated by the wind that whistled down from the North Col. There was no way to tell where the song began or ended; the wind looped it over and over.

Green bottles were scattered around the campfire and piled up beside the Victrola. Such fires were a luxury. They had brought only a small amount of wood with them, had a few crates to burn, but they would run out soon. The deaf boy leaned against the Victrola, absorbing its vibrations, feeling the music. He stared at the Englishmen, mouth wide.

Near the Victrola, Teddy and Somervell danced, stumbling on the uneven terrain. Teddy pinwheeled his arms, and Somes turned himself in circles, doing some kind of box step. George glanced over at Sandy and smiled, then heaved himself up from his camp chair. "Come on." He reached for Sandy. "It's good exercise. Helps with the acclimatization."

"My head hurts," Sandy protested.

"Of course it does. And that is why you need to dance."

He pulled Sandy to his feet and the boy swayed against him for a moment. Briefly they struggled for the lead before Sandy began to follow. George could feel Sandy's heart beat. He counted it out. One. Two. Three.

The men fell into one another again and again as the jazz played, their laughter becoming raucous. Eventually the coolies slipped away to their own sleeping arrangements, gathered in the mess tent, or tucked under the shelter of boulders. The Englishmen danced, became dervishes as champagne and whiskey took fast hold in thin blood, thinner air.

An avalanche of notes, like death on the mountain.

The deaf boy was watching him. George thought about waving him over, lifting him in the air to the music, but Sandy faltered. He held Sandy up instead.

George hadn't meant to hurt the boy. He was frustrated, exhausted from having to trek back down from Camp I because he'd forgotten his damn crampons. With no way to move into the Icefall, he'd lost a day. All he wanted was to collapse in his tent, sleep, and get ready to do it all again tomorrow. But the child was in his tent again.

"Give me those," George said, holding out his hand.

The boy gaped up at him, his eyes only half focused, spittle and crumbs on his chin. When the child didn't respond, George grabbed the crampons away. Their sharp points caught the boy's flesh, and blood welled up before dripping from his hand in bright red threads. The boy stared up at him, his mouth jawing around the pain, his eyes panicked and wide. George thought of Berry tumbling on the back walk at the Holt, the scrape of blood on her knee, the way she screamed as if she would never stop. He waited for the wail of pain but the boy didn't make a sound. George grabbed the white vest that was drying across the peak of his tent and tied it tightly around the child's hand. Then, turning the boy by the shoulders, he pushed him out of the tent toward a group of coolies gathered around a small cooking fire. "Someone needs to bloody well keep an eye on him!"

When he found Sandy outside his work tent, soldering a length of pipe, George held out his crampons. They were slightly twisted, a smear of blood on one of the points. "The boy broke them and I need them on the ice tomorrow. I haven't even started and already I'm a day behind."

Sandy wiped away the blood and peered at them. "I'm sure it was an accident."

"He's always underfoot. This isn't the first time I've found him in my tent. His parents ought to be minding him."

"They're probably working."

"This is no place for a child. What kind of parent brings a child here?" He wiped a sleeve across his face. The sun was blaring down on them.

They'd been at Base Camp for only a week, but already he reeked of his own sweat. It dripped down his back while he was breaking trail or sorting loads, and pooled and froze when he slowed or stopped, exhausted to stillness. He pulled off his hat, ran his hand through his greased mess of hair. It stayed standing at odd angles, held up by its own oils. His fedora smelled acidic, sharp. A few more days and he wouldn't be able to smell the stale stench of it on himself anymore, but he would know the odor was there, coming off all of them. They reeked of the latrines. There was shit on the cuffs of his trousers, hidden beneath puttees, the backsplash of piss from when the wind changed direction suddenly, inexplicably.

He felt feral.

"Where is he?" Sandy asked.

"Some of the coolies are looking after him."

"Maybe Somervell should have a look at him."

"I'll mention it to Somes later," he said. "Can you fix them? I need them tomorrow."

"So you said, George. I'll get to it tonight. I was actually just on my way to talk to Somes."

"What for?"

"At breakfast he mentioned he'd broken something. You just reminded me. I'll get to these later. Promise."

Sandy left the crampons on the ground outside his tent and walked across the camp toward Somervell's makeshift infirmary.

After tea, George sat alone in his tent, reading the most recent letter from Ruth. *Don't forget Clare's birthday, all she wants is to hear from you.* As if he could forget his children. As if Clare, Berry, and John disappeared when he left.

Still, he knew that altitude could make him forget, that the mountain had a way of unmooring things. He scratched Clare's name into the margin of his journal, scrawled *birthday* beside it, and then counted back the days it would take for a letter to reach her. Four weeks, to be safe. He'd have to send her something soon. The letters he sent from now on would travel down valleys in yak trains, drift backward away from him, and board other ships bound for England, relaying old news, old worries. Letters to Ruth, to Will, to each of his children. He would remember Clare's birthday, send her a poem from her daddy. Nine years old. Impossible.

For now, he pushed aside the journal and turned to the letter he'd been writing to Will.

Ruth tries to sound happy in her letters, light. But I know her too well for that. Thank you for being there for her, Will. You are watching out for her, aren't you? You'll keep Hinks in line and not let him badger her? It's enough for her to deal with already.

Is she getting out? Seeing people? It seems unlikely. She'll lock herself in to be stoic all on her own. Don't let her. Perhaps you could suggest a dinner party? All our close friends. It would be good for her to have you all around, I think. Maybe even invite Hinks and you can handle him head on.

It was growing dark outside by the time he finished the letter. He checked his watch. Where was Sandy with his crampons?

As he approached the work tent, he heard Somervell's voice through the thick canvas.

"He is good. It's true." George flushed a little. They had to be talking about him. "But sometimes he doesn't always do what's . . ." Somervell paused, seemed to contemplate his words carefully. ". . . prudent."

"What do you mean?" Sandy asked.

"Last time there was the avalanche. You read about it, I'm sure. It was in the book, in all the papers. I guess it could have happened to any of us. But it didn't. Maybe it was just dumb luck that George was leading that day. There was fresh snow. He should have called it off. It wasn't safe. We could see where the snow wanted to slip. But George pushed up anyway. Teddy should have been more adamant, or I should have been, maybe. But it was George's insistence. 'We'll lose our window,' he said. So we went."

That wasn't how George remembered it. They had agreed to push up together. Yes, there had been fresh snow on the mountain, but the sun had warmed it. It should have bonded to the colder layer of older snow underneath. He knew about avalanches. They saw them often enough here—first the low thud, like untamped gunpowder, and then a building rumble, like the whole world collapsing. And then the rolling waves of snow, picking up speed and crashing down the rock face, carrying off everything in its path.

No, he and Somervell had made the decision together. It was going to be their last attempt, that much was clear. They had the burst of good weather that always preceded the snowstorms that the wet monsoon weather swept up and across the Himalaya. They examined the face of the mountain, tramped up away from Camp IV, and jumped up and down on the snow, watching for it to ripple, to pull away. It didn't.

Avalanches happened on mountains. It was one of the risks. They all knew that. Foolish to pretend otherwise. Yet here was Somervell again, saying George had been the reckless one. That it was his fault that seven men had died.

He pulled back the tent flap and ducked inside. "Telling war stories, are we, Somes?" When Somervell wouldn't meet his eye, George turned to Sandy. "Did you get those crampons taken care of?"

"Yes. Yes. Sorry. I was just on my way to bring them to you."

"You just got sidetracked?"

"They'll hold," Sandy said, handing him the crampons.

"Thanks." He turned to leave.

"George," Somervell called after him. "We should run another series of tests when you get back. See how the stress is getting to you. Maybe I'll get you to take Sandy with you so I can check him too. He's doing remarkably well, actually. Come see me."

"I'll see how the schedule looks when I get back." He held up his crampons. "We're already behind. Teddy and I will talk about Sandy," he said, turning away.

He'd always suspected that Somervell thought him reckless. Ever since he put up his first solo route in Wales. It didn't really much matter what Somes thought, though. As long as he had Teddy's confidence, Somervell could bloody well go to hell.

✦ ✦ ✦

IT WAS QUIET, blessedly quiet. Sandy hadn't been interrupted in his work tent for at least a half-hour. George had warned him back on the *California*, when Sandy had sought him out, that he should guard his privacy when he could. "It will be hard to find a moment to yourself once we're on the mountains. You might want to enjoy some solitude while you can." But the quiet was too good to last. Outside the tent was the crunch of footsteps, the whisper of the canvas. Sandy inhaled deeply and looked at the list of repairs he had to make—*camera, Unna cooker, Hazard's camp bed?, torch, oxygen*. A silhouette fell across the page.

"What is it?" he said, more sharply than he meant to.

"Not quite the greeting I expected," Odell said. Sandy could hear the smile in Odell's voice, but even the grin he couldn't see aggravated him.

"Sorry, I assumed you were another one of the porters with something else to fix."

"Well, still no reason to be so short. Could've been anyone, really."

Sandy didn't respond. He'd forgotten this side of Odell—the instructing, headmaster side of him. In Spitsbergen, Odell had always been correcting Sandy's glissade, how he pushed his skis forward, no matter that Sandy had won a race his first week on the damn things.

Odell pushed on into the silence. "Teddy's hoping you might have another of the oxygen rigs ready. George is due back from the Icefall today. Teddy would like him to take a look at it."

Sandy stood and stepped toward the flap, and Odell backed up to allow him to duck out. "I'll get to it," Sandy said. "There's just so many interruptions." He inhaled again. "I'll get to it," he repeated before turning and storming away toward the far edge of the camp. He didn't know where he was going, but he had to get away from Odell. From everyone. No matter where he looked, though, there were people—porters scurrying about, Shebbeare sorting through a pile of ropes, Norton stepping out of the mess tent, paper in hand. Sandy tried to head away from all of it. Past the mess tent, past the Victrola, toward Noel's tent at the far edge of the camp.

He wished he could conjure the affection he'd once felt for Odell, but he was still irked by what Odell had done the other night at one of Norton's after-tea war councils.

"Sandy's done a complete overhaul of the oxygen system," Odell had told Norton.

"That's a waste of time," Somervell interjected.

"We haven't made a decision yet, Somes," Norton said. "But if the oxygen will get us to the top and back down safely, we'll use the oxygen."

Sandy had been surprised by Somervell's resistance to the idea of using oxygen. During one of their debates on the topic, Somes had made his case: God created man. God created earth. Man should be able to reach the highest point on earth on his own. "God doesn't make mistakes like that," he argued.

"Right, Somes," George had responded. "Forget that man can't get to the bottom of the blooming ocean."

Not that Sandy was in favor of using oxygen. "I'd much rather get to the base of the final pyramid without than to the summit with it," he'd once told George, though he wasn't sure he meant it, not even at the time. Everyone had an opinion on the oxygen question: Was it sporting or not to use it? Would it even work? But the sheer mechanics of the system fascinated him.

"Sandy, why don't you fetch the prototype you've finished for Teddy to take a look," Odell had said, making him feel like a child asked to show off the good work he'd done at school. By the time he returned, Odell was showing Norton the sketches Sandy had made. He didn't remember giving his drawings to Odell.

"Maybe I should show him?" Sandy said.

"I was just trying to explain what you've been up to," Odell told him. It seemed to Sandy, though, that Odell was trying to take some of the credit for his work.

Even so, Norton had been impressed and told him to carve out some time to get a few more rigs overhauled. He'd added it to his ever-growing list of chores and repairs.

The sun beat down on Sandy now as he moved toward the edge of the camp, and he squinted against the sharp light. His face had been scoured by the sun, burned early on during the trek, and the skin hadn't had a chance to recover. His bottom lip was swollen and blistered. He ran his tongue over its pulpy tenderness. He'd left his hat in his tent. He could go back and get it, but Odell was still standing nearby, reviewing his own list of duties.

The work tent was sagging and pathetic. As he watched, another porter approached it and scratched at the flap before pulling it open. He put something on the floor and then backed out. No doubt something else to add to the bloody list. The number of things that got broken, damaged, or lost at Base Camp was staggering. And with someone always carrying another broken thing in, it was impossible to get anything done.

At home, no one ever bothered him in his workshop. If the door from the garden was closed, that was all there was to it. It had been that way since he was eleven, when his father let him start using the workshop on his own. They had painted STAY OUT on a sheet of wood that they banged to the door. For some reason they all respected the sign—his parents, his brother and sister, even his good friend Dick, the few times he'd come to visit.

As Sandy rounded the corner of Noel's work tent, he stumbled into Hazard, who was wrestling with a large mound of canvas. "Sorry," Hazard said, looking up at him. "Noel wanted this for something. Says the tent's not dark enough for developing. Maybe you could give me a hand?"

God, he just wanted a minute alone. "Just on my way to the latrines. Then more repairs. Your camp bed's next on the list." He stalked off in the direction of the latrines before Hazard had a chance to say anything else. If there was solitude to be had anywhere, it was there. They all gave one another a wide berth when using the privies.

As he approached the latrines, the smell wafted toward him and he almost turned back. Calling them latrines was being generous. *Imagine, a shallow hole behind a low wall of piled stones. That it's cool here is the only thing that keeps the stench down. An open pit used by nearly a hundred men . . . The ancients had it better than this!* It seemed a safe enough thing to write to Dick about. Latrines couldn't have less to do with Marjory. And he certainly wasn't going to share this with her. Sandy dropped his pants, the cold air shriveling him, then squatted, peering over the wall.

Base Camp was crowded, a small city of tents. A hundred porters, lowing yaks. Not at all what he'd imagined. He'd pictured a vast emptiness, the luxury of being alone in the middle of nowhere.

"Oh, it will all be so glamorous," Marjory had said from the claw-foot bathtub, her hand dangling over the edge. He lit her cigarette and put it in her outstretched fingers. "Exotic," she said, with a puff of smoke.

"No, that's you. Glamorous and exotic."

"You're such a charmer." She splashed at him. "But really. Think of the food and the spices. They say India is so dark and secret. And you're going farther than anyone else has. Nothing around you but the wilds and local men to carry your champagne and caviar." She kneeled in the tub, leaned over to kiss him where he sat on the floor. She tasted of nicotine. "I wish I could go. What an escape from all this."

He hauled up his trousers. It *was* an escape, of sorts. At least here he didn't have to think about what to do about Marjory or Dick. It really was just them and the mountain. He didn't have time to think of anything else. Or at least that's what he told himself. He promised himself he'd straighten matters out with both of them when he got home.

He had thought things would be simpler on the mountain, but relationships were strained. He understood how it happened in these extreme circumstances. In Spitsbergen, after only three days on the glacier with Odell and Simon, he'd grown sick to death of them. Of Odell's instructing and Simon's ongoing optimism. *You can imagine,* he'd written to Marjory at the time, *how such close contact can breed contempt.* She'd written back, jokingly, *It certainly did with my husband.* Now he was avoiding Odell, and Odell was peeved at Norton for some perceived slight Sandy didn't know about. Somes and George were barely speaking after their terse exchange inside Sandy's work tent. Only Norton seemed to be above it all. Yet for all the sparring, they seemed confident in each other. He'd be able to count on every one of them farther up.

His work tent was, mercifully, deserted when he returned to it. If Norton wanted the oxygen rig ready by the time George got back, he'd do his best to get it done. He threw back the tent flap and the bright sun cast his shadow darkly across the empty tent. All right, then: the Unna cooker first. Then back to the oxygen. Then lunch. Leaving the flaps open for the fresh air and light, he sat cross-legged on the floor.

As he worked, his thoughts drifted back to what Somervell had told him the other night.

"That's precisely what I was talking about," Somes had said, after George stormed off with his crampons. "He's impetuous and he lets his temper take hold of him. When he's excited, there really is no way to stop him. But the Lord knows he's good. When George is focused, Sandy, there's no one better." Somes shrugged a little. "Of course, publicly, we can't say things like that. Publicly, we have to present a united front. George was the easy target, and perhaps that wasn't fair."

It had been George's name associated with the avalanche. George who was singled out for blame.

Sandy tried to fire up the cooker. It still wasn't working. He pulled the tubing from it, unscrewed the cap.

"Maybe," his mum had said, after reading the articles and editorials, "maybe we shouldn't be going over there if it's going to be like this. Too many have already died." Her voice was tight, as if she wanted to say more, but couldn't. It was the same voice she used for talking to his father when he came home too late from the pub. "And these Sherpa men. Well, it isn't even for them, is it? They're just farmers or whatever it is they are. Maybe we should leave them alone."

Maybe. She said *maybe* when she believed something was true.

"Nonsense," his father responded. "There's a cost to pay for something worth doing. Anything worth doing. Isn't that right, Sandy? Isn't that what I've always taught you?"

"Yessir."

"*Sacrifice* is the watchword."

"Yessir."

"Maybe," his mother said, "this isn't our sacrifice to make."

Sandy fired up the Unna cooker again and flinched back from the static sparks. Everything was so bloody dry here, there was a constant tingle of static electricity. The cooker was giving off a distinct hiss now, a whiff of gas. A leak somewhere. If he had been at home, the job would have been done in a quarter-hour. There he had the tools. Here he had only the most basic kit, and the grit of dust that stuck in everything.

"But you didn't," he'd said to Somes. "You didn't stand by him in the press. The Committee did, but none of you said anything."

"We weren't allowed to, Sandy. You know that."

Until he'd had to sign his own contract for the expedition, he hadn't realized that expedition members weren't allowed to speak to the press unless they had express permission. "But George did."

"He shouldn't have. And he's lucky he was invited back. Finch was let go for talking without permission and he didn't say anything near as controversial as George did."

"What do you mean?"

"George said he wished that one of us had been among the dead. One Englishmen among the seven porters, so that we could share the grief. As if we didn't."

He hadn't wanted to challenge Somes, but he wondered if that wasn't what George meant. Maybe he just felt they didn't really share the burden.

He set the cooker aside. He'd have to ask Odell if there was any spare tubing left. Might as well get it over with. Then he could get back to the oxygen. If Norton was expecting George back at Base Camp today, that meant they'd start moving up in a day or so. The oxygen had to be ready. *He* had to be ready. He didn't want to be the one left behind here, supplying the higher camps, playing nanny to the porters. He didn't want to be forgotten.

◆   ◆   ◆

GEORGE WAS ON his way to check the mail after being away from Base Camp for almost a week. He was hoping for a letter or two from Ruth. He had another one ready to go and a poem for Clare's birthday, if the post hadn't been dispatched yet.

Sandy called to him from near the mess tent. "George, you're back. Norton wanted you to look at what I've done with the oxygen as soon as you returned."

"Can it wait? I was just going to check the post." His lungs burned as he moved. By the time he came down from the summit, this would be easy.

"There isn't any. Hasn't been since you left."

"Nothing?"

Sandy ignored him. "I've overhauled the oxygen rig. Norton had a look at it and liked it."

"I thought you weren't interested in using the oxygen."

"Well, if it'll work. And maybe it will." Sandy led George toward the work tent. "I mean, I've been thinking about the oxygen. About acclimatization. It's practically evolution in fast motion. Our bodies are changing while we're here." Sandy reached out and placed his palm over George's heart. "Since the air gets thinner the higher we go, our bodies make more and more red blood cells, so they can carry more oxygen. We can't *make* oxygen, so our bodies make the most of what they can get. If *they* want to carry more, well, maybe *we* should carry more. I mean, if it's lack of oxygen that makes us so sluggish and seedy up here, causes us to make bad decisions, then we really should take full advantage. Shouldn't we?"

Sandy pointed at the scattered canisters outside his work tent. "The biggest complaint last time was that the benefit wasn't worth the weight of the apparatus. Or the leaks. Well, I've fixed all of that. If it's light enough, reliable enough, maybe now it'll be worth the energy of lugging it up there."

"Let me try it," George said.

While Sandy strapped him into the contraption, George put on the mask and breathed through the tubes, sucked the cold dry air from the cylinders.

The stale smell of the mask, the dryness of the forced air. His breath quickened, came short and tight. It was too much. Claustrophobia pressed in around him. He couldn't breathe. His lungs froze. He heard the gas alarms, the panicked voices: *Gas! Gas! Gas!* The fumbling prayers. Fingers slipping off metal clasps that wouldn't fasten. Praying your mask wouldn't leak. Wouldn't clog or falter. Praying that the lack of air, that fear, wouldn't smother you as you lay in a mud ditch, gas creeping down on you. Yellow green. He gagged. The smell of decay.

There was a puddle of gas at the bottom of the crater. The walls were almost impossible to climb. They crumpled, melted under him, wet with blood, with rain. Why was everything wet all the time? Gaddes knew the walls wouldn't hold, that his mask was failing.

George could see that in the jerky movements, the desperation, as Gaddes clawed at the walls, mud sliding down on top of him. He couldn't get away from the gas. Couldn't get up above it. Couldn't climb. The walls were collapsing on Gaddes at the bottom of the shell hole, sucking him back down. George scrabbled about him, grasping for something that he could use to help Gaddes. But there was nothing he could do.

"Are you all right?" Sandy asked, peering at him. Concerned. God, what did Sandy see?

He forced himself to focus on Sandy, on the weight of the pack on his shoulders, on the peaks surrounding him, the blinding white air. The mask pinched at the flesh on his cheeks. His pulse thudded at his temple, his throat, his ears.

He might need the oxygen to get to the top. He couldn't panic like this. Sandy's voice was a muffled burble over the beating in his ears. Waving Sandy off, he peered up toward the summit, the bleached sky. He needed this. He took a deep breath. Pushed it back out. Breathed in and out. In. Out. The air expanded his lungs. With the oxygen, his head cleared somewhat, the ever-present headache receding. It would work. It had to.

His hands shook as he unfastened the mask. The mountain air in his lungs felt thin again, anemic. His face was clammy.

"This is good, Sandy."

"Really?" Sandy looked pleased.

He reminded George of some of the other boys he'd taught at Charterhouse. They all wanted to impress so badly. Had he ever been like that?

"Yes. It's lighter and the gas is coming faster. I can feel it."

"And I can repair it," Sandy went on. "If something were to go wrong with it, higher up. I could fix it on the fly."

"And the others? What do they think?"

"Somes is still against it. Odell seems ambivalent. And even though Norton seems impressed, he's still noncommittal."

"Sounds like Teddy."

"Maybe you can convince him," Sandy said, looking past his shoulder.

Teddy was coming toward them. "I'll do my best," George said, turning toward the expedition leader.

"Have you seen him?" Teddy asked, out of breath, before he even reached them.

"Seen who?"

"The boy. He's missing."

He hadn't noticed the shouting until now. It wasn't unusual, the loud babble of Tibetan, but this time the noise was different, the voices more urgent. There was no laughing, no lightness in the sound. One man yelled, bawled, louder than everyone else. He was standing in the middle of the other coolies, his head tossed back. A few others stepped close to comfort him, while beside him a woman collapsed. There were people moving in all directions—coolies, Shebbeare and Hazard. Noel hurried after one of the coolies with his camera.

"He probably just wandered off," George said. "We're in the middle of nowhere. He won't be able to find his way out of here." He gestured around the Base Camp, set in the bowl of mountains, surrounded by peaks and sheer walls in every direction except for the glacial valley, down which they could see for miles. "There's nowhere to go but up. We'll find him."

"He loves the Victrola," Sandy said. "Maybe he's there?"

"Maybe." Scanning the camp, George rotated slowly on the spot and thought about John.

John was dogged. He'd worry at something for what seemed like hours. "Unusual in a boy," Ruth had told him, though he wasn't so sure. Couldn't he work on a climbing problem for hours until he figured it out? That must have started when he was a boy. How did women know these things about children, anyway? John, at least, could entertain himself. Not like the girls. The girls always wanted his attention, were always grabbing at him, clinging to him.

That's why he hadn't worried about leaving John alone in the back garden with his football. John would happily kick the ball for an hour. More. Until he exhausted himself.

"I'll be right back, John," he said. "Stay here. Kick the ball, yes?" He kicked the ball once at the wall and John stumbled after the rebound and then kicked it back. It stopped short of the wall. John looked up at him.

"Kick the ball, John." And he did. He watched John kick it twice, three more times, and then he stepped away. John hadn't even noticed. He'd left John alone for only a few minutes. He couldn't even remember why. What had been so important?

When he came back, John was gone. There was a metallic taste in his mouth. His heart hadn't beat faster but slowed, painfully, even as he told himself John must be there somewhere, that he was being ridiculous.

And of course he was. He found John by the small stream at the back of the garden, poking at the wet dirt, hunting for bugs or frogs. His football, stuck behind a rock, spun in the quick current.

Dear God, his heart thumped back into his ears, his temples. He swore he'd never let the boy out of his sight again and hugged John, squirming, to his chest, even as he was making plans to return to Everest. The memory brought with it a rising feeling of panic. His heart slowed. He feared it might stop.

Near the camp the melting glacier resurfaced from under the moraine in a small rush of water. He loved the small stream, fresh and so cold it hurt his teeth. It was so dry here, they were all perpetually thirsty.

Maybe water attracted all little boys.

"Teddy, have some of the porters check toward the Icefall," he said before moving off. "It's where I would go."

✦   ✦   ✦

SANDY HAD BEEN STANDING not far from where he stood now, just a short distance from the mess tent. He had scanned the near horizon, the jumble of the boulder field, the hundreds—thousands—of places to hide. A repeated combination of syllables bounced around him. The Sherpas were calling the boy's name even though he wouldn't be able to hear it.

"Anything?" Sandy asked as Hazard approached from around the side of the mess tent.

"No. You?"

Sandy shook his head.

There was a lull in the shouting, a brief respite that drew Hazard's attention over Sandy's shoulder. Sandy turned to follow his look. Across the moraine, one of the porters was carrying the boy back into the camp. He was so small in the man's arms, yet he seemed heavy too. The man staggered slightly, and then Sandy was running toward him. He reached him just as Somervell tried to take the boy from the man. The porter's face was impassive, dark, and wrinkled, but calm in a way that was unsettling. He stared blankly across the camp, not seeming to see anything, and clutched the child tight to his chest. The boy's clothes were wet, dripping, his hair plastered to his forehead. His lips were blue, his face tinged with it too.

Sandy wanted to look away but couldn't. He couldn't move at all. He stared—at the boy, at the man holding him in his arms, at Somervell trying to examine the child. One of the women was crying. No, keening. A sound he'd never heard before. It slid along the full register, articulating her grief.

Norton was beside them now, drawing Somervell back and saying something in a quiet, calming tone to the porter in Tibetan. The man didn't respond, said nothing.

"Sandy, you don't need to see this. Come on." George was at Sandy's elbow, pulling him back toward the mess tent. "Sandy?"

"Sandy? Are you with us?" Norton's voice cut into his thoughts. "Sandy, I need you to focus. We need to finish this."

Sandy closed his eyes, squeezed hard, willing the image of the dead boy away. When he opened them again, he stared hard at the loads lined up in front of him. Tomorrow, the first group of climbers would be heading up to the next camp. They had to stay on schedule. They couldn't afford any delay. Not for the drowned boy. Not for anything. "We only have so much time on the mountain," Norton had said. "If we want to succeed, we can't get derailed now." Sandy tried to understand. Tried to believe that they didn't have the luxury of showing the simple respect of waiting one day.

"The list for the next five camps," he said now, handing the manifest to Norton. "And what needs to go to each one."

"There isn't much leeway," Somervell cut in.

"There never is," Norton said.

"Why did you let them bring him here?" Sandy's voice was louder than he meant it to be, sharper. It sounded like an accusation. Norton and Somes exchanged glances. Somes turned to walk away.

"These loads look good," Norton said, ignoring the outburst. Then, "They're not children, Sandy. They can make their own decisions. Decide what risks they're willing to take. We don't force them to do anything. Bad decisions get made. By all of us. The only thing to do now is not make any more and not make things worse."

"Right. Don't make things worse."

Norton squeezed Sandy's arm and then handed him a tangle of ribbons and garters. "Put one of these on each of the loads."

"These are the porters'," Sandy said, taking them.

"They'll recognize which ones are theirs tomorrow and they'll take that load when it's time to go. No squabbling, no complaining. It's the fairest way. You, George, and Odell, you'll take the lighter loads. If the coolies run down, that's one thing. There are only a few of us who can climb. You need to take care of yourself."

"And the oxygen?" Sandy asked.

"It'll go up soon. The food and tents first. If those aren't up there, people die," Norton explained. "Oxygen we'll take up later."

Sandy nodded.

"You'll be fine, Sandy." Norton stared hard at him. "Just do as you're told."

"And don't make things worse," Sandy repeated.

"Right. I have to check in with Noel, see how he's coming along."

Noel had his own miniature expedition arranged and would be heading off after they'd established Camp III to set up his own high camp across from the Col on the flanks of Pumori. From there he'd have a clear view of the summit ridge. He'd wait and film them from there. Noel documented everything. Sandy was surprised he hadn't taken pictures of the boy's body. Or the parents. No, maybe that wasn't fair. Noel just wanted a record of what happened. He'd make his movie and secure his own fame. That's what he was there to do.

Each member of the expedition had his role to perform. Sandy had somehow forgotten in the sweep of the journey, the exotic locales, that he had a job to do. There was so much more at stake than just their lives. They couldn't get waylaid. By anything. He'd thought he understood that. After watching the boy's body brought back to camp, though, he was unsure. But Norton had made it clear: no matter what, they were going up the mountain tomorrow. *He* was going up the mountain tomorrow. That's what he'd come here to do.

BREAKFAST

Seven O'Clock

When I enter the nursery, the children are still tousled in their beds, the room under the eaves stale from having been closed up all night. I open the window onto the long back garden. The color of the willow tree is deepening and I am reminded of how George always comments on the tender green of spring growth. He hasn't seen this garden in spring yet, missed the press of shoots up through the black soil.

Sliding into bed behind John, I pull his body to me, damp with sweat and sleep. He mewls like a small animal and pulls away from me. On his shoulder I trace landscapes, the great bulges of mountains and vast troughs of seas. He calms under these images, my touch.

The three of them are just beginning to wake; there is the slightest shift of breath as they climb slowly from the depths of sleep into daylight. Part of me wants to hurry them along, pull them toward wakefulness so I can hear the chirp and cry of them, for the distraction of them. They are always wanting something, their insistent demands giving shape to the long days, creating the comfort of routine. Hours can be filled attending to their needs: meals and naps and lessons and playing.

John rolls over in my arms and smiles widely when he sees me. Pure joy. He puts his small, sticky hand to my cheek, pushing at it. Then he is holding his arms out over my shoulder, past me, to Vi, the same smile turned to her. Vi has been with us since Clare was born, and she is as familiar to them as I am. Maybe more so than their own father. I keep my back to the nurse, facing my son. Our son.

Sometimes I wonder what he thinks of George, if he does at all. He knows his father is gone, that much is obvious. *When I finally returned home after seeing you off,* I wrote to George, *John wandered from room to room, stood at the bottom of the stairs and called up them: Papa? Papa? It was enough to break my heart.* But in the last few weeks he hasn't done that. I worry he is more accustomed to his father's absence than his presence, though if Berry or Clare ask about Daddy, he will ask too.

When it feels as though Vi has turned away, I roll over and watch as she touches the shoulders of the girls and shifts John to her hip. They rise silent from their beds and I am struck anew by the height of them, tall and thin. Their nightgowns were new when you left, too long on them; now the gowns brush their shins. Clare will need a new one: Berry will take her sister's hand-me-down. Another task for the list that is filling up in my head.

I sit up and the creaking of the bed stops the girls, who look at me. Berry smiles automatically, as John did. Clare doesn't.

"Good morning, Clare-Bear," I say, their collective nickname.

"Say good morning to your mother, girls," Vi instructs them.

"Good morning, *maman*," they chorus.

They have taken to calling me by the French term since Cottie began her lessons with them, and I love it. It warms me, even when prompted, like this.

"I think, Vi, I'll have breakfast with them this morning. Have their things ready for their French lesson. We'll leave by ten."

Berry smiles. John is curled into Vi's neck. Clare stares at me. I don't wait for a response from Vi. She considers me silly, I think, as I step past her and make my way back down the stairs. That I suffer George's absence poorly. That I spend too much time "wandering like a little lost lamb," she says. Drifting from room to room, piling and unpiling books, papers, linens.

It isn't hard to understand why. She lost her husband in the war. As did so many others, of course, God rest them. But his body was destroyed and never found.

"Where was he?" George asked when he was evacuated home. I hadn't told him in the hospital, but George had asked after him during his weeks at home, before his return to duty. Not to France as he wished, but to train recruits not far away. He wasn't glad to be home. His safe return was all I had been praying for, for months, and he wanted to be somewhere else.

How could he feel that he should be away from us, I wrote to Marby, forgetting she had just recently married a career military man. *It's his duty, Ruth,* she wrote back. *It isn't a want, it's a duty. And you have a duty as well. It's time for you to grow up.*

"Ypres, I think," I told him. I should have remembered. It was important to remember, wasn't it?

George looked grim. "I'm not surprised they didn't find anything. She wouldn't have wanted to see what they would have found." He had forgotten he was talking to me. His usual indomitable calm had vanished. When he saw my face, though, he shook his head. "I'm sorry, I didn't mean . . ."

"Let's not talk about it."

But the idea of those smashed bodies stayed with me. More so when word came only a few days later about Trafford. There was no body to bury, only the empty coffin at the front of Reverend Mallory's church. For days George's mother and sister were silent, and we sat in Mrs. Mallory's overwarm kitchen, the light outside bright and sharp. She drew the curtains. In the next room George and his father argued. "I wish they'd stop," his mother said. "If Trafford were here, he'd make them stop."

"What's the use of being home," George told me, sitting outside the rectory, his red-rimmed eyes squinted against the sun, "if I can't even make my father care?"

I was stung by his wanting to be away from us. "He does care. Of course he does. But he knows that the rest of his congregation need him too. He has to care enough for all of them." For my part I was glad George was home. Glad I could see him, touch him. Glad he was far from what had killed Trafford and had almost killed Geoffrey.

Maybe Vi is right. I should be more stoic. It's not as if I haven't been through this before—there was the war and Everest twice already, then the long trip to America. There have been seemingly countless lonely mornings.

During the war, though, there was a different sensibility: it was something we were all in together. There were the church knitting circles, and Marby, when she came to stay with me in Godalming, insisted on hosting weekly first-aid classes, showing us how to wrap bandages, how to dress wounds. She would give us—me, Millie, Mrs. Graham, and Mrs. Parker from down the road—the same instructions every time. "Idle minds dwell," she'd say, before making us repeat the directions she'd given the week before for treating burns or head wounds.

"*This* makes me dwell," I protested at first, cutting and then rolling the long strips of cloth into workable bandages. And it did—made me think about how many ways a body could be injured, destroyed, and how insufficient our homemade bandages would be for patching it up.

"No it doesn't," Marby insisted. "It gives you a sense of control."

We didn't talk about where our husbands were, or what they were doing. After Mrs. Parker's husband died, she continued to join our first-aid drills, but her face was gray all the time. Millie would bring the newspaper and she'd sit by the window reading out loud from the casualty lists, all of us listening for names we knew. I couldn't bear reading the columns of names myself. There were so many familiar names there: Vi's husband, Captain Parker, Trafford.

I'm startled by the noise of the children tramping down the stairs, the small parade of them, their footsteps a chaotic beat. There is a chatter of questions from Berry and then the kitchen door opening, closing.

On the side table under the window is a copy of *The Times*. I should just cancel the subscription. I try to read it and try not to at the same time. I used to read the newspaper over breakfast—scanning for interesting news to write to George, things that made me feel connected to the wider world. But now the whole of England seems to be caught up in Everest fever. There have been stories about everything: what the expedition members wear, what they eat, how these details find their way to the most esteemed editors.

I do want to know. But I want only good news. Briefly, I allow myself the luxury of imagining George's success. *He's done it*, I think. *He's done it.* And the certainty of his success wells up in me so that there are tears in my eyes and I can't help but smile. It's as true as anything, as the newspaper in my hand that I won't read. When he comes home, he will be ecstatic and tell me it's over, all of the leaving, the absences. And we will celebrate.

It might have happened already. Perhaps Hinks knows something.

Without reading the headline, I fold the paper over and drop it in the wood box. If it is cool this evening we might build a fire after dinner. It can serve as kindling. The feeling of his success calms me. I wipe the newsprint from my hands, straighten the clock on the mantel.

Under the clatter of breakfast in the kitchen, I keep one ear cocked for steps on the front stairs, for the drop of the post through the door. I check the time. Nearing nine. But the clock here is always fast. Edith likes it that way. "I can cook properly for the table then, mum," she says. She says *mum* instead of *ma'am.* As if I'm a lady. As if she's a lady's maid.

I love this kitchen with its old oak table that used to belong to my mother. It is pocked and scratched across the surface from chopping and spills and burning pots. The whitewashed cupboards make the room bright and welcoming, big enough for all of us, yet still small enough to feel cozy. There is toast and jams, soft-boiled eggs, milk and tea, all of it laid out on the china I painted when George and I were first married. Pieces of it have been lost and broken, so it's relegated to the kitchen now, to the children's breakfast. John dips his toast into the yolk of his egg, misses his mouth slightly as he bites down.

"Why is there a party without Daddy?" Clare asks as I lean over to wipe at John's face. He squirms away and I give up and refill Berry's milk.

"Pardon?"

"I think," Clare goes on, "and Berry thinks that Daddy will be very sad if he misses the party. He might be very angry at you if you have a party without him."

A smile, reassuring. *It's a balancing act,* I wrote to George after he left for Everest the second time. *I try to make the children feel that everything is normal, as if you've just gone out for the evening, or climbing with Will for the weekend. But they also know that isn't true. They know you're gone a long time, somewhere far away, and while we say it is an adventure, they sense the risk. I have to take some care with that—respect that they might be apprehensive.*

"I shouldn't think he'll mind terribly," I tell her. "He wants us to enjoy ourselves. Mummy thought it might be fun."

Clare nods. "Berry would like to have a party."

"Would she, now?"

Clare has taken to using Berry as her excuse to ask for things. Conveniently, what she wants, Berry wants. Berry wants biscuits. Berry wants a party. Berry wants to know when Daddy is coming home.

But Berry isn't listening. She and John are bickering over something, snapping at each other like little sparrows, small hands grasping hair, pinching. I press Berry's hands to the table and John lets out a piercing shriek, part victory, part complaint.

"What kind of party would you like, Berry?"

Her nose wrinkles up as she thinks a minute. "A tea party. Like Daddy promised."

"That would be fun, wouldn't it? Perhaps this afternoon. In the back garden." Clare looks triumphant and for a brief moment I want to recant, to take it away so she won't use her sister or her father's absence to get what she wants. "After your lessons," I say directly to Clare. "French and then maths." Pouting now, she slouches back in her chair. "Sit up straight."

She does and then tries to make amends. "Berry likes to go to French lessons."

"Do you, Berr?"

"*Oui.*" Her voice is a small cheep.

"*Oui!*" John echoes, yelling it at the top of his lungs and kicking at the underside of the table. His glass wobbles and then tips, milk spreading across the scored surface. I reach for the tea towel near the stove and John rubs his hands in the milk, then sticks tight fists in his mouth.

"John, no!" I grab his hand and he yells again.

The milk runs onto the floor as I reach for the bell to summon Vi.

"Yes, ma'am?"

"Please take them and get them cleaned up. We need to leave in half an hour. This afternoon, if they're good, there will be a tea party in the back garden."

Vi surveys the mess and I bristle, feeling reprimanded. She only obeys me because it is her job. There is no affection there. Not for me. Perhaps there is for George; he is at ease with the servants. I am not good with them. When I was small, I would go out of my way to clean up after Millie and Marby so as to not have to talk to my father's maids. Somehow they make me feel a stranger in my own home. If there was a way to join Vi and Edith—for a chat, a cup of tea—I would. But it isn't done and they wouldn't have it. When I sit in the parlor and try to read, I can hear them chattering to each other, their small bursts of laughter. There is a creeping fear along my spine that they are talking about me. Laughing at me.

Usually Vi would take the children to their lesson, but I'm rest-less, my nerves taut from lack of sleep. It would do me good to get out of the house and get some fresh air. "I'll take the children to Cottie's—I mean, Mrs. O'Malley's—this morning. You'll have enough to do for dinner. Please ask Edith to join me here and then you can get the children dressed."

I begin to gather the dirty plates, piling them and then the sau-cers, toss the wet tea towel in the sink.

"Mum?"

Edith is flushed red from some exertion or other in the pantry. There is sweat on her lip and I wipe at my own face. She doesn't notice. She huffs and stares past me, a spot over my shoulder. There's nothing there. Like Vi, she is stocky, thick legs in slouching stock-ings. They're like squat bookends.

Vi and Edith are all the things I am not. Solid and reliable. There is a kind of physical power to them that I cannot really imagine. They would be rough in bed with their husbands and lovers. I can almost picture them, shuddering against their partners.

Edith folds her hands in front of her. She is holding this morn-ing's post.

I cross the kitchen to the window, to distance myself from the mess, from the letters that I want to snatch from her sweaty hands. We are awkward with each other; she's only been with us since just before George left. I know so little about her and feel she knows everything about me.

"We need to . . . I mean, I would like to discuss this evening's menu."

She nods but doesn't say anything. Looks from me to the spill of milk on the floor and back, then puts the letters on the sideboard and begins clearing up.

"I think lamb," my mouth is saying. I crane my head to see the handwriting on the topmost envelope. "Spring lamb. Fresh-butchered. Potatoes. Some sort of green vegetable." How did I not hear the post arrive? Were they from yesterday? Would she have kept them from me? No. It must have come while John was screaming or when he and Berry were fighting. "A dinner that George, Mr. Mallory, would enjoy if he were home. You take care of the other courses. Nothing extravagant. Simple."

The writing on the top envelope isn't his, but it could contain news of him.

"The good china is still packed." A pause and then, "Mum."

"Oh. Of course. Have Vi unpack it while you go to market. She'll have the time. I'm taking the children to their lesson." A flush across my face. *Don't explain yourself,* Marby's voice hisses.

She bobs her head but is still waiting.

"What is it, Edith?"

"The seating, mum? And candles? Flowers?"

"No need," I say. My hand is reaching for the letters. "The seating we will discuss later. I'll buy the flowers while I'm out."

I wait to flip through the envelopes until I am back in the sitting room and the door is closed. Outside, the bells at one of the colleges toll. If George were here he would say, "Ah, King's." Or, "That's the alma mater." And I would hum—*Oranges and lemons say the bells . . .*

There is nothing from George. A bill for his boots still to be paid. A request for an interview from the *Evening Standard*; they've heard something about the climbers' diet being one of sweets and want to know more. Absurd. And a letter from the Reverend Mallory, which I don't want to read. Not now. It will be full of the usual self-serving pity for me. He uses George's absence—or my *situation*, as he calls it—to further pontificate on his son's failings. I've become a convenient tool for him. A blunt one. It was better when he thought me strange and unsettling.

"He doesn't," George said, after I'd met his father and mother for the first time.

"Oh, but he does. I can see it. He peers at me as though I'm some strange, exotic animal. Part of him is entranced, part of him appalled. He likes my father's money but loathes my father's politics."

"You mean your father's habits."

"Yes, fine then, his habits. I think your father is terrified he'll find me naked some Sunday morning in his sacristy. I'd never do that. One's parents being naturist is enough to purify any child."

I did try to make him like me, though. I thought if the reverend and his son were able to reconcile their differences, it might make things easier for me. Now he seizes on me as a means to steer George toward a more conventional life. That the reverend doesn't like it is the one small pleasure that I take in George's being away.

I drop the post on the side table and go to sit in the window. Unless a telegram comes, there will be no more news until late this afternoon. Six long hours.

Below me the garden is a lush green; the grass will have to be trimmed soon. From here I don't see individual blades but a swirling carpet in shifting tones. As I watch, the lawn darkens, like sea grass, and the air above it too. Just a cloud moving in, but there is the plunging in my stomach, a flash of déjà vu.

It was the week before George left, and I was waiting for him to return from his run.

Some days it feels as if all I do is wait.

That particular day was gray and the rain on the window blurred the world beyond. George should have been home by then. He had promised to go to church with me. In the sitting room, I stood at the window, staring at the cascade of rain so I wouldn't see his presence everywhere. The house was cluttered with his belongings—mine and the children's were still in so many boxes, but George's possessions were everywhere. Maps and books and lengths of rope to be carefully measured.

On the floor at my foot was an envelope with his scrawl: *Blue socks, letters, book, metal flask, Burberry*. I lifted my head so it was out of my line of sight.

The rain slipping down the window pulled my eyelids downward with it. The night before George left, he didn't sleep and so neither did I, jostled awake by his ongoing arrivals and departures. When I came down for breakfast, he was already gone.

I dressed and waited by the window. My hands were cold. And then there was a scraping against stone, a tapping at the window. My name. "Ruth."

He was pressed against the window, clinging, like a drowned cat, to the sill. Everything was wet.

"Don't let go," I cried, and opened the window out, carefully, as he shuffled aside. He pulled himself up so his waist was even with mine outside the window. "Get in here. You'll catch your death."

"Kiss me first."

"You haven't done this for a long time." And I shook my head, leaned back out of the rain, but couldn't help smiling.

"Kiss me," he insisted again. His face was wet from rain, from sweat. He hauled himself in the window and grabbed me, water dripping onto the carpet, onto my dress.

"I'll have to change."

"Then you'll have to change." We were warm and damp where our bodies met. He pulled me to his lap on the floor. "Do you remember how I used to do that, Mouse?"

"Of course, when we were first married. You would climb the wall beneath the loggia at the Holt and pounce on me." I didn't say how much I missed it. "When you come back, don't ever use the door again." I kissed him and stood. "To church, then."

He was sheepish. "I'm sorry, Mouse. You'll have to go without me. I have so much to do." He gestured around the room. "The truck is coming tomorrow. I'll make it up to you. Go every Sunday when I get back." He kissed me again.

Did he want me to stay with him? I wanted to ask, but it was as if he had read my mind. "Go on. You'll be late."

"They're ready, ma'am." Vi stands in the sitting room door with the children.

I've been staring at the book on my lap, the words swimming on the page. If I were asked, I'd never be able to say what I'd been reading, though I'd been turning the pages.

I put it down and look at the three of them, lined up, waiting for inspection. "Go get your shoes on," I say. "Your hats."

I close the book without marking my page. It doesn't matter anyway. The last page is missing.

Each time George has left, he has ripped out the last page from the book I am reading. Has done since our very first separation— when he left me in Venice to go climbing with Will.

"What are you reading?" he asked, leaning over the back of the sofa. He smelled of soap.

"Henry James. *The Aspern Papers.*"

"Is it good?"

"You don't know it?" I was surprised.

When he shook his head, I handed it to him for his inspection. He stood up, leaving the soap smell lingering. "I can lend it to you when I'm done." He turned right to the last page. "No," I cried. "Stop, you'll ruin it!"

I meant the ending. Instead, he folded the page carefully against itself and then ripped it out. I said nothing, only watched.

"I'll keep this," he said, and slipped the page into his pocket. "And you'll never know how it ends unless you agree to see me again. I'll keep it with me and the next time you see me you can have it back."

"That's ridiculous."

"Maybe. But it's also the way it is."

Since then he's taken a page with him every time he's left. To France, to the Alps. Even to Everest and New York. Whatever book I am reading, no matter how close I am to finishing. I pace out the rest of the pages, reading slowly, timing the end with George's return.

This time he almost didn't take the page. In the hotel room, as I packed, I realized it was still there.

"You forgot this," I said, and ripped the page myself. It wasn't as neat as when George ripped it; words were left hanging in the book.

He took it, folded it in his journal, kissed my forehead.

When he comes back I will find it hidden, somewhere, on him. Tucked into a pocket, the waistband of his trousers as I undress him.

"We're ready, *maman*!" Berry's voice, impatient, from the entry.

"*Shhh.*" Vi's tone is scolding.

I go to them; they are neat and clean, the mess of breakfast washed away. Their faces are damp at their hairlines, their jaws.

"Shall we be off, then? We've a busy day."

"To Aunt Cottie's?"

"Yes."

"*Oui, maman.*"

Clare turns to leave, with Berry shadowing her. John reaches to me and I lift the solid weight of him. "Lay the table while we're gone, please, Vi. I may be a while."

"Yes, ma'am."

I take up my own hat and gloves from the hall table and quickly inspect the three of them. *You won't believe how big they've grown*, I'll write. My own reflection in the mirror is presentable. I step with the children into the bright day.

ICEFALL

———✦———

19,325 Feet

Gentlemen, please?"

Noel stood outside the mess tent, his arm around his camera on its tripod, a massive mahogany and brass contraption weighing better than a stone. Sandy had been learning to calculate the weight of everything at a glance. "Don't carry anything up you can live without," George had told him. "Every ounce will try and drag you back down again." It seemed true enough. The summit was still a long way from here.

"Over here, gentlemen," Noel called again. "Please?"

"Have you noticed," George had pointed out to him on the trek, "that Noel always speaks in questions?"

Since then Sandy hadn't been able to help but hear it, and Noel's persistent questions grated on him. It would be a relief when Noel no longer shared a camp with them. They wouldn't have to worry anymore about being filmed, being photographed, of always being asked to pose and do it one more time. For the camera.

This, though—the official photo—this Sandy didn't mind, really.

This would be in the papers. In the history books. If they made it. He wished he felt more like smiling.

He couldn't stop thinking about the boy, but he hoped that by moving up the mountain he'd be able to put the death behind him. The others seemed to have done so already. No one mentioned the drowning, and now, only a day later, they were back to teasing and joking with one another. Somes had sat next to George in the pre-dawn dark and asked him about his sleep, about the route up. It was as if nothing had happened between them. The porters were quieter than usual, but they were lining up to compare the loads they would soon shoulder through the glacier and stamping their feet against the cold. They were ready too. Now, the only thing that remained to be done was to pose for the expedition photograph, but Noel had insisted they wait for more light. Sandy just wanted to move up the mountain. To get on with the bloody thing.

Noel's camera bellows were cracking in the dry air, even though he slathered them with petroleum jelly throughout the day. The arid cold was taking its toll on everything. Sandy's own face was parched and scabbed and hurt constantly, as if the skin were being flayed from his skull. Noel pulled off his fingerless gloves, expanded and collapsed the bellows, loosening the folds. He exhaled loudly, showily, and his breath fogged the lens.

The others—Odell, Shebbeare, Hazard—were milling about, the early morning light setting them in sharp relief against the gray of Base Camp. As Noel tossed his arm over the camera again, in an almost intimate gesture, and peered into the glass eye of the lens, the men arranged themselves in some sort of composition they remem-bered from school photographs—a tableau of rangy lines, one seated in front, one standing behind, deciding how they wanted to be seen, to be remembered. Shoulders were pressed back, chins jutted out.

"Come on." Norton waved to him and George. "Let's get this done."

George sighed, then dropped the rope he'd been uncoiling and recoiling and moved off to join the others, Sandy trailing after him.

Odell gestured to the space beside him, but Sandy stopped and stood next to George, behind Shebbeare. George turned to him and reached over to straighten his scarf, pushing it down under his chin. It hurt like hell, the wool brushing against his face, but Sandy forced a smile. George nodded, squinted his eyes a little at him, then lifted his foot and set it on Shebbeare's shoulder.

"We all know you want the summit, George," Odell said from down the line, "but you don't have to climb over our dead bodies." No one laughed.

All around them were tin plates of half-eaten food, teacups balanced precariously on rocks. But Noel would frame it perfectly. Sandy pressed his own shoulders back.

"Really, Mallory?" Noel asked. "Like that?"

George tensed beside him and he tried to hide his smile. "Take the bloody photo, Noel. I've things to do."

"We've this to do." Norton's voice was quiet from the other side of George.

George didn't shift. They looked a fine lot, though. Strong. Well kitted out. Ready to take on the mountain.

"Right," Noel gave in, walking around behind the camera. "This way, gentlemen, please? And a one, two?" The shutter opened; he could see the fanning eye of it, imagined the silver of the chemicals. They waited long seconds, standing still in the sun and wind. When Noel dropped his hand to indicate the shutter's closing, Shebbeare shrugged George's foot from his shoulder.

Stepping away, George spoke over his shoulder. "Ten minutes and we're out." Then he bent to retrieve the coil of rope and walked off alone.

◆   ◆   ◆

EVEN WITH THE EARLY START, the sun was over the near peaks by the time they reached the glacier, washing the landscape in pinks and golds. George had settled into the rhythm of the climb, the crunch of his crampons cutting into the ice. He could see the route in his head and on the ice in front of him, like lines on a map. The ropes paid out behind him.

Sandy came next, then the coolies with their loads, followed by Odell, Shebbeare, and Noel with that bloody camera. "You'll have to keep up, Noel," he'd told him as he checked the ropes earlier. "I won't wait for you."

"Don't worry about me, Mallory."

"It's not you I'm worried about." There were too many risks on the glacier to stop or slow for more than a few minutes. Despite the cold temperatures, this high up the sun was merciless, scorching the atmosphere, which was too thin to provide any protection. They had to be through the ice before the full heat of the sun was upon it. This part of the mountain was alive: the glacier lay in wait for them. And even at this relatively low altitude there were risks.

"The first time, we had no idea what to expect," he told Sandy during the trek. They'd been sitting next to one of the glacial rivers in the foothills, drying after a brisk swim. The air was warm after the shock of the roaring water. "We were pushing up the ice. We didn't know what we were doing, where it was going. And then one of the coolies just stopped and screamed."

"One of the porters?"

"Young fellow. Virgil's nephew, I think he was. It was a shock.

We don't expect the altitude to get to them, but it does. Impossible to say who and when it will strike. When I could get the lad to speak again, he said it was like an ice pick in his head. We all had headaches. The one consistency on Everest, the headaches. Like a rotten hangover. I thought he might just be lazy, didn't want to do the work. But he couldn't go any higher up. Every step, he said, was an agony."

"But he was all right?"

"He had to go back down to Base Camp and then on back home. Longstaff said later it was a hemorrhage. If he'd gone any higher, he would have died. Might even have died if he'd stayed at that height. We weren't even that high up."

The rope pulled at George's waist. The ice carried sounds up to him, the gasping breaths behind him sounding close in the narrow passes of ice.

And now a faster sound, the quick crunch of footsteps coming even closer. He turned to see Sandy dashing toward him, more a hurried walk than a run. With their short breath, running was impossible. What was Sandy doing? Had he missed something? Quickly he tallied the coolies who trudged monotonously upward, heads bowed.

Sandy dropped to his knees on the smooth ice, gliding along it until he reached George. Then he dug in one toe, pivoted, and stopped, smiling up at him. Sandy was gasping, flushed. All raw exuberance. "The ice has certainly gotten to you." George reached out and cuffed Sandy lightly on the back of his head. "All right," he said more loudly, the ice carrying his voice, "we'll rest here a minute."

"How on earth did you find your way through this?" Sandy asked, amazed, his voice a raspy breath. Sandy stood, and George felt his breath warm his face briefly, leaving his skin cooler than it was before. He shrugged out of his pack and sat down on it, in the shadow of an overhang. It was true—there was no obvious trail to follow, no exit; they were hemmed in by ice walls.

"The ice shows you, if you know how to read it. It's like following a slow river."

"Very slow." Sandy laughed, crouching down beside him. Then he pulled his hat low over his own face and rummaged through his rucksack for his canteen.

For the most part the coolies coming up seemed strong, despite the massive loads on their backs. None of them wore crampons—there weren't enough to go around and that slowed them some—but all in all he was pleased. A short break would refresh them. Keep them from getting frustrated, from dropping their loads or refusing to go on. Keeping them focused was important. A single misstep could send someone stumbling into a crevasse, pulling everyone on the rope down with him.

"How are we doing for time?" Sandy asked, taking a long drink from his canteen.

Somewhere the steady drop of meltwater was a ticking clock.

"Not bad." He checked his watch—ten-thirty—though the hour meant less than how hot the sun was, beating down on them through the thin atmosphere. "But we'll have to keep pushing. It's getting warm. And once that happens, the ice starts to melt, to shift. That's the real danger."

"I really didn't think I'd have to worry about getting too warm on Everest."

The coolies were beginning to reach them now. They said nothing to him, but murmured to each other and dropped their loads. It would take some work to get them going again.

To a man, though, the coolies looked good. None of them was the worse for wear, just slow. They always needed to be pushed. Unmotivated, he thought. They had nothing at stake. They'd get paid so long as they finished the expedition. If they quit early, their pay would be docked. One of the female porters opened her red coat to breast-feed the child strapped to her chest. He turned away, avoiding the sight of the swollen, drooping flesh, the blackberry-colored areole so exotic and blatant.

He pulled out Ruth's recent letter, delivered last night. He'd been parceling out reading it, wanting to make it last. *What I want you to know, darling, almost more than anything, is that I am appalled, I really did behave terribly in the months before you went. I should like to be able to go back and do them over again and have nothing but support for you. But it is so terribly difficult, despite all my best intentions.*

He stopped there and turned to his own half-written letter. If he tried hard enough, he could almost imagine that this was a kind of conversation they were having, as they did at the end of the day, lying in bed together. *No,* he wrote, *I've been terribly selfish and you completely justified. It was a terrible tug, you know that. But in less than a month's time I shall, with all luck, be on my way back to you, and you already trumpeting my success. It's closer than you think, love.* He paused, gazing out over the gathered coolies, the Icefall below him. "Where's Noel?" he asked.

He folded the letter away and stood. Bloody Noel. If something had happened, if he had to turn back . . .

Odell slipped into the shadow of the overhang, breathing heavily. "It's been two hours. Another—what?—hour and a half before we're through?"

"No need to check up on me, Odell. It's Noel I'm more concerned about."

"He's right there." Odell pointed down the ice to where Noel was climbing slowly toward them. "It's a good route, Mallory. Well done. But we shouldn't wait on Noel. We'll be too delayed."

"I'll decide how long we wait," George said, withdrawing and lighting a cigarette. He inhaled deeply before he answered. "There's an hour or so. But the next bit will be tricky. We'll have to belay some of the loads, break new trail."

"We should get going, then." Odell bent to pick up his pack from where he'd dropped it, patting Sandy's shoulder as if to hurry him up.

"Not yet," George said, and stood to peer down the line to where Noel was now trudging up with Shebbeare and two coolies carrying a camera, a tripod. "I'll let you know when we're ready to go." He took Odell's canteen, drank deeply from it before taking a long final drag on his cigarette and making for Noel. Odell would just have to wait for him.

Noel should know better. George truly loved this part of the mountain, but it was changeable and dangerous. The East Rongbuk Glacier was a frozen river that churned and flowed down the slope of the mountain until it finally melted and raged into the Himalayan watershed. It was never the same. Not even day to day, let alone year to year. Here, on the ice, was real climbing. Technical, precise. Noel couldn't be left to wander through it on his own.

◆   ◆   ◆

THE BICKERING made Sandy uncomfortable. Not bickering, exactly, but he didn't quite know what else to call it. It was an intimate sort of squabbling that somehow reminded him of how his mother didn't quite say what she meant to his father when he came home a bit tight.

He shifted his weight where he sat on his pack as George stalked off to talk to Noel.

"For chrissake," George started in, gesturing to Noel's two porters, to Shebbeare. "They, at least, need to stay on the rope." Sandy looked away, took a drink from his canteen. Over and over again, Noel had stopped, unroped, set up his camera, and then tried to catch up to them. It was reckless. George had made it clear they shouldn't dawdle on the ice.

"It's all right," Shebbeare said. "I don't mind."

George turned on Shebbeare. "You may think you're being useful, but you aren't. I'm the one in charge here. For a good reason."

"I needed the shot, George," Noel said.

"I don't care about your shot. That's not why we're here."

"You'll care when you're headlining the film again in New York," Noel shot back. "If I remember, you had a pretty good time playing celebrity last year."

"You might want to use this," Odell said, handing Sandy a tube of petroleum jelly. "For your face."

"I'm fine," Sandy said, taking and opening the tube anyway.

Odell nodded and sat down. "You're moving well. Not that I'm surprised. But not quite like Spitsbergen, eh?"

He glanced over at Odell. "No. It really isn't." Spitsbergen had been rolling fields of ice and snow. This was more like a vast labyrinth.

"Because of the extreme temperatures up here," Odell said. "It melts and freezes so quickly. Day in. Day out. It shapes the ice. Spectacular, really. You sure you're feeling all right?" Sandy just nodded. "Good. George will likely set a quick pace in the next while. He thinks everyone can move like him. It's good to push, Sandy, but if you need to slow down, do it. Sometimes George needs to be reined in."

"I'll be fine. I can keep up."

"You know what can happen on glaciers. You remember what

happened in Spitsbergen. Simon delayed us for hours because he pushed too hard. You want to stay sharp."

"I don't really need the lecture."

"Sandy . . ." Odell began, then paused, inhaled deeply. "That's not what I meant. I'm just looking out for you."

"I know. Thanks." Sandy stood and shrugged into his pack. It felt heavier than when he'd put it down. His legs were heavy too. Too bad they couldn't rest just a bit longer. It was pleasant out of the sun, in the cool shadow of the ice. Back out in the full glare, the sun would rip at him. "Looks like George is ready to go," he said, stepping away from Odell.

It seemed to take a long time to get moving again, to get the porters back on their feet. Sandy moved down the line, checking the ropes they'd looped around their waists, one to the next, a great length of it paid out in between. The Sherpas were so small he had to bend to check their jumbled knots. This close to them, he caught the scent of soot and grass. Unfamiliar smells amidst all the snow and ice.

"Odell," George said, "bring up the rear with Noel, will you? It'll give you a few more minutes to rest too. Sandy, let's go."

Sandy kicked his crampons into the ice and followed George through the pinnacles rising up all around him. After creeping through a narrow pass, the ice so close he could feel the cool of it on his pained face, he entered into an open-air ballroom. The ice surrounded them. Great towering seracs rose up and encircled a pond of perfectly smooth ice that glinted in the sun.

He would never be able find his way out of this. Not on his own. Everywhere there were walls and walls of ice, fun-house mirrors that painfully reflected the glaring rays of the sun, even through the dark tint of his goggles. George could be leading him anywhere.

As he glanced around, the rope tugged at his waist, drawing him on. There was a fairy magic here. It was changeable, beautiful. It almost returned his breath to him, lightened his load. Almost.

"You wouldn't believe it," he'd tell Marjory when he got back. "It's like your diamonds, all that sparkle and fire captured in something solid." He'd hold it up for her, the necklace she'd lied to her ex-husband about, telling him she had lost it somewhere because it was one of the few things that she had wanted to keep. "Look at it, Sandy," she'd pouted, holding it up so it flashed. "Wouldn't you keep it too?"

He wouldn't have. Not then. But now it might conjure a little of the magic of this place in a way she would understand.

The rope tugged again, so he picked up his pace, feeling the strain in his lungs. It was good, though, to feel his body work. "This is amazing," he said when he caught up with George, his voice coming in gasps that he tried to hide. "Really. I've never seen anything like this."

"'Before me,'" George said, spreading his arms, "'nothing but eternal things were made, / And I shall last eternally.' Dante."

"I think I was supposed to study him this term," Sandy said. "Dante." His tongue was thick in his mouth, woolen. "Actually, the term's over by now. Isn't that strange? How time keeps passing there even while we're away? Just exams left to sit now. Dick, all the rest, they'll be graduating. I'll still have to go back."

"You only have one term left, Sandy."

Sandy closed his eyes against the vicious sun and opened them to his light-dappled room at Oxford. His sister, Evie, was shaking her head at him. "I know that, Evie," he said, tossing a pair of wool socks at her. "I thought you were here to help me pack." She tossed the socks back and then dropped onto his neatly made bed. He pulled the corner tight where it had come untucked.

"But one more term and you'll be finished. Then you can go off and explore anything you want."

"Mum's already tried that tack. By the time summer rolls around, there will be one less place to explore. Come on, Evie, don't pretend you wouldn't go if you could."

"Sure, I'd go. But I'm not doing that well in school anyway. It really wouldn't be a great loss."

He ignored her, opened his wardrobe, and pulled out the new windproofs he'd had made for the trip. When they first arrived, he had tried them on, admiring himself in the mirror, striking climbing poses with his ice axe. Since then he had kept them folded neatly in the box they were delivered in.

"And how does *Miss* Marjory feel about your going away again for so long," she asked, reaching for the framed photograph on his desk.

He dropped the box and took the photo back from Evie. "Actually," he said, "*she* thinks it's a grand idea."

"Really, Sandy." Evie picked up his dropped windproofs and began folding them into neat packages, the material crinkling in her hands. "You can't keep this up. For goodness' sake, poor Dick is devastated. Humiliated. You know he tries to pretend it's all fine, because he loves you. But imagine what it's like for him—his best friend and his father's wife. How could you do that to him? She's a married woman."

"She's divorced."

"Barely. And that doesn't make it any better." She'd folded and refolded the pants and jacket. He took them from her, put them into his footlocker. "Are you in love with her?"

"Jesus, Evie."

"It's probably something you should figure out," she said.

"Here."

Sandy squeezed his eyes against the dark shadow George made against the blaze of sky and snow, and glanced around for his sister. She shouldn't be here. Slowly, he realized, she wasn't.

"I just need to sit a minute," he said as he slumped to the ice. "Just a minute." George wavered and shimmered in front of him. He'd sort it all out in a minute.

"You're dehydrated, Sandy. Drink this." George was holding out his canteen.

"I'm fine. You drink it." He pushed George's hand away, but George was insistent.

After Sandy drank, George took the canteen back and then leaned down to haul him up by his armpits. "We need to keep going."

"No. I'll just stay here."

"That's the lassitude talking. You can't stay here. The water will help. You'll be fine." George tugged at the rope. "Come on."

He wobbled a moment, then picked up his foot and stumbled on, measuring his own limbs against George's. The cold water sloshed in his stomach, but it was already leaching into him. His vision sharpened. Foolish. A beginner's mistake. He should have recognized the signs of dehydration, of glacial lassitude. He could quote them by heart: indifference, lethargy, drifting thoughts, distraction. George shouldn't have had to tell him.

Ahead of him George moved like liquid, lazy and easy; there was no panic in his movements, even when the ice seemed to shift under his feet. His own movements were awkward, jerky. His knees too stiff, his legs unsteady. He wished they were back on solid rock.

The glacier was draining him. At least he hoped it was only the glacier. It couldn't be the altitude. Not yet. There was still so far to go. But he'd have to tell Somervell. "I need to know everything," Somes had told him when he and Teddy had seen them off this morning. "How you feel, good or bad, all right? Write it down when you get to Camp Two." He didn't want to tell Somes about this.

The cold from the ice rose up his body in convection currents. Farther ahead there was an echoing boom, followed by the shiver of the ice moving beneath him as a chunk the size of a house broke away.

George slowed down and motioned to him. With his hat pulled low over his ears and his dark goggles blocking most of his face, George looked inhuman. Sandy's reflection in the goggles was warped and bent. The reflected heat and sun illuminated George from below so he appeared to be floating.

"How are you feeling now?" George asked, and coughed.

"Parched. I can hear water. Sounds like it's everywhere."

"It is." George nodded. "It's all melting, dripping down underneath the glacier. There's a river under here. Enough to drive you crazy."

Sandy thought of breaking off a piece of ice and dropping it in his mouth. The slow, cold drip down his throat, smoothing the edges of his cough. Heaven. It must have shown on his face.

"You can't chew on the ice, Sandy. It's tempting, I know, believe me, but it takes too much energy to melt it. It's not worth it."

I know that, he thought but didn't say out loud. He swallowed dryly. "We're almost there, right?"

"That's only the half of it. Then we have to get the camp set up or we'll be sleeping in the snow. We need to unload the coolies and send them back down, at least to Camp One." George gestured with a mittened hand. The line was fully stretched out below them now. He hadn't realized how much height they'd gained. The porters were tiny, threading their way between ice spires on glacial roadways, making their way up to where he stood with George.

"It reminds me of Oxford," Sandy said. "All the ice. The shapes of the towers."

"Reminds me of Manhattan," George said. "I climbed Manhattan once. Ever been?"

He shook his head, but George wasn't looking at him. Maybe if things went well, if there was another film, maybe this time he could go to New York too. He'd love to go to America.

✦   ✦   ✦

GEORGE IMAGINED SHAPES in the ice. Outlines and memories.

The seracs towered over him like the Manhattan skyline: great jutting façades of ice and stone, canyons thrown up around him. He was exhausted and sweltering. They were almost there. He felt as if he were dragging the line behind him up the mountain, up the side of a skyscraper.

Climbing the side of a building had been easier.

After the last expedition, he'd been sent to New York to tell stories. In the blue-white spotlight of the film projector, he had narrated Noel's photographs to raise money for a new expedition by reliving the second expedition on Broadway. Pointing to features in the filmed landscape, he told the audience the color of the ribbons in the hair of the *dzongpen's* wife—red, if he remembered correctly. But the truth didn't really matter. Not then and there. Not anymore. *Remember, you're there, Mr. Mallory, to give the audience what they want. To tell them a good story.* Hinks's letter on the matter had been explicit.

He used the words that he knew they wanted to hear: *ascent* and *angles, altitude, scree, degrees of frost, attempts.* He tried to conjure up the cold, the desperation—everything the ridiculous poster plastered outside the theater had promised. When he first saw it he had cringed, though later, when he described it to Ruth, he tried to laugh about the melodramatic image of two figures against a violent blue sky. "One of them—me, I suppose—" he told her, "was saving another man from falling, with just a single handhold. Ridiculous!"

When he stumbled in his delivery, he knew he had to be disappointing the audience, and his usual enjoyment of being the center of attention slipped. But the small group had applauded enthusiastically and swelled to their feet like the tide. When they finished, he walked backstage, threading through the darkness, around the pulleys and flats from the show in rehearsal, past a beach scene, a canal with Italian buildings.

In England, the Everest lectures had been a rousing success. They'd sold out over and over again, and he was feted at dinners and drinks before and after. He basked in his newfound celebrity, even as Ruth shied away from it, insisted he go alone. "I just can't do it, George," she'd said when he asked her to come with him to America. "You'll be so busy you won't even notice I'm not there." This was after George Finch, who had toured with him some in England, had complained loudly about the attention lavished on George and was dropped from all future speaking engagements. None of the others wanted the bother. Noel was happy to let his film speak for him. Teddy and Somes wanted nothing to do with the spotlight. George bathed in it.

The same could not be said of his experience in the New World.

George had collapsed into his chair in the star's dressing room in New York. His name wasn't on the door. For the first time, he noticed the flowers by the lit mirror, wilting slightly. The heat, he told himself, as he read the card. They weren't for him. They'd been left there. His face in the mirror looked old.

"Come on, old chap."

He tried to smile at the representative from the National Geographic Society, but couldn't remember his name. Neil? The fake accent grated on his nerves more than it should have done.

"Time to celebrate." Neil clapped his hands together emphatically.

"Yes, of course."

At the reception there was an ice sculpture on the table, shaped like a mountain, though not at all like Everest. American ice, molded and chipped. Misshapen. It looked more like the mountain logo of that film studio than any real summit. No one here was going for accuracy. The room was too warm, the lighting too soft. As Neil ushered him from guest to guest, someone handed him a cup filled with shaved ice topped with red raspberry syrup. Like blood on snow.

"Straight from the summit." A woman's voice near his ear.

"The summit of what?" he asked.

"The mountain over there."

There was a slight trace of an accent, carefully covered. She nodded toward the sculpted mountain, at the waiter standing behind it in a sharp tuxedo who shaved ice into glasses. The mountain was melting in the warm room, the edges of it softening, pooling around the bottom. Cigarette smoke wreathed its flanks.

"Ah." When they pulled him away for photographs a short while later, he still didn't know her name.

"Gentlemen, please?"

And he thought of Noel taking photographs in other rooms just like this. There were always the official photographs. He handed off his melting red ice and settled into the routine of it: shaking hands or standing between older couples, smiling or serious—morphing into whatever it was they wanted him to be, whatever it was they were looking for. He desperately needed a drink. How did Americans get anything done being so bloody dry? The inevitable round of questions was coming. The hows, the wheres.

The whys.

Between the popping of flashbulbs he had looked for her, the woman who had spoken of the summit, craning for her neat blond bob in the darkened room, electric lights turned low to match the candles. He could hear her mid-Atlantic accent somewhere. It was something between here and home. She had smelled of the city, a little acrid, sharp, but somehow there was also a fading scent of green. From a greenhouse maybe, New York being too cold in February to dream of anything growing.

Someone handed him a cup of tea; it looked weak, already cooling, but he sipped it anyway. Then she was beside him again.

"Take mine," she said.

"No, I couldn't. Thank you."

"I insist. You'll need it. For the reporters. Oooooh." She shivered exaggeratedly and the cap shoulder of her dress slipped down, revealing a sharp angle of bone, the ribbon strap of a silk slip. She pulled it back up and exchanged her cup for his. It was warmer and smelled of whiskey and lipstick.

He tried to remember the taste of whiskey on Ruth's lips, of alcohol radiating from her skin in the morning. How would this woman taste?

He turned to face the reporters.

Why. That was what everyone wanted to know. Or at least the ones who had never been on a mountain before. He'd never been able to explain it properly. What was there to explain? It was the aesthetics of the climb, the pull and lure of what lies just over that oh-so-close horizon. It was the pure pleasure of turning a route, a wall, of having your body do exactly what you need it to, when you need it to. But it was more than that too. There was a supremacy he felt when he stood on a summit. An ascendency.

His limbs were tired and tight. He'd been still for too long. He wanted to climb something. Anything. Or go for a run through the park that was only a couple of blocks north. Maybe no one would miss him. He was exhausted. He wanted to flirt with that blonde. He wanted to sleep.

But *why?* He had waited for it all evening. Dreaded it.

"Why, Mr. Mallory?" began one. "What exactly is the point of climbing this mountain?"

"It seems like an awful great risk, don't you think? Is it worth risking your life for?"

"Or the lives of others," another man cut in.

"How many people have died so far?"

"Mr. Mallory, what exactly do you hope to prove?"

The voices and questions merged together. They were beginning to sound like accusations. He took a long pull from his teacup, wondered if any of the reporters were drinking too.

He wished Ruth were there with him.

The weight of the climb was in his legs, but George had no choice but to continue breaking the new trail. No one else could take over. Sandy, the closest behind him, was too inexperienced, too weak. Besides, they were almost through the glacier, and the pleasure and anxiety of a new route kicked up adrenaline in him, eroded his exhaustion. His body made the decisions for him, carried him around weak spots in the ice and crevasses covered with a rime of snow. George leaned his forehead against the ice wall he was scaling, so cool after the glaring sun reflecting all around him. It melted against his skin, water running down his face. He licked his lips.

He wished there were stone under his bare fingers instead of this ice under his gloves. He dropped all his weight onto his right foot and the toe of his crampon dug into the ice. There was pressure on his ankle, a familiar ache, as he pulled his ice axe from the wall and slammed it back in a few feet higher. Ice chips rained down and melted on his cheeks and lips. He pulled himself up on the axe and pressed his forehead to the ice again. Just a moment, then the next placement.

He could see into the ice, only inches from his face. There was a boulder in the ice in front of him, petrified, frozen in place for a millennium. More, maybe. Sliding slowly down the mountain in the river of ice.

His wrists, his elbows, his shoulders—they ached from the stuttered impact of his axe into ice. How many times had he wielded the axe today? In his lifetime? His fingers were tight and swollen from dehydration. No matter how much he drank, the dry air sucked all the moisture from his breath, his body. There was too much tension in every one of his joints. He exhaled and pulled up again, wrestled himself over the lip of the wall.

His body had forgotten grace.

From the top of the wall he could see the rest of the trail ahead, as clear as a line on the white of the Icefall, leading off the glacier and onto the flank of the mountain. Ruth's words circled in his head—*I really did behave terribly.* George dug himself in at the top of the wall and waited to feel the pull of the rope at his waist and in the grip of his hands as Sandy climbed up behind him.

"Why climb Mount Everest?"

He always wanted to be witty—like James or Vanessa—quick

with the perfect retort. But he couldn't find it. Exhausted, resigned, he exhaled.

There was a furious scribbling and he knew the reporters liked what he'd said, though some of them looked confused by it. There was a knowing nod from Neil, as if what he'd just said was incredibly wise, but he'd forgotten it already. What did they like so much? He still wouldn't remember when he read his own quote in *The New York Times* the next day: *Because it's there.* Had he really said that?

He was slightly drunk. Well, more than slightly. Throughout the evening, the blonde had continued to materialize and pour more whiskey into his tea. His head was foggy, the way it was at altitude. The way it would be at the summit. His body kept itself balanced without his telling it to. He stepped out of the room onto the winter balcony. The wind whipped northward along the skyline to the black rectangle of Central Park. That's where he wanted to be. He glanced at his watch. It wasn't too late. He ducked inside to find his host and make his excuses. Early morning, another lecture to prepare for.

"Are you going?" She was beside him again.

He smiled involuntarily and covered the dregs in his teacup. "No more," he pleaded. And then, "Yes. I need to be on my way. But thank you. For this. Miss . . . ?" He left the question open and waited for her name.

She waited longer, watching him. He waited her out.

"Stella." Her name was a breath. She extended her hand, her short blond hair shaking around her jaw. She was so American. "Stella Jones."

"A Welsh girl? I knew it." He shouldn't be flirting. He should go back to his hotel room and write to Ruth. She should have come to New York with him.

"Something like that," she said.

He followed her to the door.

Out on the street she turned to him. "I want to see you climb. Everyone says that's the only way to really see the beautiful George Mallory." She shivered exaggeratedly yet again, and pushed up against him.

Blushing in the city's darkness, he wondered who "everyone" was. "There isn't anywhere to climb here."

"Maybe we'll find something later."

She took him to a speakeasy where a jazz band played, dark and smoky in the corner. She danced and bought him a record in brown paper from the saxophone player, introduced him as a hero, a great explorer. With the pressed shellac under his arm, he walked away from the conversation.

Outside the club he thought of Ruth and tried not to. He thought of rules and roles and wondered why he bothered. He thought of who it was they all thought he should be and leaned down to kiss Stella.

She shook her head, her lips brushing past his. "No."

It surprised him; he'd thought that was the game. He stepped back but said nothing, wondering how he had so badly misread the situation.

She spoke first, stepping into him, her body so close he could feel the heat off her. Her hair was thick with the smell of smoke from the club. "What are the walls of the Waldorf like?"

"Is this a dare?"

He had sobered up a little, spread talcum powder on his palms. They were dry and smooth in the winter air. Stella stood in his overcoat on his balcony at the Waldorf-Astoria. She sipped at her tumbler of rum, her scarlet lipstick smearing its rim. All of New York lay below him. He knew it was an optical illusion, but the sheer walls of the building dropping away to the avenue below made it seem as though he were higher than he had ever been on any mountain.

"Yes!" she said, cradling her glass in the crook of her arm and clapping her hands together. The sound snapped in the crisp air. Her accent had thickened through the night, with alcohol and comfort. "A dare!"

He stood on the balustrade where it met the wall, and the world fell off to his left. His fingers found the holds in the brickwork the way they always did. He pulled himself up, made his way above the doorframe, and traversed the width of the balcony. He forgot about his audience, the woman watching him, and felt more at ease than he had since he'd arrived in New York.

The stone felt strong under his fingers. His patent leather shoes scraped against its surface, transferring black to the gray stone, leaving traces of him on the building. On the rock.

He descended to the balustrade on the other side of the balcony and thought briefly of the dark emptiness below him. What if he just let go? Why didn't he?

When he came down, Stella's arms were immediately around him. Sometime in the evening, she'd told him she knew him. She was a friend of a friend, knew his mother's sister's daughter at school. She insisted they had met before when they were young, but he didn't remember her. He wished he did. He descended and kissed her.

She tasted of tea and whiskey. Of America and jazz.

"Is there a Victrola?" he asked. He wanted to dance with her.

He found his way through the billowing gauze of curtains into the room. It was opulent, the blue carpet lush and yielding under his feet, the sinking depths of wingback chairs, the soft expanse of the enormous bed. He would have to leave it the next day. The expedition couldn't afford for him to stay there another night. They could barely afford one, but appearances had to be kept up. Tomorrow he would move downtown, before leaving the city in two days from Penn Station.

There was a Victrola. He played his new record and airplaned his arms in time to the music.

Stella laughed. "George Mallory, this isn't you."

"It is."

He walked toward her.

"Well, then, I think I like him."

She was a woman of angles, sharp like ridges. The narrow bones of her hips, the declivity of her collarbone, so different from Ruth's rounder softness.

They danced to jazz and he wished there was more to drink.

In the morning he would read his name in the newspaper and order room service. That night he led Stella to bed. She was long and thin like the girls he had watched in the speakeasy.

When he kissed her again he thought of other kisses, thought of Ruth and his absences, thought about how she would probably understand this. There was no guilt. That was the story he told himself.

He was almost certain Ruth knew nothing of Stella. He'd written her only once, from the Alpine Club. He still hadn't opened her letters.

It was early afternoon when they finally arrived at what would be their campsite.

"Camp Two. Just as we left it."

Well, not exactly. The remains of the old camp—the metal skeleton of the tent, the canvas shredded by wind, by ice, and by rocks that had been hurled at it for the past two years—sat in a drift. There wasn't much to salvage beyond a forgotten tin of beans and some tent poles. The site had been utterly destroyed. They'd erect a new camp in its place, occasionally tossing aside old bits of equipment, frozen rubbish.

It took them hours to raise the tents. Later, they would build small walls from stones he'd ask the coolies to drag from the edge of the Icefall, which they'd drape with canvas to provide a small measure of protection from the mountain. But for now they'd make do. Odell tasked the coolies with making tea, that interminable chore he avoided at all costs. Everyone moved in slow motion, despite the effort. In the thin air they were all half drunk.

"It's cool enough now," he said a few hours later, giving Shebbeare directions for leading down most of the coolies. "It'll be stable. Just stick to the ropes and you'll find your way back easily enough. It should take you only a fraction of the time going back down." Shebbeare nodded a little nervously. "Tell Norton and Somervell to start bringing the oxygen up tomorrow. And give this to Somes." He handed Shebbeare the notes he'd made on how everyone had fared on the push through the Icefall.

"Yessir."

George turned back to camp. The rest of them would stay—Sandy, Odell, Noel, a handful of coolies. They'd settle Camp II and finalize the plans for the next camp. By the time Shebbeare returned with Teddy and Somes tomorrow, he'd be on his way up to establish Camp III. Four more camps and then the summit. They had three weeks, maybe a month, before the monsoon made landfall on the subcontinent.

. . .

George sat on a small box of supplies and watched Odell hover over the coolies as they melted snow for tea and prepared food. Odell would take the first serving, no doubt. He always did.

"Odell," he called. "Could you check those packs? Make sure everything survived the trek." When Odell nodded, he looked away. "We all have to do our part," he added to himself.

Near one of the tents Sandy paced, moving back and forth between crates and tents, stacking and restacking the boxes and packs, digging them into the snow so they wouldn't slip. He hit at chunks of ice with the head of his ice axe. Sandy burned with nervous energy, and the sight of so much activity churned George's stomach. He dropped his head so Sandy was out of his sightline. He needed to focus. They would start to move up to Camp III tomorrow, the day after at the latest. He had to sort out what to take, who would carry it.

Moments later Sandy stood over him, looking down.

"What? You should relax, Sandy. Tea will be ready soon. Don't believe this burst of energy. It'll disappear soon enough."

"Come on," Sandy said. In one hand Sandy held a small palm-sized stone he'd plucked from the edge of the glacier, worn smooth by the ice. In the other, his ice axe. He held them both up, gestured with his head back toward the Icefall.

He shook his head. "Don't be ridiculous."

"Come on, George. You said exercise was good for the lungs, the head, didn't you? Besides, it'll be fun. Odell," Sandy called, raising his voice, "bring your axe."

He followed Sandy back onto the ice, to a smooth, flat pond a quarter of a mile deep. In the heat of the afternoon it had been an oven. Now it was cool and blue. Perfect.

Sandy dropped the flat stone to the ice and grabbed the shaft of his axe. He slapped the puck with the blade, sliding it toward George, who stopped it with his foot and then smiled. With his own axe George slid the rock forward, shuffling his feet along the ice, skating.

"One of the fellows back at my college," Sandy called, "traveled to Toronto one winter with his father. He saw these blokes playing this on the harbor there and thought it looked ripping. So he tried to teach us. We tried to freeze the courtyard at school with buckets of water. It didn't work. This seemed the place to give it another go."

George had been to Toronto just once. After New York. The place had been unbearably cold. Ruth had laughed at him. "Cold? After Everest?" Yes, he'd told her. Cold. Even after Everest. And gray and dark. The cold there pinned you down. He'd never had any desire to go back, but if he did, maybe he'd have a look at Sandy's game.

Virgil had grabbed George's spare axe, and another of the coolies was gripping a broken piece of crate that Sandy had handed him. The ice cooled and snapped around them as they played. Here the sky remained bright long after they could no longer see the sun. George made a false rush at Odell's goal but was blocked by Noel, who slammed him hard from the left. He lifted his elbow to block the ricochet. The sound of his axe on the rock and ice, Sandy's short burst of laughter, echoed off the ice walls. Virgil held his net for him, moving slowly, steadily, between the rocks they'd placed as goalposts. George moved around behind him, nudged the goal markers in a bit. He felt fit in his body. Odell slapped a shot toward him. He blocked the shot, felt the ache of the hit in his cold-numbed leg, then raised his elbow to check Noel, smiling. This was just playing. Noel smiled back. They were having fun. He didn't remember having any fun in '22.

George kept score in his head until they were panting and sweating, too tired to play anymore. It was his win. He wouldn't tell them that, but he knew it. The game had probably lasted only a few minutes, but it felt as if they had played forever. The air was too thin to support Sandy's enthusiasm.

"Come on!" Sandy yelled. "One more point? Winner takes all?"

"What's at stake?"

"The loser melts snow in the morning. Makes the tea."

They seemed to think about it even as they lay spread-eagled on the ice, their chests heaving.

"Maybe a rematch," George said. "On the way down."

His head pounded now. Foolish, this burst of activity. The water they'd have to drink to make up for the dehydration. But everyone was smiling. Even the coolies.

Maybe it was worth it.

"Speaking of tea, we'd better get it on," Odell said. He turned to lead them back to camp.

"Come on." Sandy put his arm over George's shoulders. It was comforting, welcome. "Wasn't such a bad idea, hey?"

"No," George said. "It wasn't. You should keep them coming."

Sandy was flushed. He smiled and his sunburned lip cracked. George wiped at the small spot of blood.

MAGDALENE

Eleven O'Clock

Cottie opens the door with her arms spread out to sweep around Clare and Berry before she realizes I am with them today instead of Vi. She cocks her head at me and then says loudly, brightly, *"Bonjour, mes petites!"*

The entryway is a sunny yellow. Everything in Cottie's home is vivid and boldly colored—paintings and photographs on every conceivable wall space, flowers rotting in the vases, giving off a sickly, overripe scent. Against this backdrop she is a dusty lark, always in tan trousers, a man's white shirt. "Come in, come in! *Entrez!*" She ushers us in, scooping John from my arms. Everything about her is welcoming. "I didn't expect to see you until this evening," she is saying while she swings John from side to side and he giggles. "Can I do anything for you?"

"Could you keep him for me for a few hours?" I bob my head at John in her arms. "If you don't mind."

"Of course. Some time for yourself. That I understand." She says it as if we're conspiring and then turns to Clare and Berry. "What do you say, girls? We'll teach John the colors *en français*." A few hours on my own—away from the house, from Vi and Edith. From everything. The luxury of it washes over me.

The two of them nod. "Then we'll need some paints and papers." Cottie's arms sweep out in a wild gesture; the wood bangles at her wrist knock against each other. "You know where they are. Go find them." They scamper out of the room, toward the kitchen. John toddles after them. Doors bang.

We listen a long moment, waiting for a crash, a wail. When there's no emergency, I carry on, apologizing. "No, it isn't that. It's just Edith and Vi are busy with the dinner party and there are things to take care of before everyone arrives. It's easier without—"

Cottie cuts me off. "Ruth, there's nothing wrong with needing an hour or two—or two months!—to yourself. But you'll have tea first? It won't take a minute."

I walk to the mantelpiece. The clock is ticking close to eleven.

"No, please don't bother. I won't stay long." Cottie's hands are at her short, frizzy hair, trying to smooth it down. If the Reverend Mallory thinks me strange, what must he think of Cottie, whose husband and children are away in London so she can live her "bachelor's life" here, as she calls it, writing and thinking.

"But I haven't seen you in an age. You look well."

"Thank you, but there are the errands to run and it feels like forever since I've been out in the world. I've been staying close to home. It's easier." The words pour out of me like water. "It's just, if word comes, I want to be there. And so many people ask about him. But I can't take it today, sitting there, waiting for the post." I collapse to the sofa, laugh a little. "I sound ridiculous."

"Of course not. It must feel as if everyone is after you. After him. Impossible to talk about anything normal."

"Precisely! Look at us, even now, talking about George and his being away. Sometimes I just don't want to hear his name anymore." There is a long beat as we both try to find something else to fill the conversation. "I knew I was in love with George when I wanted to say his name over and over again. It gave me a thrill in my stomach just to hear it, to taste it."

"I remember that feeling. Even if it's a name like George—not a beautiful name, that."

I smile despite myself. "No. But I would make up excuses to say it." I laugh, embarrassed at the memory. "'By George, Papa!' I used to say. So silly."

"No. It isn't. And it isn't silly to want a break from it."

"Thank you, Cottie."

In the back of the house the children are making noise, opening cupboards. Clare's voice imperious over everything.

"I have had a letter," Cottie says. "I'm sure it's nothing compared to yours. But would you like to read it?"

"You wouldn't mind?"

"Of course not! Just give me . . ." She is already up and crossing the entry into her study. Through the open door there are piles of books, scraps of paper everywhere. Cottie rifles through them, searching.

I picture my letters gathered together under George's pillow, raising it from the bed.

"Ah!" There is a triumphant sound and she pulls pages out, others fluttering to the floor. I am a crow gathering scraps of news about George wherever I can, all of them outdated, irrelevant. None of it tells me about how he is right now, only how he was three weeks ago, a month ago. I count weeks, days, hours. I've become an expert at time. First how long he has been gone, then how long until he returns. But this leaves everything open. In this moment, every possible ending is open to us. He has climbed the summit. He is coming home victorious.

Cottie folds the pages sloppily back into the envelope and hands it to me. There it is—his handwriting. The Mount Everest Committee crest on the reverse, a small sketch of a mountain in blue ink.

"May I?" I hold up my handbag. "I'll give it back to you this evening?"

"Certainly. Take it with you. Take your time."

When I stand, she gives me a quick hug.

"Thank you," I say, though I'm not sure if she hears me. "Vi will come for the children. At the usual time. Thank you," I say again, louder this time.

"I haven't done anything. I'll see you tonight."

Outside I take the letter from my bag and lift it to my face, hoping for some trace of him, but there's nothing. If anything, it smells now of Cottie's home, of ashtrays left full for too long, of ink, maybe. Still, I tuck it inside the top of my blouse, in under my slip, so its corners dig against my skin.

The early-June light is watery still, but the lawns and the foliage are blushing green. Even the gray buildings of Cambridge sprout green moss on their shady sides, which makes them verdant, soft. Walking toward the town center, I feel a sense of ease. The children are taken care of, I have errands to occupy my hours—a nightgown for Clare, flowers for the table. A letter to read. There is peace in the choice of solitude.

In the narrow streets, fellows stream by on their bicycles, and I imagine George here, in his dark, flowing robe, his long, floppy hair. Is this the life he imagined? Am I?

I think of Cottie with her short hair, her trousers. Her ambitions. Even the way she smokes is glamorous. The way she stays so long away from her children, her husband—so she can write. I wonder if I could live like that, be so driven by my own desires and interests, the way George is with his mountains, that I would send the children, my husband, away. There is something to admire, I think, in that kind of commitment.

Like so many of my friends, Cottie was George's friend first. At first, I was intimidated by Cottie—jealous, even, though I hate to admit it, even now, even to myself. But she had climbed with George for years and she, more than me, had once seemed the right girl for him—bold and adventurous. Foolish to imagine ever feeling that way now.

I didn't meet Cottie until after our wedding. At dinner. At the Woolfs'.

"They'll love you," he'd told me, to calm my nerves. "They'll love you because I love you."

He kissed me hard against the Woolfs' front door, his hand under my coat, against my breast, until the maid answered.

I hoped he would be right—but what an audience! Virginia and Leonard; Maynard Keynes; Cottie and her diplomat husband, Owen; James Strachey; Lytton Strachey with whoever his lover was at the time. Aside from family dinners, it was our first invitation as a married couple. Our wedding had been tiny, intimate—family and just a few close friends.

I changed three times before George recommended a dress that his sister, Avie, had given me, cut in loose lines that somehow showed my body underneath. "I can imagine you naked when you wear that dress," he said.

Cottie was kindest to me from the start. She leaned across the loud table, the sleeve of her blouse dipping into her plate, and said, "We were so sad to hear about your honeymoon."

"Yes, a shame to have one's romance derailed by war." James sounded bored by the whole thing.

"It must have been dreadful, really. Porlock, did you say?" Virginia looked at me. It wasn't the honeymoon we'd hoped for. There had been talk of the Alps, but then the war broke out. Still, it was a week for just the two of us and that was enough for me. We camped in a canvas tent on the beach with the sigh and rush of waves on the shore, burbling over fist-sized stones. We brought lots of blankets and piled them under us. We stayed in the tent for days. Eating, talking, reading, making love. We only left to splash into the water, in the rain, wet before we'd even entered it. We were damp for days but it didn't matter. All that mattered was he was there to reach for me, to be reached for.

"Yes," George said. "Porlock. And no, not at all."

I felt a glow radiate down my body and thought of every place he had touched me. We'd lain head to feet, leaning on elbows, on each other. I examined him, crawled over him, drawing lines across shadows of bone, scars, bruises.

"It's not the honeymoon I planned," he had apologized to me at the time. Climbing up to his face, I kissed him.

"It wasn't a bore at all," George told the table. "It was all too much excitement, really. We were arrested for being spies."

He didn't look at me, but his hand under the table scrunched up my dress so that he could touch the bare skin at the top of my stockings. I couldn't look at him.

"You weren't," said Lytton, incredulous. They all were. But there was much talk of spies then. The street signs had been removed from the coastline all the way to London to foil foreign agents. It wasn't impossible that people camping on a beach might be viewed with suspicion.

"We were in the tent, reading. It was pouring rain. Not only didn't we get a honeymoon on the Continent, but we were rained on the entire time. We were keeping each other warm, reading together, and there was a scratching at the canvas flap. Ruth looked at me. We hadn't heard anyone calling. We hadn't even seen anyone else for days. I reached over and untied the flap and there was a soldier crouched at our tent—wet from head to toe. He smelled of wet wool. I thought maybe he wanted to come in out of the rain and I'd already started to lean back out of the way. Then I noticed his gun, pointed at us, but only just. 'Papers,' he sputtered. 'I need to see your papers.'"

In George's story we were stunned, laughed at the absurdity of it. At the dinner table I shifted in my seat, reached for George's hand under the table as Maynard poured me more wine, which I drank deeply. I squeezed his fingers as hard as I could. He didn't even flinch. Didn't blink. Just went on. "We handed him our identification. Our new marriage certificate, which Ruth had tucked into the book she was reading. What was it, darling? The book."

He squeezed my hand as he said my name.

I was meant to conspire with him. To lie. I was flattered and taken aback. The books I had taken with us went right out of my head. I was worried I'd pick the wrong one. Everyone would laugh at me. Glancing around the table, though, I realized they all believed him. They had no reason not to.

"That one by Whymper," I said, finally. I gulped at the wine. "About the disasters in Switzerland. You recommended it. What was the title? I can see it in my head. Small book with etchings. Men falling. Oh!" I grasped at the title. *"Scramble Amongst the Alps."*

"Of course." His smile was dazzling. "It practically gave you nightmares. You tried to forbid me from climbing anymore." He wrinkled his nose at me, the same way he had when we had met, in the drawing room, overlooking the canals in Venice. Us against the world. And there was a thrill to that.

"I'd never forbid you from climbing, though," I corrected. "I know how much it means to you."

There was an approving nod from Cottie, a smirk from James and Lytton.

George continued with his story. How the soldier demanded we go with him, in the rain, and took us to a small stone building overlooking the sea. The waves hammered at the bottom of it, and we were certain the whole cliff would collapse. When they asked if we were spies, George said of course not. Still, we stayed overnight, but at least it was dry. "In the morning they sent us home," he said. "Told us to honeymoon elsewhere." There was appreciative laughter around the table. I felt a flutter of excited nerves at the ruse, but at the same time a swell of embarrassment that I had to be apologized for.

As I gaze in a shop window, I catch my reflection and wonder, not for the first time, if George would rather have married the girl in the story. And what if he had? Even here there is another me, reflected back, darker and wavering.

In the glass behind me, a man in a gray flannel suit walks by, a fedora pulled low over his eyes, and my heart skips. I glance quickly over my shoulder toward him, but he has moved off down the street without even looking at me. Still, I step into the shop, to be sure.

I thought he might have been a reporter, not likely from *The Times,* but the *Standard* maybe, or the *Post.* They send notes. There had been one this morning, asking questions, wanting information.

I don't answer them, and they've never come in person, but I've been wary after what happened at St. Pancras Station, when the press descended on us after the last expedition.

I finger the bolts of cloth on the large wooden table, try to find something suitable, and inexpensive, for a nightdress for Clare. My heart is still racing, but it's slowing now in the cool of the shop. This, too, I could do without—the scrutiny of it all, the constant demands.

"Can I help, Mrs. Mallory?"

"I think this one, please." I hold up the length of cotton and the shopkeeper nods, takes it from me to cut it.

"Would you like us to make it up for you? Or will you be sewing it yourself?"

The light comes in sharply through the store windows, cleaving the floor in two, so that the back half of the room is still dark and cool, while the front is too hot. I step into the shadow so I don't have to squint at the shopkeeper. She's an old woman. And much better at sewing than me. I am about to ask her to make up a simple night-dress, when I realize I haven't measured Clare and she has clearly grown. Foolish. Well, so be it. Clare will have a nightdress made by me, uneven hems and all. At least it will be thriftier.

"I'll take it as it is, thank you."

I should have Clare try on her new dresses again. I had two made up in this very shop for her birthday and she may well be near out-growing them already the way she has sprouted up. If that's the case I'll need to have a photograph taken soon so George can see what it was her daddy gave her for her birthday last month.

I had wanted to make her birthday special.

"What would you like to do today, birthday girl?" I had asked her when she finished her breakfast. "After school, of course."

"Do I have to go?"

"Of course you do."

"Berry doesn't. John doesn't."

"Berry and John aren't big like you."

"Will Daddy be home for my birthday?"

"No, pet, you know that." I had his letter for her. I wanted to wait until the end of the day. "But he did send something." Her face blossomed, she became a different child. "But you'll have to read it here. You can't take it with you to school."

She took it to the window and opened it carefully, trying to pull back the flap without ripping it. Her face was a bold smile. "What does he say?" I asked.

"That the wind tried to carry his hugs and kisses away and the letter ended up in a stream." Then, when it was time for her to go, she handed it back to me. "Keep it somewhere safe for me."

Later, Will arrived with the dresses I had had made. "These came," he whispered to Clare, "straight from Everest."

"They've got *Cambridge Milliners* on them."

"Yes, well, that was the only box your daddy had, wasn't it?"

She looked dubious. She's too old for these sorts of tricks, but Berry and John aren't and they wanted to see what had come from Everest.

"Do coolie girls look like us, then?" Berry asked when she saw Clare's very ordinary dresses.

"What a strange sort of question that is," Will answered. "Let's have pudding!"

Thank goodness for Will.

The shop woman is wrapping the cotton. Perhaps I should have gotten something nicer. Something prettier. But it is only a nightgown. And if all goes well, then perhaps we can afford shop-made nighties for both the girls, and Berry won't have to wear her sister's hand-me-downs.

"Can you send the package to my home? It's only that I have more errands."

"Of course, Mrs. Mallory."

Outside, the pavements are warming under the midday sun and the bells of the colleges all begin to sound. The narrow promenade echoes with them.

It was Will, of course, who suggested the dinner a couple of weeks ago. He'd been by just after the post was delivered. He thinks I don't notice his timing, but I do. He wants to be there should bad news arrive, but also wants to have news from George. I don't mind either way. There had been no letter and so we wandered in the back garden, me bending to pull a weed now and again or to check on a fresh pea shoot, Will following after me. The garden was a surprise, seeing what had been planted before we'd moved in come to bloom.

"The Woods have invited me to dinner on Thursday. Why don't you come with me?" he asked.

"I haven't even been introduced to the Woods. It isn't appropriate."

"Nonsense. They'd love to have you."

"What you mean is they'd love to quiz me about George." I leaned over the just-blooming tulips, their red heads vivid against all the lush green.

"No. I didn't . . ." Will tugged at the leaves of one of the rose-bushes. I lightly slapped his hand away.

"It's all right, Will. I know you didn't mean it like that. But they"—I gestured over the garden wall, at all of Cambridge, all of England—"do."

"Still, it would be good for you to get out."

"I'm fine." I stepped away from him, deeper into the garden. "We're fine."

"Then what say we have a dinner party here?"

I thought about the mess in the house: boxes still piled in corners, the drapes mismatched while I decide on a color. I shook my head. "The place is a mess."

"It'll be a good reason to get everything cleared away. And what we don't, we'll put into George's study. No one needs to go in there. And you'll just invite the people you like. Your sisters. Me?" He cocked his head in a question.

"Of course." I tried not to smile.

"Geoffrey and Eleanor."

"Yes. All right."

"And Arthur Hinks."

"No." I shook my head. "No, Will."

"Hear me out."

"No."

"If you invite Hinks, we can both deal with him and his questions head-on." He could see me listening. "And aside from that, he might know something we don't. That *you* don't. It's almost time."

Will was right. It was almost time. The monsoon, unpredictable as it was, has arrived in India. It will sweep the snow up onto the mountains and shut them off completely. We would have to receive word soon. "Fine." I spread my hands, bobbed a little in a mock curtsey. "A dinner party. But nothing too fancy. And you have to come early."

"Of course."

. . .

Ahead of me the pedestrian promenade widens into Bridge Street. Up ahead is Magdalene, George's old college. I'll walk through, pace his steps. It will be something to tell George: I will see what roses are blooming, what the fellows are discussing. Small things collected up to fill the letters, the hours. I have some time still before I need to be home, and right now the narrow streets seem warmer than the empty house.

I've almost forgotten the man in the fedora, the gray flannel suit. I shake my head at my own foolish thoughts. Will is right: I need some distraction, some company. But when has Will not been right? I've known Will for almost as long as I've known George. He introduced us in the days before we married, when the two of them returned from Wales—"my last jab at bachelorhood!" George had proclaimed, and I had sent him packing. How easy it was then to say good-bye, when it felt like our lives were just beginning. He came home with Will, who would stand up for him at the wedding. "At anything, really," George told me.

Will had found me alone at breakfast—my last, I'd hoped, in my father's house. George and I had already bought our own house across the valley—the Holt—which I could see from my father's veranda. I was staring out at the Holt when Will came to sit across from me.

"Can I show you something, Ruth?" Will asked, accepting a cup of tea. Early risers, both of us.

"Of course."

"George is very happy. It seems you both are."

"Yes. Very. Thank you."

"I've known he was in love since he first met you. What I

mean . . ." Will stuttered a little, flushed. "George isn't the most . . .
restrained person."

"That's part of what I love most about him."

"Me too. When I met him in the Alps in the spring, after he'd
been to Venice with you, he was already saying he would marry you.
I'd never seen him quite so swept up." Will laughed a little. "To tell
the truth, I worried his mind wasn't on the climb. He wrote this and
gave it to me to keep for him. Until you married him."

Will handed me a folded piece of paper.

Now I am lost in listening
That the same lark winging the universal blue
Wakes the same trembling ecstasy in you.

"He said if you'd already agreed to marry him, then his poetry probably wouldn't scare you off."

I stop on the bridge just before Magdalene. Cambridge is becoming my home. I am beginning to love the shape of it, the sounds.
To love the silent college courtyards and the formality of the buildings pushed right up to the road. To love the river that lazes its way
through the town.

Below me, the punts are out, the fellows in their robes resem-
bling great hulking birds, the flapping black cloth like great wings.
Because it's Saturday there are fleets of the small boats drifting the
length of the river and back. Their calls echo along the water, under
the bridge.

"I want to show you something," George said when we first moved
here. We'd held hands all the way to this bridge and I could feel his
excitement, how much he wanted to share. As we walked past the

colleges, their Gothic spires catching the sky, he pointed out routes and angles, loose mortar and deep cracks in the stone.

"Geoffrey taught me to climb them. Look." He pointed up to the spires of Trinity. "That's the most dangerous one. We'd go in the night, in the dark, and try not to get caught. There's even a book. Everyone knows Geoffrey wrote it when he was a fellow, but he denies it. Still. *The Roof-Climber's Guide to Trinity.* I wanted to climb every one of them. I did, too."

I took in all the towers and spires and sloping roofs, wondered what it would be like to scale them. The freedom of it. The terror.

With one hand George reached to show me the best routes, the worst—while his other clasped me about the waist, held me fast. "But this," he said, ushering me down a walkway beside Magdalene, "was one of my favorite places."

The garden in front of me now is just the same, only more lush with its spring growth. The willow hangs low over the wall of the river, washing the couple who sit on it, leaning against each other, in an underwater green. There's a hush here; with the bustle of Bridge Street left behind, there is an almost sacred air.

"Oh, it's lovely," I said. And we lay on the grass, my head against George's chest.

I glance at the couple on the wall and think about us. They're so young. *Oh, George, when did we get so old?* I don't feel old, but thirty-two. *Thirty-two!*

Suddenly I'm exhausted. Insomnia has left my eyes dry and my head thuds slightly. I sit on a bench, lean against the rough bark of the tree, and wish someone were here to hold me, to stroke my hair and my back and send me to sleep. Instead I pull Cottie's letter from my breast. Out of habit I sniff it again briefly before I read, but catch only the scent of my own perfume.

Dear Cottie—These mountains here are unlike anything we've ever seen and only you would know what to call that colour, that blue, that snow and ice turn when the sun disappears.

I try to picture it, think of the paints I have lined up in front of the easel at home, wonder if I could mix it for him. But it would only be guessing.

The climbing here isn't real climbing. Not like you and I have done.

"When did you first climb?" We are on our honeymoon, curled naked together under the blankets.

"Once when my father grounded me to my room."

"You told me he used to make you write out his sermons as punishment."

"Yes! But that was later. Probably the climbing changed the punishment. Clearly I couldn't be left to my own devices. I certainly don't think I deserved to be punished, at any rate.

"Avie dared me that I couldn't lie between the train tracks while a train went over. I said I could and tried to prove it, and when I wouldn't get up again, she ran home to tattle on me. I was locked up for scaring my sister. But as I sulked at my window, I realized I could probably get from there to the roof of the rectory."

"You didn't!"

"I did. I lifted the sash and started to climb out. Just then, of course, Avie came in and screamed. She grabbed hold of my ankle and begged me to come back in. I'm sure that was the only dangerous moment of the whole thing—Avie clinging to my ankle, trying to drag me back in.

"So I kicked her. Not hard. Just enough to get her to let me go. I kicked her and took off like the devil for the roof. I wasn't even thinking about climbing, just about showing them they couldn't punish me for something that wasn't my fault. I stayed up there until they apologized to me. Then climbed down the bell tower. I must have been seven or so. That's how it started. As an escape, I guess."

"Is that what it still is? An escape?"

George Mallory. I am startled by the sound of his name. *Everest.*

I must have drifted off, and I cast around briefly to get my bearings. The light under the tree, dancing off the river, is sharper. The couple by the river have pulled apart somewhat and I notice now that he is in uniform. Perhaps I didn't hear those words, didn't hear his name. Rubbing my eyes, I turn my attention back to Cottie's letter.

Then there it is again. Clearer. "Can you imagine what it would be like on Everest?" It is the woman sitting on the wall. Her blond hair is pulled back tight into a low bun, her profile is elegant, but weighed down by too strong a jawline. "So cold. So uncivilized. Everything is against them. Oh! How brave!" Her face is rapturous as she looks up to the man next to her. His face, though, is stricken. That's the only word for it.

He's not as young as I thought—there is gray in his hair, lines around his mouth. I assume he served in the war. The girl next to him doesn't see his stricken expression or how she has hurt him with the word *brave*. Cruel, foolish girl.

"Didn't you say you knew him?" she asks now.

His response is muffled, carried off down the river.

"George Mallory," she breathes, and leans her head back against him. "Imagine what it would be like to be married to a man like that. I bet she's beautiful. Glamorous. It's all so romantic." Her voice is a sigh and I feel my stomach rise.

Not a foolish girl, then—a stupid one. Anger flashes hot across my body. There is some power in this feeling. Then I am on my feet, Cottie's letter tight in my hand, and I'm walking toward them.

"How glorious it would be if they succeeded. Think what it would mean."

"What would it mean?" I am standing close to them now. Did I say it out loud? I check their faces for a response. I must have. They're staring at me. He swallows and looks away, makes to stand up. Her face is haughty, her chin thrown back.

"What could it possibly mean?" I say, more clearly now, because I do really want to know. I need to. What could it mean? To this woman. To anyone. Whether someone they have never met climbs some damned mountain. She pulls back from me as if I've spit at her. My voice tightens. I barely sound like me, but I can't stop. "You don't know anything. Certainly not what it means to be brave. What is important."

There is a pounding, a wash of noise in my ears, as though I am back by the seaside. The taste of adrenaline, like cloves in my mouth, tinny at the back of my throat. It tastes like betrayal.

Her soldier is panicked. He pulls her from the wall and navigates her down the walk, the click of her heels like the ticking of a clock, speeding up and then slowing, slowing and fading.

I don't want to cry, but it comes in sobs, full racking shudders across my body. I haven't cried like this since before George left.

I was in our room. I'd gone to dress for dinner and it was like a sudden wave crashing over me. I wanted to call for him. I wanted to be comforted, but I couldn't let him see me like that. I rubbed at the tears on my face as he came to me.

"Ruth, it will be all right. It will. I'll be back before you know it."

"You don't know that."

"But I do. I have to."

He sat beside me in front of my vanity, pulled me to him, and dropped my head to the hollow below his collarbone, his chin on my head. We stayed like that and he let me cry. Let me shake against his body, solid and holding me.

I would give anything for him to be here now. So much so that I won't allow myself to name the things that I would do without. I'm appalled by my own selfishness. My whole body hurts with crying. Burns with it. I don't bother to collect myself. There's no point. The garden is empty; I am entirely alone.

ADVANCED BASE CAMP

———•◦•———

21,200 *Feet*

He was finally getting used to this.

Sandy leaned over the cooker, placing chunks of snow inside the tin pot. After a week of climbing up and down from Advanced Base Camp, of bringing up supplies from the lower camps, putting the necessary pieces in place for a summit push that would hopefully come in the next few days, he was finally getting used to the hour it took to make one bloody cup of lukewarm tea. If he had to make a cup quickly or for more than one person, he needed to coddle more than one cooker to life at a time.

There was no one else to do it, though, since the rest of the porters had been sent back down. If he couldn't be climbing, then at least he had the camp to himself, which was more than could be said for poor Hazard, stuck at Base Camp, coordinating loads and supervising the porters. George and Somervell had left yesterday, as had Noel with his own miniature expedition to set up his Eagle's Nest. Everyone, save Noel's team, was due back at ABC anytime.

"Climb high, sleep low," George had told him, explaining the plan of attack.

Sandy repeated the refrain in his head, a mantra that marked his footsteps when he was feeling slow. *Climb high, sleep low*. It was the key to acclimatizing—press up and then drop back down. He was adjusting well, he thought, and Somervell seemed to think so too. "Looks like Hinks was right," he'd said after his last check-in, patting Sandy on the arm. "Our best bet at a superman." He was more than ready to push ahead. Maybe tomorrow. Or the next day, if he wasn't sent instead to bring up more supplies like Shebbeare and Hazard. Those two were little more than glorified porters. Pack mules. Of course, the two of them were still retrieving loads that the porters had dropped short of Advanced Base Camp when they could no longer carry them any higher. Sandy hadn't realized before how much work it was to make sure the higher camps were all properly stocked, or how enormous the undertaking. But if gear or supplies were inadequate or not where they needed to be, it could derail an attempt. Or worse. He couldn't imagine being snowed in above the Col without enough fuel or food to eat. With a spoon Sandy poked at the melting snow. The Col had shocked him when George took him to see it the day after they arrived at ABC. He'd stood at the bottom of the long saddle that connected Everest to her neighbor Changtse and looked up: thirteen hundred mostly vertical feet. All ice and snow. Above the Col, nothing was protected. Above it, the wind screamed down in a terrible way that he couldn't quite grasp. That was where they got turned back in '21. Where the avalanche had occurred in '22. George pointed. "On the lower section we'll cut steps and haul ourselves up them. But the last twenty feet"—George drew his attention to the chimney that they would follow, the route he would try to take—"might as well be rock."

Even then Sandy was certain he could come up with something to make scaling the Col easier. An idea was already ticking in the back of his mind. Yesterday he had broken down some of their empty crates and used lengths of climbing rope to fashion a packable, portable ladder that he would show George when he got back. It might be useful for moving loads up the Col. The rope ladder had turned out well. Maybe a little heavier than he had hoped, but the added weight would be worth it if the ladder made that last stretch easier. They'd need an extra man to carry it or they'd have to leave a load of supplies behind so that someone could cart the ladder up there instead, but delaying a load for a day or two couldn't hurt that much, surely.

Advanced Base Camp would be full that night. He was expecting George and Somes to return from higher up, Odell and Norton to arrive from lower down, and both teams had their own set of porters. He'd enjoyed the night on his own; he'd kept the lantern burning longer than he should have, read a little, and written letters to Evie and Marjory without feeling that anyone was looking over his shoulder; a rare luxury. He probably should have taken the opportunity to write to Dick.

For weeks already he'd been trying to finish his letter, but nothing he wrote seemed adequate. If only they could have resolved the whole messy situation before he'd left, but Dick had remained recalcitrant and Sandy hadn't been able to think of a way to bring him around.

"For God's sake, I could die out there," he'd pleaded the last time they saw each other. "And you'd let this come between us?"

"You've put it between us. You humiliated my father. My father. Who's done everything for you. He thinks of you as another son. And you slept with . . . you're sleeping with that woman." Dick had taken to calling Marjory "that woman" ever since the discovery of their affair almost a year ago.

"Ending it won't change things, Dick. It will still have happened."

Dick said nothing.

"Can't you just wish me well?"

"Of course I want you to do well, Sands, but . . ."

"But nothing." Sandy had spread his arms, an invitation. "You've got to put it behind you."

Dick extended his hand instead, grasped Sandy's. "Good luck. And I want to hear from you. You'll be in my prayers. But when you come home, you'll have to make a choice."

For now, all he could do was try to fill the gap between them with descriptions of the day-to-day business of the expedition. It seemed ridiculous. But it would be days before he got the chance to try again. Having others in the camp again would be a welcome distraction, in a way.

And someone else could take over the responsibility for the camp. It had to be done: someone had to stay at the camp, readying food and support in case any of the climbers higher up stumbled back in, but he didn't much care for being the one left behind. Even if it did prove he was capable of running things on his own. He wanted to do more. Like actually climb the damn mountain. God, what if George and Norton thought boiling water was all he was good for?

George would soon be announcing which teams would be making the push for the summit. Sandy longed to be able to write home with that news. *That* would be something to tell Dick. A chance at the summit would mean all sorts of opportunities: job offers, more expeditions, lecture tours as George had done.

He looked up to see Odell coming into camp from below, a

half-dozen fully loaded porters following close behind him, and Norton bringing up the rear with one flagging porter. Sandy left the cooker to carry on melting the snow and got up to go meet them. At least there was nothing to catch fire up here.

"How was it?" he asked as he reached Odell.

"Same as always." Odell sounded strong. Sandy reached to take his load, but Odell waved him off. "No. Could you help Teddy with Tsering?" Odell gestured at the porter stumbling ahead of Norton at the end of the rope. "He's slow. There must be something wrong with him. He's not usually like this."

The man was limping, his face a grimace of pain. As he approached, Sandy pointed at the straps of his pack, but the Sherpa shook his head. Sandy nodded, emphatic, aware of his own silence. He felt awkward in front of the porters, all miming and half-sentences. "All right?" he asked loudly. The porter shook his head again, but this time he let Sandy take the load before he turned and limped toward the camp. Norton caught up to him then.

"Thanks, Sandy." Norton stepped past him, head down, plodding on. "He's been dragging all day."

Sandy followed, dumped the load, and then sat the porter down on the camp chair he had vacated. Tsering was pale under his sunburned skin. Sandy stood over him. "You're not all right," he said too loudly, shaking his head.

The porter nodded, pointed at his left foot. Sandy kneeled down and took the cramponed boot in hand. *Boot* was being generous. The Sherpa's footwear certainly wasn't meant for climbing, trekking like this; the leather sole was thin, the upper already cracking. Tsering moaned as Sandy touched his foot. Sandy held up his palms, a calming gesture, and then moved back to the man's foot.

The crampons were tight. Maybe too tight. He unstrapped them and Tsering grimaced again. The foot was swollen; he could tell even through the leather of the boot. It was misshapen, like a rotten fruit.

He pulled at the boot and Tsering screamed.

"Dammit," he cursed.

"What is it?" Odell was over his shoulder, pulling off his gloves.

"Frostbite?" Sandy guessed.

"Damn." Odell crouched down. "We'll need to get the boot off. That's why we don't let them use the crampons. They don't know how to use them properly. Now we've lost a porter and a pair of boots."

"Why didn't someone check him?"

"We can't nanny them. Go find something to help."

By the time Sandy came back with scissors from his pack, Odell had enlisted another porter, who was crouched next to Tsering, talking to him in Tibetan.

"I can take care of this until Somes gets back," Sandy said. There wasn't much to be done beyond getting the boot off and slowly warming the Sherpa's foot. Other than that, they'd just have to wait and see.

"Hold his foot," Odell said as he took the scissors. Sandy took hold of the porter's leg, just above the ankle, and braced it for Odell as he slipped one of the blades into the soft leather of the boot. Tsering moaned and bit his lip as Odell began to cut. The anguished expression on the man's face made Sandy nauseous.

"If he's in that much pain, it can't be that bad," Odell was saying. "If it was frozen solid, he wouldn't feel a bloody thing."

Sandy tried to think of what it would be like to have your feet frozen solid, or your hands, imagined the sound they might make knocked against each other. A dull thump. Dampened and slightly soft.

Tsering's wool sock stuck to his skin as Odell tore it from the swollen, blistered flesh. The exposed foot was white, like a fish belly. "We'll have to warm him. Slowly."

"I know."

"Then we'll have to get him back down as soon as we can. Someone will have to take him through the Icefall." Odell looked up; the sun was already dropping to the high horizon. Tsering was breathing heavily through his clenched teeth. "Tomorrow, maybe. If the weather holds."

The sky was clear, the spindrift off the summit a white flag. There weren't any signs of bad weather as far as he could see.

"You don't think it will?"

"I don't know. It's so hard to tell here, but it's awfully calm. That's always cause for suspicion." He returned the scissors to Sandy. "You get back to the tea. Make Tsering a beef one. I'll get him settled. Hopefully one of the coolies can warm him up. Shouldn't George and Somes be back soon?"

Sandy pointed. He'd been watching the two spots moving down through the wide snow bowl of the Cwm for the past hour. George and Somes looked as if they were moving well. If they kept that pace, they'd be back in another hour or so. Just as the sun was setting. He'd never have enough tea ready in time.

✦   ✦   ✦

"WELL, WE GOT UP THERE," George was saying. "Got the loads up. A couple of tents, but it took us longer than I'd have liked. There's still too much work to do."

"And bloody hell," Somes added, "the wind up there will cut you in two. It just comes screaming down the ridge. One moment you're tucked in behind it, sheltered. The next it's tearing you apart."

They were gathered in the larger of the tents, spacious enough for the five of them to sit close but not on top of each other. They'd eaten cocooned inside their sleeping bags, hats pulled over ears, fingerless gloves on their hands.

Somervell had come in late after checking on Tsering. "You two did well with him, no damage in the cutting at all," he said to Sandy and Odell. "He might lose a toe, but if he keeps his foot warm he should keep everything else."

"His crampon was too tight," Sandy said. "He didn't have enough circulation."

"How many times do we have to tell them?" Teddy cut in. "Now we're down another man. We're two days behind schedule because of the cache left down at Camp Two. George, you need to establish Camp Five tomorrow. That's all there is for it."

"I know," George said, slumping after the lousy night on the Col.

"Speaking of," Sandy began, "I have something that might be of some help. I made a ladder—for the top of the Col."

"A ladder?" Teddy sounded incredulous.

"Yes. A rope ladder. One person can climb up with it, get it in place; then everyone else can climb it."

George nodded. "Could be a good idea, Teddy. We need to save all the time we can up there."

"But we'll be down another load," Odell said. "And we're already down a porter."

"George is right," Teddy said. "We'll have to take extra care. Make sure we get those next loads up as quickly as we can. But we'll give the ladder a try. We need to get the camp up. That has to be the first priority."

. . .

George woke with his feet numb from a small drift of snow that had gathered in the tent near them. The flap had come undone in the night and the canvas rumbled and snapped, almost tearing apart as the wind ripped at the material. The roar of it was deafening, but they weren't snowbound. Not yet. The tent was tossing too much for that. A hefty gust picked the whole thing off the ground and then dropped it hard back down to the scree. Next to him, Odell grunted. He hoped the guy ropes would hold.

George sat up, hunched under the angle of canvas. A rain of rime from his condensed breath fell on him. "Odell?" His throat hurt and he couldn't hear his own voice for the sound of the wind, the whipping canvas, the pressure in his ears. "Odell?" He kicked at the shape in the sleeping bag, which grunted, moaned again.

He pulled a jumper around his shoulders, tugged his leather hat down around his ears, and hunched deeper inside his sleeping bag. The wind whistled. He tightened his scarf and exhaled into it; his breath condensed and froze again in an instant. They would be pinned down for the whole day. This was more than another one of the mountain's almost daily skirmishes. It was really bearing down. It would mean a day's rest, but it also meant another day's delay. And they were already behind. Loads were still too low down on the mountain. They needed to establish the upper camps. They didn't have much longer before the monsoon began its sweep across the continent. Two weeks at most, and then the clear break that always preceded the heavy snowfall. If they were lucky.

But the idea of just staying put in his sleeping bag—not moving—was appealing. His whole body ached. Everyone could take care of themselves. If they stayed put in their tents, they'd be fine. The coolies could make do. They stole food all the time anyway, even if they thought the English didn't notice. Besides, they were used to this. The weather if not the altitude. He thought about checking on the injured porter, but even if he dragged himself out into the snow now, Somervell would still need to see to the man. That was *his* responsibility. He was the doctor.

It would be so easy. To just give in to the torpidity. To just sit here and be rocked by the snapping, rolling tent. But the delay would make his head ache, his cough worse. With every delay the summit receded just a little farther. Dammit. He couldn't afford this.

He roused himself and coughed again with the effort, phlegm on his scarf. The muscles that wrapped around his ribs wrenched painfully. He fumbled into his boots, huffing with the effort, with the cold. He didn't bother to tie them, his fingers stiff and clumsy in mismatched gloves. On the way out he kicked Odell again. Harder, maybe, than was necessary.

"How many hands is that you've lost, George?" Teddy tallied numbers in the air, licking at the lead of an imaginary pencil. "You must owe me your firstborn by now."

"Maybe if you'd quit looking over my shoulder at my cards." George tried to sit up straighter.

With all five of them now gathered in the largest tent, they were able to fend off the cold, taking shifts sitting near the barely closed flap. They were relatively warm, easy, lounging against one another, leaning on their elbows.

"Let's play something else." George put down his cards and lit a cigarette before handing his lighter to Somervell.

"We've already played whist, rummy. What else is there?" Odell sounded hoarse. They all did. It was easier to hear each other talk now that the wind had let up some after the long hours they'd spent sitting there. At one-hour intervals George fumbled from the tent into the buffeting wind and snow to check on the coolies. To get away.

Somervell tended the small cooker in the corner. He'd coaxed it all day, methodically melting snow for tea, water to make their weak lunch of bully beef, tinned berries, and chocolate, which Sandy had hidden away in his pack.

"Careful you don't use all the fuel up, Somes," Teddy warned.

"There's plenty."

"We don't know how long we'll be here."

Somes turned down the flame a little.

They didn't talk directly about the mountain, about the delay.

"No point, really," Teddy said. "Not until we know how long we'll be pinned down. We can hold out a good while yet. A good few days. We'll make a plan when we can make a plan."

George drifted in and out of the conversations, in and out of half-sleep.

Somervell talked about his family, his daughter's upcoming wedding, his new position at the hospital in London. Teddy about heading back to the military staff college at Quetta to welcome in the latest batch of recruits. "Don't want them getting too lax before I get to them," he said, laughing.

"Tsering's foot should be fine," Somes said when he came back from checking on him, "but I'd really like to get him down tomorrow at the latest."

George lolled in the late afternoon, exhausted and bored. Through the dull silence he stared lifelessly at nothing. Odell held a notebook in his hands, open to a sketch he had been drawing of a plant he had seen weeks ago. The lines were shaky and weak. He talked about rocks and animals, about the vast diversity of the subcontinent. He droned on about insects and flowers, about a recently translated work he'd read by Alfred Wegener, who proposed something called "continental drift" that could explain why the Yellow Band looked for all the world like deposits of seabeds. Odell might as well have been speaking to himself.

Sandy sat silent. Like an acolyte. Still and quiet. Not how George was used to seeing the boy. He was reminded of the lamas meditating far below them at the Rongbuk Monastery, the ones who took food to the old monk in his stone cave. The anchorite who hadn't left his dark cell since retreating into it twenty-three years ago. He had lived there since before Sandy was born. Amazing. The lama had walked into the cave as a young man and given up everything. He meditated while others sealed up the mouth of the cave and left only the smallest opening through which to pass a daily ration of rice, of water, for the anchorite to pass out his buckets of waste. George couldn't imagine a world that narrow. Nothing but his own thoughts. No one to speak to. Or touch. Twenty-three years of silence.

He leaned back and closed his eyes. Everest enforced this, this isolation and enclosed intimacy, both at once. They were gathered together here, separate from everyone else in the world. They were crammed together in this tent, but the roaring wind, the thin air, kept them speechless for long stretches of time. He climbed into the cave of his head and sat silent in a stupor, leaned against Teddy and Sandy for warmth.

He envied the anchorite, his choosing to be still. Choosing to stay. He wished he could make that choice.

He wished for that kind of commitment.

His father had always known that making George sit still was the worst punishment he could inflict.

"Copy these out. Neatly." His father believed in medieval punishment. He handed George a draft of his Sunday sermon to be copied out: eight pages, each covered in his father's tight writing. "And don't just copy them out. Make sure you understand what they say. We'll be discussing it before supper."

"Yes, Father."

Trafford rarely got these punishments, but then, Trafford rarely did anything that required them. Even when his brother was caught out doing something wrong, Trafford would be sent outside to tend the grounds, to pile leaves. Trafford was never made to sit still inside while the world went by without him. Maybe it was because, unlike him, his brother was happy to sit still with their father in the study anyway. Sitting still, thought George, was for old men. He'd have plenty of time for that later.

He leaned over his father's desk and wrote out the words. He jiggled his legs, swung his feet. His handwriting trailed off into blots and smudges. It would never do. If he took this to his father now, he would only make him start again from the beginning. He'd likely give him extra work just for good measure.

He hated it even more for the fact that Trafford never took his side. Despite being the older brother, the firstborn, George was always in his shadow.

"He never does it to you," he complained to Trafford.

"I've had mine, George."

"Not hardly."

"You're impetuous. He wants to calm you."

"You don't even know what that means. And calming is for girls. Calming is for old men. And goody-goodies."

"That's not fair, George. He only needs you to listen. Only slow down and listen to him. If you did, then maybe he wouldn't have to be so hard on you."

"I do listen, I just don't like what he has to say."

"You can't just always listen to yourself. Sometimes other people do actually know what's best."

He crumpled up the pages and started again. Everything would have to be perfect. He forced his legs to stay still and copied the lines.

His father's study was dark. Reverend Mallory hated the distractions of the outside world, and so the windows were shuttered against the churchyard, against the flowers that bloomed just outside the windows. "It keeps the mind clear," his father said.

It made George angry. He hated the dark room, knowing that there was a world outside that he wasn't allowed to be a part of. How could his father not love it, want to keep it out? It made no sense to him.

He went to the window and opened it, and stood there dazed by the light. Until his father cuffed him on the back of his head, he might as well have been out in the world.

Now he fidgeted in the cramped space of the tent; his hip ached from sitting cross-legged, hunched on the cold tarp.

"What do you want most?" Odell asked. "Right now."

It was a game they played, conjuring the luxuries of home.

"A hot bath."

"Perfect, yes."

"My wife to draw it," George added.

There was laughing, in gusts, with the wind.

"Hot tea."

"Mmmmm."

"Hot soup."

"Hot anything." Sandy poured insinuation into the words. They paused and the silence hung in the air, blown about by the wind. He was surprised by Sandy's joke, enjoyed the blush that spread up Sandy's cheek. He could imagine the heat there. The moment ended and laughter exploded again.

"A flush toilet," he said.

"Clean clothes."

Their voices rushed together.

Somes said, "A soft bed to sleep in."

"Any bed to sleep in."

"New books to read," from Teddy.

"Fresh food."

"God, yes," agreed Somes. "Anything green and crisp."

"The summit," he said.

That stopped them. Maybe he shouldn't have said it. Maybe they needed a break from it. But the summit was there, behind every word and thought, even if they didn't say it out loud.

"The summit," Teddy repeated quietly. He might have been the only one who heard him.

"I should go check on Tsering." Somervell put his hand on George's shoulder as he passed, squeezed it a little.

He lay back, stared at the roof of the tent, and imagined the shape of the mountain leaning down on him. It was what they all wanted.

Most days it's sitting and waiting. That was what he had told Ruth.

"That's what you said about the trenches in the war," she said, rolling her eyes slightly. But it was indulgent, a look she gave him when he repeated a story she'd heard before, or told her something that she had originally told him, as though it were his own thought. There was a swell of something in his throat. He swallowed against it. "You tell me that so I won't worry."

She was right. It *was* something he told her so she wouldn't worry, but it was also true. The waiting was interminable. He used to hope for something to happen and then curse himself for the hope. But even in the sitting still there was danger. During the war. On Everest. At any moment the world could fall down on him. The dirt of exploded trenches. The tumbled avalanche of snow.

"Does it work?"

He'd only just returned from his second trip to Everest, in '22. Less than a year after his first. How did she put up with it? All this picking her up and putting her down. In the past few years he'd spent more time with Everest—traveling to or from the mountain, planning for it, thinking about it—than he had with his wife. What kind of a husband did that make him?

They were in Paris. They had decided to meet there instead of in London or at home. *I want you to myself,* she'd written him in a letter. It was what he wanted too. Her to himself. Time alone together was what they needed. What he needed. Before he left again for the lecture tour, for New York.

They had met at a hotel just off the Seine, opulent and rich after the confines of tents, the rigors of expedition life. He sent his bags up and stood watching her from the doorway of the salon. She was perfect, waiting for him. He'd imagined her like this for months. She picked up one of the salon's delicate miniature desserts and bit it in half, taking her time, savoring it. Her eyes were on a book but he knew she wasn't reading; she was trying to look as if she weren't waiting.

He imagined her in their room, the swelling curves of her on the still-made bed. He wanted to undress her, peel off the loose coat she wore, the lace gloves, find her underneath, the smell of her—a faint perfume of rose hips, of paper. His own body swelled in response. There was sweat on his lip.

He walked over to the table and stood over her. She glanced up and barely had time to smile before he bent and kissed her. Her teeth scraped against his lips.

When he stood back up she blushed, smiled wider and scanned the room, embarrassed yet hoping everyone had noticed.

He sat down in the chair opposite her, and when he reached for her hand on the table, it was cool, but warmed quickly in his. He ate the remaining bite of her dessert, had a sip of her tea.

"Let's go upstairs," she said.

Afterward she rolled herself in the plush coverlet and ran her fingers over him, drawing the leaner lines of muscles in his arms, his legs, the hollows beneath his cheekbones. She navigated bruises and scrapes.

"You always come back so different," she said. The bumps and bruises were part of any climb, and she would catalog them when he returned, asking for stories—*How did this one happen? Did it hurt?* Most times he couldn't remember. She jokingly counted his fingers, his toes. Her hands on his body were cool, soft. He could have stayed there forever.

She marked each change on him, each fading bruise, each scrape, with her lips. "You'll want to be careful," he said, pinning her to him. "I'll start to make a point of hurting myself."

"Let's go for a walk," she said. "I haven't been here in so long and we've never been together." She stood up from the bed, tossing the blanket over him, and stepped into her discarded dress before bending to pick up from the floor the page he'd torn from her book.

He'd tucked the folded page into the back of his waistband, and she had found it as she undressed him, smiling quickly before dropping it to resume kissing him. He dressed slowly, then followed her out of the hotel.

The streets were noisy and crowded, and he reached for her hand. She grasped it tight, but out in daylight now she seemed more distant from him, as if she didn't know quite what to say or where to look. When she met his eyes, she smiled shyly and then glanced away. They walked through the Luxembourg Gardens and she talked about the children. "They miss you so much. Well, of course they do. That's rather a foolish thing to say."

But after supper, after cocktails on terraces and the walk back to the hotel, she was bold and easy. In the darkness of their room, her body damp and heaving beside him, she said, "Oscar Wilde used to live here. I think he might have died here." She paused a moment— "I almost forgot. The children sent these for you"—and slid down to hug him, first around his thighs and then his waist. The heights of the children.

He pulled her up to him again, kissed each cheek, her forehead, and they fell asleep clasping each other.

After two days everything felt normal again. She'd stopped telling him how he had changed, and she reached for him casually as they strolled the city, leaned against him when they stopped on bridges.

They were sitting on the Pont Neuf. The sun was rising and it was already hot. They would be taking the train to the coast in the morning, be home by evening. He wanted to see his children.

"Tell me the words again," she said. He could feel her voice vibrating through her back, into his chest, where she was pressed into his side. The small hum of her. Could feel her inhale and exhale. He didn't want to move, didn't want her to move. He remembered this, how easy she was against him. "Tell me all those foreign words."

The words had been slipping into his conversation for days— *monsoon, coolie, yeti, bandobast, metch kangmi*—Nepalese, Tibetan, Sherpa words.

"You wouldn't believe it, Ruth. Any of it. Me and six stinking men." He pressed his nose into the space behind her ear to smell her, erase the memory of the camp. "You wouldn't be able to stand me."

"What makes you think I can stand you now?" she teased and kissed him lightly. It felt as though he'd never left.

She shifted away to look at something on the river. He watched her a minute, the line of her curved spine like an echo of the bridge. She kneeled on the bench to peer over the edge of the bridge at the faces carved along the length of it. "Did you know that all of these people were dinner guests?" she said. "One of the kings—Henry, maybe, I don't know. Weren't they all Henrys? At any rate, he wanted to remember them drunk and rowdy."

He reached for her on the bench and pulled her back to him. He was almost convinced by what he had told her about the long, lazy days reading in camp, almost believed in the boredom, the dull routine of it himself.

"I missed you," he said, and she made a small mewing noise. "I don't want to leave again. Let's just stay here for good."

He'd almost believed it himself.

And yet, less than a year later, he'd gone back on his word.

"You're considering it," Ruth spat at him. "Don't lie to me. Please. After everything, I know you're considering it."

"Yes. Fine. I am considering it. It would be foolish not to."

"Foolish? If anyone is foolish, it's me for believing anything you say."

"That's not fair. I meant it. But I don't know that I can let anyone else climb her. I started this, Ruth. I have a responsibility to go back. To finish it. For them. For us. You must see that."

"I don't give a toss for your bloody mountain."

"Ruth, please—"

"You say you love us, George. Me and the children. And I believe you. But every time you're asked to choose, you choose the mountain. Do you know how that feels? And if you go again now, when does it end?" She gestured around the sitting room. Ruth's book was spread open on the sofa where she'd left it, John's blanket crumpled next to it. The photos of the children lit by the wash of light through the window. "Why can't this be enough for you?" When he had no answer, she turned and walked out of the room. He hadn't gone after her.

He pulled a tin of condensed milk from a small packet of food rations. The tent was cramped, a littered mess of open tins, dirty cups, crimped playing cards. Something was jabbing into his right thigh from beneath his sleeping bag. Probably the pencil he had lost earlier after he'd drawn, for Sandy, the route that he would take through the Yellow Band.

"There should be fossils up there," Odell interrupted, "in the Yellow Band. All those layers of limestone, laid down over millennia. Lifted up. Imagine what's hidden up there."

"There's no wandering in the Yellow Band," he told Odell, then turned back to Sandy. "It's like crumbling roof tiles. Dangerous territory. We'll cut a diagonal line up to the ridge, I think. Straight up and along."

Sandy had made his own sketch in his notebook, clean lines, more precise than what George had drawn.

Ignoring the jab in his thigh, he poked two holes into the top of the condensed milk with one of Odell's crampons. His hands were stiff and cold, clumsy in his gloves. When he pulled them off, the flesh looked almost dead. So white. Gingerly, he poured the milk into the small pot of strawberry jam, swirled it with a small spoon. It blended, the cream into the red, to make a lumpy, fleshy pink. It looked alive. More so than they did. They were blue-gray in comparison, drawn and angled. All the soft flesh that used to pad their faces was already gone.

Somes was talking again about faith. They'd run out of polite conversation days, weeks ago. He loved that about climbing. The small spaces, the long hours together, gave them a freedom to talk about big things, important things. Being in the mountains seemed to demand an accounting from them. Each of them had to know where he stood, where the others stood. It wasn't the first time he and Somes had had this conversation. It wouldn't be the last.

He'd been surprised last time by Somervell's faith. He was a doctor, after all. "I expected you to be a man of science," he'd said on another day when they had found themselves pinned down by weather.

"They don't need to be mutually exclusive, George. Who knows, maybe someday science will prove God."

He doubted it and had told Somes so. And now here they were again.

His teeth ached. A persistent stabbing in a right molar, his jaw tensed against anxiety and cold. He dished out dessert to the others. The altitude played tricks with their taste buds, making things too sweet or causing flavors to disappear altogether. Eating was done for survival. There was no pleasure in it. He missed dinner parties, the service of food—hot and cold, a range of flavors, vegetables, anything fresh.

"With God's help, and not the oxygen's, we'll make it." Somervell's tone was affirming, emphatic.

"Somes, the only thing that's going to tame this thing, this . . ." He wanted to say *bitch*. He wanted to curse the mountain but held his tongue. "The only thing that matters here is us."

"Exactly, George. Us! We're the instrument designed for climbing. You pretend to be a skeptic, but you have faith. You believe you're destined for it, for the top. Don't pretend you don't. That's faith, George. That's a plan." Somervell turned to Sandy. "And you? Do you share his skepticism? His humanism?"

George watched Sandy as he glanced from him to Somes and back again.

"I don't know." Sandy's tone was slow and measured, or perhaps it was the altitude. George leaned toward him and Sandy's voice picked up. "All that religion seems an excuse. I'll keep God to myself, I think. I want to climb Everest for the achievement of it, not because it's for or against someone's idea of God."

George leaned back. Somervell was about to cut in when Teddy piped up, looking up from a letter he was writing. "He sounds like you, George."

"Hardly," Odell interjected. "That's far too moderate a tone."

"You're right," George agreed. "And *God knows*, being moderate won't get us anywhere near the summit." He thrust his hand skyward. "It's going to take a damn sight more than faith to get us up there. Moderation has never led to greatness. Robert Scott was hardly a moderate kind of man. He couldn't have made the South Pole if he was. No, give me a wild temperament and the summit."

"There's no need to be melodramatic." Somes shook his head. "And besides, Scott died."

The five of them settled into an uneasy lull.

Melodrama. He'd been accused of that before.

In his room at Magdalene, Will had asked him, "Don't you think you're overreacting just a bit?" passing him a long shot of whiskey in one of George's chipped teacups. "You must have known how all this would end."

George took down the photograph of James that was pinned above his desk. Ripped it in quarters and dropped it in the wastebasket before pacing the length of his room to the ivied window that overlooked the courtyard. He leaned his forehead on the leaded pane. "He said I was a bore. In front of everyone."

"You're not a bore. James Strachey is a bully. He always will be." Will paused while George tossed back the shot and passed his cup back to have it refilled. "I think you're well served to be done with that whole lot. So blooming smug." There was satisfaction in Will's voice. He'd never been partial to James and his whole Cambridge School of Friendship. "The Cambridge School of Snobs, more like. Only the vainest and most dramatic need apply."

But Will had never understood the allure, the glamour of the Stracheys, of Maynard Keynes, of Rupert Brooke, while George had plunged headlong into the group and embraced their ideals of examining every emotion and motive over carousing evenings in James's rooms. "Welcome to our little salon," James had said with a bow when he first joined at Rupert's invitation. James had focused on him. And George had been determined to impress them. To try anything they did. For James, every breath was meant to be savored, every interaction scrutinized and embraced. As if each decision were sharp, could cut either way. There wasn't a moral judgment on anything. At least there wasn't supposed to be. Pleasure and experience were the endgame. It was libertarianism at its finest. Until it had fallen apart.

"You don't understand, Will. You can't."

Will looked taken aback, hurt. "Fine," he said. "Then I'll leave you here to revel in your own heartbreak." He gulped down his own slug of whiskey and moved toward the door. "I forgot, George, just how much more capable of feeling you are than I am."

"No, Will. Please. I'm sorry. I didn't mean it like that." Why did Will always have to be so much more measured than he was? "Let me explain?"

Will left his hand on the doorknob. "Why?"

"God. Because we've been mates forever. Because I just need you to sit here and get drunk with me."

"All right." Will sat back down and George threw himself on his bed. "But only if you'll stop being so bloody melodramatic."

"But that's the point. With James, everything mattered. What I said, what James said about me. Every word, every action, had the potential to change things—even the future. Anything was possible." And it was true. He felt raw, hyperaware of every word, its myriad meanings, every tiny insinuation. "It's a bit like being on a climb. You know that feeling—when you're pushing yourself and pushing yourself and then you leap for that hold you think is just out of reach. You know you're going to fall. Then you don't. And for just that moment, the world sharpens. Comes into focus." He threw back the shot in his hand, then tossed the teacup to Will for a refill. "That's how every moment felt with James. I wouldn't trade it for anything."

"Don't you hear how ridiculous that is?"

"But it isn't. Not at all. Isn't that part of why we go out there? The fear, the possibility of it all ending? To really feel alive. And when you come back down, the world is different. For an hour, a day, it's so vivid, it hurts."

"Still, one can't live like that."

But he *had* lived like that. For the few months that James had courted him, seduced him, taken him along to lavish parties. Maybe Will was right. Maybe this was the only way a relationship like that could end—with him cast aside and heartbroken. That he might have been able to bear. It was the humiliation that hurt most. He'd seen the letters between Lytton and James Strachey, how toying with his affections had just been a game to them. Still, he'd do it all again. He'd throw himself in body, soul, and mind the next time around too. "What's the point in going halfway? If you're only going to go halfway, why even bother?" How could he make Will understand? Will was too cautious for anything as messy as love—cautious even in the mountains. "You know, Will, you might be a better climber if you risked a little more."

"Jesus, and you might be a better friend if you'd temper yourself a little. I watched you throw yourself into this. And it was as though it took you over. Maybe that kind of obsession is best left to mountains. Not to people. They aren't problems you can solve like a climb."

"Maybe I should be more like you, but I don't know if I can be. I don't want to hold anything back. Not ever."

"All right, then, George." Will held up his teacup. "Here's to living life to the hilt."

"To the hilt." He knocked his teacup against Will's and relished the burn of the whiskey down his throat. Will followed suit, grimacing against it.

He supposed now that Will had been right. He hadn't held

anything back from Ruth. Nothing. From the first moment she'd slipped into his thoughts, he had declared it. He'd wanted to sweep her away. He still wanted to. Perhaps Everest had stolen too much of his focus for too long. But when he got back, everything would be different. He'd be different. There would be no mountain to come between them anymore. There would be just her.

In the gathering gloom he glanced around the tent. There was maybe an hour before dark.

Odell was doing it again, taking seconds, taking more than his share. Someone had to watch him. The rations only went so far. Not having enough would derail an attempt. Odell wiped strawberry jam from his mouth.

"Did you enjoy that?"

Odell looked over at him, eyes narrowed. "I did, George. Thanks." Odell moved to stick the dishes outside in the snow, now that there was nothing left to eat.

It was the stillness that drove him mad. He had sat here for nine hours. For nine hours the storm tore at the camp, at the mountain. They had lapsed from conversation to silence. The wind was finally still. Suddenly everything was still. The only sound was ragged breathing. In. Out. In. Out. Long and painful. A dying metronome.

George fell back and stared at the canvas overhead. It lifted and fell with his breathing, as if he lay inside a great flexing lung. It was pressing down on him, clinging to his face, over his nose and mouth.

He couldn't breathe.

He screamed into the almost silence and the tent receded. He screamed again to push it off him.

The others jolted and tensed with panic. He pressed his fist to his temples, his eyes squeezed closed.

"I hate this bloody mountain!" he yelled. And then, "God damn it!" Refilling his lungs, he screamed again into the air, the scream trailing off into laughter. Somervell punched him in the shoulder and the rest of them began to laugh too. Relieved. He wasn't dying. His brain hadn't hemorrhaged. He could smell their relief.

"Jesus, George," Somes said. "Go outside and run around the tents."

"Don't forget your crampons, though," Teddy added.

"Yeah, you might fall down the glacier."

"Tumble miles to your death."

"We should only be so lucky."

They were all laughing now, rocking back and forth, cabin fevered and giddy. Odell squeezed tears from his eyes. Sandy's shoulders shook until the sound finally pushed out of him in gasps. George tossed someone's blue jumper at Sandy. It fell across his face.

"Bugger off," George said, smiling, as he climbed out of the tent.

Outside, the camp glowed in the late-afternoon light. The sun had sunk below the rim of the peaks to the west of the camp, and the sky was a heavy dark blue, the stars already piercing through, illuminating the sharp angles of Lhotse's nearby peak with tiny pinpoints of light. Everything was blue: the dusk-white of the snowfields, the indigo-bruised shadows of the rock face. Even the crumbling Yellow Band above him was blue in the twilight.

He shivered, which surprised him; he'd thought he was past shivering. Still, it was refreshing to be out of the tent, to have a few moments alone.

The storm had reshaped the camp, the landscape around it. There were new drifts and banks against the tents, scooped-out gullies and channels. The snow still swirled in the occasional eddy, skittered loose under his feet. He kicked into it and walked across the camp, his hobnails scratching at the icy crust hidden beneath the layer of new snow.

He stretched as he walked, thrusting his hands above his head, arching and flexing the long muscles in his back. He was creaky. His body was warring against him, not yet dying, but it would be soon. Somervell believed that past a certain height there'd be no more acclimatization, that they'd just start dying from lack of oxygen. He hoped Somes was wrong, but he was probably right. Maybe the oxygen would help some. Maybe it would make the difference.

The wind had scrubbed clean portions of the old camp that had been buried when they'd arrived. Remnants of the previous expedition were now exposed—perfectly preserved carcasses of half-empty oxygen tanks, sloughed-off canvas skins of abandoned tents, a cache of bully beef tins, frozen solid, the filthy streak of shit and piss along the western edge of the old camp.

Two years ago he'd kicked out that tent pole and the canvas had slumped across the snow. He would have stayed if he could. Even after the avalanche. Everyone else was done—Teddy, Somes. But the mountain had been mocking him. He hadn't wanted to go home.

He'd stood here, right here, after the avalanche. He could still hear it in his ears, the roaring rush of it. He remembered it vividly and felt, even now, the ground shift a little under him. They'd been moving well—himself, Somervell, Virgil, and the line of coolies behind—not that far above camp when the snow above them slipped and the whole side of the mountain crumpled and ripped apart as it gathered speed. There was a low rumble, louder than the incessant wind, than the chug of a steam train. And then it was on him. There was a brutal pull at his waist and he was off his feet, bullied by the wall of snow. He paddled, stroked, pulled as though swimming in a riptide. He was drowning.

Below them was the drop off the Col. Almost three hundred feet straight down.

The cold, the snow, was all over him, filling his mouth, his ears. He could no longer hear the rumble of the falling snow, though he felt it in his chest, his organs. The snow was in every crease, finding its ways through zippers and seams; it was like a fist around his chest, what little air he had in his lungs was being squeezed out. For a moment he was back in France, earth tumbling around him, collapsing, blacking out the world. But he could taste the mountain on his tongue where the snow was forcing itself inside him.

He swam against the snow, turned, was moving through the current of it. His body fought for the surface. The snow around him ground to a halt; his body was pinned, but loosely. He couldn't breathe. Couldn't open his eyes.

He tried to churn his arms in the snow, which gave a bit. He gasped, tried not to inhale snow. Searched for air.

He rocked his head back and forth, making a small space to breathe, to open his eyes. He gasped into the hollow as if surfacing. Even the mountain's thin air was a relief. It wasn't the dark he expected—it was light, a wet blue, lighter above than below. He was close to the surface.

He struggled against the wet cold where the snow had melted against his waning body heat. His skin, his fingers, were already numbing. He pressed his arms down and arched for air. First his head, then his torso, breached the surface as he sputtered snow and water from his lips and gulped at the air. He could feel the weight of the snow around him, now that he was almost free of it; could feel it clinging, sucking at him.

When he'd pulled himself free, he lay there feeling the burn of cold and sun on him. His bare, cold hand, flung on the snow, looked dead. He'd lost his goggles, his hat. The light hurt. Then the tug at his waist. There were others on the rope. It disappeared into the snow beneath him. He kicked free and started to dig.

He dug out the rope until he found Somervell, a foot below the surface of the snow, breathing, but barely. His lips already discolored. But he was unhurt. He pulled the other climber free. They were yards from the precipice of the Col. And for a moment they'd been relieved. They were alive. Disaster diverted, adrenaline rushed to his limbs, warming him.

The mountain had been preternaturally quiet just then. The rumble of the avalanche had faded. There was no sound. Just their rough breathing. Even the wind had gone quiet.

Then they'd heard the voices—muffled yelling, like his children playing in the back garden, Clare and Berry calling to him. He turned toward them.

And the sounds resolved themselves. Into panicked yells, sharp in his ears. There had been others, on another rope, carrying supplies. He staggered to his feet.

At the edge of the cliff there were two blurs of panicked movement, dark smudges on the horizon of snow. They gestured down, over the Col, to the base of the cliff.

He stumbled toward them over the fresh, tossed snow. With no crust to hold him up, he floundered and stumbled.

The men on the rope had gone over. He knew it before he reached the lip of the precipice. He waded toward Virgil. Somervell followed slowly behind him.

Automatically he pulled Virgil and the other coolie, Tranang, back from the edge. They were still in danger and he didn't want them to fall too. He stepped to the edge, feeling for it to give, and looked down.

At the bottom was nothing but tumbled blocks of snow and ice, troubled but silent. Seven bodies down there and not an Englishman among them. "One of us should have been down there," he told Somervell.

"This was a mistake," Somes said, shaking his head.

Even then he was being set up to take the blame. In that first moment Somervell was already working out his own innocence.

Then Teddy ended it. "We're going home. Now."

"We can't. Not yet. I need to have one more shot at it, Teddy. Please. One more. We have to. I have to."

"It's the monsoon." Teddy was apologetic but firm. "It's pushing in the snow and storms. We've missed our window. Seven men are dead, George. I shouldn't have let you go today. I'm certainly not letting you go tomorrow."

At least Teddy had tried to shoulder some of the blame.

Time here was meaningless. Days bled into one another, were differentiated only by certainties of weather, a specific conversation, an accident or death. He couldn't remember the order of events or days. The altitude, the repetitiveness, the emphasis on pure physical survival, dulled his memory to a shiny reflective surface. There was no perspective. No means of measurement, no tick of a clock.

He tried to keep track of details in his journal—clean notes of times, events, meals that were eaten. All of it in an unrecognizable shorthand, a map of occurrences so that someday he might make sense of it, create a narrative with an acceptable ending.

Nearby there was another camp. Another body. He'd find it again, maybe take Sandy. That death wasn't his fault.

Glancing around, he made a mental note to have someone scavenge the camp's remains in the morning, see if there was anything worth salvaging. He knew he'd forget otherwise.

He hoped he'd remember tomorrow. That was all he could bring himself to hope for.

◆　　◆　　◆

"I UNDERSTAND HOW YOU FEEL," Sandy said. "I've never been much good at keeping still, either." His breath puffed in the dark. His throat hurt. He and George had been talking in a Morse code of short sentences, long pauses. "My mother once tied me to my chair at supper. She'd always threatened to." He paused longer than he meant to. It hurt to think of his mother. He hadn't had a letter from her since he'd left. "If you go," she'd said, "I won't forgive you. But I'll pray for you." He hadn't really believed her. "I deserved it," he said to George now.

He tried to lighten his tone. Odell might still be awake in the tent. Odell had met his mum, had tried to convince her that his going to Everest was a good idea. He didn't want Odell to think it hadn't worked. "I was forever getting up and running off to do something, finish something. Me and my brilliant ideas. Always wanted to show my da' something. Never her. Then one supper she did it. She tied me to my chair. With garden twine. It wouldn't have held." Thinking of her, he smiled, tearing the scabs on his lips. He licked at them, which only made them sting more.

"Are you two going to keep talking?" Odell's voice cut the darkness in the tent.

Somervell and Norton had retired hours ago. Only he and George had remained, curled near each other, talking in the gloom. They stopped, and silence filled the black space of the tent. After a moment George spoke. "Odell, why don't you take Sandy's tent? I can't sleep anyway. Too much sitting. Being cooped up. Better Sandy and I keep each other company than keeping you awake."

Odell huffed loudly. In the quiet of the passed storm it was clearly aggressive. His sleeping bag rustled, snapped in the cold. He fumbled for his boots.

"If I slide into a crevasse, George, you are dead."

"Maurice Wilson," George said. "He was here before us. I found his body in 'twenty-two." George lay next to him, head to foot, his body radiating a small heat.

"Who was he?" Sandy asked. "A climber?"

In a thin voice that sounded as though it came from a great distance, George explained that Wilson had been a soldier wounded at the Somme. "I was never wounded. Never," George continued. "Why not? Everyone around me. Everyone but me. Wiped out."

Wilson was wounded and invalided out to a hospital in London, where he came down with tuberculosis. George's voice was low, hoarse. It slipped through the air between them, a tenuous rope holding them to each other. Sandy felt tethered, as if he were floating just above the mountain.

"Imagine, surviving that battle, that war, and then almost dying from some damned disease. He refused their treatment. Said he found God in the trenches. I don't know how; most of us lost Him

175

there. But he thought if God wanted him to go, then he'd go. And if not, then he'd survive.

"He prayed. Meditated. He got better. He thought it was the praying. The meditating. Maybe it was. Or maybe he just recovered."

Sandy closed his eyes. The weight of sleep pulled at him. He was tumbling. Falling down the mountain. He jerked awake. George was still talking beside him. Had he missed something? How long had he been asleep?

"Wilson thought he had a calling—to get people to pray, to believe. The doctors said it was battle fatigue."

"He had to make people believe him," Sandy said. "In God."

"Exactly." He felt George nod in the darkness. "And he thought of Everest. As close as you can get to heaven. Decided he would get to the top."

"But you said he wasn't a climber."

"He wasn't." There were long pauses between George's words, between thoughts. Sandy repeated the words to himself, puzzled them out. "He'd do it with belief. Fasting. Meditation. If he got to the top they'd have to believe him. Divine intervention. He was doing God's work. That's what he actually said. 'It's the job I've been given to do.' He didn't have anything we have. No permissions. No guide."

Sandy tried to picture coming here by himself. Without George, Odell, Somervell. It seemed impossible. He wondered if George had imagined it all, if he was just toying with him. Maybe the altitude was getting to him too.

"How did he get here?" he asked.

"Bought a Gipsy Moth," George said. "Called it the *Ever Wrest.*"

"Good name."

The government had tried to stop him, but somehow Wilson

made it to Darjeeling and hired two Sherpas to guide him. Then he walked to the mountain, dressed as a monk, with just one tent and what they could scavenge and beg. "He made it at least as far as the North Col," George said, "at least once."

Sandy whistled low, the sound thin. It had taken an army to get them to the Col.

"His last camp wasn't far from here. That's where he prayed. Fasted."

Beside him, Sandy could feel George move as he lifted his arm and pointed into the darkness, could see the darker blur of him on the backlit canvas. George pulled his arm back into his sleeping bag. Sandy waited. He could hear George's breath rattle in his throat, dry and ragged.

"He just sat there," George continued. "Cross-legged. Prayed and meditated until he died. Not a hundred feet from supplies, food. His tent.

"He's still out there. Frozen solid. His clothes are gone. Shredded by the wind. Torn apart. One of those great bloody birds has ripped a hole in his cheek. He's like a marble statue. A Buddha."

George was quiet now.

Sandy imagined the body tight and solid, head bent in supplication. "That's Somervell's divine intervention, I suppose," he said. He wondered about being alone out there in the cold. Just him and God. "I'd like to see him."

"Hmmmmm." George was drifting, barely awake. "Maybe tomorrow."

The next morning Sandy kicked into George's footprints, pushing through new snow, powdery, like confectioner's sugar. His breath was heavy already, his pulse raced, thudding at his throat where his muffler choked him. He didn't have to stop every few feet to catch his breath anymore and there was some relief in that, some pride, but George still moved faster ahead of him. He pressed to catch up. Felt the rhythm in his head again. *Climb high, sleep low. Climb high. Sleep low. Climb. High. Sleep. Low.* Each word a step, a breath.

George had woken him early, pulled him from the tent before the rest were up. There wasn't much time for this. He would be taking Tsering down later, while George would be pushing back up the Col.

After the storm the light was high and bright even through his goggles. The sun would be painful today. It hadn't been up long enough yet to turn the snow basin of the Cwm into a heat box, but it would by afternoon, and his face was already burned and torn. After the confines of the tent, though, the tight, cool air was refreshing.

He felt his limbs loosening, warming. He was enjoying this—the sweep of mountains around them, the brilliance of the sky. The total silence after yesterday's wind. There was only the sound of his breath. The swish of his boots through the new snow, the crunch of ice below. He thought maybe now he understood why George loved mountains. He would go to more of them, he decided. Everything seemed impossibly perfect and far away. There was just him. And George. And the mountain. He felt the confidence of early morning. They could conquer this thing. They would.

He stopped behind George, who cast about, searching for something. Everest changed all the time, shifted constantly, the drifts and stones of it moving and swirling. He was learning to read his position from the angles of distant ridges, solid lines, like Pumori in front of them. George waved to him over his shoulder and moved down the slope.

There was a splash of color, washed-out, red and blue against the gray and white of the mountain.

Wilson's body sat just as George had described, cross-legged and patient, facing the summit. His body and face relaxed, frozen in position. His skin marble white, bleached and burnished to porcelain refinement by the sun, the wind, the arid desert conditions of the mountain. A mummy. Wilson's stomach had been hollowed out by the *gorak*s, the huge ravens that floated over the lower camps, and his clothing, in tatters, flapped in the brief breaths of wind. The hands in his lap covered the groin, but Sandy could imagine the small, shriveled organ frozen there.

George stood watching as Sandy dropped to his knees, gasping into Wilson's frozen face. Wilson's eyes were open, milky, iced over.

The boy. Wilson. Sandy hadn't expected to see so much death. In Spitsbergen there hadn't been any deaths.

He reached out to touch Wilson's placid face, his movements slow, measured. He stopped, touched the air around him instead. He didn't want to wake him. He'd never imagined something so blatant as this, this kind of giving up, giving in, to death.

He gazed up at George, who was staring away, at the ribbon of spindrift that stretched out from the summit. A brushstroke of white on the blue sky.

"He looks so . . . calm."

George nodded, pointed. "His tent was just there."

There was a scrap of material, a stretch of green cloth maybe a hundred feet away from where they were. The storm must have uncovered it. "There was food," George said. "Water. Some shelter."

"And he just sat here and died?"

"He wrote in his diary, *This will be a last effort, and I feel successful . . . Off again, gorgeous day.*"

"Why?"

"That's the question, isn't it?"

He thought about George finding Wilson here. Finding his diary, reading it. Thought about being stripped down to this. A body. A few words.

WILL

One O'Clock

After stalking through the old streets, the narrow cart paths that have been here for centuries, sloughing off the words, the face, of the woman by the river, I find myself at Will's door. It's cool here—the sun barely slipping into the slender passageways—and quiet, as though the buildings and their occupants are accustomed to keeping to themselves.

Of course I have come to Will's. I'm shaking and I just need to be with someone. Someone who doesn't need anything from me, want anything. I pound out the rhythm of my thumping heart on Will's door, the heavy wood of it under my fist and my stinging palms.

The door opens and I collapse into the entryway, propelled by the force of my own desperate fists. I strike Will hard on the chest and he catches me, holds me tight a moment, then pushes me out to arm's length. There is the flicker of panic—the fear of George's death written all over his face—and I am already apologizing, pulling back, my hands to my hair, sweeping it back where I'm sure it's run wild. I'm a selfish fool, coming here like this, sobs still in my throat. He reaches for me.

"What's wrong? It isn't . . ." He doesn't say your name and it's a relief. I don't want to hear your name right now. It only reminds me of everything I don't know.

"No, no, no," I'm saying, but this sounds panicked too.

I shake my head, lift my hands in some kind of apology. "I'm sorry, Will . . ." There's a suitcase just inside the door. Its canvas cover is fraying and covered in worn travel stickers, the whole thing dark and stained, like something left too long in the rain. "Are you going somewhere?" My hand is pointing at the suitcase like an accusation. Everyone is leaving.

"What? No. No! It's there for a friend to borrow."

His arms are around me again and it's hard not to want to stay there. It feels different, being in his arms. Will is solid, larger than George. It's comforting to be held, to be touched. It's been so long since anyone has touched me besides the children, their hands small and demanding. And then I'm conscious of my body, of it shuddering against him, of the feel of the softness of me against the solidness of him, and he pulls back, or I do. Maybe both of us back away.

"Come upstairs."

He steps back against the heavy door and ushers me with one arm, up the stairs. At the top there is a mirror in the hallway, and, vain creature that I am, I look at myself, and I'm surprised by what I see. My eyes are red, my face pale, my hair has indeed run riot. But it isn't unattractive, this wild, panicked face. Still, I swallow it all down—the panic, this abandon.

Will doesn't see me looking at him behind me in the mirror. He is softer than George, his features are easier. Pleasant. Where George's features are honed to fine edges and can stop you in your tracks,

Will's are less confrontational. More forgiving. He is carrying a book, his finger stuck between the pages where he has been reading. His tie is loose and this intimacy makes me blush more than if he'd not been wearing one at all. He glances into the mirror then and catches my eye. "Tea," he says. "I'll make tea."

Pressing my throbbing hands together, I move to the tidy sitting room he gestures to. "I'm glad you were home." I try to joke. "Your neighbors might have summoned the police, thinking me a crazy woman." My voice is too loud. Circling the room, I touch Will's belongings—the covers of books, stacks of papers, the eyeglasses that he has only started wearing in recent years. There are photographs too. Him and his siblings. His father. They are smart in morning dress, some formal occasion. I admire his orderliness. I run my finger along the spines of books that all have their final pages intact.

I think of the mess in my bedroom at home, the things I allow to pile up the longer I am on my own. Scraps of paper, books, and letters in stacks around my bedroom. A way to make the space mine. I ask Vi to leave all of it be. Before George comes home I'll tuck everything away. Everything in its place. A place for everything. It is becoming my mantra.

"Yes," Will calls from the kitchen, startling me back to his sitting room. "It could have been quite the scandal."

He brings me tea and we sit next to each other on the sofa. He drops two lumps of sugar in my cup and lets them dissolve before he stirs. George doesn't have that patience; he grinds them instead against the side of the cup with the back of the spoon. An annoying habit. One that I wish I were able to gripe about this morning. "George, please. It sets my teeth on edge. Stir it like a reasonable human being." And he would have ground them all the more, then reached for my cup and done the same.

"You don't even need the sugar," he'd say. "Too sweet already."

The spoon makes a quiet clinking against the china, and when Will hands me my tea, the warmth of it floods the whole of me, even though I didn't know I was cold. It's bitter and not quite hot enough. I recognize the china. Holding the teacup toward Will like a salute, I ask, "Is this because I'm here? You don't use these to entertain, do you?"

"Of course. I don't think I drink out of anything else."

I had meant the tea set for George. A gift for when he returned from Everest the first time. Painting them was a task to keep me occupied during his months away. I started them the week he left and agonized over them, hoping for uniform perfection. On each piece there is the faintest line of a mountain in green against a gray-blue background. Somehow, after they'd been fired, they'd seemed too delicate for George. He sees the world in grand views, sweeping vistas. In bold archetypes where everything is clear. Right and wrong. Duty and disregard. Not me. I am always too distracted by tiny details—the warm pressure of Will's hand on my back as he walked me up the stairs. The feel of a name in my mouth.

The restraint of the image on the cup made me think of Will, the consistency of the line my paintbrush made over and over. There is an anticipation to the line: it reads like a pause, a foot about to step into nothingness, above cold water.

"George?" Will pulls me from my thoughts. "He's all right, then?"

"I assume so." I laugh, nervous and high. "It's all so stupid, Will. I just keep hoping, thinking. *Today. Maybe it will be today.* It's as if the words are running through my head on a ticker tape."

"I know." He lets the lull stretch out between us. There is a rattling, like a storm tapping at the window, and Will is taking the cup and saucer from my hands. "Do you want to tell me what happened?"

"No. Not yet. It's all too embarrassing." The woman sitting on the wall, her bared teeth flashing at me. Her laugh. Beside her the soldier and his yellowed skin, papery, dry. The way he'd looked at both of us as though we were exotic creatures from somewhere far away. But it was he who was from a different world altogether. I could see the alienation in his eyes. How he'd never really come back. The woman next to him didn't see any of this at all. "Tell me what you've been doing," I insist to Will.

"Oh, not so much. A letter to my father, well, a report really. And staring at the painting I've been working on."

"And is it going?" I don't ask to see it. Will keeps his paintings to himself until he's ready to unveil them, which he does with a small ceremony—a certain type of Spanish wine, a particular dark cloth over the painting. First we drink and then he reveals it to us. It is always us. Sometimes there may be one or two others, but George and I are always there.

"It is. But slowly." He doesn't want to talk about it, so I don't push. "How about you? You hadn't even unpacked your paints when we last talked about it. Tell me you have by now."

I shrug my shoulders, an apology, an explanation. "I'll unpack them as soon as I get home."

"You should. It might do you good before this evening." Will's dark eyes are wet with concern. His hair is close-cropped. Neat. Everything in its place.

"Shall we make a battle plan, then?"

"For Hinks?" His name is a hiss, conjuring someone long and thin, tapering fingers that could dig into anything. The exact opposite of how he is.

Since I first heard of Everest, Hinks has been a stone in my shoe. A constant irritation. He is all accusations and demands—accusing me of *withholding information* from him and demanding copies of George's letters in case there is something of import written there. *You must understand, Mrs. Mallory, your husband is on official Crown business. We have the right to know everything he has written.* Though he feels no such obligation to share anything with me. In all likelihood, *The Times* will have news before I do.

Will talks and fills the space between us—talks about Hinks and how he will handle him this evening. I get up and wander around the room. When I linger too long in front of a book on birds, he tells me it's the guide he will take with him the next time he goes to France. When he goes climbing again. "Don't worry," he is saying. "I won't go until George gets home."

George's name hangs between us.

"Do you think I've been a good wife, Will?"

It feels as though someone else is making me ask the question, as if I'm watching myself from afar.

"Of course," Will begins automatically.

"It's just that I've never been good at anything." I turn away to the window, look toward the shops down the road where it widens. Women scurry from the shops—all of them, I suppose, with families to attend to, husbands at home. I wonder if Edith has finished the shopping for dinner. What she has bought. How much it will cost me. She knows all the vendors, takes it as a point of pride to haggle and get the best bargain. Behind me, Will is beginning to object—to list my qualities: kindness, honesty, and so on.

"I was terrible in school. My papers wandered everywhere. Geography and poetry mixed up with Latin conjugations." I glance at the papers on Will's desk, hoping for a letter. I don't see anything and I know if there were one Will would have shown me. The clock in the hallway strikes. "Once, one of the mistresses returned my French paper to me with a rebuke. The middle of it was a muddle of Italian. Italian! Not even the right language. I couldn't keep anything straight.

"It should have been me that was kept home from school after Mother died. Instead of Marby. I would have loved to take care of Papa and not have to worry about school. Taking care of people I was good at. That's why I thought I could be a good wife. I thought I would be good at taking care of George."

"You do. You are," he protests.

"I was so terrible, before he left. It was so hard." My throat aches and the room dissolves through my tears.

"No, Ruth." Will stands, comes toward me, but I back away. He stands in the center of the room, unmoored for a moment, then returns to the sofa.

"I said terrible things. Called him selfish. And cruel. There are so many things I need to take back. Worse than that, there are so many things I wish I'd said. Wish I'd done."

I lean against the window; the cool glass is soothing against my forehead. I want this day to end. All these days, until he comes home.

"Did you know he asked me to go to America with him? He so desperately wanted me to go. Over and over in his letters he writes how he wishes he could share with me everything he sees; that's the regret. 'Come with me to New York,' he said. 'It'll be our adventure.'"

"Why didn't you?"

I want to tell Will I should have, because that's the truth. I did want to go, I should have gone, and yet I couldn't. I wanted to punish him for leaving again. I couldn't just go with him and be there when he wanted me to be, then disappear when he didn't.

"A million reasons, and no good one. The children had already had one parent gone for so long, it didn't seem fair to leave them with none. And because I would have been extraneous. All those people crowing for a bit of him, for his attention. I didn't want to compete with it. None of it seemed appealing, the parties where I'd stand off to the side, the dinners talking about how wonderfully proud I must feel. And, frankly, because I wanted George on my own terms for a while. Not someone else's."

"That's all right, Ruth. George understands that. I do. We all do. Besides, there will be time enough for that."

"But what if there *isn't*?" Will doesn't understand. It would have been so easy for me to go with George, and yet I chose to stay here, without him. "What if he doesn't know how much I love him? I should have told him how sorry I was for all the arguing. For not going. For not being supportive. There are so many things I want to tell him.

"I'm sick to death of saving up things to share with him. The stupid little things like the mouse I found in the wardrobe, or that Berry has taught John to stand on his head. Things too small and stupid to share in letters, where everything should be important. But you build a life together by sharing the insignificant things, the things you don't bother telling anyone else. George and I don't have those anymore. It can't be done in letters over days and weeks and months apart. It just can't."

It is Will who has these things now. He's the one I tell these things to. Maybe that's what George wanted—a way to ease his guilt, his responsibility. And so he gave me Will. Or maybe that's just more foolishness.

"He will come back, Ruth."

I turn on him. "And what if he does, Will? And what if he isn't done with it yet?" My voice is an ugly sneer. Every word, every sound, is a betrayal. "Then what? It will keep eating at him and it will blind him. It's what happened last time. It's humiliating, to come second to a mountain. Don't I deserve that kind of loyalty?"

I collapse back onto the sofa and Will's arms are around me.

"George loves you. More than anything. You know that. That's why you wait for him. Why you save up those things to tell him."

"I know part of him belongs to the mountain, just as there's a part that belongs to Geoffrey, to you. I used to content myself with knowing there was a part of him that was just mine alone. But it's not enough. Not anymore."

What I want to do is tell Will I won't wait. That I've waited long enough. That it's too much to have your life swept away from you, your choices made for you. It's gone on long enough. I'd like to make him recoil, to shock him out of his insistence about who I'm supposed to be. I want him to see me. Who I actually am. Maybe I'm not an artist like him or Cottie—but I have my own needs and desires. Once I thought I might have my own adventures. Once I thought maybe I'd go to America on my own. But I was young and even more foolish then.

Leaning against Will is like falling, being pushed from a ledge. Hovering. Waiting. His clavicle is hard against my cheekbone, his hands clasp mine. Just below his chin is a spot that he missed when he was shaving. A tiny scrape of stubble, tender near his pulse.

"I'm a horrible wife. A horrid person."

"No." His lips move near my temple and the touch radiates across my skin.

"Has George ever told you that story about our honeymoon? The one about our being arrested?" I pull back slightly from Will, can feel my temple cool where his breath warmed me. "It isn't true. It never happened. None of it. He made up that other version of me. I've always wondered if he preferred her. She seemed braver than me—bolder."

"It's what he does, Ruth. We all know that. George tells us stories. And all of us are better in his stories."

"But I'm only me."

"I know. And he knows. And we both love you for it."

I can feel his breath on my skin, his lips. I want to feel them on my cheek. On my closed eyelids. For a moment I imagine staying here with Will. A life with Will. Going with him to look for his birds.

I stand. "I should go. I still have flowers to pick out. And the children will be back soon. But you'll come early this evening, yes? You promised."

"I'll be there." He stands, too, more slowly than me, as if hoping I'll change my mind.

I gather my handbag and Will follows me down the stairs. At the door he blocks my way, steps close to me. He smells of tea. For a brief flash I imagine what it would be like if he leaned down and kissed me. Imagine the taste of him. What would I do? What would change? Maybe everything. Maybe nothing. Once, things could have been so different. I try to envision another life, another me. And what I would have done. Will has smaller ambitions. He would come home every evening at the end of the day, smelling of paper and ink, and tell me about the report he'd compiled for his politician father. And I would tell him, every day, of the ordinary little things that made me smile or frown, that aren't worth noting in a letter.

I rise up slightly on my toes and there is a rush of relief when he kisses my cheek. But it's just another reminder that George isn't here to kiss me. It will be weeks still before he reaches for me, before it is his lips I rise up to meet. The thought is a sharp pain behind my ribs.

When I was small I imagined love as something safe, something without sharp edges, only the sweeping, enveloping curves of romance and happiness. But it isn't. Not now, anyway. There are edges and they cut.

THE NORTH COL

23,200 *Feet*

Sandy crawled out of the tent at Advanced Base Camp in a quick, clumsy maneuver that made his head pound against his skull. For days now, any movement had increased its tempo, as if the throbbing was connected to his pulse, thudding harder every time he exerted himself doing something as simple as climbing out of the tent. He stood as still as possible, hoping the ache would subside, and finally felt the pain well up and crest, then break and ease. Even with the discomfort receding, the world continued to swim around him. Snow came at him almost sideways in fat, heavy flakes. Everything was softened and furred, so different from the storm that had kept them pinned down at Advanced Base Camp almost two weeks ago. Still, a bad day for climbing. It was bitingly cold. Already the tip of his nose stung. He rubbed at it, then tugged at his hat, the pain in his head rising up to meet it, bringing a wave of nausea too. Swallowing the queasiness down, he turned in the direction of what he hoped was the North Col. On a clear day he could see all the way up the ridge, watch the climbers, microscopic figures, moving up or down, for hours. Today, aside from the tent behind him, he could see no recognizable landmarks through the heavy curtain of snow.

Without the anchoring of the tent, it would be impossible to tell where he was, impossible to tell in what direction safety lay. Maybe Wilson hadn't chosen to sit there and die after all. Maybe he couldn't find his tent only a hundred feet away, through the snow and his own blinding headache. Sandy squinted in the direction he thought George and the others had taken the previous day. The snow had long erased all trace of them.

George hadn't even had the decency to tell him himself when they'd made the decision. It was Somervell who had climbed into the tent, pulling in a wedge of frigid air with him. Feeling ill, Sandy had bedded down right after dinner, not wanting to move or even think. Somes pulled out his stethoscope and made him sit up. He swallowed against the rising bile. It had to be bile, he hadn't been able to eat much at dinner.

"God. Not now. Please, Somes."

"It's no use if I just check everyone when they're feeling good, Sandy. But you do look seedy."

The stethoscope was cold and his heart contracted against the bite of it.

He tried to slow his breathing. His heart. Everything came in thin, shallow gasps. Looking at his watch, Somes murmured something Sandy couldn't make out.

"Am I not doing well?"

"No, Sandy, you're doing fine. All of us feel terrible." He could hear the truth of the statement in Somervell's voice: it was raw, hoarse, hard to hear over the continual white noise of the mountain. "Can you do these for me?" Somes handed him a sheet of maths problems. He'd seen them before. Where had he seen them before?

Somewhere warm, but he'd been out of breath then too. Out of breath, but feeling strong, clearheaded.

Of course. In Bombay, in Darjeeling, and on the trek as well; he'd found the problems easy then, but here at ABC the numbers swam on the page. He narrowed his eyes to focus on them, willing them to stay still, and slowly worked them out. He had the sense they were the same problems from before, but he couldn't remember the answers he had come up with so easily then. When he completed the test, he handed the sheet to Somervell, who wrote Sandy's name and the camp number on it, then folded it away without checking it. Then he turned back to Sandy.

"We're going tomorrow," Somes said.

A surge of adrenaline cut through his thrumming head, his lethargy, and fluttered in his stomach. "When? Who?"

"Two teams. Teddy and George," Somes said. "And me with Odell."

He waited for Somervell to say his name, to tell him who he'd be climbing with. It took a minute before he realized Somes wasn't going to say anything more. "Is it because of the tests? Did I do something wrong?"

"We need you to run support," Somervell said, avoiding the question. "Come up a day or two behind us. Make sure that Camp Four, on the Col, is ready for us when we come down. Or that you're ready to push up if something goes wrong. If things get dicey." Somes paused a moment and then added, as if in consolation, "It's an important role, Sandy." Somes coughed into his palm, winced, then looked into his hand before wiping it on his pants.

He didn't want to be consoled. What had been the point of all this if he wasn't even going to get a shot at the summit? Now there would be only the painful monotony of the mountain. Melt snow.

Steep tea. Fill canteens. Climb out through the waves of nausea into the snow to relieve himself and check on the others. None of it mattered. They were going on without him. "I should be going. I'm as strong as the rest of you."

"We'll be taking Virgil and Lopsang. You'll follow with whoever else you can rouse. There should be at least two porters that are in good enough shape to go higher. I'll check them tonight. Let you know who to count on. Probably not that fellow Lapkha, he was flagging last trip up. He and everyone else should go back to Base Camp with Shebbeare. Hazard will tell them what to do from there. But we need to get people down if we can. We've been up here too long. That storm didn't do us any favors. If this doesn't work—"

Somervell coughed and grimaced some more, took a long, slow sip from his canteen, and then crawled into his sleeping bag, rolling onto his side to ease his cough. "If this attempt doesn't work, we'll have to go back down. All of us. We can't stay at this altitude much longer. We're falling apart."

That had been two days ago. Now it was just him and Shebbeare and a half-dozen porters. It wouldn't be easy to rouse the porters and get them moving. Not in this blowing snow. If he could crawl back into his own sleeping bag and lie there, he would. But he had to go up. And Shebbeare had to go down. There weren't enough supplies left at Camp III for them all to stay. And most of what remained he'd have to take with him to restock Camp IV for the climbers' return. There was no margin for error. He had to get everyone moving.

When Sandy climbed into the tent, Shebbeare was staring at the porter. What was his name? That should be one of Somervell's bloody tests: name the porters at altitude. He was the smallest man on the team, but strong. He'd pushed up to the high camps as often as any of the others had. More than Sandy had.

Lapkha. Lapkha Sherpa. That was it.

"I don't know what to do." Shebbeare's voice was thin, distant. He had to force himself to focus on Shebbeare's words, leaning in closer to hear what he was saying. "I don't know," Shebbeare gasped, forcing dry air over drier vocal cords. "I don't know what's wrong with him." Shebbeare hadn't taken his eyes off Lapkha, and for the first time Sandy turned to him too. Lapkha's lips smacked against each other, dried white spittle gathering in the cracked skin. His tongue lolled out to lick them, thick and slow. But it was his eyes that were terrible.

Lapkha's eyes bulged like balloons out past his browbone, forcing his lids open. When he tried to blink, his eyelids only closed partway. He looked possessed.

"Jesus." Sandy recoiled, closing his own eyes and then opening them again. Lapkha's eyes continued to bulge at him. "What do we do?" He struggled to sound calm. Tried to feel it in his roiling stomach.

Lapkha muttered something, his voice a low, gurgling sound in his throat. Sandy reached out and touched Lapkha's hand, hushing him, trying to calm him as he might a trapped animal. Lapkha stared past him, straining to blink, to pull his eyes back into his head.

Shebbeare said nothing and Sandy wanted to shake him. Why wasn't he helping? As he tried to consider their options, there was a sharp ice pick of pain in his own head. He winced against it and remembered George telling him about the young porter. Virgil's nephew, was it? About how his brain had hemorrhaged, bleeding out into his skull. "It's the pressure, maybe," Sandy said. Lapkha's brain was probably swelling, pressing out against his skull, out into the thin air of the mountain. "I don't know. It's just a guess." Getting the porter down, George had said, was what had saved his life. "Shebbeare, you'll have to get him down to Base Camp."

"Me?"

"You all have to go down. Those were the orders."

Beside them Lapkha lashed out, his hands flew around his head, fighting something off. Shebbeare pulled back farther from him.

But how to get Lapkha down. He couldn't walk, let alone climb. "I'll find something to use to get him down." He grabbed Shebbeare, shook him by the arm. "You stay here."

"No. Maybe you should—" Shebbeare began, but Sandy was already out of the tent, moving through the blurred white snow. He turned in place, squinting through the flurries. It was dying off. Maybe. He needed something to get Lapkha down. He couldn't let the man die here.

"Be calm." He could hear his father's voice. "In an accident, always be calm." His father had been showing him his tools, his workshop. Sandy turned the wood plane in his hand. It didn't look dangerous, but his father pointed at the sharp metal blade. "That'll cut your finger right off," his father said. "And if that ever happens, be calm. Be calm and think. You're a smart lad. Stop the blood. Elevate it. It's all science. You'll work it out."

He hadn't cut his hand on his father's plane, hadn't lost a finger or thumb. But there'd been other accidents. Like the time he tried to climb the wire fence near school. He'd been trying to catch up to Dick, of course. The wire had come untwisted at the top of the fence and his hand went down on it, the wire piercing through the base of his palm and back out just below his index finger. He'd stood, the toes of his shoes hooked into the fence, keeping his weight off his hand, and watched the well and drip of blood. There'd been no panic, just a gentle *whoosh* in his ears, in his stomach. His heart slowed and he was calm. All he had to do was work out how to get his hand off the fence. If he put any weight on it, his hand would rip open. The only way was to move his hand up, slowly, off the wire. He'd lifted his arm straight up and then fallen back off the fence, pulled off his jumper, and tied the sleeves tight around his forearm, careful of the blood, before he made for home. His mother was livid. "That's my lad," his father said. "A calm head's worth more than an old jumper."

He had to work it out that way now. He couldn't wait for Somervell to come back and examine the porter. The only thing that might work was to get the man down. It was clear that the altitude was affecting them all. "Be calm," he repeated out loud. He murmured it over and over, until: *canvas*. They could use the canvas from one of the tents to move the porter. If they wrapped him in canvas and rope, they could lower him down the mountain. It would work.

He found an unused tent, half buried in the snow, and retrieved some lengths of rope he had left over from the ladder he'd made. He urged himself to hurry but would find himself sitting still and stunned and wondering how long he'd been like that. Impossible to tell the time without the sun. It didn't occur to him to look at his watch.

On the way back to Shebbeare, Sandy stopped at the other tents. He couldn't remember the Tibetan word for *hurry*. Why couldn't he remember it? He spoke to them loudly.

"Hurry. You go down. Now. Hurry."

From where they were slumped in their tent, the porters glared at him. Compared to Lapkha, they all appeared fresh and capable. Good. They'd have to help Shebbeare transport Lapkha. "Down," he said, pointing at the ground. They nodded but didn't move. Shebbeare would have to come speak to them.

"I need you to get the other porters going," Sandy said as he dropped the rolled canvas outside and climbed into the tent. Lapkha seemed to have calmed. The man was lying on his back. Good. It would make it easier to move him.

"Too late," Shebbeare said.

"No. We just have to haul him out. We'll wrap him up in canvas and then you can pull him or lower him down. Whatever it takes. Now." His voice was still calm, but the feeling had left him.

"It's too late," Shebbeare said again. When Sandy looked at Lapkha, his balloon eyes were still open and bulging. The whites red with blood.

The canvas and rope came in useful after all. After Shebbeare and the other porters had started to descend, the remaining two, Tsutrum and Nawang, watched him wrap Lapkha in the canvas. They wouldn't touch the porter's body at first, but as soon as it was covered, they helped Sandy lower the corpse into a nearby crevasse.

The cold weight of Lapkha's body had surprised him. As did how difficult it was to move him. It. Just days ago Lapkha had been carrying loads and slowing them down. Now he was gone.

Sandy wished he could have sent Tsutrum and Nawang down to safety with Shebbeare. They'd been quiet since they moved Lapkha's body, murmuring to each other while looking sidelong at him. Somes should have seen the man was sick. Should have done something before he'd headed up. What if the same thing happened to one of them? If Somes had been here, Lapkha might still be alive.

Maybe they were right to blame him.

He made the porters weak tea and soup, poured it into enamel bowls, and made motions for them to eat. Once they were done,

they'd have to head up the Col. If he could go on by himself, he
would. But he had his instructions. He'd take good care of them,
make sure they were all right. He motioned to his mouth again as he
handed Tsutrum the bowl. Tsutrum nodded but looked away as
he ate.

+ + +

THERE WAS A SCRAPE of daylight left when the four of them arrived
at what would be Camp VI, only fourteen hundred vertical feet up
from Camp V. George collapsed in the snow, turned his back to the
weight of the wind, and lowered his head into the hollow space
between his legs and chest, searching for a still spot to breathe in.
His body thrummed with exhaustion.

They'd establish their last camp here, then tomorrow he and
Teddy would push for the summit. George searched for the towering
peak of it but couldn't see it for the snow that was screaming skyward off the ridge above them, a curling wall of it, like the blown
silk of Ruth's wedding gown. He stared, hoping for a glimpse, until
Teddy knocked him on the arm, held out his ice axe to him, and
pointed with gloved hands at the snow.

They had to get the tent up. Quickly. This high up the temperature plummeted to unbearable lows with the sun. The altitude, the
lack of oxygen, amplified the cold.

He bent over the tight, dry snow, swung his axe into it. One
knock per breath. The snow came apart in great blocks that they
kicked and pushed down the slope. As the blocks fell they shattered
into thousands of pieces, each grabbed by the wind and lifted up to
join the curtain of snow falling above them.

They carved out a narrow platform that was just wide enough for
their tent. By the time he urged Virgil into the flapping canvas to

ground the tent, the sky was a deepening purple. Only the light reflecting off the white snow illuminated them. The wind was constant, a roaring white noise, more inside his head than outside it. He thought he might be going mad. "Lie down," he yelled over the pain in his throat, and Virgil climbed into the roiling tent, threw his weight onto it. As if in retaliation, the wind lifted the entire tent, coolie and all, high into the air before slamming it back against the mountain. There was a yell from Virgil that cut through the wind in his ears. He hoped Virgil was just scared and not hurt.

George and Teddy and Lopsang scrambled to pull out the guy-lines from the tent, then loop and tie them around nearby boulders. The ropes, coated with ice, were whipping and dangerous. When one of them knocked across his frozen hand, George cursed. His hand felt as if it might shatter. In the gathering night they tied off the first tent. They should have erected a second, but it was too dark and they were exhausted. He leaned over the buckling canvas, which still tossed itself into the air and looked as if it might well tumble down the slope.

"Virgil, lift."

Virgil put in the first pole, giving the tent some shape, and then the second. George waved Teddy and Lopsang in, handed them their snow-covered packs, then went in behind them. The tent settled somewhat with their cumulative weight. Though the sides of the tent continued to snap and ruffle, it held close to the ground, save for the occasional slight tossing that reminded George of being at sea.

"The other one?" Virgil asked after a long while.

"No." George could barely talk for the dry scraping in his throat, and when he coughed or breathed deeply, his muscles squeezed and spasmed around his ribs in clenched pains. He pressed his hand to his side, coughed again into his other hand. No blood. That was something, at least.

"We all?" Virgil said, pointing at the ground. George nodded. They would all sleep in the one tent. They'd make do. It might actually help to keep them warm. Virgil grimaced, translated the plan to Lopsang.

He imagined the sound of their strained breathing under the wind, the snapping tent. It would be a bad night. They sat in the pitch of the tent, hunched, each of them holding on to his pack as if it were a life vest, a buoy, holding them up. He should find a torch, a lamp, a cooker. They needed food and water. And it would take more than an hour to melt enough snow for each of them. He'd finished what had been in his canteen long ago. It felt like forever.

He couldn't bring himself to move. Couldn't will it. But couldn't seem to will Teddy to do so, either.

Under the sound of the abating wind was a low moan. It came from Virgil.

Without his torch, he couldn't see what was wrong with the porter and didn't want to ask. Maybe it was all in his head. He listened to the wounded sound and wondered if Teddy could hear it. Wondered if Teddy cared.

He had to do something. Get snow melting, get sleeping rolls unpacked. The thin shelter of the tent alone wouldn't be enough to keep them alive overnight. Not here.

He fumbled at his pack to find the cooker.

There was no sleep. Not even the hint of it flirting at the edges of his consciousness. Just the mountain all over him, the press of the summit above, the rough of frozen, uneven snow below him, poking into his kidneys.

He tried not to move. His skin ached, his joints. Even the marrow in his bones hurt. Beside him Teddy hacked and tossed, not sleeping, either. The wind crashed over him like waves and he thought about being at the seashore with Ruth. Their honeymoon. Her body beside him. He ran his fingers along the curve of her waist, her hip, his hand hovering just above her skin, the hair standing straight up in goose pimples, the heat radiating damply off her.

"I didn't mean anything by it," he told her. "Telling that story at dinner. It was just for fun."

She shook her head. "It doesn't matter."

"Clearly it does." She was right, though, he shouldn't have told it. He'd loved their honeymoon—in fact, loved that for seven days they had only each other for company. That it was just the two of them in a tent together. If they'd gone to the Alps or back to Venice, they couldn't have just lain together for days on end, talking silly talk about children's names and the color of linens. But he couldn't have said that in front of Virginia and James. They'd have thought him soft or, worse, sentimental. He knew James would declare there was nothing more dreadfully boring in the world than curling up in a tent and reading together. They wouldn't have understood what was so marvelous about Ruth, wouldn't have seen her goodness. He only wanted them to admire her as he did.

"It's nothing," she said, and pressed her lips together to try to smile, to try to pretend nothing had happened. It only made her look sadder. She rolled over and he pressed against her.

She was cold. Why was it so cold here on the beach?

"Are you cold?" he asked, pressing himself closer.

Teddy's voice answered.

He pulled back, tucked his arm back into his sleeping bag, remembered he was on the mountain. They were going to summit tomorrow. He tried to remember how much he wanted it.

A long time later, he used his torch to look at his watch: six a.m. "Teddy. We need to go." He clenched his jaw against his chattering teeth. He'd feel better when they were moving.

He sat up slowly, the world blurring slightly at the edges of his vision, and reached down into his sleeping bag, groping at his boots until he found the canteen he was looking for. They'd spent hours the night before melting the water they needed for the attempt. The water might stave off some of the headaches, some of the drifting thoughts, but the altitude was the real danger. He sipped at the water now, not wanting to drink too much. There wasn't time to melt more.

"Teddy?" He reached down and shook him.

They'd eat a cold breakfast of jerky, some tinned custard, and be out of the tent before the sun had crested the neighboring peaks. They'd have to travel fast to make the summit and back before nightfall. Being caught outside on the mountain that high after sundown would be deadly. There wasn't enough air up there to survive for long. And at night they would freeze to death in an hour if they weren't moving. They had to be back in the scant shelter of the tent, if not all the way down to Camp V, before it got dark. Which meant that time was already slipping away from him, and with it the summit.

Teddy moved beside him, jarring him so that there was a stabbing pain in his kidney, his bladder. He needed to piss. Outside he'd have to stand in the frigid dark and fumble himself out of his trousers. He tried to put it off, think of something else. Damn.

He put down his canteen and hauled himself from the tent.

Protecting himself as much as possible from the constant wind, he turned to urinate. The wind had died down some since they'd arrived but still chugged across the camp. The sky was beginning to lighten, the blowing snow off the ridge haloing the mountain. *Please give us a few good hours.*

When he returned to the tent, Teddy was swearing.

"What is it?" he asked, even before he was inside. Had Virgil been injured more seriously than he'd thought? Had they forgotten something? Anything could derail the attempt. They were balancing so precariously.

"The water. The. God. Damned. Bloody. Water." Teddy spat each word in a gasp.

Teddy's sleeping bag was wet through. His puttees. George just stared at the spreading stain. "What happened?"

"You left the goddamned canteen open."

"What?"

"It was open, spilled everywhere."

"You'll have to dry." His voice was mechanical, didn't sound like his at all. "We'll have to melt more. We can still try."

Teddy wasn't looking at him. "We'll never get away in time." Virgil bent to the cooker, coaxing it to life. Lopsang was tightening his boots.

"We could go. With what we have. You could wear Virgil's—"

"We'll finish this and head down," Teddy said. It sounded like an order. "It'll be up to Somes and Odell now." There was a long, empty pause. Teddy's disappointment was palpable. "You shouldn't have left it open, George."

"You shouldn't have knocked it over!"

The air was brightening around the tent, the sun already too high for a serious attempt. They'd never make it back down before night-fall. Teddy was right.

It was over. Before it had even begun.

"At least the camp is established," Teddy said. "They'll have an easier time of it. Probably for the best."

"How could it possibly be for the best?"

"We'll go down. If Somes and Odell don't make it, we'll be rested for another shot. It's not over, George."

He nodded. Somes and Odell would have their chance. His chance. Maybe they'd make it, but he had his doubts. Odell didn't have the drive for the top. He wouldn't push and Somes would play it safe—the danger of knowing too well the risks. But George wouldn't be counted out yet. It was still early. There would still be the window of good weather before the full force of the monsoon was upon them in a week, maybe more. They still had time before the weather closed in, cutting them off from the mountain. He'd go down. Wait. Regroup. He'd have his chance yet.

They met on the ridge. Somervell and Odell were well below where they should have been. Still, they were surprised to see George and Teddy with their coolies heading down when they should have been pressing up. The sun had come up clear and hot and Teddy suggested a rest. He'd been moving slowly. Neither of them had mentioned frostbite, but George wondered about it now. Teddy's puttees had almost dried, but the wet in them had frozen and stiff-ened around his legs. His trousers underneath had to be the same. The cold might have already begun to seep into his skin. The six of them sat for a long hour breathing heavily on the leeside of the ridge, their backs to the mountain as it dropped away recklessly beneath their feet. George grabbed a chunk of frozen snow and threw it down the mountain.

What would it be like to fall? he wondered. He'd seen others fall, but he'd never fallen himself. Well, almost never. He'd fallen only the one time. With Geoffrey.

How many times had Geoffrey told him: Rest when you can, not when you're tired. "You can't rest on an overhang, no matter how tired you are," Geoffrey had said, correcting him from below on an easy climb. "Your legs will hold you up all day. Your arms, though, they'll let you down. You have to climb with your legs."

And George had forgotten that. No, he hadn't forgotten. He'd been uncertain about a move on one of the pinnacles up to the summit of the Nesthorn, and he'd clung to the overhang for too long. Below him the rock face dropped away, to Geoffrey twenty feet below, and then another hundred feet to where they'd camped the night before.

His arms had been so heavy, the blood draining down them, into his shoulders, leaving his hands tingling and cold.

He had known what he had to do. He had to pull his leg up to his chest, press his foot into the rock wall, and leap to the next overhang, a little more than an arm's length above him. It was a move he'd made dozens of times before. Hundreds. But he didn't know this face. Didn't know the overhang.

On the belay below him, Geoffrey had called up, "Go for it, George, or drop down to rest. You can't stay there." The rope and Geoffrey's hold were the only things that would save George if he fell.

He'd been hanging for too long, but finally he launched himself at the thin shelf just out of reach. His dead arms flailed at the over-hang, his fingers clawing at rock, dirt, air—and then he was falling.

He didn't yell or scream. Just plummeted past the rock face, past the blur of Geoffrey. The rock looked smooth, a soft fabric. Maybe it wouldn't hurt to land. And then the pain as the rope tightened around him. The constriction at his ribs, the burning skin on his chest as the rope pulled taut. The sound, like a popped paper bag as the air was squeezed out of him. But the rope held. He remained suspended, his body arced out over empty space, the rock face swing-ing nearer to him, then away.

He had turned himself on the rope. He needed to get to the wall, take the weight off Geoffrey, who might be straining to hold them both to the mountain.

He had reached for a fist-sized hold. His arms felt like his own again. He should have made the leap. It was a good hold. Shouldn't have waited. He pulled himself to the wall, pressed himself to the rock, and breathed against the easing in his ribs. After a few minutes he climbed back up to Geoffrey.

It was the only time he'd ever fallen. And it was because he'd doubted himself. He couldn't imagine falling again.

"George and I will head down to the Col," Teddy was saying to Somes, "and wait for you there."

"Leave your men at Five," Somervell said, gesturing to Virgil and Lopsang. "Just in case."

Teddy nodded.

George looked over at Virgil before insisting, "I'll stay with them." *The coolies are children where mountain dangers are concerned*, he had written to Ruth after the avalanche. *And they do so much for us.* He didn't want to leave them alone on the mountain.

"No," Somes answered. "Not enough fuel. You'll end up using it all before we get back down."

George nodded. Somes was right. There wasn't another choice. They all climbed to their feet, stamping them to return feeling to their frigid toes. "Good luck." They shook hands and then George watched intently as they climbed upward. He watched until he felt a hand on his arm.

"Come on," Teddy said. "It's theirs for now."

They were moving strongly. Maybe they would make the summit. He wished them well and then turned his back.

After leaving Virgil and Lopsang dug in at Camp V, they waited out the next day at IV, at the top of the Col, scanning the upper slopes until the weather came up. George hoped the weather was staying low on the mountain, that it might be clearer farther up. They tried to play at cards. Tried to read. He thought about letters he should be writing—to Ruth, to Geoffrey—but he could say nothing reassuring to them now. George pictured Somes and Odell's climb—their slog upward—across the ridge, or dropping down into the couloir, the gorge that ran up the face of the mountain. They might have done it already.

Sandy kept quiet, kept to himself. He seemed drawn, the raw flesh of his windburned skin angry against his paleness. The previous night, Sandy had described Lapkha's death to him.

"It was terrible," Sandy said. "I'm glad I wasn't there when he died. Shebbeare said he choked and then gulped at the air, as if he couldn't get any into his lungs, but he kept trying and trying." Sandy's voice was remote, as if he were trying to puzzle something out, thinking aloud. "Then he just stopped. That was it."

"I'm sorry, Sandy."

"Maybe if I'd been quicker. There might have been something more I could have done."

"There wasn't. You're not a doctor. I wouldn't have known any better, either. It wasn't your fault." He hated the sound of the platitudes, wished he could think of something better to say.

Ruth would have known what to say. She always managed to say the right thing. When Trafford was killed, she held him while he sobbed. "You can't look for fairness, George," she said to him. "Not here. Not in this war. The regular rules don't apply. Trafford's death will never be fair."

"It's a different world up here," he told Sandy. "The regular rules don't apply. We have to be responsible for ourselves. All of us. There's no rescue, not up here. We're barely surviving. That's what no one back home seems to understand."

George hoped Virgil and Lopsang were all right up at Camp V. He should have sent them down and stayed there himself in case Odell and Somes needed assistance. But that wasn't his role. He needed to rest, to regroup in case they didn't make it, in case there was still a chance at the summit. Virgil would be all right. Virgil knew the mountain.

"But that can't be right," Sandy said. "We're responsible for each other. I should have done something. I just didn't know what."

"That's the point. There was nothing to be done. Lapkha should have told someone or gone back down."

"Or maybe someone should have noticed he wasn't fit to be here."

Now, as he dealt another hand of cards, he tried to catch Sandy's eye, tried to think of something reassuring to say. The wind howled down the ridge, the tent flapped. "Do you hear something?" George asked.

"How could you?" Teddy answered.

They turned back to their cards, played for cigarettes that they would share anyway.

"No. There it is."

A yell on the wind. Like the *yeti* the Tibetans claimed lived on the mountain, cloaked by the weather as it stalked them, tried to eat them alive.

He reached for his boots and climbed out into the wind and snow. It felt as if the mountain were punishing them this year. The previous years hadn't been like this, bad day after bad day. In the lee of the tent, he crouched down and cupped his mittened hand to his ear. The wind screamed like some monstrous thing bearing down on him. Maybe it was nothing. Somervell and Odell should be well above the storm, pushing forward.

But it was there again. He moved toward it, wading through snow and wind that cut sideways, pushing him off track.

So as not to lose his bearings and wander in circles or into a crevasse, he noted the tents directly behind him. If Odell and Somervell were coming down, something had gone wrong. Or what if it was only one of them—the others lost in the blinding snow, or simply disappeared off the face of the mountain?

Then they were there, their soft, dark outlines mere smudges in the snow. "Somes?" His voice cracked in his throat. A failing yell came back to him. Squinting, George made out two figures—Odell and Somervell. Virgil and Lopsang must be following close behind.

When he reached Somervell and Odell, he pulled their arms around his shoulders, one on each side, and tried to take some of their weight. By the time he'd turned them around, his own footprints had almost disappeared, but he was able to make out the faintest trace.

"Where are the coolies?" Teddy asked back in the tent before George had a chance to.

"I'll go back for them," George said, peeling off his mittens and breathing into his cold hands. "Just give me a minute."

"Have something to warm you up some before you head out again," Teddy said.

"They need it more." He gestured to Somes and Odell, who were shivering uncontrollably, snow clinging to their beards and eyebrows.

"What happened?" Teddy asked them, handing them mugs.

"Just couldn't get up there," Somes said through clenched teeth. "I turned us back before we even got to Six. Couldn't feel my toes, couldn't think. After we left you the wind just sliced down at us. We spent the night at Five and could barely get out this morning."

George climbed back out to search for Virgil and Lopsang and swept his arms through the white blurs of snow. No sound. Nothing. It felt as though hours were ticking by.

"Maybe they turned back," Odell said when he returned to the tent. Odell looked comfortable now. Warm. The tea had returned some color to his face, but he still rubbed at his feet.

"Turned back?" Teddy repeated. "To Five?"

"But there's not enough fuel at Five." He could hear the fear in Sandy's voice, gauging the possibility of yet another death. "They won't be able to melt water. Warm anything to eat. They'll freeze to death without fuel."

Odell and Somervell were silent.

George wasn't. "You were supposed to bring them down, Somes."

The anger swelled through him, hot under his skin. "You don't descend in front of the coolies. They're our responsibility. How do you know they turned back? Maybe they fell. Maybe they're injured. How could you just leave them out there?"

"You don't know what it's like out there right now," Somervell said. "It's just dumb luck that we got back alive."

"Besides, you're one to talk, George," Odell muttered. "After last time."

"But that was an accident—" Sandy began.

"That's enough." Teddy's voice was calm, even. "We all know what it's like out there. And tossing blame around will have to wait. There'll be plenty of time for that after we get them back down."

"Now?" Sandy asked. "I'll go."

"No." Teddy was firm. "We'd never make it up there now. We wouldn't be able to see a thing. And as Somes said, they're lucky to have made it back alive. We have to believe the best right now. They're at Camp Five. They'll use what little supplies are there. They'll be fine. George, you and I will go at first light and get the porters. And then we go down. All of us. We can't keep pushing like this."

The next morning Sandy continued to press his case to Teddy. "I haven't been pushed yet. You all have."

Teddy was dumping stuff out of his pack, trying to decide what he'd take. A length of rope. Some small rations. Nothing else. Every ounce would count. George did the same.

"No," Teddy said to Sandy. "You don't have the experience. If you got into trouble up there, it would be one more person for us to deal with. George and I know what to expect."

"Then let me go too. Why not the three of us?"

"Sandy," George said, "Teddy and I are going. That's all there is to it."

"But if they're hurt, if they can't walk, you'll need an extra hand."

Teddy's voice rose. "I am *not* putting anyone else at risk."

"What if something has happened?" Sandy said, his tone dropping. "Will that be it?"

"No," Teddy said. "We're not done yet. We'll still get our shot."

George tried to agree with Teddy, but the summit seemed farther away than ever.

"We'll have to restock the camps," Sandy said.

Somervell stepped in. "We'll worry about that later. Hazard and Shebbeare will already have loads prepared down below."

George loaded his canteen inside his jumper, against his chest, to keep it warm. On the ridge there would be thirty degrees of frost.

"We keep moving," he said to Teddy just before they set out. "No slowing. Not for anything. If we keep moving, we'll stay warm enough." Teddy knew that. They both did, but he needed to say it out loud. "Stay in the lee of the ridge, but not too far down." Too far down and the new snow might give under them, send them careering down the mountain face. "Light and fast," he said.

They pressed up against the wind, trading the lead, stopping only to peer up the ridge, hoping to see the coolies coming down. Not that he expected they would. Not in this. They'd be near frozen already, without food or fuel for nine hours.

"It's all suffering," he remembered telling Ruth in a weaker moment. "That's all there is to climbing mountains. Suffering. You only need to be better at it than everyone else."

"You think you'd be the best by now," she said. She might have been joking. He chose to take it that way.

"I am." He pulled her to him then. "I suffer for you every day." He thought of her hands on him, how they were always cold. The wind cut through his ill-named windproofs.

When he'd heard his new gear had arrived from London, he couldn't wait to get home and open the packages. It was like Christmas morning. The windproofs, the silk puttees, the new boots: he wanted to pull them all out of their packaging, turn them in his hands, though he knew they'd have to be packed right back up and sent off to the shipyards. When he'd walked in and seen the empty boxes, he was furious. He knew it was juvenile, but they were his— and his to unpack. He was about to walk out of the house when Ruth called to him from up the stairs.

"George, darling?" she teased, in a tone he loved but wasn't in the mood for. He stood at the bottom of the stairs like a pouting child.

"What is it?" He heard a loud *clomp*, like a heavy footstep.

"Come upstairs, please, darling."

He knew he should humor her, he owed her that. But he didn't want to. He didn't want to climb the stairs.

He didn't want to climb.

He stopped on the ridge. Ahead of him, Teddy tugged on the rope. He stepped up again.

"Please?" Her voice again. A question, doubting. He climbed the steps. She was at the top of them, peeking around the door of their room. "Come here." Then she backed away, sounding heavy, fumbling.

He stepped into their room, dull and gray in the damp of fall. She was dressed head to toe in his expedition gear. Her tiny hands invisible in his gloves, her eyes hidden behind his goggles, below his hat. His windproofs sagged over too-big boots.

"What do you think?" Her voice was muffled through the wool of his scarf. She turned, laughing, her feet shuffling on the wood floor. His anger, his petulance, evaporated. She was perfect, playing the fool in his clothes.

"I'll pack you in my trunk," he said. "You could almost pass for one of the Sherpas."

"I thought I'd keep them. Wear them to market. It gets cold enough here."

"I need them."

"Then you'll have to come get them."

They climbed above the storm, George in the lead, the snow tossing below them like foaming surf. They couldn't be far from where it had happened. The avalanche. Instinctively George stopped, stomped down on the new snow. He wouldn't make the same mistake twice. He watched Teddy, below him, surface out of the storm and then turned to see the camp a short way above them. It looked deserted.

He dropped to the snow, leaned back against the angle of the mountain. They couldn't be dead. They couldn't be. If they were dead, it would be all over. And this time the papers would be right when they printed his name beside the names of the dead. This would be unforgivable.

"Almost there, Teddy."

"They'll be fine, George." Teddy paused a moment beside him. "They're sitting there waiting for us. We'll get them down. And then we'll see about the mountain. Still plenty of time to be bloody heroes."

Teddy patted his shoulder roughly, then plodded past him toward the tent. He stood slowly and followed.

. . .

They found them cowering in the back of the tent. Virgil sat up as George climbed in. "Sahib Mallory."

"Virgil," he said, pulling the cold tea from under his jumper before he even had his gloves off. "How are you?" Coughing, he collapsed into the tent. God, he was tired. If only they could rest here, just for one night. But the camp couldn't support them. And Somes was right, they'd been up here at these altitudes too long.

"Me, good. Lopsang, not good. He not make it down yesterday." Virgil's voice was creaky, dry.

"Neither did you."

"I come back with Lopsang."

"We need to get down. Now. You're both dehydrated. When did you last eat? Drink?" He gestured at the canteen.

"Yesterday. Maybe before."

Teddy was examining Lopsang. "We need to get him down." The coolie was muttering, his head lolling back as Teddy tried to haul him to a sitting position. When Teddy let go, Lopsang slumped back into the sleeping bag. They'd have to drag him down.

"We need to hydrate them first."

"Lopsang," Virgil was saying, ripping a piece of pemmican with his teeth, "not go down. You must make him to go down."

He wished it was that easy. This might be a rescue, but the Sherpas would still have to get themselves down the mountain. He and Teddy were little more than moral support. Bullies.

"We'll have to short-rope him," Teddy said, forcing Lopsang to drink.

Outside the tent Lopsang was able to stand, but he wavered on his feet. The weather below them had blown clear, the route lay crisp before them. George tied a rope from himself to Lopsang and from Lopsang to Teddy. A short line, only ten feet between each of them.

"I'll go first," he said, and moved off, feeling resistance, then a grudging movement. Behind him Teddy stood still until his own rope to Lopsang was taut between them, then he followed them down, holding the coolie up.

They worked their way back to Camp IV in this way, inching down the mountain, forcing Lopsang down from the front. It was laborious. Lopsang stumbled, fell in the snow, and George would pull on the rope like a pack animal while Teddy arrested his fall from behind. Ahead of him George kept an eye on Virgil, who plodded down mechanically. At least they would get the coolies back down. He tried to feel the success of that.

◆　◆　◆

"SHOULDN'T WE GO LOOK?" Sandy asked Somervell. He'd already spent most of the day staring up the ridge, blinking away spots in his eyes that he thought might be the others returning.

Dusk was creeping up the mountain. They'd seen no sign of torches, no light from the higher camp. At least the sky and mountain were bright with the moon. But the temperature had already dropped, and now it was too cold to stand still, keeping watch for them. But unlike him, they were moving. They had to be, Sandy thought. That might be enough to keep them warm.

"No," Somes said. "There are too many people already in danger. You heard what Teddy said. He isn't putting anyone else at risk. And we don't know if they're even on their way back down. No. We stay here. At least until morning. If they're not back by then, we'll go look for them."

Sandy didn't want to wait. What if they were injured, or sick from the altitude? Lapkha's bulging eyes rose again in his mind, and an anger with it. "Maybe you should have gone," he said to Somes.

"Teddy made the call."

"But you're the doctor. You're the one who's supposed to make sure we're all all right. If you'd been here, maybe Lapkha wouldn't have died."

Somervell inhaled deeply. "I can't be everywhere, Sandy." His voice was calm. "I can't be climbing and waiting behind. Right now, all we can do is wait. Hope for the best. Pray, maybe."

Sandy wasn't much for praying. When he was a child, he would lie in bed when his parents had gone out to the pub. He'd wait for them to come home, convinced something *nefarious* had happened to them. That was the word he'd thought. He'd read it somewhere. Some *Boy's Own* or the like. He didn't know exactly what it meant then, but he knew it was bad. It meant someone had tried to hurt them. He would make promises in his head to try to keep them safe. If he could keep his eyes closed until he counted to one hundred, five hundred, one thousand, they would be home by the time he finished. He usually fell asleep before he reached the end, but if they still weren't home, he picked a larger number and started again.

He closed his eyes now, murmured under his breath. He knew it was foolish. Still, he continued counting in his head.

"Hallo?" The sound of someone out there, far away. He waited and heard it again. Somes heard it too. "Come on," he said, and climbed from the tent, handing Sandy a canteen. "Come on."

The dark was pressing in on them now and Sandy lit a lamp so George and Norton would be able to see it, follow the smudge of light.

The air outside felt as though it might snap. Sharp and fragile, edged like crystal. When he inhaled, it cut into his nostrils, his lungs. The moonlight was cold on the mountain, iced blue. Sandy slogged through the snow after Somervell, the snow filtering into his mislaced boots, melting against his skin and cooling fast. His feet would freeze in his boots. The cold in his brain hurt. He pressed forward.

Then he saw them. "There," he said, squinting, and pointed past Somervell. The group was a huddled mass stumbling slowly toward them.

George's face was pale and white, frostbite beginning to settle in. Sandy brushed at his own face. The scabbed skin hurt. The pain reassured him. Behind George, Lopsang hung on the rope between him and Norton, kept up only by the tension on the rope.

"What happened?" Somes asked.

George didn't speak, just waved over his shoulder at Lopsang, and fumbled at the rope at his waist. Sandy stopped him, handed him the canteen, and leaned in to untie the short rope. As he did, George collapsed to the snow.

Somervell cut the rope between Norton and Lopsang and took the weight of the porter on his shoulder. Sandy tried not to look too closely at Lopsang as Somervell urged him past him. He couldn't be as bad as Lapkha, he was still on his feet.

"Sandy, get them to the tent," Somes said.

He nodded and moved to support Norton before he collapsed too. If they both dropped to the ground, he'd never get them moving again. Norton leaned on him and Sandy almost fell as he bent to pull on George's coat. "Come on, George. Just a little way."

Virgil trudged past them, not looking at him or at George, still on the ground. As he passed by, George heaved himself up and stumbled after him, ahead of Sandy, who was dragging Norton's weight.

They were back. And safe. Though only just barely. He wondered if the expedition was over, if Teddy would send them all home. They would know more when they got lower down, had a chance to regroup. For the first time, Sandy considered just what the chances were of his getting home safe.

MARKET

Two O'Clock

These medieval alleyways curve and wander every which way, and I follow this one past Trinity College with its sunlit rectangle of green out front, past All Saints' Passage and its tiny shaded square of gardens and dirty paths around the squat trees. On my right are the windows of shops, people moving behind the displays of oxford-cloth shirts or books or sweets. To my left are the fortressed walls of Trinity and St. John's, each with its own chapel, the stained glass catching the sunlight. The market is behind me, but I need a few minutes. I want to sit, quiet and alone. I had thought, on leaving Will's, to go to St. Mary's, but there I might run into people I know, at the very least Reverend Winterson, who would insist on being a source of comfort. Instead my feet lead me back toward Bridge Street, to the Round Church.

I've adored it since the first day George and I came across it as we walked about the town. It sits squat on its corner, where it has been for eight hundred years. Eight hundred. So long for something to stand steadfast as it has. The stone, brown-gray like the feathers of a dusty sparrow, describes a curve perfect for open arms.

Inside, the rotunda is dark and cool, and the arches sweep upward in a gesture so expansive, it makes the space beneath them seem larger than the curved walls can contain. The four columns that hold up the ceiling could hold up the whole world. The carved faces glaring down from the top of the columns are like demons, judging and cold. I find a spot to sit where I don't have to see them. Where instead I can watch sunlight dapple through the stained glass.

What if Will had kissed me? I might have wanted him to. To abandon myself to him, the way that I have been abandoned. It would be easy to love Will. To love someone who was always there for me, someone I wouldn't have to wait for. Perhaps, though, beginnings are always easier.

Once upon a time, I think, the world must have been flat. It was our minds that made it round, our desire to circumnavigate it. Our desire to leave home, certainly, but just as strongly our desire to return. But in making it round we crumpled it up, pulling it apart in places, crushing it together in others, thrusting them up into the atmosphere. Bullying the deserts, the tundra, the plains, into George's beloved mountains, peaks that stretch up from the rest of the world.

I prefer the cracks and crevasses, the gaps and holes, the bottomless depths of oceans and valleys, where you can see below the surface. Or small spaces that hold me secure and safe. I prefer what is hidden away.

Everything is about to change. Is changing. The slow smolder of desire is reshaping our landscapes. Maybe the oceans continue to plunge and Everest to grow higher, piercing into the heavens. Even if George were to reach the top of it, Everest will keep growing higher. Someone else will reach that height first. *It won't be you.*

Around me there is the hum of prayers from scattered supplicants, the smell of candles being lit and blown out, wax and incense. I think about lighting a prayer candle in George's name, but I don't want to tempt fate. I've lit candles for him before. In hope. In desperation. In good faith. First in Venice, to keep him safe, now that I knew he existed, on the sides of mountains. And then at each of his departures. I think the one I lit recently at St. Mary's must have been burned down for weeks now. When I attend service tomorrow, I'll light another one.

In the hollow silence of the church I catalog George's departures. So many memories of good-byes and leave-takings. I name each train station, the names of enough ships to raise a flotilla. It is my own rosary, each name a prayer.

I find comfort in ritual, in controlling what I can, in developing routines. Tea served at the exact same time, with one biscuit, set into the saucer. Saying prayers with the children and then tucking them in, in order, foreheads kissed, one, two, three. Letters scooped from the floor and sorted into stacks, each to be dealt with in its turn. With the arrival of each letter from George, there are steps to go through. First, I sit, carefully, in the window of our bedroom, the door closed firmly so I won't be disturbed. Then I hold the pages to my face, taking in the smells of where it has been. A deep inhale to steady my nerves and to push the hopes and fears aside so I can read what is there, and not what I want to be there. One sentence at a time. One paragraph. And then back to the start. Then read on to the next one. I draw it out, knowing it will be a long time before another letter arrives.

When I finish reading the letter, I fold it back into its envelope, slip it into my pocket, but I won't read it again until I go to bed. Try to remember it all day, test myself about what I remember he has written, how he has written it.

Once, I used to keep all his letters in order, neat and tidy in a box, but that's a pastime of youth. I no longer hold fast to that. There have been so many. There have been letters from George since the very start.

The morning after he arrived in Venice there was a note slipped under my door—*Would you do me the honour of walking out with me to Asolo tomorrow? I hear the hills above Browning's villa are a thing to see. Just the two of us. Don't tell your sisters.* The writing was messy and careless. The ink splotched on his name.

It was a beginning. An opening up.

At my feet the stone is cast in jeweled light from the stained glass placed high under the eaves. I wonder if I could catch that dance of color in paint—the sharpness of it, the sparkle, so that it is the color of the glass and the dark stone all at once. How it changes as the sun moves across the sky, as clouds move across its face. I could paint it from moment to moment, just this square of floor, just get this right. Just this.

What would George think I had come to if I were to write, *I'm painting floors—no! Not painting them like a house painter, like a real painter. Like Will or your friend Duncan Grant. Trying to capture the light.* Some things just don't suit letters.

Like proposals. *I wonder if maybe we should be married.*

The letter came from the Alps, a scant three months after we'd met. We barely knew each other and it was thrilling and disappointing all at once.

Without question I knew I wanted to spend my life with him.

There had been other offers before—there could have been any number of other lives I might have lived. But all I could think of was the luxury of reaching for him whenever I wanted, to claim possession of some small part of him for myself. Reaching across a bed that had never seemed empty before and feeling his skin.

Yes, I started to write back. Immediately.

But this was already a kind of ending. If this was the proposal, there'd be no grand romantic gesture. No getting down on one knee. I didn't know if I was ready to be a wife when I'd barely become a sweetheart.

The letter continued: *Forgive me. But I am better on paper. I will ask you in person, if you think you'd agree, but my heart stops just thinking that you might refuse.*

I couldn't refuse. But I didn't tell anyone. I wrote back, lightly: *I wonder a great many things too and would love to talk them over in person. I am worse on paper. I cannot spell, which you often point out. And I prattle on about nothing of consequence. Let us save important words for when we can be together.*

George came back from the Continent tanned and healthy, and had lunch with my father and me. When my father retired after the meal for a nap, we sat in the walled garden. The lilacs were already spoiling, the air was pungent.

"What do you think?" George asked.

"About what?"

"About what I wrote."

I knew exactly what he was talking about. At lunch he could barely look at me and flushed when he did. His hands fluttered across the table, picking up utensils, putting them down, turning the water glass in his hand to see the blower's signature.

"You'll have to refresh my memory."

"I already spoke with your father."

"Yes, you did. You had a rather extensive conversation about rope. I was there."

"You're going to make me ask properly, then?"

"I'm going to make you ask something."

"Ruth Turner. Will you marry me?"

He offered me a small, plain ring, nothing like Marby's had been. I touched the hair that still fell over his collar.

"You'll get a haircut first?"

"If that's what it will take."

"Then yes. I will."

Ahead of me, near the altar, is a small memorial to the members of the church who died in the war, a wreath draped with purple and black. The flowers are wilting, need to be replaced. The number of flowers England goes through for all her lost sons must be staggering. Gardens full of them. There are flowers for Trafford, I'm sure, at Mobberley. I'm glad there is no need of them for George.

"We all have to do our bit." That's what he told me before he went to France. But he didn't have to. He volunteered, begged them to take him, even after he'd been refused three times. *You're a teacher,* he was told. *Crucial to the war effort.* But he couldn't abide that.

"I can't stand by. Everyone's over there. Geoffrey, Trafford. Robert. Dear God, Ruth, boys I taught are over there fighting. I have to go too." It was as though he was afraid of missing out on some kind of adventure. "I can't just stay here. Safe. With you."

The *with you* sounded like an indictment. When he was finally accepted, George brought home champagne to drink to the future. To victory. I sipped at mine and hoped the whole war would be over before he got to France. Too many times I have drunk champagne at his departures. I hate the taste of champagne.

This time he said, "I can't imagine coming down defeated." I tried not to parse that sentence—the ways it could be interpreted.

The quiet of the church is calming. The traffic outside is muffled and far away. I am in a tiny, perfect fortress. A fortress for faith, for comfort. How many people have prayed here in eight hundred years? And so many of them are dead now. Forgotten. I know that George believes if he succeeds he won't be forgotten. It's a way to stave off death, grasp some immortality. He believes it's a way to make things right—with Trafford and Geoffrey. With his father. A way to establish a new life for all of us. Maybe he's right, but for what it's worth, these sacrifices don't add up to much of a life.

In the alley beside the church there's a sign: *The Occupiers give notice that they will take Proceedings against all Persons committing a Nuisance in these entries.*

I laughed the first time I saw it. We'd only just moved to Cambridge and George was showing me the town. The day was damp and cold, we leaned close together. We'd go to the pub, he said, to get warm. But not yet.

"What kind of nuisance should we commit?" I asked.

"We could drink and curse."

"No. Too simple. University stuff, really."

I leaned back against the wall, under the sign. I wanted him pressed against me. He was close. Everything else seemed so far away. The calls across the Cam, the *drip, drip, drip* of rain. I pulled down my hat and looked up at him from under it as he leaned against the opposite wall. Our feet crossed each other, and our bodies made a vee.

"We could fall asleep. They'd have to step over us." He gestured down the carriageway.

"I think we can do better than that."

"What did you have in mind?"

I pushed off from the wall and fell against him. I kissed him hard.

"That's not a nuisance," he said when I finally pulled back.

"To them it might be."

"Let's make a nuisance of ourselves all around town, then, shall we?"

I nodded, kissed him again. We made a joke of it on the way home, stopped in doorways and alleys, alcoves and narrow passages. We kissed everywhere, getting sillier and sillier.

"Like the Eskimos this time," I said. And he rubbed his cold nose against mine.

"Like the French," I said, and he kissed me long and hard and deep.

When we reached our new doorway, I said, "Like it's the first and last time you'll ever get the chance to."

The Saturday market is a chaos of sound and I plunge headlong into it, drowning myself in the noise, the swell of people all around me: students, wives, kitchen maids, and cooks. They are a tidal pull, brushing against my arms, legs, and back. This anonymous touch is somehow soothing, as if I've become a part of something, a churning life that surges on regardless of wars, disasters, and deaths. It won't be stopped. I am bumped and jostled, I knock into someone and don't apologize. The bell at King's tolls two. The children will be home by now and I promised Clare a tea party. I should hurry.

For an instant the crowd parts in front of me and I see the man from this morning in his gray fedora, his gray flannel suit. This time he looks at me, and then the crowd closes in again. Surely he is a reporter. I duck between two stalls, make my way to the northeast corner of the market, where I know there is a flower stand.

The man looked just the same as the reporters who met us when George and I got off the train at St. Pancras Station; the crush of their bodies against us, the smell of sweat and cheap booze, had repulsed me. Then the accusations thrown at George. I glance over my shoulder again, but don't see him. Maybe I'm being foolish again. I'll buy the flowers and go home.

Of course, it's not just reporters I need to watch for.

"Mrs. Mallory." The woman had approached me outside of St. Mary's. I was just leaving the service, the children clustered around me. "I'm Dorothy MacEwan. We haven't met," she said, waving away my response. The long feather on her hat bounced as she talked, a fleeting shadow over her face. She was a large woman, broad, packed into a corseted, high-necked dress. Severe. I felt small in front of her. But I remembered myself and tilted my head up. I wouldn't judge. I was new to town and could use more acquaintances.

"Pleased to meet you."

"May we speak?" She looked down at the children around me.

"Clare." I dug for a coin. "Take your brother and sister. You can share one sticky bun. One." I held my finger up for emphasis. Clare nodded seriously and led the other two off.

Mrs. MacEwan took me by the arm, began to promenade me in front of the church. I felt as though I were being displayed. "I wonder if you would consider coming to talk to the small women's salon that I host?" she asked.

I began to protest that I had nothing to say, but she cut me off.

"You see, they, all of them, lost their husbands in the war. There's about eight of them, and we gather and talk and I try to make them see how they can be strong, move past their grief." She didn't wait for a response from me, and I pictured another eight women as severe as Mrs. MacEwan. "I thought you, of all women, must surely be able to provide them some advice. Your husband is so far away, you must sometimes feel as though he's dead. And yet you carry on, and your strength is a shining example for your children. It could be for these women too."

"Mrs. MacEwan, my husband is not dead."

"Oh no, I know. It just must seem that way sometimes. And you're so brave. You could tell them how to be like that."

I recoiled from her, pulled back my hand. All I could think of was George being dead, a thought I usually kept, with effort, from ever quite surfacing. I shook my head at her. "I wouldn't. Never," was all I could manage. I won't be caught unawares again.

The flower stall is in front of me, a sudden blossoming of color, of perfume. The nodding heads of peonies and gladioli droop in the afternoon sun, funereal and sober.

Now the thought is here again. *What if he doesn't come back?* It is as sharp and clear as if someone had said it, and I glance around for the source. No one. No one is even looking at me.

What if he doesn't come back? What if he is already . . .

I can't even think the word, and yet I see myself walking up the aisle of Reverend Mallory's church. The same steps I took when we married, but now I am draped in black taffeta, accepting condolences instead of compliments, congratulations. There are deep-colored blooms, their heads drooping, on the altar, in the aisles. There are the children. Will and Geoffrey. My sisters and his. His parents, so sad I cannot look at them, the reverend's face a terrible grimace. I would like to reach out to him, but don't. Can't. My limbs are dream heavy. I will not cry. I do not.

I've written a eulogy in my head. *He wasn't mine alone, but he was mine.*

What if people knew I sometimes imagine what would happen if you died?

"Help you with something?"

I shake the thought from my head. There will be no flowers for funerals—instead something that George would appreciate. Something delicate, to remind me of him. Like the bones in his fingers, his wrists.

"Do you have something lighter than this? Not quite so weighty. For a dinner table. Like falling snow?"

The woman glances up at me now, and I see the flicker of recognition. She is tall and bends down some to address me, to peek under my hat. I stare at the ground and see that she wears men's boots, her skirt short enough to show them. Perhaps they're more comfortable for standing all day than women's shoes. Though I doubt they were designed for comfort.

"Of course, Mrs. Mallory. Something for a dinner party. Lilacs, perhaps? Picked fresh this morning." Clearly she has never thrown a dinner party. The scent of the flowers would overpower the food. Too thick and pungent. I shake my head as she prattles on. "And how is Mr. Mallory? Have you word from him?"

I try to smile indulgently but ignore her questions. I don't know her name. Have seen her only once—twice, maybe. I don't know what I could possibly tell her. I have no answers.

"No. I don't think so. Too strong."

She doesn't really want to know anyway. Like that horrid woman by the river, like Mrs. MacEwan. Even if I were to explain exactly how I feel, they still wouldn't understand. They can't. And what difference could it make to them, anyway? But as she shuffles her large boots through the buckets of flowers she is watching me, waiting for some tidbit. A scrounging dog.

"I have," I finally concede. "But it's much delayed. They are going strong."

I don't tell her that there may be a telegram waiting for me at home and I should hurry. That perhaps Hinks is waiting to bring word in person this evening. No, my response is automatic: I tell her the only thing that people really want to hear—that he is fine. I almost believe it myself.

I don't want to give her anything that she can use later as gossip. I will not crack here, will not confide. This is who I am to strangers now. Stern and cold. Efficient.

"That's wonderful." Her head bobs among the flowers, her long blond hair stringy across her shoulders. "We're all of us thinking of him. My youngest boy, Jack, is just excited to bursting with what your husband is doing. Has a scrapbook. Cuts out every mention of George Mallory from the papers. These?"

She holds out a bouquet to me: tiny white flowers, dotted with dark in the middle—purple, maybe, but it's hard to tell. Their scent is light and I can't stay any longer. "They're perfect."

I reach for them, but she begins to wrap them, prattling about her son wanting to climb, that he's heard some of the fellows climb the buildings at night and that seems a right sight dangerous, don't I think? She seems to think we are friends. "Perhaps Mr. Mallory could have a chat with him when he gets home."

She says *when* and I think *if*. I'd like to spit it at her. *If.* If he comes home.

"We do pray for him," she says, and hands me the flowers.

Nodding my head, I hand her the coins. This anger is misplaced, that much is clear. This isn't her fault. She probably thinks I want her good wishes, her thoughts. It's supposed to be a great adventure.

As I move off, she says my name to someone nearby, as though she owns me.

"Mrs. George Mallory," she says, and there is pride and sincerity. *Your name haunts me.*

RONGBUK MONASTERY

16,340 Feet

The monastery was a collection of low, fat buildings terraced behind the large chorten, a bulbous tower painted bright red. After almost two months in the wasteland of Everest, the monastery seemed ablaze with sound and color, its whitewashed walls a harsh contrast with the dun landscape. George noticed his steps falling into sync with the rhythmic chanting that rose from the place, almost operatic after the wash of wind on the mountain's slopes. Nearby, yaks lowed, and his mouth watered at the sound. There would be raw milk for his tea. At a table. Under a roof. Compared to the frigid cold of the higher slopes, the air here was warm, soothing; George imagined drowsing in the late-morning sun.

Behind him, at the end of the valley, Everest stood out in sharp relief against the sky. It seemed so innocuous from here. Another peak in a sea of them. The wind whipped across the summit, shaping what appeared to be a flag of surrender from the white snow. He knew better than that, though.

Things had fallen spectacularly to pieces. The day before last he'd lain in his tent after returning with Virgil and Lopsang, his body aching in a pulsing rhythm, his blood sludging through his veins, thick from dehydration and starvation. When had he last eaten? It didn't matter. Even the thought of food made his throat constrict, his stomach roil. He'd sipped at some water, his teeth aching from the cold. He tongued a back molar, swollen and angry.

Teddy had crawled into the tent. "George?" A weak croak. "I talked to Somes. We need to retreat."

"We can't. Not yet." He had wished his own voice sounded stronger, more compelling. "We can still make it."

"No, we can't. Not like this. Somes says we can't stay here any longer." There had been a long pause. "We have to go down."

At the time he'd assumed Teddy meant down to Base Camp, but he'd meant to take them farther down.

"It'll do us good," Teddy had said when they had stopped temporarily at Base Camp to gather the rest of the team—Shebbeare, Hazard, Noel. "We need to regroup."

Regroup. Had Teddy meant that, or was it just a ploy to get them back down and comfortable, ready to quit?

"This place"—Odell's voice cut into his thoughts—"is more than two thousand years old. Can you believe it, Sandy? They've been praying here since long before Christ was born."

Odell's obsession with dates, with stones, with the tiny, infinitesimal parts that made up the mountain, that made up time, was grating on George's last nerve. God, he'd like to punch him. That would keep him quiet for a while, anyway. He shoved his hands into his pockets, inhaled deeply. The air was dense here, wet. It flooded his lungs.

Sandy didn't answer Odell but pushed on ahead, past him and Somervell, toward the monastery. "How's he doing, Somes?" George asked.

"Sandy? That porter's death has really affected him, I think. And probably the altitude. This is all new for him. You and I know what to expect, have a sense of what's coming. The unknown can be incredibly troubling. How about you, though?"

"I feel good now. Best I've felt in weeks, to tell the truth."

"That's what I thought. I told you, the altitude up there was killing us. It wasn't a metaphor, George. Seems descending cures most mountain ills, and if I'm right, we'll likely handle the next crack better."

At least Somes thought they would have one more attempt at it. But Teddy was a cautious one. He might have decided to put an end to it. And then? He didn't want to think about that. His legs felt light, quick, as he pushed himself toward the monastery. He could sprint down if he wanted to, and part of him did. He hadn't been indoors in almost eight weeks. Almost as long since he'd properly bathed. The smell coming off him must be disgusting, the filth of seven weeks of sweat. He was looking forward to having a bath, imagined the water cascading down his skin.

As they entered the monastery grounds, monks appeared from under shadowed overhangs to meet them, some wrapped in gold sashes, others wearing elaborate headdresses. He winced at the vibrancy of their clothing, almost lurid against his own bland tweeds and cottons, the browns of them dulled further by dirt. They bowed to one another, the monks in scarlet and saffron, the English in trousers and fedoras, templed fingers raised to their foreheads.

With Shebbeare translating, Teddy conferred with one of the monks, and George withdrew into the shadow of an overhang. He was actually craving a cigarette for the first time in weeks. Leaning against the white wall, he let the smoke fill his lungs.

George watched as Virgil and the rest of the coolies were enveloped by the monks, two of them moving to support Lopsang, whose fingers were swollen and black from frostbite. How had Teddy failed to notice that Lopsang had lost a glove during the descent? The coolies would ask for a *puja*. They believed the blessing would purify them, cleanse them after the deaths on the mountain. If only absolution were as simple as lighting candles and saying prayers.

In the courtyard, Noel stood beside his tripod, documenting everything, chalking up their failure.

Teddy looked over to him. "Three hours. Then we'll meet in the main hall. I'll have food arranged." Then he turned his attention back to speaking in his faltering Tibetan to one of the more elaborately dressed monks.

It was typical of Teddy. Give them all some time to themselves, some space to think. There was a hand at George's elbow. He followed the monk into the depths of the monastery.

This was the first time he'd been alone in months.

Naked, George could see where his clothing had demarcated itself on his body in lines of pressure and dirt. He splashed water across his skin, cupped it to his face, watched it darken with dirt in the bowl.

Lying on his pallet, he found the gloom of his cell a relief. Even the reek of scalded butter from spent ceremonial candles, the sharp, acrid tang of dung fires, was appealing, if only because it smelled of something other than rock or snow. His body felt unmoored from the yak-hair pallet beneath him.

There were only two choices. Each of them inevitable.

If Teddy decided to put an end to this bloody thing, they could all go home. He could go back to Ruth, thousands of miles away.

Too far away. He wanted her beside him. To wake up in the middle of the night and feel her pressed, naked, against him, her breasts against his back, the soft sureness of her. That was all. Just the simplicity of a shared bed, the litany of her day, her desires. Surely that would still be his, even if he returned empty-handed? Maybe Ruth wouldn't care. Maybe she did just want him to come home. Hadn't she said as much the last time he saw her?

He conjured his last image of her: her face pale in the winter cold. She'd kissed him good-bye on the deck of the *California,* and he watched as she walked down the gangplank. But then she stopped, turned, and climbed back toward him. She lifted her gloved palms to his face, cupping it in her hands. There was her perfume—some spring flower—and the scent of the sea already clinging to her. She stared up at him, hard and earnest, the way she did when she needed him to believe her. "I only want you to make it," she said, measuring every word, "because you want it. If you want it, then I want it. Your heart is mine. Mine is yours. But it really doesn't matter to me, you know. Just you matter."

He wanted to believe her. Even then, on the gangplank. But she couldn't have meant it. Not after everything he'd put her and the children through. "It feels as though we've spent more time apart than together, George," she'd said as they battled about his return to Everest. "That's not a marriage. I want to be with you. Isn't that what you said you wanted?" If he came home empty-handed, all the sacrifice would have been for nothing.

"It's for something greater, Ruth. I promise you. If I do this, then I'll never have to go away again. We'll be able to have a real life together. We won't have to worry." He'd grasped at her hands, needed her to understand. "I want you to be proud of me. I want the children to be proud."

"But we already are," she said, as if she couldn't understand how he didn't see that.

If he left now, if they abandoned the summit, what then? Then it would be back to teaching. The day in, day out of it. Ruth had lived for the past five years on the promise that he would reach the summit and then everything would change for them. Disappointing her would break his heart. And Everest would still be there, between them. The great mass of it and the years it had consumed. For nothing. Only claiming the summit could make things right between them.

The mattress rustled under him as he rolled over. It wasn't only Ruth who would be disappointed in him.

He could hear his father's chiding tone already: "Time to put away childish things," his father would say, as if giving a sermon. "It was about time a long time ago." He pictured his father's shaggy head shaking at him. "You'll go back to teaching. That's an honorable job. Trafford, all those boys, they didn't die so you could gallivant around the world. We all make sacrifices. This one is yours. Show your boy how to be a man."

His father would add this to the catalog of disappointments: his being evacuated from the front, while Trafford died; his drifting across careers; his resigning from Charterhouse; his leaving before he'd even given so much as a single lecture at Cambridge. All the maybes. Somedays. Whens and ifs.

"He only wants to see you well situated," his mother would say, yet again. "He doesn't mean to sound so disparaging. Spend some time with him and you'll see."

"What he wants is for me to be more like Will," he'd replied the last time. "And he's probably right." Will, who was always there, with his steady job and his holiday climbing. It was Will who John had clung to last time he'd come home. They teased each other about it. "Somewhere between the two of us, George, there's the perfect man."

Deserting Everest would follow him everywhere. He would be crucified, the failure pinned to him, attached to his name once again. *The Times* would love that. He could picture the headlines already: *Two Dead as Mallory Fails Again to Reach Everest Summit.* And that was if they turned back now. If they pressed on, there was always the possibility of more injuries, that others could die. And then what?

He'd heard it all before. When he and Ruth had disembarked from Paris, a wall of reporters had been waiting for them on the platform at St. Pancras Station. He'd feared he might suffocate from the crush of their flannel suits. Then Ruth seized onto him and he felt a flush of lust and excitement—that she could see him like this, sought after, desired. There hadn't been this many reporters the first time; Hinks had discouraged them. But then the questions had started, innocuous and polite enough at the beginning.

"How do you feel, Mr. Mallory?"

"Exhausted, but glad to be home." He had wrapped his arm around Ruth's shoulders. She was still smiling.

"And you're pleased with the way it all went?"

"Would've been more so if we'd made it."

"And the avalanche? Can you tell us exactly what happened?"

"It was an accident."

"But you were leading. The conditions were right, weren't they? Shouldn't you have known better?"

He had looked for where the question had come from, but all he could see was a wall of men pressing in with notepads and pens. He pulled Ruth tighter to him.

"You can't understand what it's like up there. We did everything we could."

"Do you think it was worth it, Mr. Mallory? Is Everest worth it?"

And then his name in the papers. *Reckless. Porters in danger. Everest at what cost?*

He'd canceled their subscriptions, refused to talk any more about it with Ruth.

Geoffrey had sat on his gray sofa, in his tailored suit with the leg turned up at the knee, and tried to comfort him. "I would have done the same thing, George. You know it." But there was pity in Geoffrey's voice. He might have done the same thing, but he hadn't had to. He couldn't do it again. The cost had been too high, the reward not high enough.

He needed the summit. After everything, the *want* of it was still on him. It crept across his skin, slipped into his groin. He flushed with sweat in the cool room.

Teddy had to say yes. Of course Teddy wanted the summit, too, but only to a point.

"How far would you go?" he had asked Teddy once, a long time ago. It was after the reconnaissance, when Teddy's name was being tossed around for the '22 expedition. They'd met at the Alpine Club on Savile Row, where they had drunk too much and their conversation had grown too honest.

"For the summit?"

"How far would you go?" he had repeated, leaning forward, jabbing the air between them with his finger.

"It would be remarkable," Teddy said. "But—"

"But," he'd cut in. "But nothing. I don't need to hear any more. I don't think there is a but for me."

"That's why you'll need me, then."

He was right. If Teddy let them have another run at it, he didn't know if he could turn back. *At what point am I going to stop?* he'd written to Geoffrey. *It's going to be a fearfully difficult decision . . . I almost hope I shall give out first.*

He wanted to sleep, but his thoughts continued to churn against one another. Forget it, then. George pulled himself from his pallet and stepped back into his filthy clothes. In his bare feet he walked back to the courtyard, reclined against the wall in the warming sun, and lit another cigarette. Here the exhaustion pulled heavily on him. His head nodded.

"Sahib?"

He opened his eyes to Virgil, then patted the ground next to him. "You go again?"

"I don't know."

"You want go." Virgil sounded disappointed.

He wouldn't explain himself to his porter. Not now. "It's the job," he said. Virgil crouched down beside him, not sitting but leaning against the wall. He smelled slightly of incense, of rice wine. They'd already done the *puja*, then. Maybe he had slept some after all.

"No. Better if you go home." Virgil pinched some sand between his fingers, tossed it three times into the air, the way George had seen him do before with rice flour, an offering.

"You don't think I can do it?"

"Maybe no. Maybe Chomolungma say no."

"I don't believe in that, Virgil."

"She not care if you believe."

As the silence drew out between them, George sucked smoke into his lungs, then exhaled it slowly through his nose. "It doesn't matter," he said finally.

Virgil nodded. After a long beat he said, "You give money for Lapkha family."

After the avalanche, he had given Virgil the money he'd had on him to split amongst the dead coolies' families. He'd felt compelled to do something. It had been an empty gesture, but the only thing he could think of to do. It had changed nothing then, and wouldn't now—not for him—but it might make a difference for Lapkha's family.

"I'll see what I can do. Later. Yes?"

"But if you not come back, his family starve. They on other side of Khumbu. Not able to harvest."

"Jesus, Virgil. I will come back," he snapped, his tone harsher than he'd intended. Virgil didn't look at him but tossed another pinch of sand in the air. "I'll talk to Teddy, all right?"

"George?" Odell was standing in the shadowed cave of the doorway. "You should see this." An escape.

"I'll see what I can do," he said to the porter, and stood. He had to talk to Teddy about a lot of things.

"Look at this," Odell said, leading him farther inside.

Whatever Odell was gesturing at was hard to make out in the shadowed gloom inside the monastery. George narrowed his eyes to focus. It was a painting on a back wall, far away from what little daylight infiltrated the room. Odell reached for a lantern and held it up before them.

The light bounced off the paint as if it was still wet. *Drippy* was how Duncan Grant would have described it, as if that were a technical term. These lines were more savage, more primal, than the vague impressions of shapes and colors he had watched Duncan create at Cambridge—the washed-out watercolors of so many English painters—and they were all the more powerful for that.

In bold blocks of color, the painting showed an Englishman lying at the base of a sharp outcrop of mountain, fallen, collapsed, ripped down from the summit. One demon stood over him, driving a spear into the man's bloody gaping chest. Another was about to devour him or drag the man back into the frozen innards of the mountain.

"Is that supposed to be one of us?" he asked.

"One of the younger monks said it was dozens of years old. Well, seasons, actually. That's the way they measure their time here. In seasons. So it can't be us." Odell looked at him sideways. "Can it?"

"Of course not." But there was no mistaking the paleness of the skin on the victim, the clothing he wore. He reached out to touch the open wound in the white man's chest, then looked at his fingers, expecting to see a smudge of color there. Nothing. The paint was dry. "Let's not mention this to anyone else. If we start looking for portents now, we'll start seeing them everywhere. And if the coolies see this . . ."

"Right, none of them will go back up." Odell cocked his head and looked at the painting again. "Still. It makes you think."

"Don't. There are enough monsters up there already."

Next to him Odell fidgeted slightly; he could feel the man studying him before returning his gaze to the painting. "Do you think Teddy will let us back up?"

"You want another crack at it? I'm surprised. After your last retreat, I thought you'd be done."

"That was Somervell's call. He turned us around before we even made it to Six. I could have gone on. I would've made the attempt. Somes didn't like the look of the weather, he said." Odell turned away from the painting, moving into the long prayer room. He ran his hand along the wall of prayer wheels. They were supposed to keep the world turning. Odell spun one.

In the gloom at the far end of the hall was a glitter of gold, the belly and massive shoulders of a Buddha rising up into the darkness that gathered below the eaves. It was surrounded by thousands of flickering butter candles, their smoke and incense curling up into the air, the statue wavering above them. At its feet a monk sat cross-legged, his robe gathered around his shoulders. He looked as if he hadn't moved in a very long time. There was a plate of rice flour beside him, a dish of water. Every so often he reached in for a pinch of one or the other and tossed it in the air the way Virgil had tossed the pinches of sand outside.

If only he could find whatever it was that this monk had found. Or his father. Or even Somervell. There was comfort in ritual, he could see that, even sense it here, but he was shut out of it somehow. "You expect too much," Ruth had said to him after she'd persuaded him to accompany her to a church service. "Faith doesn't come like that, crashing down on you. It's an opening up. You just have to open your-self up to it." But he couldn't. Maybe if he had more faith in some-thing, he wouldn't be here. Maybe that was what he was missing.

But then, Somes had faith, and he'd turned back. What if Odell was telling the truth? Odell himself had looked good on the way down to the monastery. He'd kept pace with George the whole way. And it wouldn't have been the first time that Somes had turned back. Last time he'd managed the height record but had pulled back when he still had good hours of daylight ahead of him. He'd said he just couldn't see his way to finishing. Maybe Somes's faith was in the wrong place.

"I guess we'll know soon enough, though," Odell said, moving past him toward the main hall. "But it would be damn nice to knock it off."

"What are you thinking, Teddy? Which way are you leaning?"

"Maybe it can't be done, George."

"Come on, Teddy, I'm supposed to be the cynical one."

"No. You're supposed to be the hero. I'm the one who will take the blame."

"That's not fair. It was me last time. It will be me again this time."

"Just because it's your name on everyone's lips doesn't mean I don't pay a price for what happens up here. I'm the expedition leader, George. I'm the one who's accountable." Teddy picked up a telegram from the table in front of him, put it down again, shuffled his papers. "All you have to do is climb the mountain. That's all anyone wants of you."

"That's all they want from any of us."

"No, they want me to bring everyone home. Safe. With all their fingers and toes. They want better maps and new species of plants. They want Somervell's groundbreaking research on the effects of high altitude on human physiology. They want Odell's goddamn fossils. They don't want to hear about drowned boys or dead porters."

"They want us to make it all worth it."

"What?"

"The bloody war. They want this last crowning jewel, don't they? Isn't that what this is all about? The sun never setting on the glory that is the British Empire?"

"I don't know, George. But maybe we've gone far enough."

"So you're turning us around?"

"Virgil came to me. About money for the dead porter's family. You said it was a good idea?" Teddy put down the cup of tea he was nursing, the thick yak's milk curdled across the top of it. It smelled slightly off. "Are we just buying our way out of our responsibilities?"

"That's not it." Was it? He had told Virgil he'd look into it. Virgil shouldn't have gone to Teddy.

"Do you really think we can do it, George?"

"I don't think we have a choice."

✦   ✦   ✦

GOD. SANDY JUST WANTED to be left alone. Just for a little while. Granted, the place to do that would have been his cell, but the dark air in there felt solid and heavy after the nights at the higher camps, where the snowfields brightened everything. Even though the whole way down from Base Camp he'd been daydreaming of sleep— thought he wouldn't be able to get enough of it when he finally lay down in the quiet, on his own—he couldn't sleep now that he was here. His eyes felt as though they were swelling, pressing out until he had to open them to the dim room.

Out here in the courtyard the sun was gentle, lulling. More benign than it had felt higher up, where it glared down on them, close and hard. He wanted to stretch out under it, hat pulled over his eyes, and doze.

"Couldn't sleep, eh?" Somervell was standing over him, blocking the sun. He shielded his eyes to look up at Somes, a black shadow against the stark white sky.

He didn't want to talk to anyone, least of all Somervell, who moved to sit beside him on the ground. The sun beat down on Sandy again.

"I think Teddy and George are in there deciding our fate," Somes said. Sandy didn't respond. There was a long silence between them. "You did well, Sandy, you should know that." He hoped Somervell wasn't talking about Lapkha. He really didn't want to talk about that. Somervell went on, "I'm not sure anyone else could have done any better."

"You weren't there."

"I know. But I know what it's like."

"How can you? You can't know what it's like for someone like me. You're a doctor. You know how to cope with things like that." He couldn't stop now. "You told me you were going to check on the porters before you went. You should have seen he was sick. You should have sent him down days earlier. Then he'd still be alive. I shouldn't have had to see him like that."

He wanted Somervell to snap back. He was spoiling for a fight. None of this was fair. None of it. They had left him behind to tend camp and to watch Lapkha die. This wasn't how things were supposed to happen.

Somervell was quiet for a few long minutes. "Did you really think it would be easy?"

Of course he hadn't thought it would be easy, but he hadn't expected it to be like this. It had all seemed like a great adventure at the beginning. Had it only been two months ago that they had sat in Richards's back garden in Darjeeling, drinking champagne? It had all seemed like a grand lark. At least then he'd felt that they were all in it together.

"No, of course not," he said finally, feeling small, petulant.

"If it was easy," Somes said, "everyone would do it. My dad used to say that to me when I was little. When I said school was too hard. When I lost a race. I hated when he said that."

He didn't want Somervell's platitudes, wasn't going to let this be easy for him. "If you'd been in camp, Lapkha might still be alive."

"He very well might be. But then, maybe not." Somes leaned his head back against the wall, closed his eyes, pinched at the bridge of his nose. Then he turned to stare hard at Sandy. "There's a price to pay, Sandy, for something like this. An acceptable price. Everyone knows what's at risk. Everyone shares the rewards. If you were a little older, you might understand that a bit better."

"That's what this is about? I'm not a bloody child."

"No." Somes leaned back, shaking his head, surprised. "No, you're not. That's not what I meant. I just meant we had to figure that out for ourselves. Over there. During the war." Somervell let his words sit for a moment. As if he wanted to say something else but wasn't sure he should. "We didn't get an inch of land—not an inch—without paying for it. We've all watched men die. Brutally. Unfairly."

"That was war, Somes. This isn't."

"You're right. It was war. And I'm sorry, Sandy. I'm sorry you were there by yourself. But you handled it well. You should be proud of what you've done. But you have to decide for yourself what price is too high. I can't decide for you. Teddy can't. George can't. A lot of people thought the war cost us too much—that maybe this will as well."

Sandy thought of what his mum had said: *Too many have already died.* "What do you think?"

"I think we do what is required of us. Then. Now."

Somes put his hand on Sandy's shoulder to heave himself back to his feet, grunting as he did so. "You'll have to make your own decision. And soon," he said and started back toward the monastery. "Teddy wants us in the main hall in a half-hour."

"So that's what we'll do, then," Norton was saying when Sandy walked into the narrow room a half-hour later, still not having slept. Norton sat at a long, low table with George, their legs crossed under them. George nodded, gulped at the stew in front of him.

Noel entered from the other end of the room, through the arch of daylight, a backlit shadow, shrinking and solidifying. "Ah, the war council, eh? Well, let's get it on film, shall we?"

But Noel was too late. It seemed Somes was right, things had already been decided. There was a brief surge of excitement in Sandy's stomach, a flash of hope that ebbed away as he slipped onto a cushion at the low table, across from George. With the light coming at him sideways, George's eyes glowed like fevered spheres. Noel instructed a porter to set up his heavy movie camera at one end of the table, then fussed over it, wiping the lens, fogging it with his breath, and then wiping it once more.

Sandy had almost forgotten about the camera. How much had Noel seen from his Eagle's Nest? Had Noel watched him stumbling around ABC, trying but failing to help Lapkha? What if it had looked as though he weren't doing anything at all? He remembered that there had been long moments when he'd found himself sitting still in the snow, unable to recall what he was doing or why he needed to be moving. But then he *had* moved again. What if Noel's film only showed him sitting there, wandering, useless?

Before he'd been invited to join the expedition, before he'd even gone to Spitsbergen, Sandy had gone with Dick to see Noel's film of the 1922 attempt. Dick had offered to buy them tickets for one of the lectured showings so that Sandy could hear George speak. "Look," Dick said, "I know Spitsbergen's not Everest, but there's bound to be some similarities, at least. Setting off into the great unknown, wild adventure, and all that."

"That sounds fantastic, Dick. But you don't have to do that. We'll just go to the film."

"When have you ever refused my generosity?" Dick had cuffed his arm and he'd felt the flush across his face, the perspiration on his lip. Dick always treated. What was Dick's was Sandy's. It had been like that since public school. But it didn't feel right anymore. He kept wondering, God, what would Dick say when he found out about Marjory?

"Well, we can't go on like that forever, can we? Actually, why don't you let me treat?" he'd said, though he couldn't afford it, really.

They had sat in the dark theater and he tried to imagine being that cold. He believed what he saw on the screen. All the camaraderie, the smiling faces of porters. The hope that they'd make it the next time. Now he wondered how much of it Noel had manufactured. Whether those smiling faces might have been from before things went wrong, the hope from before the avalanche.

The rest of them filtered in—Odell, Somervell, Hazard, Shebbeare. Odell came and sat beside him, placing his hand on Sandy's shoulder as he lowered himself to the table. "All right?" Odell asked.

"Fine, thanks. You?"

Odell nodded and smiled an easy smile. He knew something. He knew what was going to happen. Had Norton already told them who was going?

Norton looked around the table and then at Noel, whose film camera clattered to life and then whirred loudly. Across from him, George put his hands palms down on the table and inhaled deeply as if to focus himself. As if he were preparing for battle. "This is from last week." Norton held up a small piece of paper. A telegram with a scramble of words on it. "The monsoon hit the continent a week ago," Norton explained. "It's on its way."

The monsoon was their warning bell. The weather would change. There was no way to know for certain how quickly, but it would turn, and they'd have to be down from the high camps before it did. Lower down, when the spring winds swept in, the monsoon brought rain and warm weather—the crops would grow, the rivers might flood. Up here, it meant blizzards, feet of dumped snow. Up here it meant the summit would be impossible.

Norton cleared his throat and started again. "We go back tomorrow. George and I have set the teams. We'll try one last blast for the summit. Two teams, a day apart. With God on our side, with luck, that's all it will take. George?"

George's eyes skimmed over him as he looked around the table. "We'll go in two teams. Light and fast. Teddy and I talked about who should go. Who was strong, ready. It hasn't been an easy decision, but this will be the last shot. I'll be on the first team, of course." There were nods around the table. Even from Noel, who had moved out from behind the camera. "Teddy and Somes will be the second team."

George seemed to be finished. He leaned back slightly away from the table, then placed his hands back on it as if to push himself off.

"And?" The word was out of his mouth before Sandy could stop it.

"And what?"

"And who is going with you? On the attempt?"

"Oh." George looked away from him and stood up so he towered over the table. "Odell. Odell and I will take the first assault."

Norton took over. "Hazard, Shebbeare—you'll stay below. Sandy, you'll run the support for both attempts. Start at Four and then move up a day behind us." Sandy didn't hear the rest of the conversation.

Slowly, everyone drifted out of the hall, leaving only him and Shebbeare to confer about provisions. Shebbeare flipped through the pages George had handed him. "Most of what we need is already at ABC. We'll need to send some more fuel. Some more food. And what about the cooker at Five? You said it had broken down?"

"I've already repaired it."

"Ah." Shebbeare crossed something off the list in front of him. "That's taken care of, then."

Sandy's face was hot under his sunburn. He felt like a fool. Like when he had had to sit out the Oxford–Cambridge race last year because he'd been away at bloody Spitsbergen with Odell. He'd been in better shape than anyone else on the eight, but he wasn't allowed to row because of a stupid rule about missed practices. He sat on the sidelines and watched Oxford win, and he was thrilled for his team-mates, for his school, but still he ached during the course.

He turned now on Shebbeare. "You're all right with this? That we'll just be pack animals for the attempt?"

"Of course. That's what I was brought on for, Sandy. I know you thought maybe you'd get a crack at it, but I didn't. I've got my job to do. We're still a part of it."

"We're not. We're being left behind to wait. What if something goes wrong?"

"It won't." Shebbeare gathered up the rest of the papers from the table. "You should get your things together. Norton wants to get going at first light." He stopped at the door. "I think we might just do it this time."

When he was alone again, Sandy thought about what Somes had said. About what price he was willing to pay. What Everest was worth.

If he was on the attempt, he might think it was worth anything, but not this way. This way it wasn't worth watching another man suffocate, his lungs flooding, his brain expanding until it exploded. Sandy swallowed down the image.

They were going to make the attempt anyway, whether he thought it was worth it or not. But he wouldn't watch anyone else die. No matter what Somes or George had to say. If his job was to make sure they were safe, that's what he'd do.

TEA

Four O'Clock

There is nothing on the table in the entryway. No afternoon post. No cards. I drop my hat on the empty surface and make my way to the dining room, where Vi is wiping and stacking the unpacked plates. One of the serving bowls has been chipped in the move, but I don't want to see it. "It's fine," I tell her, handing her the flowers to arrange. "It will be fine." She looks at me as if this is some enormous mistake.

"We're working hard, Mummy," Berry greets me as I step out the back door.

"I can see that."

The three of them are on the veranda, where Edith can keep an eye on them from the kitchen without their being in her way.

"Letters for Daddy!" John yells, some kind of battle cry before he goes back to work and Berry holds hers up—all wobbly letters, a heart. Some X's and O's.

The tip of John's tongue sticks out between his teeth, his brow furrowed as he tries to draw a picture of himself and his daddy climbing a mountain together. Clare's is neat, her letters bold and round. "Where will they go this time?"

The atlas is on the floor in George's study. Before he left, I sat with them and we wrote letters to hide in his cases. "A surprise for Daddy," I told them. "You know how much you love surprises, right? Well, guess what? So does Daddy."

Clare folded hers and gave me strict instructions not to look at it. Berry did the same because Clare did.

Together we made our way to the front hall, where crates were piled, waiting to be taken to the train. We made a small expedition, with Clare in the lead. She climbed up to tuck her letter into one of the boxes at the top. Berry found another one that she could slide hers into. John handed me his.

"Will he find them?" Berry asked.

Clare answered. "Of course he will. When he gets to the mountain, he'll unpack everything and it will make him happy." She climbed down and looked to me for confirmation. "Right, Mummy?"

"Yes. When he gets to the mountain, Daddy will be happy."

I bring the atlas out to the veranda, but I don't know where to tell them their father is.

Clare takes the book and opens it up, traces the route, around and up, all the way to the mountain. She knows it well now.

"Here." She taps the map. Mount Everest.

"Can we take them to post now?" Berry wants to know. What she really wants is to visit the sweets shop next to the post office.

"No," Clare proclaims. "Now it's teatime." She turns to me. "You promised."

"Of course." I force the cheer into my voice. "We'll go to the post office on Monday. Everyone—hats and gloves. Time for tea in the garden!"

. . .

We sit under the willow tree in the deep back garden. *It is so lush,* I'll write to George later. There are a thousand shades of green, and the tulips and roses are like bright paint splattered against it. Bees tumble from the flowers and the air is soft and cool. If we're quiet we can hear the little stream burble at the end of it, but of course John and the girls are never quiet. The four of us are at a small table draped with a lace cloth that is folded so its stained edges won't show. There are scones and jam and milky tea.

Clare officiates at teatime, directs the conversation. Today she is talking about the seaside. About the pier.

"Cottie said that perhaps we should all go to the seaside to distract ourselves from what is at hand." The words are imperious.

"And what is at hand, Clare?" I ask.

Her brow furrows and she glares at me. I shouldn't have said it, though it doesn't matter, as Berry has taken up the refrain. "The seaside! We could have toffee." She had toffee once and it is what she thinks of whenever any mention is made of the seaside. Not the smell or the roll of waves to the horizon. Only the toffee.

John gets up from the table and wanders a short distance away. Not too far. He wants the treats but doesn't want to sit. Instead he turns himself in circles faster and faster until he falls over, giggling.

I've never understood how you could have been so disappointed when Clare was born. Superfluous, *you told Geoffrey. Having a girl was superfluous when so many young men were dying. As though it were her fault. As though we should just breed replacements for the men killed in the trenches. As though they could be replaced.*

George wasn't around for any of their births, though he promised to be there for John's, so certain the baby would be a boy after Clare and Berry.

"I'll be there, Ruth, I swear," he said as he packed his bags again for the Alps.

My stomach pressed out into the space between us. I refused to help him pack.

"You could just wait. Go with Will after the baby is born. It's too close. He or she is going to be early." My voice was a whine. I hated the sound of it.

"He," George said, and then, "Don't be like this."

I wanted to ask, *Like what?* It didn't seem strange to me that he should want to be here when his child was born, that I should want him to.

I knew he would miss it. When he left, John was already so heavy in my belly, it was as if I could almost taste him waiting to be born, as if he had looked out, through my eyes, to watch George leave.

"He's on his way," Marby said two weeks later, sponging my brow, and maybe she meant John or maybe she meant George. As I strained against John, trying to keep him in, trying to push him out, George was on a train traveling from the coast. When he walked in he still smelled of the mountains.

The bedroom reeked of blood, pungent afterbirth, the sea. Marby had wrapped John's umbilical cord in a tea towel for me to plant under a new tree in the garden. It was wrapped next to the bed and the smell of it made me want to retch, my stomach still sensitive from exhaustion and giving birth.

George breezed in like spring. "It's a boy!"

It wasn't a question. Marby must have told him.

John was asleep on my chest, his small head nestled under my chin. He smelled like me. Like himself, specific and familiar and mine. There was nothing of George on him yet. In that moment he was mine. Only mine. George stared at him, cupped his head in his palm.

"John," I said.

"John? What about Trafford?"

I knew George had wanted to name a son for his brother. I would have agreed if he'd been there. "John Trafford," I allowed.

John mewed, opened his eyes and stared up at his father, unseeing, as George took him from me. "John Trafford," he said, nodding.

In the garden John throws himself at the ground, rolling down the small incline in a tumble of somersaults, and then laughs maniacally. The girls I know I can take care of, raise properly. But John, he needs his father.

Vi steps out onto the porch. "Your dress is hanging, ma'am."

It's time, then. "Clare, want to come with Mummy to dress?"

She nods as if it's a solemn duty and leads me by the hand back into the house.

The dressing table is an array of small bottles, combs, brushes. For years, Clare has sat with me while I dress, and each time she removes every cosmetic from the small middle drawer and spreads them all out, lining them up across the silk runner that George brought back after the first expedition. It's a patchwork of dark purples shot through with silver and gold threads. Today she does it as if by rote, then rises and wanders around the room until she reaches for the silver frame beside the bed. A photograph of her father and me taken just before he left for France.

"You should try to smile," George said. "Then I can see your smile every day when I look at it."

"If you stayed here," I told him, "you could see this smile every day." I scrunched up my face into an exaggerated, crazy grin.

"If only. But it's impossible."

Except it wasn't impossible. He hadn't been conscripted. He had chosen to go. He could have made the choice to stay. I've tried to understand why it is that he goes away so often. I tell myself it is a matter of duty, of honor. But duty seems to be different for men than it is for women. Duty is something men step inside and fasten around them, like uniforms. For women, duty is a cloak draped over us, that weighs us down.

The photograph had been my idea. "We could each have one. One for me to keep, next to our bed. One for you to take with you to France. You can carry it in your pocket. Over your heart."

"Ruth, I won't forget what you look like. It's emblazoned here and here." He put his hand to his heart, to his temple. But a small part of me worried that he would forget. Worse, I worried that I would forget him if something were to happen. I needed the physical token of him, like a talisman. As long as I could look at him, he would remain alive.

We sat for the photograph—him in his new uniform, which even I had to admit made him all the more handsome. We each thought the other looked better.

"But that's how it should be," I said when we received the prints. "I think you're strikingly handsome, you think I'm pretty. We both think the other one is a fool. Perfect. Just how it should be when you're in love."

Darling, he wrote, *I carry the picture in the small notebook in my pocket. It's always on me, though it's gotten wet and dirty, it is there.*

And it was easy to believe. When he was invalided home, it

came with him, crumpled at the corners, soft. I didn't ask if he ever pulled it out, just imagined it. When he felt alone. Scared. I needed to keep that.

"Put it away," he said of the photo I kept next to our bed when he knew he wouldn't be going back. Not after Trafford's funeral, after Geoffrey's leg. "It reminds me of going away and I don't want to go away anymore." So I did. I wrapped both of them in some folded paper and put them into a cupboard.

The first time he went to Everest, I pulled the photograph out and placed it back on the nightstand. He didn't say anything when he saw it.

I saw his copy scattered amongst the papers on his desk. "Are you taking this?"

"Of course. I always take it. Whenever I go away. Anywhere."

"You don't. I saw it in the linen drawer. It's been there for years."

"I take it and put it back. Every time." I imagined him opening the drawer, unwrapping it, then wrapping it back up when he returned.

"I'll leave it at the summit. That's where you deserve to be, at the top of all things," he said, and kissed my forehead. "And I won't need it anymore after that, I shan't go anywhere. I'll stay right here. You won't need yours, either. We'll get rid of them both."

But we didn't. We just continued to fold them away.

Clare traces the lines of the photograph. "You look very pretty."

I don't know if she means then or now, but Clare has become an authority on what is pretty. Soon, I think, she'll be too old for this. How long do little girls watch their mothers dress? Until they're eleven? Twelve? I'll have to let Berry come and join us soon, although I love this time alone with Clare. Berry I'll have for a few more years. I imagine Clare as a young woman, dressing herself to impress someone. I touch Clare's lips with color. Her cheeks with rouge. I pin glittering butterflies in her hair.

"We should have waited to write to Daddy. I would tell him how pretty you look."

Her face becomes a rain cloud when she mentions you. There is this tug-of-war as she shifts from anger to protectiveness. Like me. There are moments when she lashes out, is angry that you are not here.

Like she does sometimes with Will, I think. "Daddy should be here to do it," she said when Will helped to tie up a swing in the garden. Her anger was sharp with the injustice.

"Maybe Will can be our daddy now," Berry said, and Clare turned on her.

"Don't be stupid, Berry. We have a daddy."

Poor Berry hardly knew you when you returned from Everest the first time. Do you remember how John fussed when you tried to hold him? And your face, when you saw how comfortable they were with Will, asking him to lift them up. It was terrible. There were repercussions none of us had expected.

Clare, though, has her memories of her father and holds fast to them. The other day she drew a square on a piece of paper. More squares inside it.

"What are you doing?" I asked her.

"Trying to remember."

"What are you trying to remember?"

"You won't know. Only Daddy knows." She huffed, then showed me the paper. "It's Daddy's magic square. He made it and showed me how all the numbers added up to nine. I couldn't find the one he made me. I want to make a new one."

I left her alone so she wouldn't see me cry. I could practically see George leaning over her, trying to help her with schoolwork. She was frustrated to tears and he pulled her to his lap, whispered to her, "I'll show you some magic, Clare."

And as I watched, he lined up numbers in a square and made her add them up. He held up his fingers for her to count on.

"Nine!" she gasped, and giggled in surprise.

I didn't tell her I could show her how it worked. She wouldn't have wanted that.

"I'll ask him when he gets home," she said. "How many more days?"

"I don't know exactly, love. But we shall, very soon."

I turn to her now as she examines herself in the mirror. "You look lovely too," I tell her. "We'll write Daddy again, don't worry. We can write him every day if you like."

"We don't need to do that."

"No?"

"He doesn't write us every day. He's busy. We're busy." It is a simple declaration.

She is quiet awhile, staring at our reflections side by side in the mirror. She is so much like her father, but I doubt she can see that. *What would she ever do without you?* I wonder so much what I would do that sometimes I forget how hurt they must be. But I know she counts the days, marks them off on the calendar she asked for.

"I think John and Berry miss Daddy," she says, as if she can read my mind. I try to smile. "They're sad, I think. And you miss him, too, right?"

"Of course, darling."

"So why do you want to look pretty when he's not here?"

I don't know what to say to her. What could I say that she would understand? That it feels good to put on one's best. But also that it is part of my duty. To behave the way that I am expected to behave.

We have roles, all of us, and maybe sometimes that looks like be-trayal, but it isn't. What she wants is for me to mourn so that she doesn't have to. So that she doesn't have to be sad that her father is gone. And I will do that for her. Willingly. But not tonight. Tonight I need to feel as though everything will be all right, that everything is how it should be.

And it is also a kind of armor—the makeup, the dress. One that Clare is already learning. I must be properly armed to get through this evening. To manage with Arthur Hinks. I imagine what he might say to me:

They are still making the attempt.

I had word this afternoon, they're on their way home.

I'm sorry, but I wanted to tell you this in person.

I tie a silk scarf around Clare's pale throat. She cocks her head in the mirror and then takes it off, drops it to the floor.

"Because it's a dinner party," I say, bending to pick it up, and my voice sounds like a sigh. "And Auntie Marby is coming. And Cottie and Eleanor. And they always look so pretty, don't you think? And Uncle Will."

"He isn't really an uncle. Not like Uncle Trafford was." She doesn't remember Trafford, was only a baby when he died. But her grand-father talks about him as though he were still alive.

"No, he isn't. But he's a good friend, almost like a brother to your daddy. And a good friend to me too. And to you. So we call him Uncle. To make him part of the family."

"Oh."

"And don't you like that you're pretty?"

She looks in the mirror again. Her eyes are huge with the slight gloss of tears that I ignore. She nods. "Can I come to the dinner party?"

"No, sweet. You're too young. Soon enough, though. How about we have a dinner party with Daddy when he comes home? You and me and Daddy. Just the three of us. We'll dress our best and use the fine china."

"But what if I break it?"

"It's only china."

She smiles. "Daddy will be sorry he missed this."

"I'm sure he's sorry to miss a lot of things."

THE ASSAULT

27,000 *Feet*

No one had yet been this high up on the expedition.

After a cold night at Camp VI, George had left with Odell just before dawn. If they kept up a good pace, George wagered it would take them ten hours or so to reach the summit and make it back to camp. Ten hours of straight climbing. He'd had longer days in the Alps, but never at this kind of altitude. And the cold here was unbearable. He couldn't even begin to imagine what it would be like to be caught out here, unmoving, at night. Still, their progress had been slower than he would have liked in the predawn glow. Yesterday, on the way up, Odell had challenged him all the way to VI. He liked being pushed and found himself feeling certain they would make it. Him and Odell. He never thought it would be him with Odell, and now here they were. Teddy was right about leaving yourself open to other possibilities.

But this morning Odell was already waning, slowing before the sun had even crested the peaks to the east. Maybe he'd pushed too hard yesterday, trying to prove himself. He stopped after every step, staring at his feet, inhaling three, four breaths for each step upward. George was at least making two, even three steps before he had to stop and catch his breath.

"You should wait here," he finally told Odell.

"I'm. Fine." Odell's voice stuttered. Slow but vicious, as if he couldn't believe that he would be left behind. But Odell was an anchor. As long as they were tied together, George couldn't gain any ground. Odell had to see that. This wasn't about either one of them. Not anymore. They had to go all out if they were going to succeed. *He* had to.

At this rate, the summit and back would take more than the ten hours he'd estimated—much more. "You're slowing me down. We need to move faster. I can move faster on my own."

Odell looked up through the gloom at the glowing snow cone of the summit and slumped to the ground. He tried for a moment to haul himself back up before fumbling with the rope knotted at his waist. "Go," Odell nodded. "But I'm not turning back."

"Fine. But be careful. Go down. If you need to. I'll meet you back there at the end." He pointed down toward the smudge of their tent.

That was forever ago. He'd left Odell just after dawn and pushed on alone. As noon rolled over him, the summit was still so far away. He couldn't even see it past the mountain's nearer shoulder. Couldn't tell anymore how long he'd been climbing, how much farther it was. The guilt of leaving Odell behind buzzed in his head. If Odell got disoriented he might walk right off the mountain, and if he wasn't moving he would grow colder and colder. He could freeze to death. George imagined climbing back down and finding Odell dead beside the route, frozen solid. He shook the image from his head.

He groped for his watch, the cold burning the exposed flesh of his wrist. The summit was there. Maybe just over the next rise. He could reach it this time. He trudged toward it. And toward it.

It was hard to measure the distance. He set markers—an outcropping, a strange dog-shaped rock formation nearer to him—to count it off. Pressed himself to reach it and then allowed himself a quick break, a gulp of water, when he did. Picked another marker and pressed forward again.

He stepped forward, and again, and again—a dragging rhythm like a slowing Victrola. One step. Followed by another. And then another. Then a sickening lurch in his stomach and he was falling. And the wrenching stop, his right arm over his head, a tearing at his shoulder. He screamed in pain. Above him, his ice axe was caught widthwise across the top of a crevasse. The loop of leather cut into his wrist. He couldn't breathe against the pain that thudded in his arm. Below him a gape of emptiness.

He was being held together by his skin, his windproofs. He imagined them ripping, his flesh tearing, and dropping him a mile inside the earth.

Light came in from the crack above him and to his right. He'd stepped through a cornice of snow masking a fracture in the mountain. He tried not to think. He was hanging between sheer walls of ice and snow that grew deeper, more violet and indigo as they sank down toward the bowels of the mountain, away from the wind and cold and light. If there was a monster on the mountain, it lived down there. His fingers were growing numb with his weight on them. With the cold.

This was how it could end, then, this easily. He wasn't tied to anything. Not the mountain. Not Odell.

Odell. He was too far away to help him, even if he could have gathered enough breath to get Odell's name out through the searing pain in his lungs, his shoulder. He closed his eyes. Breathe. Slow. Steady. Don't panic. His breath came in ragged gasps, squeezed out by his position. There was nothing but ice and rock around him. Nothing. He dangled over the empty darkness of the mountain and imagined letting go.

"Hold on," Ruth said.

He was hanging from the loggia at the Holt. He'd climbed up to where she was reading in the back garden. "If you don't kiss me," he warned, "I'm letting go."

"No!" And she giggled. "Please hold on." Then she leaned over and kissed him.

He opened his eyes and tightened his grip on the axe.

He was still clinging to the overhang. He couldn't find the hold, couldn't make the leap. "Go for it, George," Geoffrey was saying. "Or drop down to rest. You can't stay there."

There was a ledge just in front of him. A hold. Big enough for his foot. He kicked his crampons into the ice, putting his weight on the metal spikes. It held. Frozen for a millennium, the ice was solid, didn't splinter or flake. He fought to dislodge his axe and then threw himself against the wall of ice, its coolness washing over him. He was sweating, though, in the cold, the false warmth of it a relief. After catching his breath some, he swung the axe and dug into the ice, which rained down on him, lifted his right foot to kick in again.

Hours passed, and the sun crept slowly over the opening of the crevasse, its shaft of light moving faster than he was as he fought to climb free. Ignoring the burning in his muscles, he inched up the ice wall until he surfaced and hauled himself out of the crevasse and back onto the mountain. Exhausted. Terrified.

The peak was there, its spindrift racing across the sky. He closed his eyes. The dull pulse in his shoulder was warming somehow, and his lungs heaved as he swallowed down frigid air that dried his mouth and throat until he was coughing, his body racked with muscle spasms.

"You can't stand by, stay here, and just let someone else climb her," Geoffrey said.

"What if she just can't be climbed?"

Geoffrey didn't say anything. George huddled himself in a ball. He had to move. One way or the other. It could be done. She could be made to yield.

He fell back onto the mountain again and cursed upward into the screaming wind. He couldn't even hear his own voice. Couldn't hear Geoffrey.

But it couldn't be done now. He was exhausted from freeing himself from the crevasse, and even if he wasn't, he'd lost too much time. If he pressed up, he'd be caught out by nightfall for sure. Even if he made the summit before dark, he'd never make it back to camp before the temperature plummeted. The image of Odell's frozen body came back to him. No, he had to turn back.

Finally he hauled himself to his feet, swaying before he steadied himself on his ice axe. Then he trudged down the ridge, poking the snow in front of him. Moving down toward Odell, toward the camp.

He would have to watch someone else try to take her. It would be up to Teddy and Somes now. He turned back to give the assault to the second team, trying not to hope for their failure.

❖　❖　❖

"IF THEY MAKE IT, I'll be a footnote. After all this. A footnote." George was slumped over the cup of tea Sandy had brought him, though he still hadn't taken a sip.

"Don't be ridiculous, George. Everyone knows what you've done on this mountain."

"Right. How many men I've killed, you mean."

George had never spoken to him about the avalanche before. Sandy wasn't sure what to say to that. George certainly wasn't responsible for Lapkha's death. That much was obvious. He was. "There's enough guilt to go around, it seems."

"You don't realize it now, Sandy, but you've got everything in front of you. Everything. This isn't the end for you."

"I don't think this is the end for you, either."

"It is. Either Teddy and Somes will claim the summit and it will be over or we'll go home and it will be over. And by the time the Committee is ready to make another go of it, I'll be too old. I'll have failed too much. It'll be your turn. You and yours."

"You wouldn't go again?"

"No. Not like this."

George put down his tea and they sat in silence in the tent. It was growing dark. They'd know tomorrow. Sandy couldn't decide anymore what it was that he wanted. If Norton and Somervell reached the summit, maybe he would just be a footnote, but at least it would be a footnote to success. That had to be better than being a footnote to failure. And there wasn't any guarantee that he would get the chance to come back, despite what George said. Hinks dismissed climbers all the time. And so far he hadn't done anything to set himself apart.

"What would you do differently?" he asked after a while.

They were both blue shadows in the tent, their skin the pale blue of clean water, their clothes darker, like the depths.

"Everything."

"No. Really, George. What?"

"I don't know. Maybe I should have just stayed home. Maybe

nothing would have made a difference. Maybe setting out earlier or using the oxygen would have."

The oxygen. What if it came down to the oxygen?

"I wanted an attempt with the oxygen. I told Teddy that. But he thought if we just had the one chance, it was better to reach the summit without it. That way no one could dispute it. And it would be a greater glory. Of course, no one would call us unsporting. But to hell with *sporting.* What if it's the only way?"

"There's oxygen here, George." He hadn't meant to tell anyone that, certainly not George.

"What?" George peered at him. Even in the dimness of the tent it was clear something had shifted, a switch had been thrown. The air between them sharpened.

"I brought it up."

"Why? You weren't supposed to. It wasn't in the plan."

Sandy could feel the flicker of irritation from George, all because he'd done something he hadn't been told to do. He'd followed orders up to now, and look where it had got him—left behind, nannying the porters and watching one of them die. How could George be so bloody clueless?

"Dammit, I brought the oxygen up just in case. If it had been up here all along, maybe Lapkha wouldn't have died." His voice was harsh and there was a sharp pain in his throat, but the anger felt good. To hell with it. It was over anyway. "All any of you ever talk about is how hard it is up here. How the altitude gets to us, is slowing us, killing us. So I brought the oxygen in case it would keep someone bloody well alive."

He panted, short of breath after his outburst. There were small explosions of light in his head.

George didn't respond.

"Forget it," Sandy finally said, and moved for the flap of the tent. He didn't know where he was going to go, but he didn't want to sit there with George anymore.

"No, wait." George's hand was on his arm, insistent. "How much?"

"What?"

"How much did you bring?"

"Six bottles. Two rigs."

"You're a genius, Sandy. If Teddy and Somes don't make it, if the weather holds, then you and I will get one more shot." George clapped both his hands on his shoulders, leaned forward, and kissed him, hard and fast. Sandy's chapped lips swelled and then they split as he smiled.

"Sahib! Sahib!"

At the end of the following day there was shouting, and Sandy was out of his tent. George was beside him, a smile fixed to his face. This was it, thought Sandy. If they'd done it, it was all over. If not, then he'd finally get a crack at the summit. But they were back, and they were alive, and that was something. His own smile spread across his face in a ripple of pain.

George hurried on ahead while he grabbed a Thermos of tea and some cups. Were they celebrating? Disappointed? They were huddled close together: Norton, Somervell, and now Odell and George, hugging. They had to be congratulating each other. He raised his hand in greeting as he moved up the slope; there was no response.

Then he realized Norton wasn't walking on his own. George and Odell weren't hugging or celebrating; they were holding him up, with Somervell collapsed behind them. The three of them lurched into camp like a dying creature.

He hurried toward them. They didn't look good. His heart throbbed. Norton and George stumbled past him, Norton's eyes covered with a piece of cloth torn from his puttees. Snow blindness. It could have been so much worse.

But the snow blindness might have happened on the way down. After the summit.

He went to Somervell, hauled him to his feet, took some of his weight on his shoulder. When Somervell met his glance, he shook his head. There was a smear of blood near his mouth. Failure was written all over him.

The possibility was physical, a rush of adrenaline in his stomach, so that his limbs tingled and he tasted blood. He stumbled and Somervell grunted in pain.

He and George would have their chance.

✦   ✦   ✦

"How was it, Somes?"

"Bloody awful."

Somervell's voice was a rough scratch, barely audible in the small tent. George handed him a cup of tea and settled him back into his sleeping bag, propped up against a pack. When Somes was comfortable, George settled back next to Sandy. Sandy's leg fidgeted against his. "Tell me," he said.

"I thought we were doing well," Somes croaked, so it hurt to listen to him. "Made it into the Yellow Band." Somervell's hands fluttered close to his throat, touching it under his muffler, stroking it like a pet.

So they had gone higher than he had with Odell. They had done better. If they left now, thought George, he wouldn't even hold the height record. He'd have nothing.

"I stopped. Coughing. Teddy kept on." Somervell sipped and

winced. "Left there for hours. Only thing kept me awake. My cough. The bloody pain of it. Throat. Ribs. Everywhere."

Somervell paused for a long time, closed his eyes, his breath evening out and then coming in a gulping gasp. George was going to leave when Somes opened his eyes again and held out his hand. Sandy handed him a lozenge.

"Martha was there. Offered me tea. She wanted me to walk with her. Wanted me to follow her, right off the mountain. Told her, 'Thank you, love,' but I'd wait right where I was."

It was something Somes had said could happen at altitude. "Lack of oxygen makes you hallucinate," he'd said on the *California*, at one of his lectures. "It's your brain shutting down. When that happens, it's time to descend. Fast." As George understood it, this was entirely different from his half-remembered conversations with Ruth; Somes had really believed his wife was up there with him. That hadn't happened to him. Not yet. George imagined those were the only real monsters up there. The ones they took with them.

"Then Teddy was there. Goggles gone. And a glove. He stumbled past me. We didn't rope up. Should have." Somervell's breath was in long, ragged gasps. "The world closed in. Bloody snow. Swirled to a single white pinpoint. Couldn't see Teddy. I stopped. Don't know how long. Everything hurt. Ribs. Head. Lungs. My throat. Like someone stabbing me in the throat. Couldn't breathe. I knew. I was going to die there."

George couldn't imagine the horror of that. Of dying alone. Of dying and having no one even know it had happened.

"Tried to breathe. Wished I had a knife to cut my own throat. Emergency. Tracheotomy. Then coughed and coughed. I was being ripped apart. I coughed it up. Blood on the snow. And something fleshy. The whole bloody lining of my throat."

Somervell slipped a stained cloth from his pocket, unwrapped a lump of flesh like a skinned animal, and poked at it with his surgeon's fingers. "It was frostbitten," he said. "You can see. Here . . . and here."

There was bile at the back of his own throat; he wanted to spit.

"Felt better after." Somes smiled a little, then folded the flesh back into his pocket.

George wanted to let Somes rest, but first he had to know what had happened. "And Teddy?"

"Couldn't see this morning. Didn't tell me. Tried to melt snow first. Almost set his sleeve on fire. Didn't want me to know. Said he felt stupid." Somes shook his head. "I roped him up, led him down. Slowly. And here we are."

"And here we are," he echoed.

"Teddy will need. Few days to rest. Then we'll go home."

"I'll go talk to him."

"Let him rest, George."

"You should be resting too. I'll just check on him, bring him some soup."

"You go, George," Sandy said. "I'll stay with Somes."

George kneeled in front of Teddy and handed him the soup Sandy had made. A weak beef broth with chunks of some dried meat floating in it, flecks of something unnameable in an oily sheen. It made him want to retch, but Teddy couldn't see it. A damp cloth was tied over his eyes and he moaned softly every so often, seeming to forget that he was not alone. George couldn't bring himself to look directly at him, even though he knew Teddy couldn't see him.

What if Teddy said no? Maybe he should. Maybe it was a terrible idea. Teddy might think enough had already been risked for the mountain, enough had been lost. After all, he and Somes had barely made it back to Camp IV alive.

Teddy slurped noisily at his soup before groping for a flat spot near his knee to set it down on. With his other hand he reached out toward George, his fingers landing on his cheek.

"George," Teddy said, "how's Somes?"

Teddy's fingers moved over his features, into his hair, along his jawline, before cupping the back of his head. Teddy would die up here without them now. Leaving him would be a death sentence. He'd starve without food or could take a false step and tumble down the mountain.

Maybe he shouldn't be thinking about the summit. Maybe he should stay put here with Teddy, for just a day or two, keep everyone safe. Then they'd go home.

"Fine. He's fine. Worried about you."

"Worried that I'm a bloody idiot." Teddy dropped his hands. His breath heaved out of him in a cough. When he finished he said, "Home, I guess, eh, old man? Once I can see, at any rate. She's beat us fair and square." There was a long silence. He didn't know what to say. Teddy went on. "I think I'm done, George. With these mountains. Give me the Lake District and the Alps. That'll be enough for me. You?" Teddy tilted his head as though he were looking at George.

"No." He didn't mean it to sound so abrupt.

"You'll come back? A fourth time?"

"No, Teddy. I can't come back here." He laid it out carefully. "I want to make another push."

"George, it's over. We've thrown everything we have at her. We've tried."

"We haven't tried the oxygen."

"It doesn't matter. The oxygen isn't in place."

"Sandy brought up the oxygen. I want a chance with it." His voice was speeding on ahead of him. "We can't move down yet, Teddy. Not with your eyes. We're stuck here for at least another day, maybe two, until you're capable of negotiating the Col and the Icefall. We have to use the time we have left. We can't just sit here while the summit is up there waiting to be claimed." He could hear the pleading in his voice and tried to lighten his tone. "I'll be back before you're ready to descend."

"Sandy brought the oxygen up? Who ordered him to do that?"

"No one. He was thinking ahead. Showed initiative. There's enough for a final push."

"George, it doesn't matter. About the oxygen. It's not a good idea. There isn't time. The weather's going to close in on us. The monsoon is on its way whether you like it or not."

"We just need three days. That's it. The monsoon isn't a definitive indicator of how much time we have, you know that. The weather is holding. We have the time."

"Sandy's too young." Teddy's tone was measured. Careful. He tilted his head back and stared blindly. George had heard this tone before. Teddy was weighing the arguments, talking it out. He might be persuaded. "Too inexperienced—we already decided that. You and I."

"But he's fresh. Everyone else has already been beaten back."

"Including you."

"I can do this." A beat. "I *have* to do this."

"That won't cut it, George. You want to risk your life? Sandy's? I need more."

"Because I can do it." The words came quickly. "You know that and I know that. Let me do it and we'll all go home heroes. All of us."

"Pass me some water?" He handed Teddy his canteen. Listened to him swallow it down. "And you think Sandy can do it?"

"I think Sandy doesn't know that he can't. He hasn't been beaten yet."

"He'll follow you anywhere, George. He'll push himself to keep up with you. To not let you down." Teddy was waiting for him to say something, but he remained silent, determined to wait him out. "You'll be responsible for him. He won't turn back. You'll have to do it."

"I know. I will."

"I'm asking you not to go, George. Just wait it out and we'll all go home. I'm asking you."

"But you're not ordering me."

"No."

"If you're ordering me, I won't go." Neither of them wanted to concede. "But if there's the slightest chance, Teddy, I'm taking it."

Teddy nodded in the dim tent and removed the cloth from his eyes. He squinted at him and then winced. Teddy's sharp intake of breath pained him.

"George, don't do this."

He took the bandage from Teddy and replaced it gently. "I have to."

There was a lull between them. George kept still, not wanting to hurry Teddy. He was considering it. He had to be considering it.

"You and Sandy, then," Teddy eventually said. "One more chance. Take Odell to Five. Someone to carry the gas partway up for you. Then you and Sandy use the oxygen to continue on to Six." Teddy shook his head again. "Three days, George, and then we go. We are all on our way back to Base Camp. No more delays. Three days."

Three days. Ascension Day.

DINNER

Seven O'Clock

There is something interminable about the moments before a
dinner party is meant to begin. That is when you worry about
what more you should have done, when you wonder whether the
lamb will be properly cooked. And the clock on the mantel ticks,
ticks, ticks. There is one cardboard box left in the corner, opposite
the door.

"Vi?"

Her head pokes around the door. Her hair is neater than it was
this morning; there is a blush along her cheeks. I think about telling
her she looks lovely, but point instead at the box. "Can we do something about that?"

We. Of course I mean *her.*

"It's too heavy."

I walk to it, bend, the dark silk of my dress stretching over my
knees, and put my arms around the box. It *is* heavy. Standing, I gaze
at the ugly box full of goodness knows what—books or climbing
gear, or the ephemera of our life. "Is there a cloth? Can we cover it?"

There is the bob of her head and she leaves. And I pace the floor again. The light outside is the golden green of early summer evenings. The days are still growing longer. Before Vi returns, the doorbell sounds. I move toward it before I remember it might not be Will or Marby. It might be Arthur Hinks. And if it is Hinks, I want to do things formally, properly.

When Vi finally returns I grab the cloth from her—"The door?"—and turn to cover the box. Now it's a box covered with a white tablecloth, and it glows against the dark wainscoting.

"I'm here." It's Will, of course, just as the clock strikes. He hands his hat to Vi and bows elaborately to me. He's wearing a sharp linen suit, the creases pressed to crisp lines. I feel hot and cold thinking about this afternoon, my hands pounding on his door, imagining him kissing me, and hope he cannot see it on my face. Glancing around, he says, "I assume I've beaten the rest of them."

"Yes. Still waiting." I gesture to the sofa but he walks to the drinks cart, plucks ice from the bucket, pours gin. No asking, he just moves around the room and then hands me my glass. We've long since stopped having to play host to Will. Uncle Will.

"You look beautiful." And I flush again, gulp at my drink.

"So do you. Well, handsome, I mean." And he does.

But not like George. When George is in the room everyone watches him. "You're far too pretty for a man," I teased George when we were on our way to some party or other, and he stood behind me in the hall mirror, his cheek pressed to mine.

"No one even notices me," he said, "if you're there."

Which wasn't true, but it didn't matter. His glamour was cast on me, too, making me alluring.

"I'm sorry, Will," and he turns to me from where he has moved to the mantel, contemplating the photographs set out across it. "For this afternoon."

"Nonsense. That's why I'm here."

"It's just . . . some days it all feels too much. As though we're ghosts and we're waiting for life to begin."

"Not much longer."

"No. Not much."

Even though it's still light outside, the room is close and gloomy. I turn on a table lamp to hold off the dark and the air feels warmer already.

"When I come home everything will be different," George told me. He'd already decided he was going. I was trying to steel my resolve, trying to be supportive, quiet. That's what Marby recommended, what I tried to keep in mind: *Pretend! Act as if you're happy and calm and proud and eventually you will be. What you have to do is hard, but it is what you must do. So smile and be kind and loving. Be a wife.* And I was trying. How I was trying.

So I smiled, nodded, and said, "I know."

George, encouraged by the smile, went on. "Then we'll have our own adventure. Anywhere you want to go. Pitcairn? As you said."

"That was so long ago. No. Let's just stay here. You and me and Clare and Berry and John. We'll get a cat. A pony for the girls."

"And we'll plant a garden. Roses for you, vegetables for me, and we'll get old tending them. I'll build you the fishpond you always wanted. Just there." He pointed to a spot low in the back garden, shaded, quiet.

"Promise?" I tried to keep my smile in place. I tried to believe him.

"Of course! We'll fill it with water from the river and we'll buy strange, exotic fish from all around the world."

"No. Only fish that belong here. No one should be far from home anymore."

What I wouldn't give for a mundane conversation like that, the bickering over what to have for dinner or the cost of buying a new suit. The planning for the future, for trips and adventures. For home.

"Do you remember, Will, that climbing trip in Wales? You must remember. It was the only time I went with the two of you. Not that I blame George for not inviting me again after what happened. And, of course, by then there were the children. They made it hard to get away in quite the same way."

His face softens with remembering—"George was so excited you were coming. 'Finally,' he said, 'we'll all of us climb together.'"

"He said almost the same thing to me. Isn't that like him? Trying to make us all get along. All of us love one another. We were supposed to go climbing for our honeymoon. He was going to teach me. But then the war began. And then after that there was always something else. He'd be off to the Alps, or it was only the old crew going. Never the right time for me. Then finally the three of us were going to Wales. He promised it wouldn't be too challenging. Not the first time, he said. I'd be tied between the two of you and I'd be safe. It started off so perfect. The weather, the day. You two must have been bored stiff."

"How could you think that? No. It's one of the things I love about climbing—sharing it with someone. There's no point in going alone. You want a witness. No, a co-conspirator."

I wonder sometimes if you have given Will instructions to take care of me. Maybe all of this is your doing—Will's visits, the dinner party. "Please, Will," you would have written, "don't let her be too much alone."

"It started out so wonderfully. And we stopped for lunch on that ledge—it was like a green carpet laid out for us, and the whole world was below. All we had was some bread and cheese and cold tea, but it seemed so ideal. Until the weather turned. It always seems to on mountains. Something always seems to go wrong, doesn't it?"

"Maybe it seems that way. But no, not always," Will reassures me. "Sometimes it's perfect. It's just that the bad turns make for better stories. No one wants to hear about the hike you took where nothing happened." Will gives me a small smile and holds up his glass. "Let's hope George won't have many stories to tell this time." I am a small reflection in his eyes, upside down, doubled, so I'm not sure who I am.

"But then it got cold and dark and the rain came down so hard, I couldn't see two feet in front of me. I wanted to shelter somewhere, but not George. He just plunged down the slope, dragging us along. His feet just seemed to know where to land. Until we got to that overhang." I can still feel the wet on my skin, the cold all the way into my bones. I wrap my arms around myself. "George just wanted me to go over it, but I couldn't see what was below it. It looked like an empty void dropping away into mist.

"'There's a ledge,' he said. 'Just there. Trust me.' But I couldn't. I was paralyzed with fear. He pulled me to him, hugged me, and kissed my face. And then he walked me backwards and pushed me off the edge."

"He didn't push you."

"He did, Will! You know he did! He pushed me. At least, that's how it felt. And the ropes held, as he knew they would, and I was lowered to the ridge. And after that somehow we got below the storm and the two of you laughed and joked about it the whole way down."

Somehow Will and I are giggling now. With relief, I suppose. The way that you do after a terrible fright, when you realize that everything is all right, that you've escaped unscathed.

"Our George," Will says.

I imagine we will always talk of you this way.

The dining room shifts in the flickering light of the candles on the table, on the sideboard—long shadows are cast to far corners. With the wood paneling it feels as if we are on a ship, locked together for the evening, afloat, a long way from everything, everyone else. The table stretches out in front of me and steam rises from plates and serving bowls. The air is thick with the smell of the lamb and onions. The candles glint off the silver, off the crystal. Edith and Vi have done well and I feel a brief surge of pride. I will remind myself to tell them so tomorrow.

Next to me, Will casts reassuring glances in my direction, around the table, ready to jump in should it be required. He is like a watchdog.

Next to him are Marby and her husband, Major Morgan. Marby has been taking care of Millie and me since our mother died, staying home from school, and now coming to stay close to me whenever you are away. "I'll be fine," I told her when you were leaving again.

"Of course, you will," she said. "It's just I always thought it would be lovely to stay in Cambridge for a while." And she had the Major rent a house just outside town so she can keep a close eye on us. I know she means well, but at times her concern is a little overbearing. In the candlelight her skin seems doughy, soft. It suits her, strips away some of her severity.

Her husband, the Major, is dashing in his elegant uniform, the black and red of it smart in the dim room. If this were a ship, he would be the captain.

"Let's pretend," George used to say when the girls on occasion dined with us. "Let's pretend we're on a ship sailing to South America. Look out the window—dolphins!"

"Pirates!" I'd add, and the girls would race to eat the fastest before the pirates boarded and made them walk the plank.

To my left is Cottie, her short hair swept into tiny curls at her temple. And next to her, Geoffrey and Eleanor. At the door Eleanor handed me flowers—gladioli from the market—and held her hand near Geoffrey's elbow as he limped with his cane. Geoffrey seems worn. He has aged since last I saw him. He has taken care of you for so long, and it is wearing on him, I think.

Finally, Arthur Hinks. He is at the far end of the table, after arriving late and gruff and without apology. I was glad I'd chosen to seat him as far from me as possible. But I hadn't thought about the fact that I would have to stare down the table at him all evening.

I haven't seen him since the night before George sailed across oceans I have never swum, when we ate curry in honor of a continent I have never seen. *Imagine Borough Market,* George wrote, *but full of gypsies and people of every colour and oxen being driven through the crowds. Imagine exotic birds and food that burns your tongue from the spice, not from the temperature.* I couldn't. I still can't.

I may not have seen Hinks since then, but I hear from him all the time. Or rather, he wants to hear from me. Twice a week he sends me letters or wires. This man who took my husband from me and sent him to Everest again and again. He thinks we are on the same side, want the same things. I wait for him to ask me what I've heard, if he may read my letters. I have a standard reply. *I'm sorry to say, Mr. Hinks, I have heard nothing that would be of interest to the Committee, only small sentiments from a husband to his wife.*

It begins.

"Have you heard anything new, Mrs. Mallory?"

"I was hoping *you* could tell me some news, Mr. Hinks."

He begins to bluster some words about Everest that I pay no attention to, distracted by the great walrus girth of him and his mustache, which catches food and liquid so it sparkles in the candlelight. It is lewd and unsettling, how he fingers his mustache constantly.

Cottie stops him mid-speech. "Oh, let's not talk about the mountain. Not yet, unless you have specific news from George?" She looks from Hinks to me and back again. "Then let's talk amongst ourselves. How is your father, Ruth?"

I turn to Marby, because I don't know. I should write to him. Plan a visit. "How is Papa?" I ask her.

"You know how Papa is, always the same." Marby's voice runs along on its own, her words tight together, like a train speeding away from her. "He wants to put in another toilet. Another one. There are almost more toilets than people who live in the house, isn't that right, dear?" She looks to the Major. "He sent the sketches for you to look at. Maybe after dinner. Or I can leave them. But don't let me forget. He wonders if you need another one."

"I shouldn't think so." Dear Papa, always trying to change things, improve them.

"We'll probably put a new one in after the baby," says Eleanor, looking to Geoffrey.

"Oh no! So much better to do it before the little one's here," Cottie tells her, and they begin to chat about renovations, the difficulties of working around an infant.

I'm glad for all this domestic talk. It's soothing. But Hinks fumes, chomps at the meat on his plate, and waits for his opening.

I remember meeting Hinks, hearing the boom of his voice for the first time. I wanted to like him; I tried to.

"Ruth," George said after, "you don't always have to see the best in people."

It was at the Royal Geographical Society. I loved the red façade of the Victorian building, the formal weight of the lounges and lecture rooms. The men wandering the hallways with their tans and lined faces, so one wanted to ask them where they'd traveled and what they had seen. Explorers, all of them. The first time George took me there, I stood transfixed in front of the tapestry map of the world, made when Elizabeth was queen. Incredible. And still so much bigger than my own world. I stared for so long that George finally came searching for me. We drifted to another map, stopping to examine trophies, the giant tusks from an elephant that bracketed the doorway.

"Where do you want to go?" George asked then.

"Anywhere. Everywhere."

"Close your eyes." His hands on my shoulders turned me around and around. "Now point."

I stepped forward, blind and wobbling a little, until my fingers touched the cloth. Dry, dusty. "Here," I said, and opened my eyes.

"Pitcairn. A good choice. Lived on only by the descendants of the *Bounty*'s mutineers. Scandalous. Let's go."

"Now?"

"Why not?"

He kissed me again and pressed me back against the map of the world, and I was dizzy. From the spinning, from the kiss.

It was some months after that, when we returned for a gala affair—George in his dinner jacket, me in my gray silk gown—that George made the introductions. "Ruth, I'd like you to meet Arthur Hinks, the chair of our committee. Arthur, my wife."

"Mr. Hinks." I smiled. "A pleasure to meet the man who is stealing my husband away."

"I trust, Mrs. Mallory, you're in full support of this expedition. They'll need all our support for what they have to do. What a chance for King and Country, eh? The third Pole. Lost the other two to the Yanks and the Norwegians. We need this one. We must all rally to do our bit."

"Of course."

Hinks leaned in close to me, his hand on my elbow, trying to draw me into his conspiracy. "In that vein, I hope I can count on you to keep me abreast of anything you hear from our good man, then. Any bits and pieces that he might write to you but forget to tell me? We need all the details. It might be best if you just send on copies of his letters, then you needn't trouble yourself with what is important and what is not. Let me sort that out."

"Mr. Hinks, I'm sure you're not asking me to share everything my husband sends to me. A wife's letters from her husband, well, that's almost sacred, don't you think? You wouldn't want anyone reading your billets-doux, I'm sure. Think how embarrassing."

"No. No, of course not." I'd taken him aback. He expected me to be more compliant. "Your husband and I will have to discuss the best way to move forward. But for now, let's celebrate. Come sit by me."

Hinks gave speeches that night about God and King and Country. All the propaganda he could dredge up from the war. It all sounded so familiar, but so hollow now. George fairly glowed under it. "A chance to make it up to all those in the war," he said.

I've never really understood what you meant. What is it that you're trying to make up for? How can you feel responsible?

When Geoffrey lost his leg, George said he wished it had been him.

"How can you say that?" I asked, even though I didn't really believe he meant it. Not then, not now. It was an easy thing to say. He was still in the hospital then, invalided home because of an old climbing injury, and he was humiliated, wanted to prove he wasn't a coward, wasn't weak. That he would do his part if they would let him. "No one wants that for you."

"Geoffrey will never climb again. I've always climbed with him. He taught me everything I know. If I can't climb with him anymore, I'm not sure I want to."

"That's not about Geoffrey," I said. "That's about you. About what you've lost."

"It isn't."

"You're mourning the Geoffrey you lost when he lost his leg."

"I'll miss him," George said, as if Geoffrey were dead.

"I know."

But here is Geoffrey, at my table, and he has proven to be as much a guide to us as he ever was on the mountains.

"But you have heard from him, have you not, Mrs. Mallory?" Hinks's voice rises above the advice and chatter of renovations. And as everyone falls silent, he's conscious now that he has an audience and I fear he's about to start some speech about duty, remind us all of the roles we have to play. I won't have it.

"I have," I admit. I am maybe slightly tipsy on the wine Papa sent with Marby. The light over the candles is a soft blur that sparkles into drawn-out stars at the corners of my eyes. I focus on the plate in front of me. Our wedding china. The roast lamb smears across the snowfield white of the plates, the stained potatoes. The air steams, thick, succulent. I eat by rote, set my fork down after each bite, just as one's supposed to. But I would like to fly across the table at Hinks. He is still talking.

"They're doing well so far. From what we gather from the reports. That's what Norton tells us." His voice is louder now and everyone else has gone quiet. "It's hard to really know, though, what the others are thinking and feeling. Norton's in charge; sometimes you want to hear from the men in the trenches. Really in the trenches. What they might stake their chances at." He pretends it is a general statement, but it is pointed at me. It's a rebuke.

"Mr. Hinks, do you really think if George had made it to the summit that he'd keep it a secret? Tell only me? Truly? What do you think I could know that you don't? You probably know more than I do. My husband sends his love, he asks after me and our children. He says he is healthy."

My voice shakes some and I curse myself. I inhale slowly, steadily. Under the table, Will takes my hand. His is dry, mine moist with sweat. I squeeze his lightly and then pull away, reach again for my wine.

"Of course." Hinks wipes at specks of food in his mustache with his napkin, then drops it beside his plate. His fork falls to the floor. When Vi scuttles over to collect it, he doesn't even notice her. For a moment Vi and I are on the same side, both of us revolted by this man. Hinks continues on. "Of course, it's just . . . we're all anxious. We had hoped they would have already succeeded. Our George. Knocked it off already. Then we'd be celebrating, what?"

"Yes," Will says. "We'd be celebrating that George would be on his way home. Safe. And isn't that what we all really want?"

"I mean to say, we certainly can't afford to send them out again next year." Hinks is warming to this talk, to politics and money. "We've sent them three times already! Well, Mallory, at any rate. But someone will pony up for it. Everest is the new Pole. Someone will rally an expedition if we can't. The French! Or the damn Germans, of course. They all want it. And then what? We lose out to them? It may be our only hope that they will fail to get the Dalai Lama's permission. But who knows where his allegiances truly lie?"

I've had enough. He's already decided on George's failure. There is a flare of anger in my stomach, up through my lungs, and almost as if he must sense it, he begins to backpedal. "I only mean, Mrs. Mallory, if—if they should fail to make it this time. But I'm sure they won't. They'll be home safe and sound in no time. With the summit."

Foolish of me to think he would bring me news. Even if he knew something, I'm not sure he would share it.

"That is what we all want, Mr. Hinks. Our dear brother-in-law to come home. To his wife. To his children. Safe and sound. Summit or no," Marby says.

"He'll be safe," I say. I have to have hope enough for all of us. I have to believe it even when no one else will. "Has everyone had enough? Shall we have dessert?" I ask.

I try to be the perfect hostess.

CAMP VI

———◆———

26,900 Feet

Camp VI was more forbidding than George remembered. Had it really only been three days since he was last here with Odell? It seemed a lifetime ago.

One tiny tent perched on a fragile outcrop of snow, the world dropping away from them on two sides. The tent silhouetted against the sky, against the white. He stamped on the ledge to test it, almost expecting a giving way, a crumpling. The snow crunched under the hobnails of his boots, but the ledge held.

He tried not to imagine it dropping out from under him, collapsing and falling.

Once inside the cramped space, George unlaced his boot and pulled his foot onto his lap to massage it. It was numb. The boot had been tied too tight, cutting off the circulation. How had he failed to notice? He tried to remember the climb, but the memory of it was burned clean by the blaze of the sun beating down in the high atmosphere. The heat had crawled in under his skin, searing him from the inside. He couldn't have imagined frostbite.

An amateur mistake. Now his toes were tingling.

In all his years on mountains, he'd never lost anything to frostbite—not a toe, an earlobe, or a fingertip. Sandy reached over, took his foot, placed it in his own lap, and rubbed at the cold skin to aid the circulation. George's foot burned and then shattered into pins and needles.

"There was a porter," George said, cringing against the tingling in his foot. "In 'twenty-two. No, it was 'twenty-one. He lost both his hands. They had frozen solid. You hear people say that, but I couldn't believe that a human body could actually freeze solid. He'd accidentally left the tent flap open overnight. In the morning his hands were white chunks."

"Like Tsering."

"Right, Tsering. He said they didn't hurt. They were like ghosts. Something he could see but couldn't feel."

He thought of Geoffrey.

"It itches," Geoffrey had told him, scratching at his leg. "Like a sonofabitch." It was the first time he'd seen Geoffrey after he was wounded, after they removed what remained of his leg, and his face was drawn, gray under a patchy growth of beard. His hands trembled on his lap. He was in a wheelchair. For some reason George hadn't expected Geoffrey to be in a wheelchair.

At first George didn't understand. "That blanket would make anyone itchy, Geoffrey."

"No. My leg, George. My leg itches." Geoffrey looked at him. "It's not even there and it itches."

He didn't know what to say. Geoffrey tucked his hands under the blanket, tried not to scratch at the stump hidden underneath.

George pulled his foot back from Sandy.

"Then the coolie's hands thawed," he went on. "I don't know which was worse. The freezing or the thawing." Both were terrible reminders that the body was nothing but pulpy meat, easily ruptured, broken, frozen, thawed. That was the worst of it, knowing the myriad ways a body could be destroyed. "His hands turned black. Purple. Swelled up like balloons. And the smell, of rot. Like in the trenches. You weren't in the trenches. You can't imagine them, Sandy. You shouldn't." He gagged a little at the memory. The smell hadn't gone away, not for months after he returned home. The stench was in his sinuses, in his clothes, his hair. When he turned his head, it was always there. Even now he could conjure the smell. "Be glad for that," he continued. "It was constant, the stench, from all the bits of bodies we never found."

Sandy looked blanched, his scabbed skin pulled taut over his cheekbones. It had been so fair, Sandy's skin. Not translucent, like Ruth's, but more solidly pale. Not anymore. The mountain had ravaged him. He'd go home older. "It must have been agony to sit there and rot like that. He mewled. Constantly. At Base Camp, Bullock had to hold him down as they amputated his hands."

There was a long silence.

"How high are we, George?" Sandy's words were a slow staccato.

It took him some time to answer. His mind flitted; thoughts tapped against his skull. He hadn't felt this foggy when he was here with Odell. Maybe he'd been too high for too long. His altimeter was somewhere.

"More than twenty-six thousand feet," he guessed.

He fumbled in his pocket, his fingers too numb to identify any of the objects inside by feel. He pulled things from his pockets he didn't remember placing there, spread them across his sleeping bag: scraps of paper, petroleum jelly, a small knife. He found the altimeter, the small round face of it sharply white in the darkening tent. He held it in both hands to keep it steady and squinted at the numbers that circled the face. Held it until the wavering stopped. He closed his eyes.

His father was speaking.

"I'd ask you all to indulge me a moment," his father said, "and add an extra prayer for the young men who are undertaking the expedition to Mount Everest, on our King's behalf. May they not be foolhardy and may God keep them safe."

George dropped his head, embarrassed, and glanced sideways at Ruth sitting beside him, his mother and sister next to her. It was bad enough that his father continued to chastise him privately, accusing him of being self-indulgent—but now this? His father asking the congregation to pray for him?

"Your mother told me everyone has been calling on them, sending their congratulations and good hopes for your safety. Your success," Ruth whispered.

"Of course."

"He means well. You know he does, George."

"Just one moment more, please," his father said now from the pulpit, "and then I'll ask our choir to sing us out into this beautiful day. George? Will you come up here?"

Ruth's hand was at his back. He rose, walked toward his father on the dais. "For you," his father said, holding out a small box. Everyone was clapping. The choir began to sing: *Nearer, my God, to thee . . .* His father would have picked the hymn. It was just another argument, an attempt at conversion, at salvation.

"You're looking for God, even if you won't admit it." That was what his father insisted, later that evening. "He is there. In the wilds. In the mountains. But He's here too."

"Moses went to a mountain," George said, pointing his fork at his father. Jabbing at the air between them.

"But he didn't spend his life running off to them." His father sliced at the roast on his plate, dipped his bread in gravy. It dribbled slightly on his beard. He wiped at it, smearing the gravy across his napkin. "Mountains won't support your family, George. Neither will writing about them. The Mallorys have been rectors and reverends for centuries. You already have a calling."

"The mountains have been there longer even than Mallorys have been in the Church, and they're calling."

"George, you aren't going there to find God. If you were, you'd have found him already. God's easy to find if you're looking."

"No, you're right, sir. God isn't there. Everest is proof enough against God."

George inhaled deeply, opened his eyes. The dial on the altimeter was sharper.

"Twenty-six thousand, nine hundred and, ummm . . . three?" He handed it off to Sandy so he could see for himself.

A slow smile spread across Sandy's face. It took him a while to speak, their conversation delayed as though by a great distance. "Incredible." Sandy peered at the altimeter, turned it in his hands to see the engraving on the reverse. *George, may this raise you up, Rev. HLM.*

He reached to take it back. "My father gave it to me in 'twenty-one. Before I first came here."

He slid it into his pocket.

A little over two thousand feet to go.

✦ ✦ ✦

"I USED TO GO TO your father's church sometimes," Sandy said. His voice sounded strange—stripped down, weak. Everything was weak. But he wanted to talk, and so forced the sound out. "My father took me. Maybe I told you that?" Lengthy pauses dragged out between his sentences. Between his words. He was finding it harder and harder to tell what he was only thinking and what he was saying out loud. There was no way he'd pass any of Somervell's memory tests now. He tried to add up numbers in his head, forgot which ones he'd picked. "Did I tell you?" he asked again.

"No."

Sandy's hands stroked the air near his face. It was agony. It felt as if the mountain had stripped the flesh from his cheeks. There couldn't be any skin left. George reached across to him in the twilight, pushed Sandy's hands away from his face, and smeared petroleum jelly carefully, gently, on his skin. George traced the lines of his eyebrows, his cheekbones, his lips. The vulnerable spot at his temple. Sandy closed his eyes.

"I remember he took me. My dad," Sandy continued. "No, that's not true," he said after a minute. "I don't remember. But my dad, he bragged about it. Even before I was set to come here. 'Sandy and I went to George Mallory's church,' he told people. Then, when I was invited to come, he said we were clearly meant to be together." He flushed a little. Why had he said that? "I remember the smell," he rushed on. "All waxed wood and polish."

"He took me for an Easter sermon," he told George. "'The Harrowing.'"

"One of my father's favorites."

"My dad smelled of sawdust. His pipe. There was a scar in the wood seat beside me. And a woman in front of me in a dark hat."

"My father," George said, "used to conjure heaven and hell for the congregation. He told Trafford and me, live a good life and you'll never be cold."

"I guess your father never thought any of us would be here."

"No." After a moment George asked, "Did you see the mandalas at the monastery?"

"I don't think so."

"They're sand drawings that the monks make, on the floor. Intricate, tight. You'd know if you had." George spoke into the air above them. "Teddy and I watched the monks for hours. There were four of them. Always four. And they sat at the cardinal points. Chanting and bending." George pulled himself to a sitting position to demonstrate. He crouched over his hands, one tapping the other as though parsing out invisible specks. "He smelled like grass, the monk I crouched next to. Used a long red tube to place each grain. Red and white—paisley swirls on demon costumes."

"Demons?" There'd been so much talk of demons.

"With white lines around their black eyes. Red-haired and fanged on green and blue backgrounds. When you watched them, they seemed to move on their own, make you dizzy. The monks sat there for days. Weeks. Tapping. It was devotion itself." George looked up at him from where he was still hunched over his tapping hands. They shook now from the cold, glowed blue in the dim tent. "He called it *samsara*. And told us to come back."

"Who did?"

George glanced at him, aggravated at having to repeat himself. "The monk."

Sandy nodded and George continued. "They called it the wheel of life." George sat up straighter, reciting, his eyes closed. "The cause of all suffering is desire. Even if the only desire is not to suffer. But everything is moving. Everything changes, passes. Even suffering."

It was a philosophy Sandy could understand. In crew they talked about rowing through the pain, when every muscle burned. The race was finite, but the feeling of winning or losing wasn't. "You have to push through it," he'd explained to Dick. "If you give up, you'll hate yourself much longer than your muscles will ache." But he hadn't thought about applying it to anything else. To life. He liked that idea. It was a sophisticated thought. He sat up straighter with it.

What if, though? What if the monks were right and none of this was real? What if the tent, the mountain beneath him, was some kind of illusion, some kind of dream? It didn't seem possible. Not with the pain, with the difficulty breathing. His body reminded him over and over again how real this place was. How much it wanted to be anywhere else.

"This feels bloody real, George," he said, trying to smile. He reached up and brushed the skin on his nose and the pain shot through him, radiating along his skin so that it was as if his whole body were a gaping wound. No, this certainly wasn't an illusion. But he did believe it would pass. There was a time when he wasn't in pain. There would be again.

Everything would pass.

George was fidgeting with his belongings, pulling things from his pack: a journal, a silk handkerchief, matches, a folded bundle of what looked like brightly colored rags. He carried so much with him. George licked at the tip of his pencil, bent over the open book in his hand as if to write something, but he didn't.

Maybe he should write to someone too, Sandy thought. He'd write to Dick. Or his mum.

"My mum," he said, "stopped talking to me. Before I left. She wouldn't even say good-bye." His voice kept catching in his throat. He worried he might cry, but he kept talking. George was staring at him now. "She lit a candle in her window. She keeps it lit, day and night. She told Evie she'd keep it there until I walked back in the door."

She must still love him. Must have forgiven him.

"She's scared, is all," Sandy continued. "Scared I might not come back. I never thought about that before. What will she do if I don't come back?" He looked down. There were words scrawled on the paper in his lap. He couldn't make them out. Somes had told him he'd have to make a decision. What price was he willing to pay?

"I don't want to die here, George. I can't do that to my mum."

"You'll be fine, Sandy. Just do as I tell you. You'll be safe. You believe me, right?"

He nodded at George. "Of course." His voice caught again in his throat. He cleared it, said "Of course" again.

George pushed the canteen at him. Sandy swirled the water in his mouth, imagined the dry ridges of his tongue, his cheeks, and the water filling them.

George spoke again. "Do you believe Somes, Sandy? About the avalanche?"

He tried to remember what Somervell had said. That was so long ago. Before the drowned boy. Before Lapkha.

"He thinks I'm reckless," George said, "because of Bowling Green. Have you been? The little green outcropping at Pen-y-Pass?" Sandy nodded, even though he didn't know it. "We go at Easter. Even Ruth used to come. But not anymore. Not since the children. But Easter. And Christmas. You could come. Someday soon.

"We were climbing," George went on. "Will and I. And Geoffrey. Back before he lost his leg. We stopped and had lunch on the Green. We'd taken this long, circuitous route to get up there. There was a more direct route I wanted to take, but Will and Geoffrey said no.

Said it wasn't climbable. When we were done with lunch, I left my pipe at the Green. On purpose. I've never told anyone that, Sandy. Never. When we got to the bottom I said I'd forgotten it, that I had to go back for it. Sentimental value."

"Did someone give it to you?" he asked. "Someone you loved?" He had a locket of Evie's he'd brought with him. And an earring from Marjory. She had pinned it inside his jacket herself. He'd forgotten about it. He felt for it now, but it was gone.

George shook his head at him. "They said I couldn't go back for it, it would take too long." George leaned into him as though conspiring, dropped his voice even lower. Sandy leaned toward him. "But I told them there was another route and I put up the climb. It was straight and tough. The hardest climb I'd done till then. Gorgeous. They named the route after me."

George leaned back, smiled slow and long, nodding.

"Somes was there. At the lodge. When we got back. And when Geoffrey told him what I'd done, he said it was reckless. He and the guide both. The next morning I saw *George Mallory is a young man who will not be alive for long* written in the guest book." George fell silent and the smile drifted away.

Sandy was shivering. His sleeping bag had slumped down around his waist. He pulled it up, burrowed down into it.

"But I've survived everything," George said. "I keep surviving."

"You're lucky, I guess."

George nodded, pulled his pack around, and laid his head on it.

✦   ✦   ✦

GEORGE COULDN'T SLEEP. It was all he wanted. Sleep. A brief respite. He was exhausted, whittled down to only bone and narrow muscle, a filament of will. Sandy hadn't spoken for what seemed like hours, though it might have been only minutes. His own consciousness was coming in flickers, in and out, a shoal of river fish. He was numbed, stupefied, in the thin air.

The tent was dark now. The lantern had gone out. It was welcome, the darkness. They couldn't see each other. Couldn't see the summit. Nothing existed in the darkness.

Everyone else was below them. At Camp V, Odell would be staring upward for a light, the dull smudge of a lantern in the night. Odell and Virgil. He would leave a note for Odell. Tell him when to watch for them. Tell him when they'd be back.

Farther down, at Camp IV—Teddy and Somervell. Both of them broken and ready for home.

Noel across the Col, in his Eagle's Nest. He would watch the skyline tomorrow. George had written him to say he'd go up skyline. The ridge was the surest way. He would have to remember to turn and wave to Noel, to his camera.

Everyone was below them. Waiting.

"Somes will be writing the dispatches for *The Times* about now," George said.

"What dispatches?"

"It should be Teddy who does it, but he won't be able to. Not with his snow blindness. Together they'll prepare telegrams for the possible outcomes. There will be two of them. One that says we succeeded. That we've returned triumphant from the summit. And one that concedes defeat, says we're coming home."

He didn't tell Sandy there should be a third one. One that said that the final summit team was lost and all hope was gone. Teddy wouldn't write that one. He wouldn't want to tempt fate.

"They'll be written in code," he said. "So no one will know what happened until *The Times* decodes the message."

It had grown even colder. His muscles ached from constant shivering. "Jesus Christ," he cursed under his breath. Beside him, Sandy's breath was labored. A long exhalation followed by a jerk, a coughed gulp of air, his body shaking. Sandy pressed against him in the cramped space, trying to keep warm. They were utterly alone in the world.

It hardly seemed possible that it was just yesterday he'd said his good-byes to Somes and Teddy. Or just this morning that they'd left Odell and Virgil behind.

He was surprised when Virgil sought him out before he left. "Sahib?"

"What is it, Virgil?" He hadn't meant to sound so short. Virgil had been a solid companion, but he felt betrayed by what Virgil had done at the monastery, going to Teddy behind his back, warning him away from the mountain.

"You not go."

"Virgil, we've been over this before." He bent to fiddle with the straps of his pack. He just wanted to be gone. He was going to climb this bloody mountain and be done with it. "I thought you wanted this too. I guess I was wrong."

"Go home to family." Virgil pointed first at himself and then at George.

"I'll go back to them when this is done."

Virgil nodded, started to step away. George watched his shadow on the snow, saw Virgil shift and then move back, the silhouette of his arm reaching toward him. He looked up. "I don't need any good luck totems."

"Not good luck. For hope." Virgil held out folded, bright-colored flags. A tied packet of rice flour.

"You keep it. You pray."

"No. You, Sahib Sandy, leave at the summit. When you reach." When. Virgil had said *when*. "For her. Not you."

"Do you really think this will make a difference? That this will be enough if Chomolungma doesn't want us there?"

"Maybe you give to her, she let you pass. Maybe not. I hope." Virgil smiled at him, his face crinkling with it. "I pray."

George rolled over now, his back to Sandy. Unbearable cold crept in through the tent flap, up through the ground and the bedroll beneath him. Behind him, Sandy choked and gasped, waking himself with a violent jolt. His convulsions jostled George, sending a sharp wave of pain from his head to his kidneys. He gritted his teeth, tried to catch his own breath, and turned around to face Sandy.

There was panic in Sandy's gasping. His eyes were open, unseeing, bulging as his jaw worked around his stuttered breath, his arms flailing against George. He was clawing at him, climbing him.

For a brief instant the boy was Gaddes looking up at him from the bottom of the crater, through the heavy green of the gas. Gaddes ripped off his faulty mask and pleaded with him with a gaping mouth, gulping down great lungfuls of gas. Trying to breathe. He clawed at the sliding mud walls, at his own throat, leaving streaks of blood and dirt there. In his own mask, George's breath was deafening. Eventually Gaddes stopped struggling and collapsed again to the bottom of the crater, his body shaking in violent tremors, until those stopped too.

He pressed Sandy's hands down and leaned over his face, his

gasping mouth. His breath smelled spoiled, thick. "Breathe, Sandy. Breathe."

He cradled Sandy while he coughed and sputtered, tried to find his breath. "Shhhh . . . Breathe. Be calm. Breathe."

It was like soothing Clare when she was having one of her nightmares. He loved when she awoke from dreams and burrowed into him, how just his being there could calm her. "What did you dream, love?"

"You fell, Daddy."

"Shhhhh . . . It's all right. I'm right here. . . ."

Sandy's breathing steadied.

Shhhhh . . .

In the black of the tent, George shivered.

When was the last time he had been warm? He couldn't remember the sweltering heat box of the Cwm, the way the sun had reached into him. He tried to count the days backward to when they'd been somewhere lush in Tibetan valleys.

In a dream he conjured the feel of sweat dripping between his shoulder blades while sitting in the shadow of rhododendrons, the flowers like massive bloody fists weighting the stalks. He plunged into glacial pools, his skin tightening. The heavy heat of hidden forests sloughed off his skin as he dropped into the water. When he stepped out again, the water evaporated, the heat settling like a blanket across him.

He couldn't count the days. Could only count one day to the summit. A day to the summit. It was the rhythm of his breath.

He couldn't remember a time before cold.

The mountain was leaching heat from his skin, his blood, his bones. He dreamed wind like ice picks.

He drifted. He walked along a ridge, ice sharp on both sides. Then tripped. He jerked awake in the tent, his breath caught in his throat, and groped for matches. He was clumsy with them, breaking the head off one before striking another successfully against the box. It flared into a needle of light that hurt his eyes. He squinted and cupped his hands over the scant heat and thought of the candle in Sandy's mother's window.

He lit the lantern and settled it on the tent floor.

He watched the shadow outline of Sandy breathing as the match flickered out, and thought of Ruth in their bed at home. Crisp white sheets. The damp outline of her body where she had come in and lain down after bathing. He lay down next to her. It was warm.

She moved to slip away from him and sit up.

"No," he said. "Stay."

"I can't, George. The children will be up. They'll want to see you."

"Yes, but not yet," he said. "Stay." She settled back into bed, her body pressed against the length of him. This close, her eyes were flecked with sparks, like gold.

"Let's pretend," she said, "that's it's just you and me. That we're on holiday and no one can find us."

"No," he nuzzled her throat. "Let's just be here."

"Yes. Let's just be here." She rolled over and pressed her back against him. He held her there, as close as he could, her head tucked under his chin, so that after a beat he couldn't tell where she ended, where he began. She smelled nothing like rock or snow.

The mountain below him was restless; ice cracked and tumbled in the glacier, echoed up to him. He wondered when the sun would rise. They should be away before it did. Sandy's breath was rasping, shallow, but steady beside him. The boy's arm across his chest was a deadweight, making it hard for him to breathe, but he didn't want to wake Sandy yet. Wanted to allow him these last easy moments.

There was a pounding in his head, the pain concentrated somewhere deep above his left ear. It throbbed with his quickened pulse. He imagined building a brick wall between the pain and the rest of his mind, but he couldn't concentrate, kept losing his place. The wall crumbled.

He pulled his journal out of his pack again and flipped through it for the sheet of paper he'd tucked inside. The page from Ruth's book.

"What are you doing?" Sandy asked as he coaxed the lantern to a low light.

"Just writing to Ruth."

"Now?"

"It has to be now. There are things I want to say." Things he needed to say.

Sandy seemed to think about that, then sat up next to him, pulled his own notebook to his lap. "But what should I say? I'd really like to set things to rights. With Dick. Before we go."

He wasn't the right person to ask. He had no advice for Sandy. He had none when the boy first told him about his affair, weeks ago. He felt even less able to offer advice now. He thought of Ruth. Poor Ruth. How to tell Sandy not to do what he did. Not to be absent. Lost.

"I guess write that."

Sandy nodded, stared down at the paper in front of him for a few moments, then said, "Are you scared?"

"It's not an easy thing we're about to do, Sandy."

"I'm scared."

"I know." So was he. But he'd been scared before. It was impossible not to be in the trenches, and he'd talked men into other, much more terrifying situations. He talked them into standing up into machine-gun fire. He'd convinced them it was their duty, that fear was best swallowed down, if it had to be acknowledged at all. He couldn't do that anymore. "So am I," he said. "But we'll be fine, Sandy. Remember?" He took Sandy's notebook from his lap, flipped through for the drawing Sandy had made weeks ago at Advanced Base Camp, the whole summit ridge in clear etched lines.

He drew his fingers along it, showed Sandy the route again. "Up through the Yellow Band, then onto the ridge, around here. Then along the steps—one, two, three steps." He tapped each of the outcroppings Sandy had drawn, hoped they would be able to skirt them easily. "And then the final snow slope. We can make it."

He thought about what Teddy had said—that he was responsible for Sandy. That he had to make the decisions—when to push, when to turn back.

"We need to be on the summit by three p.m. No later. If we're later, we won't get back down before dark and we'll be stuck out there."

Sandy nodded. "Three o'clock."

"We'll set benchmarks." He tried to work backward down the steps, into the Yellow Band. "If we get out early and move well, we'll be on the ridge by eight. That's what I've told Noel. We'll be at the Second Step by noon." It was the Second Step that worried him. From below it looked impossible to skirt; they'd have to climb the rock wall of it. "All right, Sandy? You'll know, if we're not there by then, we'll turn around. Then we'll be fine. You'll be safe."

Sandy retraced the route, murmuring the times. "Eight. Noon. Three."

Once they were up on the ridge, Sandy would want to press on. They both would.

He turned back to the page from Ruth's book. Before his attempt with Teddy, he'd written her that the odds were fifty to one against. And now? Were they really any better? There was the oxygen. And Sandy. Maybe.

He wrote in the empty spaces of the margins, around the end of the story, then folded it into an envelope. Odell would be coming up from Camp V in the morning, to ensure nothing had gone awry. He'd leave the envelope with a note for Odell and ask him to deliver it to Ruth if something happened. Not that he would have to, but he needed Ruth to know the whole story.

George could barely move, the cold slipping in under his clothing, into his veins, his muscles and bones. He held his boots over the weak heat of the cooker, the frozen leather immovable.

The light from the flame was bright in the darkness of the tent. Sandy sipped his tea, hands in gloves, wrapped around the mug. In silence they ate chocolate and meat lozenges, their hands shaking from nerves and the cold. He couldn't look at Sandy anymore.

He emptied his pockets, lined up items to take to the summit. To leave behind.

He turned away slightly so Sandy couldn't see what he was choosing.

On his sleeping bag he laid out all the things he would take with him. This was the sum total of the journey, then: matches in a swan-marked box, a tin of meat lozenges, a pencil, nail scissors in a leather holster, a safety pin. Scraps of paper, the bill for the windproofs he was wearing. A tube of petroleum jelly. Letters from home, wrapped in a blue-and-red handkerchief. He traced the monogram but couldn't feel the rise of embroidery with his frozen thumb, the initials Ruth had stitched there. A blue glove. A pocketknife. His altimeter and watch. A bit of rope.

A photograph. Him and Ruth. Taken during the war when he was home on leave. He is closer to the camera, sharp and in focus. That was him then, in uniform, with the fatness of youth in his cheeks, a slight mustache across his lip. He looked as if he were only playing at being a soldier. Ruth is farther back in the frame, facing the camera, far away. Slightly out of focus. She is haloed. Angelic. "I'll leave it at the summit. The top of the world," he had promised her.

He ripped himself from the photograph and wrapped her image in another handkerchief, slipped it into his pocket. He was ready.

He went to haul in the oxygen canisters so that Sandy could check them one more time. But as he did so, he stumbled over the cooker set just outside the flap of the tent, knocking it out onto the icy snow and sending it skittering down the steep incline. He watched it ricochet off the mountain, traveling faster and faster until it disappeared from sight. Damn. When they got back, they wouldn't have anything to heat food or melt snow for drinking water. He shook his head. It didn't matter. They'd push down to Five anyway. Maybe even Four. As he imagined returning to Six and then descending, the wind fingered the forgotten fragment of his own image, still in his hand, lifted it from his grasp, and wafted it toward the summit.

The sun would be coming up soon.

He climbed back into the tent, pushing the canisters in ahead of him. He checked his watch before extinguishing the lamp. Four a.m.

The landscape began to glow blue dawn.

PORT AND WHISKEY

―――――――・◆・―――――――

Ten O'Clock

In the dining room there is the clatter of dishes and the remnants
of dinner being cleared away. We can all hear it because the sitting room is so quiet. I open the window to let in the fresh air, the
chirps of crickets, which improves the mood a little. Will and the
Major are at the drinks cart, Hinks sits with Geoffrey, Eleanor hovering at his side as they murmur quietly. Maybe about Everest.
Maybe something else. Marby stands between Cottie and me; she
touches my elbow.

"You should come volunteer with me," she says. "It will do you
good to get out and think of someone else." She turns slightly to
include Cottie in the invitation. "I go into the local veterans' hospital. My neighbor and I. We go in and chat to them."

I'm not sure how that helps them. "Do you know," I interrupt her,
"that when a body starts to freeze to death one actually feels as
though one is warming up? Mountaineers who have died like that
are often found without their clothes. It's the confusion, doctors
think."

For years I didn't read a word about hypothermia. I didn't want to know about the cold, the minute details, the myriad ways to die. This time I couldn't stop myself. This time I devoured it all, and I imagine every detail of it happening to you. Your blood vessels constricting, the blood retreating as your hands and feet grow numb. I think of your fingers undoing my laces, brushing my cheek. See your blood turn to slush. Hear your nerve endings freeze and snap.

I shouldn't have read those words. There is no way to take them back.

Marby's face is blanched white and I'm sorry I said anything. Her eyes flash past my shoulder to her husband and Will, who are bringing glasses to us. Port for Marby, whiskey for me. I need the heat of it.

"Thank you, dear." Her voice shakes.

The Major doesn't notice. I suspect there are a number of things he doesn't notice.

"When did you last hear from George?" the Major asks. "Have you had a letter recently?"

He is only curious, but even from him there is some recrimination. The implication that you haven't written. That if you truly loved me, you would have written more. If you loved me, you might not have gone at all.

Marby takes the Major's hand, squeezes it so he glances at her, and she shakes her head ever so slightly, but it's too late.

"I have. A few days ago." It's been almost a week, but I don't tell him that.

Somehow I still believe that absence makes the heart grow fonder.

I swallow down a gulp of whiskey and clear my throat. "He says they are doing well. He's still optimistic. The weather is holding. He is certain they still have a chance."

"But that would have been from weeks ago, now, wouldn't it?"

"Of course, Major," I say. And it is the cheery tone I use for the children. I worry that with all of this pretending to be cheerful, my voice will stay this way permanently. "But we can't dwell on the weeks that haven't passed here yet."

"Maybe we could hear something from it?" Hinks asks.

"Oh yes," Marby says. "As we used to."

We did used to. During George's previous trips to Everest, I would read his letters aloud every chance I got. These days I have been finding myself less and less inclined to share. I've shared enough. But it will please them all.

Climbing the stairs, I think about saying good-bye to him. How I climbed back up the gangplank. I had to put things to rights. I had to let him know that it would all be all right. No matter what happened.

Things had been strange in the cabin before the ship horn sounded all ashore. We had orbited around each other, pulling forward and back, moving in and then away. Neither of us still until he weighed me down on his bunk and kissed me. There was a part of him already gone. I could feel it. He'd been drifting away for weeks. And a clock ticked in my head—*This is the last touch, the last kiss. Be happy. Make it count.*

I tried again on the gangway. Told him I only wanted what he wanted. It wasn't the whole truth, but I wanted him to think it was. To know it was. I don't know if he believed me. But he has to believe I love him, and that has to be enough.

The letters sent from Everest are stacked under George's pillow. There are too many to keep under mine. But when I sleep I reach for them, worry the edges of the envelopes. They are worn and soft from traveling, from being passed from hand to hand. They are in no particular order. I used to do that, read back over the news in the order they arrived, but it hardly seems to matter now. Instead I scan the drift of handwriting, examine the weight and the heft of the lines, or where he has traced my name over and over.

I don't tie them together with a ribbon. I don't carry them in my breast pocket. But I do press them to my face in the hope that there is still some trace of scent there. Sometimes I think there is, other times I know it is only my wishful imagination.

The most recent letter is easy to find in the stack of them—the cleanest, the clearest. The one that has not been handled over and over again.

George once wrote that he kissed my name where he had written it and he wanted me to kiss it, too, and think of him. I still do—kiss his name at the end, mine at the salutation. I haven't asked if he still does that. I don't know what I would do if he said no.

Before I descend, I cock my head and listen for any sounds from the children up the stairs. Nothing. Just the murmur of conversation from below. I try not to imagine what they're saying.

In the sitting room everyone is hushed, even Hinks. Will gives me an encouraging nod. I read aloud and feel his words in my mouth, hear them in my head.

My dearest Ruth—

The mail has come tumbling in—in rapid succession. A lovely poem from Clare with which I am proud and delighted. It is a great joy to hear from you especially, but also anyone who will write a good letter . . .

I shall be with the other party. Still, the conquest of the mountain is the great thing and the whole plan is mine and my part will be a sufficiently interesting one and will perhaps give me the best chance of all of getting to the top. It is almost unthinkable with this plan in place that I shan't get to the top. I can't see myself coming down defeated.

We shall be going up again the day after tomorrow—six days to the top from this camp.

My candle is burning out. I must stop.

Darling, I wish you the best I can—that your anxiety will be at an end before you get this—with the best news, which will also be the quickest. It is 50 to 1 against us, but we'll have a whack yet and do ourselves proud.

But the anxiety isn't at an end, and as I read the letter again, I wonder why. *Why aren't you on your way home?*

There is silence, even from Hinks, though I can see he wants more and is trying not to reach for the letter, to take it from my hands. I fold the pages and slip them back into their envelope. It's all I'm prepared to share. He wants to read between the lines but wouldn't be able to. It's true. I do know more than he does.

I know George so well I can read his mind. I know what every look means. I can read the intent in the angle of a leg crossed at the knee—defensive and turned away, or open and relaxed. There is a shorthand between us. A staccato rhythm of glances and gestures, half-words and shared jokes. An intimacy that cannot be forced but has to grow over time and space.

I can read him every time he tries to keep a secret, and he hates it. Hates how I know every gift that he plans on giving, every surprise he tries to spring.

"I know you're taking me on a picnic."

It was my birthday. He'd sent the girls to his parents. John hadn't been born.

"How can you know that?"

"I just do."

"You're so clever. Where? And what are we eating?"

"Hmmm . . . the river where all the canal boats are, with that pub next to it. And the wine we had at Geoffrey's wedding, along with that cold salad that I like and Vi hates to make."

"No point in going, then, really, is there?" He pretended to sulk. "I don't know how you could have figured it out."

Because he rubs at his collarbone under his shirt or tugs at his cuff links when he tries to keep a secret. When he lies, he runs his hand backward through his hair and then smooths it all forward again. I try not to see that. I tried not to see it whenever he talked about Everest, when he came home from New York. He was hiding something; how much he had enjoyed himself.

But I also know when he is telling the truth. Every time he says he loves me, it's there, in a certain angle of his chin, a glance.

Our history is encoded in these kinds of looks, in a Morse code of touches, short and long, each with its own rhythm and meaning. There is a legend to mine that he holds, and I have his. I am unbreakable to anyone else. At least I hope I am. I don't want to learn someone else's language.

But it means, too, that I can read between these lines, where Hinks, where Geoffrey, where even Will cannot. I can see it there— your hope. But also the desperation. The need. The fear of not finishing it. Of not being capable of it. Of letting all of us down.

You will try again and again. And you'll keep going back. I can read the future there.

"It's all right, Ruth." Marby is beside me, taking the letter from my hand, putting her arms around me. My body shakes against hers. But I'm not crying. I won't. That isn't what's done. We all have our duty to attend to. The men drift away to stand by the empty fireplace. My sister coos at me as if I'm a child.

"I'm sure we'll have news soon," she says.

The evening has taken on the feel of pitch—black and slow. Heavy. My body feels that way. Exhausted, although I won't sleep. I think back to this morning, sitting on the floor of your study, the sun against the leaded-glass window. It seems so long ago.

Hinks leaves first.

He promises, if he has any word, to send it on immediately, and I think he means it. At least right now. I do not make any promises in return. He doesn't ask for one.

Marby and the Major follow suit, then Geoffrey and Eleanor. They make apologies. Or rather, Marby does; they've an early start in the morning. I don't ask where they are off to.

Just the three of us now. Cottie, Will, myself. George used to be all we had in common. That's not the case anymore. There are the children, the small moments we share with one another.

"I can stay," Cottie suggests.

"No. That isn't necessary."

"I know that. But I can."

I shake my head.

"Or better, you could come with me. I'm meeting Owen in the country for a few days. Why don't you come? You and the children. A little escape."

I imagine the mail arriving, dropped into the letterbox. The delay of having it sent on, another day at least.

"I couldn't possibly," I say.

Cottie nods, doesn't push. "You'll send word?"

"As soon as I hear anything," I assure her.

"Take care of her, Will?" Cottie rises. Will nods to her, walks her to the door.

"Be right back."

I nod.

When he returns I tell him, "Millie always used to wish the three of us had a brother. Someone to take care of us. I think she felt more lost than Marby and I did when Mum died. She told me if we'd had one, she imagined he'd be like you."

"Do you want another?" Will asks, moving toward the drinks cart.

"God, yes."

I'm glad he's staying. I don't want to be alone. The jittery feeling from this morning is creeping back into my veins and there is another night to get through. Maybe Marby's right and there will be word soon.

The whiskey burns and my head swims and we sit in the room together.

"What's that?" Will points at the box I covered earlier with the tablecloth, and I stifle a giggle. I'm so tired.

"A box. Too heavy for any of us to lift. I had to make do."

"Shall I move it?"

"No, Will, just leave it. George can take care of it when he comes home." The night outside is closing in on the house, on the town. A half a world away, it must be getting close to dawn. I wonder what you see—the view from the tent of the whole world lit up below you.

"George told me this is what it feels like." I hold out the glass, watch the liquid glint and wink in the light. "At altitude. As if you've had a couple of stiff whiskeys. A bit slow, a bit off. It can be hard to make the right decision."

"Good thing we don't have to decide anything," Will says.

"Not yet."

We sit, quiet. It seems like a long time. My glass is empty.

"They are right of course, Will," I say eventually.

"About what?" His voice is far away. Sleepy.

"The letter. It is weeks old. Everything has already been decided and there's nothing we can do to change it. We both know that. Maybe George made it. Maybe not."

I stop speaking. Will is silent. How to tell him what I'm thinking? That this is the last moment before things change. That after this, nothing will stay the same. I'm waiting to find out what the rest of my life will be like, and there's nothing I can do about it. Things have already been set in motion. It's already been decided. I say what I can't help thinking.

"Maybe George is already dead."

I expect Will to protest. I want him to. I want him to say something comforting, but he doesn't.

"What do you think?" he asks.

"That I'd know? Somehow. I have to believe that. I have to believe that if anything happened to George, I would know about it. I'd *know* it. In my head. Or in my body. I'd feel it. His absence. His stopping. I don't feel anything. Nothing at all. So he can't be."

All I can feel is Will beside me. He kisses my temple. His lips are warm.

When he leaves, he promises he'll come tomorrow. "For the afternoon post," he says.

Though I know I will not sleep, I wash my face, tie back my hair, pull on my nightdress. Before I climb into bed I turn down the heavy quilt and fold it in thirds at the bottom, slip the letter I read aloud earlier back under your pillow.

I hope that I will dream about you.

In the morning I will get up again and the floor will be cold.

I will get dressed and listen for the drop of the post.

I will write to my father and to your mother.

I will work in the garden while the children play.

In the morning I will already be waiting to climb back into bed. The end of each day means you are another day gone, another day closer to home.

I close my eyes and lie still in the darkness. Outside there is the sound of crickets, the heavy scent of the garden, the soft clicking of a clock nearby.

Perhaps tomorrow there will be word. Tonight hope will have to be enough.

THE FINAL PUSH

G od, it was cold.

George tucked his hands into the relative warmth of his armpits, but still he convulsed in tremors. He bit his tongue against the shaking, the frigid temperature, and stamped his feet in ice-stiffened boots. He was going to shatter, his frozen limbs fracturing into shards that would be blown away by the steam-engine wind. They needed to move. Not moving was killing them.

As he stepped away from the tent, the mountain swam behind a swirl of wind-driven snow. The sun was already rising ahead of him. They should have been off already, but the oxygen apparatus on one of the canisters had clogged up and Sandy had done a quick, miraculous fix. They had what they needed now.

Next to him, Sandy shrugged into his pack, his hands shaking and his face pale, almost blue in the morning light. In the thin air his lips were slack and purple.

"Are you ready?" George asked.

Sandy didn't respond, only gaped blankly at him, not hearing.

"Sandy? Are you ready?" He clasped his hands to the back of Sandy's neck, forced him to meet his gaze.

"Are you ready?" Ruth had asked. On Ruth's tongue the words sounded like an accusation.

They stood together in the empty hallway, only her small suitcase at his feet. Will would carry it home for her. Their train left in an hour. She pulled gloves onto her hands, moved to wrap her muffler around her neck. He stepped closer and did it for her. She wouldn't meet his eyes, stared over his shoulder at the door.

What was it that she wanted to hear? An apology? There was nothing he could say that would change his leaving her.

The house was silent around them. The weight of it an exhalation. Empty. The children were with Cottie. She'd come and taken them just after breakfast. When she left, Cottie had kissed both his cheeks. "Come back soon?" It was a question and a plea. She blinked back tears. He ignored them.

He hadn't wanted the children to be home when he left. He'd wanted them to be the ones who walked out the door, to feel as if they were leaving him, not the other way around.

"It only makes you feel better," Ruth had said when he first suggested it. "They still know you're leaving them. John will come home and wander the house calling for you."

"It's the last time," he said.

Ruth shrugged her shoulders, drew her lips into the tight smile she used to hold back tears.

Before Cottie took them away, he held all three of them—John, Berry, Clare. They filled his arms, squirming. He had to go searching for Berry when it was time for her to go. She was hiding in the airing cupboard.

"You found me," she said, disappointed, when he opened the door.

"I did."

"I didn't want you to find me."

"Why not?"

"If you didn't find me, you wouldn't leave."

"I'll be back before you even know it. And we'll have tea with some sponge cakes and clotted cream. Just you and me, eat them all up."

When he lifted her to him, she was heavier than he remembered. He hadn't carried her in a long time. She wouldn't let go when he kneeled to put her down, her small arms clasped round his neck. The other two clambered onto him too. He held the three of them until John wriggled away, demanded to be let go.

"Come on, then, you monsters." Cottie's voice was low and she held out her hands to the three of them. John went quickly, followed by Berry. But Clare held fast to him. She smelled like fresh laundry.

He kissed the top of her head. "Go on. Set a brave example for your sister," he told her. She straightened her shoulders and walked out without glancing back.

"Are you ready?" Ruth's eyes were recriminating.

He pulled her to him with her scarf, kissed her, and then backed her toward the door, pressing her body with his. He handed her her hat, her coat, dressing her. A reverse seduction.

"Are you ready?" he asked Sandy again now. "We're a bit late. But if we set a good pace, we can still make the ridge shortly after eight."

Sandy nodded silently. He closed the clasp on Sandy's oxygen mask, watched him pull in deep breaths and relax a little into the flow of the gas once he opened the valve.

As George sealed his own mask into place, he felt a moment of panic. The pressure on his cheekbones, the rubber smell of the tubes, gave him a quick flash of trenches and creeping gas. He flailed over his shoulders to turn the valve until Sandy reached past and turned it for him. George could feel the oxygen seep into him and spread out from his lungs to his limbs, into his brain, calming him.

Encased in the mask, the ragged rhythm of his breathing, he turned in the direction of the summit. He was utterly alone now, cut off even from Sandy except for the length of rope between them. Just the mountain in front of him, the route to the top, an imagined line that led up and up.

His nerves jittered, kept him warm, so he set a good pace. He was going to make it this time. In ten hours, twelve, it would all be over.

The morning was bright and clear. Colder than he would have liked, but at least there was no snow. Even the wind seemed to have eased. Despite the late start, he couldn't have asked for a better day to climb. Confidence and adrenaline bubbled through him, energizing his limbs. As he climbed, the movement and oxygen spread a little warmth outward from his lungs to the rest of his body. He'd made the right choice, the oxygen was working. The cold fist around his heart relaxed as he found a rhythm, as his body awoke. His limbs loosened.

As they made their way quickly up into the Yellow Band, the wind picked up and screamed down at them from the summit. But it was still clear. The plume of snow off the peak spread across the solid blueness of the sky, which was darker here. At this height, night existed almost perpetually just beyond the thin veil of atmosphere. There were stars winking above him. He squinted at them, amazed, leaning into the pressing of the wind. Even if they hadn't been silenced by their masks, they'd have been unable to speak. Still, he pointed upward and then swept his arm out to indicate the peaks around them, beneath them. He wanted Sandy to take it all in. These vistas, this sweep of the world, above everything—this was what it was for. He swelled with elation.

He looked up to measure their progress. The ridge was still far away, but they were making good time, even with the wind pushing down on them. The bloody wind. Like climbing with someone on his shoulders. Once they reached the ridge, the wind would be even worse.

"Wind will kill you," Virgil told him. "It steal breath from you. From lungs." Virgil thumped his own chest, leaned over and pounded George's, then waved his hands in the swirling wind. "Careful or wind take your breath." It was another one of Virgil's stories. "A baby left outside—" Virgil held his hand over his own mouth and nose.

"Smother," George supplied. "Suffocate."

Virgil nodded. "Before it die of cold."

The wind buffeted him, tried to throw him off the mountain. The wind was the perfect weapon.

He leaned bodily into it and tried to catch his breath.

◆ ◆ ◆

HIGH IN THE YELLOW BAND, Sandy set his feet in George's footsteps and shuffled forward. When they had set out from the tent, anxiety and adrenaline had fueled him.

Now, though, the work of the climb had set into his limbs. In rowing, the start was the easy part—the jump ahead fueled by nerves. Where the weaker teams fell apart was giving in to the false burst of energy and then flagging when the monotonous pain of the race set in. They gave up too soon. He wasn't ready to concede yet, not even close. But he was feeling the climb. The hobnails on his boots skittered on the broken yellow rock, *like broken roof tiles,* someone had said.

When had that been? Sandy tried to remember. He'd been warm and hopeful. At home. Odell sat on the settee across from Sandy's mum, the tea things between them steaming in the air. "All of it might have been at the bottom of the sea," Odell was saying as he sipped his tea. "Millions of years of petrified seabeds, and who knows what all. There are probably fossils, maybe of massive sea creatures that we've never even seen."

"Mr. Odell," his mum interjected, "we appreciate what it is you're trying to do for Sandy. But he needs to finish his studies. That should be his first priority. He's too young. It's too dangerous."

"I understand your reluctance, Mrs. Irvine, Mr. Irvine." Odell set down his tea.

His mum had used the good china and they were sitting in the front room, not in the kitchen, where everyday visitors such as Mrs. Walker, the widow next door, were entertained. Sandy had known his mum would be resistant, but he'd hoped Odell could smooth the way.

"But surely Sandy proved himself in Spitsbergen. The expedition needs a man like him. The Empire needs men like him."

"Mr. Odell, the Empire used up all the men like him." Her voice was quiet, and he could hear Odell shift on the stuffed settee.

He wished they'd stop referring to him in the third person. It made him feel as though he weren't even there, a ghost.

"The college said I could go, Mum. I'll only miss one term. Maybe a bit of another one. I'll make it up. I'll still get my first."

"And think of the opportunities," Odell said. "He'll see the world. Adventure. Discipline. Leadership. When he comes back, he'll be in demand for lectures, for future expeditions. We're a proud nation of explorers, Mrs. Irvine. You know that."

"And what if something happens to him? Can you promise me he'll come back? Safe and whole?"

"I can promise I'll do my best. After all, I've already brought him back to you once before."

When Sandy returned to the sitting room after seeing Odell out, his mother was piling the tea things on the tray. The tray shook in her hands as she lifted it, the teacups rattling. She stopped in the doorway and spoke without turning around to look at him. "I don't think you should go. I don't want you to. That's all I'll say. You'll make your own choice, but I don't want you to go. It won't be on me."

But now, now she'd be so proud. He hadn't just come to Everest, he was going to the top of it.

Sandy bent down and picked up a handful of crumbling stone. He'd find the fossils Odell had been hoping for. The stones in his hands slipped through his gloved fingers, bounced off the mountain, fractured, and disappeared. There were no fossils. Not here. Odell was wrong. The mountain had been here forever.

There were tugs at his waist, sharp and staccato. He grasped the rope and turned up the slope to where George stood forty feet above him. The rope played out between the two of them. George motioned at him, waving him up the slope. He started to move again.

He should check the time. They'd set checkpoints yesterday—the ridge by eight. The Second Step by noon. The summit by three. Setting one foot in front of the other, he followed George's narrow diagonal path. The world dropped away to his right, and he stretched his left arm out so his hand grazed the face of the mountain rising up beside him. He placed each foot carefully, feeling the slip of the hobnails. It would take only one misstep and he would be hurtling down the slope, turtled on the oxygen pack. *We could race,* he thought, laughing, *all the way to the bottom.* Maybe they could just descend that way. Be back in no time at all. He'd have to tell George that. He'd think it was funny.

Out of the corner of his eye there was a flicker of green, the same color as Marjory's dressing gown. But when he turned his head there was nothing, just the vertical drop of the rock face. Nothing green. Not anywhere.

◆   ◆   ◆

WHEN HE MADE THE RIDGE, George could see in all directions—for the first time he looked down the south side of the mountain, tried to see what the route would have been like from there. Ahead of him, the thin line of the ridge stretched out to the first of the three stone steps.

"It's practically . . . ten o'clock, George," Sandy said. His mask dangled from one side of his fur-lined cap as he drank from his canteen. They'd been climbing for more than four hours. "You said . . . we should . . . be here by eight."

"Got off late. Making up time. We're fine. Still fine." It was much too soon to give in. They'd barely even started. From here it would be easy to follow the clean line of the ridge to the summit. There was no finding the route from here. There was only the Second Step ahead. "We'll make it," he said.

George stood and climbed from where they had been resting, almost hidden from the wind. At a height of more than twenty-eight thousand feet, the ridge was a knife blade that plunged away on either side of him. Out ahead were the snow cornices, whipped and molded by the wind that swept along the ridge. It was impossible to tell where the mountain ended, where the sky began. Sandy followed. George was confident he had made the right choice. Sandy had been moving well to here. If he kept him moving, he'd be fine.

He started up; Sandy would follow.

"Well done, Georgie boy. I was never able to get up this high."

"I know. I'm sorry, Traf."

It had been his brother's great joke, how George had to climb to get to these heights. Trafford just hopped into a plane.

"I mean, if you want to take the hard road . . ." Trafford had said the last time he saw him. They'd been talking of the Alps, the Pyrenees. Trafford wondered what it would be like to fly low over them. Joked he would meet him at the top of Mont Blanc someday, much less winded than George would be.

George reached out to touch the wings pinned on the khaki wool of Trafford's lapels. "Yes, well, any old fool can take the easy way up."

"Easy?" Trafford laughed. God, how he missed his laugh. "George, you would lose your lunch before we'd been up a quarter-hour. Easy!"

"Is that so? Shall we make it interesting?"

"A wager? Yes. I'll take you and your mechanically narrow little brain up, and I'll let you take me climbing. See who takes to what better, shall we?"

"I'm not sure we can get your lazy buttocks up that high without an airplane."

"So you won't take the wager? See who can get higher? See who's better?" It was an old competition, one they'd fought regularly.

"No. It's a deal. After the war."

"After the war."

They shook hands.

And then Trafford was killed during the war. "You would have been a terrible flyer," Trafford told him now. "But you are good at this." There was a pause. "Of course you would be. All the time you spent off on your adventures. You always did whatever you wanted."

"That's not fair, Traf. You had your own adventures."

"But none of mine resulted in my getting sent home from the battlefield, did they? You didn't even have to shoot yourself in the foot. You just tumbled from a sandstone wall that you shouldn't have been climbing in the first place. No, you left the real fighting, the dying, to the rest of us. To me."

George stopped on the ridge. His blood itched, cold in his veins, in his throat and lungs. All around him were lower peaks, their white caps spreading out to the horizon in every direction. As he climbed, he belayed the rope around rock outcroppings, looping over boulders and stones in the hope that it would stop a fall. Behind him, Sandy untangled it and followed him. They negotiated the space between them, the ridge at their feet. Small cascades of rock and ice rained down with each footstep.

When he looked around, he was struck by the high contrast of the peaks around him against the deep blue of the sky, everything cast in sharp relief. No one had seen this before. No one had ever been this high. Only him. And Sandy. He had to take a photograph. The entire world was below him, bright and sharp.

As he dug into his windproofs for the camera, his body was pulled down against the ridge, landing badly, his left arm caught under him. He scrambled to hold the rope against gravity and the angle of the mountain. Thirty feet down, Sandy had slipped, was scrambling for his feet on snow. George could see that he wasn't in any immediate danger, but his movements were panicked.

Finally Sandy righted himself and George collapsed back onto the ridge. His wrist throbbed where he'd landed on it. His watch was broken, the glass covering on its face shattered and pressed into his skin. He took it off, slipped it into his pocket. On his exposed skin, the blood was a dark sludge, almost black. It moved slowly, oozed.

He watched it clot in the thin air.

✦　✦　✦

HE COULD HAVE DIED.

He could have bloody died. Sandy stared down the mountain but couldn't see past his mask, past his goggles. It looked as though he were standing on nothing.

He tugged at the rope and after a beat there was a reassuring tug back. He turned carefully to see George slumped on the ridge ahead of him, maybe thirty feet away. That was it. That was all that held him to the mountain. George and their gentleman's belay. His heart pounded at his temples. He cursed into his mask.

"Just don't take a tumble off that mountain," Marjory had said with a wink. "What would I ever do if you didn't come back?"

It had all seemed such a lark then. Such an impossibility. How could he just go back to his regular life, to the way things had been? *I've seen a man die,* he'd written to Dick after Lapkha's death. He'd meant to send it, but it sounded so melodramatic. Dick wouldn't understand. How could he? And now he'd almost died himself. He tried to move but couldn't. His skin buzzed all over him. He wanted to vomit.

"You'll have to make your own decision, Sandy." Somervell's voice was in his head. "What it's worth to you."

He moved his feet upward, each step an effort. One, then the other.

He tried to keep his eye on George, who was standing now, stamping his feet, his arms hugged to his chest. But just past him on the snow slope there was someone else. A woman, tangled in the snow as if in bed linens. He tried to point to her, but his arms felt as heavy as his legs. She rolled away from him, her white shoulders disappearing into snow.

George pulled off his mask as he neared. "You're all right," he said. It was an instruction. An order. For the first time Sandy imagined George in his officer's uniform, cajoling frightened soldiers, bullying them up over the top. He must have done that. Sandy nodded.

"No one's ever made it this high, Sandy. No one. We're the first."

Around him the world seemed to move, the peaks and clouds

drifting on some kind of current. He was at sea. He turned back to George, who stepped backward, surefooted, took a photograph of him, then folded the camera away. He was favoring his left hand. "Are you all right?" There was blood on George's cuff.

"No. I'm fine. The cold's good for it."

Sandy checked his watch. "I think it's time, George."

"No." George sounded genuinely surprised. "We can still make it."

"Of course. But the gas." Sandy said, gesturing over his shoulder. "The canister will be almost empty. Time to switch them."

George checked his own empty wrist. It was bruising slightly. "Right. Right."

They stood looking at each other until George turned him around by the shoulders. Sandy tried to focus on his feet, on the ridge of snow and ice, through the long beat of suffocation, his lungs gulping for air. Then a release on his shoulders before the gas flowed again. His vision cleared and he inhaled long and deep. George dropped the tank beside him. The tank slid, slowly at first, and then picked up speed as it plunged down the south side of the mountain, into Nepal. They weren't supposed to go there.

The border seemed so arbitrary now. What could it possibly matter which side of the ridge they stood on? No, this place was theirs. His and George's. They could claim it. Like a new continent. He turned back around. George already stood with his back to him, waiting for Sandy to remove his oxygen tank. He unhooked the canister, placed it carefully on the ridge.

They were lighter now, but still the mountain dragged at him.

◆　◆　◆

AHEAD OF GEORGE LOOMED the Second Step, a rock outcropping some one hundred feet high, like the corner of a great cathedral.

"I can turn that," he said, and passed the spyglass back to Geoffrey.

"I don't know, George. You might be best to skirt it, find a way around it."

"There isn't another way. We'd have to double back. We'd have to drop down, take Teddy's route. It would take us hours."

"He can't do it. The boy. He can't climb that."

"You don't know that. I have faith in him. You used to have it in me."

"Yes, well," Geoffrey continued, "you were the one who left me behind. I should be the one climbing Everest."

Geoffrey was right, of course. It should have been him. And it probably would have been him, if not for the war. He was a better climber than any of the rest of them—Teddy, Somes, Odell. The two of them on the rope together would have been unbeatable. "If you hadn't lost your leg." It was the first time he'd ever said it aloud.

"Lost. Ha." Geoffrey laughed mirthlessly.

He'd never asked Geoffrey if they'd found his leg.

"Why not? Why didn't you ask?"

"I didn't think you wanted to talk about it."

"Bollocks, George. You didn't want to talk about it. You didn't want to know. You wanted to keep climbing as if nothing had changed."

"That's not true."

"Sure it is, George. As long as everything works out in your favor, as long as you can continue to go along on your merry way, it doesn't much matter what happens to anyone else. As long as we're still there to play the audience to your adventures."

He started to say he was sorry, but Geoffrey wasn't there. There was just him and Sandy on the ridge. He couldn't drift off like that. Had to stay focused.

He looked down below the Step, deep into the couloir.

Geoffrey was wrong. There was no way to skirt the Step, not without downclimbing at a mad angle that would send them sliding down the face. Still, the Step appeared immovable and already he felt exhausted. With every step his head throbbed and the pain rocketed down his spine, into his joints and the small of his back, where the oxygen tank had rubbed his skin raw. But it was the last obstacle. He'd pointed it out to Sandy all those weeks ago: *The Second Step— it's the only one that counts. After that it's a clear run to the base of the pyramid.*

There was someone there, below them. He could see him. He raised his arm again, to wave, to point him out to Sandy. A man, there, curled on his side. Knees drawn up. He shouldn't be there.

Wilson maybe? No. Couldn't be. Wilson was waiting for them below the North Col. Sandy, then? He focused his eyes on the shape. But Sandy was behind him on the rope. He glanced back to check on Sandy, plodding up the ridge. Slowly, painfully slow—step and stop, step and stop.

Then who was on the mountain with them?

"Higher up, on her shoulders," he heard Virgil saying, "the demons wait." When he tried to spot the man again, the shape was gone. Resolved into gray stone.

He leaned back against the wall of the Second Step and watched Sandy climbing toward him, slowing with each long minute that ticked by. He should move, at least into the patch of sun on the snow slope, out of the shadow cast by the overhang of the cliff. Instead

George closed his eyes against the bright sky, blanched to almost white at the horizon.

The stone behind him leached the heat from his body. He was shivering, his teeth chattering in the stale smell of his mask. He tried to still his body, would give anything to be warm. How long had he been climbing? Time stretched and compressed. His watch wasn't at his wrist, just smears of blood. And slivers of glass burrowing into him, drawing the cold into his veins.

He closed his eyes and there was the dry, earth scent of tea. He reached to take the cup from Ruth, but his hands were shaking. He drew them back, tucked them into his armpits and inhaled slowly before he reached out again, trying to force them steady.

"You don't look well," she said.

"Better now."

"For the tea."

"For you being here."

"Nonsense. You like your adventures. Set off every chance you get. Tuck me away at the back of the cupboard and then pick me up and dust me off when you see fit."

"No." He set down the tea, drew her to him. He could feel her warmth dissipating. She'd be cold. "No. You're perfect. I shouldn't have left. I won't leave again. You're where I want to be."

"But you have to climb her first." He couldn't tell if it was a demand or resignation. But she was right. He did have to climb her first.

And then Sandy was beside him, slumped against his shoulder. "What time is it?"

Slowly Sandy peeled back his glove, his sleeve, found his watch. "Quarter to two?" A long pause. "We should turn back. You said we should be here by noon."

"How do you feel?"

"Tired. Good. Cold. I can make it." Sandy pushed himself to his feet.

"Good." He stood, too, held his hand up to Sandy, rotated it, and waited as Sandy turned his back to him. His hands were on Sandy's shoulders. The slightest pressure and Sandy would plummet down the mountain to the glacier far below.

He unclipped the tank, slid the straps from Sandy's shoulders. He watched as Sandy's shoulders straightened a little without the weight, only to slouch again as the gas wore off.

He would have liked to hurl the canister, to make a show of throwing it in the mountain's face, but he couldn't. He let it slip from his fingers, heard the metallic clang of it, once, as it cartwheeled into space, and then disappeared below them. He turned his back to Sandy and waited for the same release. It came, but only as a brief reprieve. Without the forced oxygen, his breath came harder, slower. He struggled to send oxygen to his lungs, to his limbs, on his own. What little warmth he had curled back into his chest, his guts, retreating from his limbs.

He had hoped they would have enough gas to at least make the summit, or even part of the way back. A miscalculation. They were moving too slowly.

The stone was cold. He'd pulled off his outer mittens, had on only the thin wool gloves. He had to feel the stone, would have preferred his skin on the flesh of the mountain—stone that had never been touched, virgin behind its veil—but the tips of his fingers were numbing already, frostbite settling in. The blood in them would expand as it froze, exploding his cells, destroying them.

One hold, then another.

There was someone beside him as he climbed. Another climber, making every move he did. A reflection just off to his side. Maybe he had the better route. George reached out to him and the man beside him reached away. He had to beat him.

His lungs filled with empty air as he lifted his right foot to a hold, a tiny indentation in the face. The muscles in his legs, his back and arms, burned, the lactic acid bubbling in them. A long pause and then the pull up. An inch. Two. Just the rock in front of him. And the wind—an inaudible roar, so constant it fell silent, just a pressure on his ears, his body. And the man beside him.

At the top of the Step, George looped the rope around a stable rock, wrapped it around his waist, and felt Sandy's weight on it, stuttering and stopping. His wrist ached with the jolts. The clouds had begun to rise up around them, swelling from below, slowly swallowing the ridge in white, cutting them off from the mountain. The way to the summit was still clear, even though it was hidden coyly behind the shoulder of the mountain.

Where did he go, the other climber? The one who had been on the Step. He cast about for him. Were those footprints in the snow ahead of him? Or just the shape of the wind?

He leaned against the counterweight of the rope.

His muscles quivered against his joints and bones. He closed his eyes. Small paws crawled all over him, digging in with their claws, sending sharp currents through his limbs. Laughter. The other climber had sent them down—these creatures all over him—so he would get to the summit first. A razored talon drew a line around his scalp, then peeled back the skin. The white of his skull reflected the sunlight. Another plucked the tendon in his ankle like a bowstring. He kicked, jerked his foot away, and his hobnails caught his other leg. He barely felt it through the layers of cloth.

He jolted himself awake. What if it was on the rope? Virgil's demon. Climbing toward him.

Maybe he should cut the rope. That would be the only way to be sure that the demon didn't reach him, didn't tear him from the mountain.

"Don't be so rash, George." Will's hands were over his, helping him hold the belay. "You're always so damned rash."

"I'm not." He squeezed the words out through clenched teeth.

"That would be a first, then, no?" Will's hands were steadying. Warming.

"Maybe. But that's why we have you, Ruth and I. Someone to take care of us both."

"I have taken care of her, George. And a damn sight better than you. She would have been happier with me. You know that, don't you? She is happier with me."

The wind hollowed him out, scraped him clean, stole away what he needed to say to Will. He could see the words, scattered like bits of ribbon, blowing out over Tibet.

✦   ✦   ✦

SANDY PULLED A TIN from his pocket, put the lozenge on his tongue to try to wet it. He could hardly believe he'd made the Second Step and George was pushing on, not even allowing him a moment to rest. He had to go with him. Had to. In another minute he'd get back up. Just a minute. Two.

"Come on, slowpoke," Marjory teased him. She was standing

in the doorway, beckoning him with her finger. "Someone might see you."

What was he doing? She was right. Dick might see him. Still, his head was bubbling from the champagne at dinner and the whiskey after, the hangover already thumping behind it.

"Just one foot in front of the other," she encouraged, opening the door wider. She had changed from the pale silk dress into a robe. It was belted loosely, plunged open to reveal the long drop between her breasts.

"No." He pressed his eyes closed, shook his head. He couldn't go to her. He wouldn't. When he opened his eyes again, his mother was standing there.

"I asked you not to go, Sandy. Now please, just come home."

He stepped toward her but was stopped by a hand on his shoulder. He tried to shrug it off, but then his mum was gone and George's fingers were digging into his arm, hauling him back from where his foot hung over empty space, pulling him back to the ridge. Sandy fought to get away.

"Jesus, Sandy. Jesus." George's breath was hot on his face, his arms clasped around him, pinning him down. Slowly he calmed and collapsed to the ground. "You're all right," George was saying, over and over again. "You're all right." But he wasn't. He needed George to turn around; they should have already.

"Sandy, I need you to stay here. You're moving too slow. We won't make it at this pace. But there's still a chance. I can go on my own. I can make it. But you have to stay here and not move."

Why wouldn't George listen to him?

"Do you understand?" George's voice creaked, slipped in and out with the wind. George leaned close to him, tightened the muffler around his neck, tugged at the earflaps of his hat. It felt as though George was dressing him, preparing him.

"No," he said as George folded his arms against him, pulled his legs up. "No."

"Sandy, I need you to stay here." George was fumbling at the knot at his waist, undoing it so that they would no longer be tied together. George was leaving him behind.

He couldn't. He'd get up. Go with him. They had to do it together. He didn't want to be left alone. Not here. Struggling, he made to rise, but George's hand was on his shoulder. There was a squeeze, and a thump. "If I'm not back in an hour, two, go down." George pointed past him, down the way they'd come.

George turned up the ridge, moved off. Slow. So slow. As if he was barely moving. He could still catch him. He'd get up and follow. After a minute. A few minutes.

Sandy stared out at the horizon—at the curvature of the earth. He was so high. He tried to work out the numbers, calculate how high they must be, how far away George was. The highest thing on earth. There were things he had to remember to do: factor the angles, their rate of ascent. It had been so slow. They'd been climbing all day. All day and they still hadn't reached the summit. It was two hours away. Maybe three. He wouldn't reach it, but George might. How long had George told him to wait?

It didn't matter. He'd wait.

His heart pounded and he thought of his blood, mapped the course of it in his system, tracing its dark red color from his heart, through the aorta and then his arteries, twisting and turning. Carrying warmth. Oxygen. He pulled off his glove and watched as what little oxygen remained in his blood was leached away as it crept back toward his heart. But it was too sluggish. It would get caught up in his heart. He would die.

He didn't want to die here.

Where was George? How long had he been gone?

He numbered the hours by the angle of the sun. Time slowed. Everything slowed. The sun was getting low. Low. Nearing the peaks to the west. "We don't want to be caught out after dark," George had said. "You'll tell me when to turn around. Can you do that?"

He was supposed to turn George around and he hadn't. And if George wasn't back soon, the dark would come. The temperature would plummet. He was already so cold.

He heard his brain cells dying from the lack of oxygen. From the cold. Each of them ended with an audible *pop*, his mind bubbling like champagne. His lungs filled with fluid.

"Darling?" Marjory was curled next to him, a champagne flute in her long fingers. He wanted a drink, but she brought the glass to her lips and swallowed it down, smiling. There was sunlight streaming through white curtains. Everything was soft, white. She smelled clean, like snow. He didn't want to talk. Wanted to lie there next to her. Sleep. "Darling, do you love me?"

Why was she asking that now?

"When you come back," she purred, "what will happen? To us?"

Hadn't they already had this conversation? What had he told her before? Something that made everything all right. But he couldn't remember.

He didn't love her.

Sandy jolted awake on the mountain.

"Then why, Sandy?" Dick stood in front of him, arms crossed. He was wet, must have just come in from the rain.

"You need a towel. You should dry off. You'll catch your death."

"I'd be more concerned about you."

"I'll be all right. I just have to wait," he explained. "I have to wait for George to come back."

Nodding, Dick sat next to him, the cold radiating from his wet clothes. He wanted to move away but didn't want to upset Dick, who stared straight ahead at the white cloud that enveloped them.

"You know, Sands, he's not really your friend." Dick jerked his thumb over his shoulder, pointing up, the way George had gone. "Not the way I am. He just left you here. He wanted the summit for himself, so he left you here. And you're dying. Do you know that? You're dying, Sands. That's what he left you to."

"No. He's coming back. He had to leave me here. I'd never make it."

"Was it worth it, then?" He tried to figure that out. Was it? Maybe. "If you don't even love her?" Dick finished.

"I'll put it right, Dick."

"I don't see how."

"If you'd been here sooner," he said, "you would have seen everything. From here the earth curves away." Sandy raised his arm, described the arc in the air. "Like that."

God, it was so cold. He tried to draw breath, call for George, but choked on the dry air. His body convulsed, racked with coughing. He tried to peer through the cloud. What if George had fallen? What if he'd turned back and passed him in the gloom? He had to go down. If he went down, he could go home and set everything right. Sandy struggled to his knees.

He looked down the ridge in the fading light. It wasn't that late, was it? It was the clouds making the sky dark. The sharp edge of the ridgeline blurred into sky. He couldn't make it down the Step on his own. He couldn't do it.

He collapsed back to the rock and the anger ebbed out of him into the cold. Dropping his head to his chest, Sandy breathed into his scarf, tucked his hands between his legs. One of them was bare. Where was his glove? His hand was numb. Sandy prayed for it to end soon.

◆　◆　◆

ALONE, GEORGE CLIMBED above the cloud that stretched out around him in every direction. No peaks broke the banks of moisture, the dense softness of it. He reached for Odell's camera. There was nothing here except Everest. The cloud was so thick, he was sure it would hold him up if he stepped out into it. He could drift and float on the currents like tides.

He spread his arms for the drop and the camera tumbled from his hand, plummeting into the whiteness at his feet. Disappearing soundlessly. He watched after it.

It was gone. There'd be no record, then. No proof if he made it. Only his word. His and Sandy's. He crumpled to the mountain and peered at the long snow slope.

What did it matter, then?

He turned his back to the summit, to the wind, slipped a piece of paper out of his pocket. Then, taking care to shelter it with his body, his hands, he looked at the photograph of Ruth, his own face ripped away from it. The photograph was blurrier than he remembered. He couldn't make out her features, the curl of hair at her temple where it had escaped the pins. He had removed the pins after, so it fell across the neckline of her dress, cut across her collarbone in an auburn frizz. He couldn't make out any of that in the photograph now. He closed his eyes and tried to picture her, draw her from the white blankness of his mind. She refused to come. He could only conjure her in memory.

"I won't go on like this, George." Her face was blotchy, she'd been crying. How often had he made her cry? "I've waited and waited. I won't wait for you anymore."

He couldn't feel the paper between his frozen fingers.

When he opened his eyes, the wind was fingering the corner of the photograph. He grasped at it, but the wind slipped the paper from his hands. It disappeared into the cloud.

He shifted his body slightly on the ground and stretched out his arm, palm up, reaching toward the peak. At this angle, he could hold the summit in his hand. So close. He could taste the wind that roared down from it, that swept up from the Indian Ocean, carrying the scent of tropical rain, cleansing, warm. He could see the route drawn out in front of him. Just the long climb of the snow slope. There was nowhere to go but up or down. Maybe he didn't have a choice anymore.

"Is this it, George?" his father asked, towering over him. "Is this what it was all for? All the sacrifice?" The cold had moved past temperature to pain. George rocked against it as it crept into his veins, his heart. It curled and snaked the length of his spine. "Not that you ever made any sacrifices yourself." His father turned to glare down the ridge, his black coat stark against the cloud cover. He followed his father's stare. Sandy was down there somewhere, waiting for him.

"They all paid the price for you," his father continued. "Trafford. Ruth. Your children. That boy down there. He will wait for you. He won't leave you behind as you have him. He'll follow orders—just like the rest of them—and he will die. For this, for you. If he isn't already dead." There was a long pause. "And for what? What was it all for, again?"

There was the bright explosion of a camera flash. "Because it's there."

"Right. Because it's there. You've always been focused on what's out there, George. It's high time you focused on what's here."

"That's the bravest thing I've ever heard," Stella sighed into his ear. Her hands were in his hair, long nails scratching at him under his fur helmet. She leaned in to kiss him. George turned away from her and pressed his hands to his face, squeezed his eyes closed.

"What will they do?" Sandy whispered to him. "What will they do if we don't come back?"

He tried to imagine it. Ruth in black. His children. He pictured the candle Sandy's mother had set in her window. The flame flickered.

He couldn't just sit here. If he sat here much longer, he would die. He had to make a decision, but there was no easy choice. No good ending.

Through the banks of cloud below him he couldn't see Sandy anymore. Sandy was still alive. He had to be. The summit above the cloud was a perfect snow cone. A small, white pyramid. Clean, untouched.

It was so close.

◆　　◆　　◆

THE SUN HAD NOT QUITE SET, but it would soon, behind the banks of clouds that smudged the edges of everything. They shouldn't be up here. They should be back in their tent, with tea, the chocolate he'd kept in his pack for when they returned. When Sandy took off his goggles, the wind stung his eyes, scraped across them. He squinted. There was a shape on the ridge. Beside him. Someone next to him. George. He'd come back. But he was just sitting there. In a stupor, eyes open, staring out over the clouds. Sandy shook him then struggled to his feet, hauled George up with him. The clouds were now rising up around them, brighter than the darkening sky as though they trapped the light. He was drowning in them.

As Sandy watched, George wavered on his feet and seemed to double before his eyes—two of him standing there. Sandy tried to focus; he had to know what happened. "Did you make it? You did, didn't you?" He nodded at George, his head pounding with the effort. Sandy closed his eyes against the double vision. When he opened them again, George stood in front of him, raising his head to meet Sandy's gaze. Had he nodded? He must have. Sandy tried to smile. His swollen lips cracked.

"We have to go," George said at last.

Sandy tried to imagine the view from the summit. What would it have felt like? He tried to remember his proudest moment, but couldn't. Maybe this was it. He wished he'd been there, seen what George had seen. Everything was going to be all right. They'd done it.

George shook him roughly. "We have to go."

The world swayed. He was on a boat, waves chopping beneath him, around him. No. On the mountain. George was tying the rope around his own waist again. They were face-to-face on the mountain, the rope between them. George turned him around, let the tension play out on the rope. He felt it go taut at his back. It held him up. He began to stumble down the ridge.

It didn't matter. George had done it. They would go down and everything would be different. Everything would be fine.

✦   ✦   ✦

GEORGE WAS WADING INTO THE dim light reflecting around him, flattening everything to two dimensions. He was leading now, Sandy close behind, the rope short between them. He didn't want to lose Sandy in the gloom. Didn't want to leave him alone again on the mountain.

Feeling for his footing, he stepped, shifted his weight forward. The scree slipped out from under his boot and rattled down the mountain. He settled his foot again and moved forward. They'd been climbing from dawn to dusk, but he didn't remember the climb up. Nothing seemed familiar. There was, he remembered, a mushroom-shaped rock. He had to find that rock again. He was parched. Hungry. Nauseous. They had been climbing for more than fifteen hours. They had to be nearing the crack into the Yellow Band. Must be. He strained for the rock, the small gully they'd followed up. If he missed it in the dark . . .

"Where's the torch?" Geoffrey asked him.

"Must have left it in the tent. Shouldn't have needed it."

"Bloody stupid, George."

Yes. Bloody stupid. There was nothing for it but to keep moving. The only choice now. If he stopped, he'd never get up again. He shuffled his foot blindly forward, sucked the thin air into his lungs.

The cold radiated up through the hobnails in his boots and burned into him in freezing points. His hand was stiff around his ice axe, weak. Humiliating—how weak he was. What must Sandy think of him?

He squinted against the blackness, against the snow that was beginning to kick up. Thick flakes of it, like moths against a window.

He could hear his breath in his lungs. Cells were bursting, like tiny fireworks in his brain. He could see them, feel them, small explosions coursing through his body.

The cold and wind washed over him like water. He could feel it everywhere. Against his skin, against his legs where they pushed through the thin air, at the seams of his clothes. The cold clawed its way in. His body shivered, contracted. Tightened around him.

He stepped forward, the mountain dragging him downward.

There was tug at the rope. By the time he turned around, Sandy had righted himself and was watching the gravel and snow tumble away from him. They plodded on, stopping every step to inhale.

He stepped forward, felt the loose fall of stones.

They had to be nearly there.

He tried to count the hours back in his head. They couldn't go on for much longer.

Ahead, there was a smudge of rock. The Yellow Band. They would make it. George moved imperceptibly toward the spot, his eyes fixed on it. It shifted in the clouds and darkness, the scattershot of snow. What if he was wrong?

He stepped forward.

❖   ❖   ❖

SANDY TRIED TO PLACE his feet where George had, each step a labor. Ordered his muscles to be ready, lift, shift his weight. He couldn't believe his legs still held him; he could barely feel them. All he was was the burn in his lungs, his head, the cold burrowing into his ears, ice picks of pain. He wanted to sit down, dig into the rock and snow. Sleep. He would finish this tomorrow.

And then there was the pull of the rope and the mountain slamming into him. The last of his breath was torn from his lungs and something seized him around his chest and stomach, crushing him. He scrambled at breaking stone that ricocheted down into the inky void. He strained against the rope tearing at him, tried to grasp at anything, his last glove ripping from his hand. He clung to the ridge.

He stilled against the weight of the rope. Nothing moved except for the wind across his body and his hands, uncurling his fingers where he tried to hold on to the rope. He was cold and wet. As he tried to breathe against the rope gripping him, his head exploded in bursts of light, of color.

"George!" It was a rasp. No sound. He held the rope. His bare hand shuddered, a pale white claw. The thought came slowly. George had fallen. George was on the other end of the rope. He leaned his weight back against it, tried to reel it in. His head was fogging, his sight contracting to a pinpoint. He knocked his head back against the mountain so the pain would keep him focused. No. George had made the summit. They had to get down.

He moved his hand on the rope. Forward. Forward.

And then it was over.

He was flung back, his spine and skull bashed against the ridge of the mountain. There was no sound but the wind and his gasping in the heavy dark. He lay there swallowing air into empty lungs, feeling the pressure on them ease slightly. Still he couldn't breathe. There were streaks of color in his eyes.

"What do I do?"

"You die. Alone. Like me." Lapkha was beside him, his eyes bulging out at Sandy, who felt his own with his frozen hand.

"No. I can't."

Lapkha's breath rattled in his throat and lungs. "You not help me. No one help you."

"I'll help George. George will help me."

He hauled himself to a sitting position and began to pull back on the rope, waiting for resistance. Lapkha's bulging eyes followed his movements. When there was tension on the rope again, he'd tug on it to let George know he was there, that he was coming. He reeled it in using the crook of his arm and his good hand.

The end of the rope slipped through his numb hand in the darkness and he pulled in empty air, the rope piled beside him. The end was broken, the fray already beginning to show, the rope unwinding from itself.

He stared at it.

"Just be calm. Use your head," his father said. "Be calm. Think. You're a smart lad. You'll figure it out."

The rope had broken and George had fallen, was below him somewhere. His breath came in choked gasps. He was going to die. They both were. He didn't know how to find George. Didn't know how to find the camp. Panic rose in him like a wave. A stumbling slide downward, the scrape of scree and gravel under his feet, ripping up his legs. He tried to grasp at the mountain, to slow his descent. He had to find George. Get down. A new rhythm in his head. With each sliding step he thought he might plunge into the empty void around him. The thought stopped him for long moments and he sat, too terrified to move until the cold made him get up again, call for George. His voice was a whisper. The mountain creaking with cold. Settling.

He would rest. Just a minute.

If he rested, he could catch his breath. Could make a decision. Find George. Get down. Find the tent. Odell might be there, waiting. Watching for them. Maybe Odell was on his way up to them. No. They hadn't had a light. Odell wouldn't have seen anything. He couldn't see anything. The stars crept out above him, the clouds peeling them back.

There were tears on his face. Freezing. He wiped at them with his bare hands. Where were his gloves? He couldn't feel his fingers on his cheeks. The tips of them were white, mushroom swollen. He touched his fingers against each other—they knocked solidly.

He drew up his knees, hid his hands down between his legs. He dropped his head and breathed into the small space between his chest and his knees. He could see his breath. The condensation of it sparkled slightly, but there wasn't enough of it. Claustrophobia washed over him and he thrust his head up, back into the cold night air, gasping, shouting with what little air he could press from his lungs. His voice sounded wounded, dead.

He had to get up.

If he didn't get up, he would die, and he didn't want to die. Not alone. Not without anyone knowing. He didn't want to pay that price. He had to get down. If he told everyone what George had done, then it might be worth it.

Another minute. It was warmer now. So warm, comfortable. Like his old bed at home. He tore at his muffler. Why was he wearing that here? Pulled off his fur hat, tucked it under his head.

"I don't want to die here."

"You won't." His mum tucked the blanket in around him. It was too tight. He couldn't move. "Do you see that flame?" She pointed. But there were so many. So many flickering fires all around him. In hearths, candles in windows. Far away. They winked at him.

"Which one?" he asked.

"That one . . ."

He nodded, could barely move his head. Didn't want to move at all.

"I'll keep that one lit for you."

He focused on the twinkling fire his mother indicated. It burned brighter. It was close by. He could see his mother's candle in the window. He dragged himself toward it and tapped at the glass. He reached for the door, but couldn't find it. His hands tore at the stone wall, at the iced glass of the window.

He slumped against the house. She wouldn't let him in.

The cold bubbled in his veins. He was freezing solid. His hands holding his legs were blocks of ice.

"We made it," he tried to tell his mum.

There was no answer.

Sandy's mind floated away from his body, calm and light, the air easy in his lungs. He was dying. A flush of warmth raced through him, soothing him. Where was the pain? He wanted it back.

The blowing snow gathered around him, small drifts around his knees and chest. It no longer melted where it touched him, just brushed his face, like the back of his mum's fingers. His eyebrows were frosted, the edges of his blond hair, his hands ghost white, the blood pulled from them, the flesh frozen.

He couldn't open his eyes, iced over by the mountain.

◆　　◆　　◆

A FALSE STEP—AND THE mountain slipped out from underneath him.

He was falling, his body cartwheeling in space. "If you fall"—Geoffrey's voice in his head—"you still have three seconds to live." He'd been falling longer than that. He'd been falling forever. It didn't hurt, this eternal free fall.

Then the pain—a crushing of his ribs, his lungs, and a wrenching up where the rope caught. The air was choked out of him. He couldn't breathe. There was only pain. In his ribs. In his lungs. He wanted to scream, but it came out as a small whimper. A breath of sound. There was a moaning in his ear. Then a tearing, a release. Another moan.

The mountain rushed up to meet him.

His right foot slammed against the granite face and he heard his leg snap, audible in spite of the wind and the moaning in his head. Then the sharp burning stab of it and the white gleam of bone through flesh.

He clawed at the crumbling stone as he scraped down against the slope. His fingers and hands were shredded by the knife edges of rock that tore him apart, flaying the flesh on his chest and stomach to ribbons as his clothing was ripped away from him. The pain came in waves of heat.

Somewhere too close there was screaming that died off at the end of a breath. Then the struggle to inhale, and another scream. It was him. He was choking.

His head snapped forward, ricocheting off stone, off ice and grit. There was blood in his eyes, the warmth of it blinding him.

The mountain clung to him, refused to let him go. He slowed and stopped, his hands still tearing at the scree, scrambling for some kind of hold. His fingers were bloodied pulp. He bled onto the frozen rock.

He crossed his good leg over the broken one and tried to lift his head. He couldn't see. Couldn't breathe. His body was burning. He was grateful for the warmth.

His hands still gripped the mountain. He tried to call for Sandy. His swollen lips could barely shape the sound. And not enough air in his lungs to push the name out.

Sandy's name was a soft moan on the mountain. *Sandy.* He was sorry. *I didn't mean for this to happen.* He had to get up and go to Sandy. He had to get him home.

He tried to lift himself up, but the mountain held him close.

"Ruth?" He needed her here. "Ruth?" Where was she?

Sandy would tell her what happened. Unless Sandy fell too. No. He'd get home. He'd see Ruth. *I'm sorry. Please, forgive me. Please. Ruth?*

He looked for her but couldn't see through the blood congealing, freezing in his eyes. His split fingers pulled at the mountain. He tried to push with his broken leg. Pain shot through him. He collapsed against the mountain's face. She held him there.

He just wanted to stay still. Wanted it to end.

The mountain clung to him, claimed him. The cold seeped into his body from the stone, the air. She was lying beside him. Her breath on his cheek. Her hand on his brow. The cold numbed him, the cuts and bruises, the shattered bone shining where it pierced the flesh above his boot.

She cataloged the injuries. Caressing them, soothing them.

He existed only in the quarter-inch of flesh below the skin that no longer felt the burn of cold. His heart slowed, the blood at his temple ebbed and sparkled with the forming of tiny ice crystals.

His breath faltered, the ache in his ribs eased. The wind fingered the edges of his clothes, peeked under them, slid in against his skin. He couldn't feel her caress anymore.

His mind slowed.

He was lying on the blank snowfield of their bed, waiting. He would wait for her now. He would wait and she would come.

He was still. His heart. His breath.

His body froze around him.

He listened for the sound of her footsteps.

VISITATIONS

The morning light in the room has that curious end-of-summer hue—yellowish, as though a storm is gathering itself on the horizon. Like a fading bruise. There are no shadows, so everything appears flat, as if cast in a medieval painting—objects sized by their importance rather than perspective. The largest object in the room is the desk, with its pile of unacknowledged correspondence. But the painting of the canals on the near-empty bookshelves seems to have expanded in size, from that of a large book to something unwieldy. With effort, I take it down from where it leans, place it in the box in the center of the room. The box, too, seems very large as his belongings disappear into it. I am the only thing that is small.

In the kitchen Edith moves gingerly. She is trying to be quiet, but in the way of people tiptoeing about, her noises are all the more noticeable for it. The single clang of the kettle on the burner is more startling than the persistent small clatter she usually makes. The smell of scones wafts in the air—lemon maybe? Or lavender. And the hint of cinnamon. It is her way of doing what she can. Her way of paying tribute. The ache that I have been holding down wells up now into my lungs. I inhale and hold my breath against it. Try to get hold of myself.

The post rattles through the front door and I force myself to step into the hallway. The envelopes are scattered on the floor. So many of them. I scoop them up and pile them onto the side table without a glance. Edith is at my elbow. "Sorry, mum. I was just on my way to get that." She takes up the post and carries it away. She has done this since that first night. As if she could intercept worse news.

It was June and the children had already had their tea. I'd had a cold supper and stood reading Cottie's invitation to join her in the country. Her and Owen and the children. *I know you said you'd think about it when I saw you at dinner, but I want you to know the invitation is sincere. We would love to be with you.* Maybe we would go after all. It would be good, a change of routine, a distraction. The mail could be forwarded, Hinks given the address to find me with any immediate news.

I remember every one of those thoughts, the words in Cottie's letter.

The doorbell sounding was a surprise. Then Edith's voice. Vi was upstairs with the children. The deeper tenor of a man speaking. Hushed, low. The both of them. Cold crawled across my skin in the warm room.

In bed the previous two nights, I'd lain half awake, half dreaming. I imagined George was in bed beside me, his body long on the white of the sheet, arms stretched above his head, his face turned away.

Beside me, George was heavy, motionless. So heavy, my body rolled toward his, and I wanted to hold myself against him, feel him against the length of me. But he was so cold, I held back, only touched him with my hand. The cold seeped into my skin, up my arm, discoloring it. When I pulled back, there was the snap of cracking ice.

In the hallway the door closed and I exhaled, though I hadn't known I was holding my breath. Then footsteps came toward me, quick and shuffling. Quicker than if Edith was returning to the dishes. In my head I urged her past the parlor, back to the kitchen. *Go past. Go past.*

She was standing in the doorway, looking everywhere but at me, her lips pressed tight.

"What is it?" I was sitting. Hadn't I been standing by the window? Hadn't I been thinking about joining Cottie in the country? Her note was still in my hand.

Edith motioned to the door.

"What is it?"

She waved her hand again. "The door, mum."

There was a man, just inside the door. A small man, young, in an old suit, the black of it faded at the elbows, the cloth rubbed bare. The collar was worn. He turned his hat in his hands. Flipped it. Flip. Flip. Flip. I didn't know him.

"Can I help you?"

"Mrs. Mallory? Mrs. George Mallory?"

"Yes."

"I'm Vincent Hamilton. From *The Times*?" It was a question, as though he were unsure of his name, or perhaps he expected I would recognize him.

The dream swam in my head again and I shook it away. He just wanted to know something, I told myself, some detail about George. Something silly he hoped to make a story from: what George ate for breakfast before a climb. Did he have a lucky hat? I had nothing to say to him.

"I'm sorry, Mr. Hamilton," I said, surprised at how calm my voice sounded as I reached past him to the door to usher him out. I could smell cigarettes on him. Stale. "I'm sorry you've come all this way, and Edith should have told you I don't wish to speak to reporters. You've wasted your time, I'm afraid."

He stopped flipping his hat, stared at his feet. His hair was thinning on top, unfortunate in someone so young. When he glanced back up, his face was pale and he backed toward the door.

"Oh. Ah . . . I see."

He was reaching for the handle, preparing to leave, but I could tell there was something. I held the door shut and drew closer to him. Below the smell of cigarettes there was coffee. Alcohol, maybe. And something else. Sweat and fear. Mine or his? He was still stuttering.

"You haven't, um, haven't heard. I'm sorry. They assured me. At the paper. Said the Committee had told you. I didn't want to come anyway. We would never . . . I wouldn't have come . . . But it will be in the paper tomorrow. They said we could print it. And I was only sent here to ask about it. But you were supposed to know. We only . . . I mean, the paper only wanted to know if you had something to say." He wasn't making sense.

"About what?" My voice sounded as far away as I wanted to be. Wherever George was.

"About your husband? About Mr. Mallory?"

"I already told you, I have nothing to say."

"But he's dead." The word exploded out of him.

And everything stopped. Just for a beat. The world was a tiny pinpoint of light and a cold wind in my mind, like a scraping away, a scraping clean. My lungs hurt, my ribs pressed against them. I couldn't breathe. There was a strange huffing sound. Uneven. It was me.

Staring at the door now, two months later, at the sunlight coming through squares of colored glass, I feel it wash over me again.

He calmed then, in the face of my panic. "We received this today. This afternoon."

He held out a piece of paper. A telegram. The sheet of onionskin in my hands. Words typed in black letters. MALLORY IRVINE NOVE REMAINDER ALCEDO. Above it something written in pencil. The word *killed*.

Killed.

"They died, ma'am. George Mallory and Andrew Irvine. Did you know him, too, ma'am? I'm sorry. They were making an attempt. I'm sorry."

He kept saying he was sorry. As if it were his fault. As if it would help.

He asked, was I all right? Was there someone he could fetch for me? Then he remembered himself—was there anything I'd like to say? For the papers? For the people?

The clock chimes. I count. Ten. Eleven.

Eleven already. Colonel Norton and Mr. Odell will be arriving soon. In the sitting room a small round table has been set for three near the window. Edith has put out the good lace tablecloth George sent me from Belgium during the war. The good china. The silver polished so brightly, it gleams in the shafts of sunlight. Edith has been baking. She has made sandwiches on fresh bread. Everything we can offer. I have set aside a bottle of wine. There is ice, should they want something stronger than tea. Whiskey. They may need it. I might.

Upstairs, I check myself in the mirror, make sure I appear put together. Calm. I don't want them to think I'm a woman who is about to break down, though that's how I feel. As though I might break apart, might shatter. I pinch my cheeks, push back my hair. My face looks pale against the black collar. Then I sit on the edge of the bed and wait for the sound of the bell.

I will have to pack up this room soon. Send the clothes, the photographs, to my father's and set them up there. He's offered to buy new furniture, and for the children I have agreed. For me, I want to take this bed.

We talked about this happening. George and I. Right here.

It was after the fights had ended. He was packing but I'd refused to help him, only half teasing that I wouldn't make it easier for him to leave.

"What happens if . . ." I couldn't say it. I took a pair of his wool socks and hid them under my pillow.

"If what?"

"If something happens? If you don't come back?"

I'd never said it before. We'd never talked about it, all through the war, or the first trips to Everest. I tried not to even think about it. Why did I say it then? Did my saying it make it happen?

"George?" He stopped then and focused on me. I didn't want to cry. "I mean it. I want to know. What if you don't come back? How do I go on?"

"You'll take care of the children. You'll be sad. And then less so. Maybe you'll remarry. You'll carry on. But don't worry, Mouse. Everything will be fine."

"Will it?"

"Yes."

It rises up like this. Not the grief; the grief is always there. As I described it to Geoffrey, *I feel numbed and quite unable to realize, there is only just pain. It has only just happened and one has to go through with it.* No, the pain doesn't scare me.

It is the other things. I can't remember when I last told him I loved him. I should have said it on the gangplank. I must have. I would have. But what if I didn't?

I try to conjure him now.

"George?"

But there's no answer.

Two months later I am still piecing the story together. From letters and telegrams. From the eulogizing newspapers. In every way that I dreaded.

At 7:45, a half-hour after the reporter from *The Times* had left, the telegram from Hinks arrived. Edith was sitting with me in the front room and jolted when the doorbell rang again. We'd been silent for so long. She had made tea, sat with me, tried to stifle her own cries. "Do you want me to fetch the children?" she'd asked.

"No. Let them have one more quiet night. I'll tell them in the morning."

She peeked at me and went to the door. I couldn't cry. I wouldn't. If I cried, it might be more real. As it was, when the door rang, I thought, *At last, they're going to say it was all a mistake.*

Edith came in with the other telegram.

MRS MALLORY HERSCHEL HOUSE CAMBRIDGE

COMMITTEE DEEPLY REGRET RECEIVE BAD NEWS EVEREST
EXPEDITION TODAY NORTON CABLES YOUR HUSBAND AND

IRVINE KILLED LAST CLIMB REMAINDER RETURNED SAFE
PRESIDENT AND COMMITTEE OFFER YOU AND FAMILY
HEARTFELT SYMPATHY HAVE TELEGRAPHED GEORGES FATHER

HINKS

I told the children the next morning. Vi brought them to me in our room. In my room.

"Come sit," I said. And patted the bedclothes next to me. John scrambled up quickly, followed by Berry. Clare came slowly, perched on the edge. "Come closer, Clare. Please?" She curled her feet under her and sat at the foot of the bed, cross-legged. I barely knew how to begin. "There is some bad news, I'm afraid."

They were silent, the three of them. Still, as they never are. Clare's face creased. "What is it, Mummy?"

"Come sit by me." I scooped John onto my lap, Berry to one side, and Clare conceded, crawled to me, leaned against my side. They hemmed me in, held me up.

What were the words? *An accident? Killed*—like in the telegram? *Disappeared?* What did any of them mean?

"You know," I began, "that what your daddy is doing is very dangerous."

"Climbing the mountain?" Berry asked.

"Yes. The mountain."

"But Daddy's brave and strong," Clare said. "You said so."

John sucked his thumb, stared from his sister to me.

"Yes."

"Good." Clare tried to get down.

"Not yet, pet." I pulled her back to me. She went stiff, like deadweight. She didn't resist, but she didn't help.

"Something's happened," I said. But that felt like a lie. What had happened? Some man had come to our door and said words. A telegram had arrived. Why should those things be believed? It was only just words on a piece of paper. From day to day, nothing has changed, just the knowing. The plummeting in my stomach tells me things aren't the same. The constant ache in my bones.

And for just the briefest moment there was a flare of anger, like an electric current, in my stomach. That this is what I have to do. That I have to tell my children this.

Beside me, Clare huffed, impatient, not wanting to hear.

"Daddy's had an . . . an accident."

"Is he hurt?" Berry asked. "Who will kiss him better?"

"No, he isn't hurt. Not anymore." That is something, at least. "But he won't be coming home."

"Shall we visit him in hospital?"

I won't say the word. "No, love. He's been . . . lost."

Clare's eyes bore into me. "You said he'd be all right. You promised." She began to cry.

Berry reached over to her. "It's all right. Maybe we can find him."

Edith shows the two men in. I haven't seen them in almost seven months. They are both thin, drawn. The skin of their faces stretches tight across their cheekbones, across their set jaws. The colonel's lips are turned down, Odell's tight together.

"Colonel Norton. Mr. Odell. How good of you to come." I stand and they cross the room toward me.

"Please, Ruth. Call me Teddy." His hands are light on my shoulders and he leans forward to kiss my cheek. He steps away and Odell reaches forward to do the same.

Last week I wrote to Geoffrey: *You share George with me, the pain and the joy. I never owned him, I never wanted to. We all had our own parts of him. My part was tenderer and nearer than anyone else's but it was only my part.* And now these men can claim part of you too. They are the last men to have seen you alive. Aside from the boy. His parents are grieving, of course, and I have sent them my condolences. Odell and Norton will no doubt visit them the same way, if they haven't already. Maybe there is a sweetheart somewhere weeping for him. Someone who thought she might marry him.

"There's tea." I gesture at the table. Everything in its place. "But perhaps you might like something stronger? I know it's early, but at a time like this it's best not to stand on ceremony, I think. Don't you? My father always says whiskey—Irish in times of sorrow, Scotch in times of joy."

They both nod, standing still. I gesture at the seats and step to the drinks cart. Pour three glasses. When I turn, they are still standing. I sit so they will.

"I trust your voyage wasn't too taxing?" My mouth remembers what to say, how to be polite. There are routines for a reason, scripts that we follow, roles we slide ourselves into. I hand them stiff tumblers of whiskey.

"No, it was fine. Just fine."

Norton begins to tell me how sorry he is, and I watch his mouth move. The condolences have come like a torrent. From all over. All the people who loved him. The strangers who followed every detail. There have been reams of headlines in the newspapers. Most recently someone got hold of the telegram the King had sent to me, to the Irvines, too, I suppose: *They will ever be remembered as fine examples of mountaineers, ready to risk their lives for their companions and to face dangers on behalf of science and discovery.* They are proclaimed as victors and warriors, described as *compassionate, brotherly and the pure in heart.* No doubt it is true, but not because of Everest. Hinks is planning a memorial service at St. Paul's Cathedral. The bishop will give the address. The prime minister will attend.

But all I think about is walking with George in the hills at Asolo the day after he slipped the note under my door in Venice. Before all of this was even a thought. We took a bottle of wine with us and sat overlooking Browning's villa, the views of the terraced gardens, the vineyards and the town stretched out below. Everything clinging precariously to the hills. On the steeper portions I reached for your hand, held it tight in mine.

"You must have questions," Norton says, pulling me back. "We'd like to be able to tell you anything we can."

I want to ask if they believe it was worth it. If they will go back. "Just tell me what happened."

"Unfortunately, we don't really know."

"You must have a thought. Some idea?"

"It's likely—" Odell speaks up. Until now Norton has done all the talking, in the calm, measured tone that I remember from our previous meetings. Odell, though, seems more nervous than I recall him. He sweats a little across his forehead, wipes at it, rushes through his words as though he's rehearsed them but might forget what he means to say, and say what he means instead. "It's likely that they were benighted. Probably on their way down. They couldn't have survived a night out there."

They have agreed to this, on this order of events, on this story. There will be no discussion of accidents or falls. There will be no blood. *Dear Mrs. Mallory, your husband died quickly and without any pain.*

"There was no sign of them? Did you look? I'm sorry, I don't mean to accuse . . ."

"No. Of course. I did." Odell nods. "I went up after them, Mrs. Mallory."

The name slices through me. "Ruth," I say.

"Ruth. I did. I was running support for the attempt. Saw them off the day before. I was one camp below them. I was to follow them up to the high camp, make sure there was food, water, fuel. I would have waited there for them then, but there's only one tent up there. Not much of a place to stay. Desolate."

"Typical of Everest," Norton cuts in. He doesn't want me to picture it, but it's too late. I see one wind-whipped tent, snow tossed in the gale, feel the freezing air.

How often have they told this story? It has been relayed down the mountain, across valleys and then the sea to here. They will have told it over and over again, trying to change the way it ends. And yet it doesn't.

"Of course they had a perfect day for it," Odell goes on. He picks up his glass, holds it in his hand, but doesn't drink. "A perfect day. I was on my own on the mountain, feeling good. Well, as good as one can up there." Norton clears his throat. A warning. He has told Odell to be careful with me. Nothing discomforting. "There had been some cloud up high on the mountain and then it cleared. The clouds stripped away for a moment and the whole ridge was there. Early afternoon. Ten to one."

He is precise with the time. As if to confirm it, the clock on the mantel strikes a sharp eleven-thirty.

"I'd just found the first ever fossil on Everest. I'd made a note of it and the time. I was excited. Then I turned toward the peak. And I saw them. One tiny black spot on a crest. At the time I was sure it was the Second Step." He glances now at Norton, who isn't looking at him but gazing over my shoulder. "But it might have been the First," Odell continues. I want to tell him it doesn't matter. "It moved up and then another one followed. I yelled. I knew they couldn't hear me. But they were moving well. And as I say, I was excited. They were moving so well. It had to be them. Your husband. And Sandy." His voice catches a little on the boy's name and he glances toward the window, his eyes wet. As he blinks against the tears, I remember George saying Odell had traveled with the boy before. Had recommended him. "They were going to make it. They would have had to move fast to get back before nightfall, but they looked strong. They looked strong."

He pauses a moment and then drinks. His hands shake a little. "And then the clouds closed in. I didn't see them again. When I got to their tent, it was a mess. Hardly surprising. And a note from George that they'd knocked the cooker down the slope in their hurry, so they'd come down to Camp Five that night. Maybe even to Four. I should be ready to head down when they arrived."

"Do you have the note?" I want to have it. The last thing he wrote. His last words.

"I'm sorry," Norton says when Odell looks at him. "It was given to the Committee for the archives."

"No. Of course. It would be, wouldn't it?" It feels as if George is slipping away. Becoming something others can claim. Less mine. "Please, carry on."

"I left them what I had in my pack. Some pemmican. A little chocolate. I hadn't thought to bring a stove. I wrapped my canteen in their sleeping bags, hoping it wouldn't freeze before they got back.

George had left his compass at Camp Five. I brought it for him. Placed it carefully where he would see it. Then I closed up the tent."

Odell tells me how he lay awake most of the night, listening, crawling out of his tent to squint up at the dark slopes, hoping for a light, anything. There was no sign of them. No hint that anything was alive up there.

"We watched too," Norton says. "From down below. Trying to guess what was going on up there."

"You were watching? I understood you were snow-blind."

"Of course. Howard Somervell was, though. He was my eyes for those couple of days."

"I was out of my tent at first light," Odell goes on. He is testifying, as though the only witness in front of a court of law, and I am the judge. "The weather was even better than it had been the day before. Clear all the way to the summit, not too cold. But I was tired. I'd been several days at that height. Still, I kept moving, because I expected to see them, truly, at any moment. But I got to Camp Six and didn't see any sign of them.

"And the tent was just as I left it. Closed up. Quiet. I called for them before I got there, but nothing. Still, I hoped. They might just be exhausted. I'd rouse them, get them down. When I opened the tent, there was George's compass just as I'd left it. Everything just as I left it.

"I went out and climbed up the way they would have gone. Called for them. Looked for some sign. But there was nothing. I called for Sandy. I thought I could hear him if the wind would stop." His voice is fracturing now. He gulps down the rest of his whiskey. "You can't know what it is like up there. Impossible to do anything, to move quickly. I'd been up there for days. I was tired."

Norton glances over at him, a reprimand. The kind of look Clare often gives to Berry. Odell inhales deeply and calms somewhat. The wind has picked up and is tossing the leaves on the oak tree outside so that the light ripples. We are underwater. All of us.

"There was no trace of them. Not even footprints in the snow. Nothing." Odell picks up his glass, sets it back down without drinking. "I'm so sorry."

I see him standing there. The hope ebbing out as the cold settled on him. What it must have been like to accept that no matter how long he waited, they weren't coming back. I wonder if he realized that at that moment he was the highest living thing on earth.

"I went back to the tent to gather their belongings. To send down the message."

"There was a code," Norton explains. "So we would know what happened. So we would know what we had to do. If we should send someone up."

Of course there had been a plan for this. A plan for disaster. George would have helped determine what that would be. They all would have known.

Nothing on the table has been touched. "You should eat something," I say. "Edith worked so hard. Baked everything fresh herself. George loves these scones. Please."

Neither of them moves. Norton shakes his head slightly. "I shouldn't have let him go. I'm sorry. I said it to Somes. I even thought about calling them back down. But George seemed to need it. Still, I could have ordered him not to go. I did ask him not to, but I should have ordered it."

"There's a crate coming from the station," Odell tells me. "George's belongings. I packed up everything, didn't look through it. But there's this." He hands me the compass George had forgotten, and an envelope. "When I pulled out the sleeping bags I found it under one of them. Your name was on it. I wanted to be sure you got it."

"Thank you." I take the envelope. I don't ask if they think he made the summit.

All day I've kept the envelope with me. I am frightened by what it might contain. What the contents might say. What they might not. The weight of the compass in my pocket a small comfort.

This day, like all of them since you left, has ticked by, filled with the endless work of moving on. After tea there were more boxes to be packed, letters to reply to, the children to be fed. I am still waiting. I cannot help but feel, somewhere, deep in my stomach, that you are on your way home. So I wait.

There are so many things left unsaid between us. I sit at your desk and make a list of them. The things I should have said. All the things I've been collecting to tell you. The house is settling in for the night, almost quiet. Most everything is in its place—ready to go. The day after tomorrow we will leave for my father's. We will live at Westbrook, at least for a while. I'll teach John to swim in the pond there, to ride a bicycle, just as my sisters and I did. Will has promised to visit as often as he can.

I leave the sheet of paper in the middle of the desk. When I turn off the light, it seems to glow in the dark before I close the door.

Up the stairs the children are sleeping soundly. When we go to my father's, Clare will have her own room. Berry and John will share one for a while longer. From the veranda outside my father's dining room I will be able to see the Holt. I'll point it out to them. "That's where we used to live."

"With Daddy," they'll say.

They seem to be doing well. John has developed a limp that the doctors think is psychosomatic. "A physical manifestation of his pain," they say. They tell me to ignore it. But how can I, when it is a reminder every day of what he has lost? What *I* have lost.

I bend and kiss each of them. Only Clare stirs, rolls over, and settles again. Then I descend the stairs to our room.

The sheets are cool, and I curl my feet under my nightdress. I put the compass on your pillow, hold the envelope to my face.

It smells of paper. That's all. I open it and pull out a yellowed piece of paper, torn at the edge, words and letters missing. The last page. The end of the story.

The words you have written in the margin are shaky and uneven and blur through my tears. The last thing you will ever write. This was meant just for me. I won't share this part with anyone.

As the clock chimes downstairs, I curl on my side with this last page, and the white expanse of the pillow, the snowfield sheet beyond, stretches out in front of me.

AUTHOR'S NOTE

Above All Things is a work of fiction inspired by historical events. When I first encountered the stories of the early Everest expeditions, I didn't even have the facts; all I had was the myth.

I was first introduced to the story of George Mallory while working at a local outfitter's, selling climbing and camping gear. There was a television set on the shop floor that played gear videos, mountain movies, and adventure documentaries. My favorite documentary was one that showed black-and-white footage of the earliest attempts to climb Mount Everest. That was how I first saw George Mallory: in pith helmet and knee-high socks, crossing the Himalaya. From the very start, that image and the story of his disappearance had me hooked.

The mythology surrounding Mallory is unmistakably grand. He was one of the last of the classic English gentlemen explorers—an athlete, a scholar, and a writer with ties to the Bloomsbury Group. He was outrageously attractive: "six foot high, with the body of an athlete by Praxiteles, and a face—oh incredible—the mystery of Botticelli, the refinement and delicacy of a Chinese print, the youth and piquancy of an imaginable English boy," as Lytton Strachey described him. He was a romantic figure nicknamed "Galahad" by his friends, and when he was asked why he wanted to climb Mount Everest, he gave what is perhaps one of the most enigmatic quotes of the last century: "Because it's there."

But myths are only ever a beginning, so even before I knew I would spend years writing about Mallory, I started reading everything I could about Everest in general and, in particular, about Mallory and the British expeditions of the 1920s. I was fascinated by the sheer ambition of the first attempts—by the degree of optimism and obsession that the summit bids must have necessitated, and by the men who willingly endured the discomfort and pain of freezing temperatures and the many dangers of extreme altitudes dressed in little more than Burberry tweeds.

But early on, too, I couldn't help wondering what it would mean to be married to a man like George Mallory. What would it be like to be left behind for months at a time with nothing but long-delayed letters, delivered by steamer, to soothe your worries? How would you fill your days? How would you cope with the possibility that your husband might not come home?

Before long, I found myself writing a novel.

Thanks to a grant from the Canada Council for the Arts, I was able to travel to England, where I visited the Royal Geographical Society, the Alpine Club, and the Pepys Library at Magdalene College, Cambridge. As it was Mallory's old stomping grounds, Cambridge was my first stop; this was where he went to college and climbed its towers, where he had his early love affairs, and where, ultimately, he left behind his wife and his three children when he joined his third expedition to Everest. It was at Magdalene that I had the opportunity to read the letters Mallory and his wife, Ruth, had exchanged over their entire relationship—from his first love poem to her to the very last letter he sent from Everest.

With its dusty tomes and shafts of light filtering through leaded-glass windows, the library at Magdalene College looked like a movie set for an old English college library, and Dr. Richard Luckett, the Pepys librarian, with his cane and mane of gray hair, could have been straight from central casting.

After quizzing me about my book and what I thought might have happened to Mallory, Dr. Luckett explained to me that the Pepys Library was the official repository for all the Mallory personal papers. He apologized for some of the papers they didn't have, and then he sighed and said, "I suppose you'd like to see the letters?"

"Of course," I said gamely, though I wasn't even sure which letters he meant.

Dr. Luckett opened a large leather book he'd been carrying and slipped out a plastic envelope, which he handed to me. "Go ahead."

I pulled the thin papers out. They were folded, their edges worn and dirtied. I looked at the first one. I knew this letter: I'd seen photographs of it in books about Mallory. These were the papers that had been found on George's body when it was discovered in 1999: letters, receipts, lists of oxygen bottles. My throat caught. I'd already been living with George and Ruth in my head for more than a year. I often joked to friends that if it was possible to be in love with someone who had died some eighty years earlier, then I was certainly in love with George—and these were the documents he had carried with him when he died. I tried not to cry. This was to happen to me over and over again as I sought as much information as I could about the real George and Ruth—the surprise of coming across a particular document, or artifact, that I wasn't expecting. Eventually, Dr. Luckett took the papers back and left me to my research.

There is something unsettling about reading a couple's private letters. Here they all were, hundreds of them in some four or five boxes—loving assurances George had written to Ruth, confessions (often misspelled) Ruth had written to George of her worries that she might not be a good parent, of her "behaving terribly" before his final departure. And always, always, this lilting love that ebbed and flowed but never disappeared. "I love you," Ruth wrote to George during the First World War, "and you love me, and that ought to be happiness enough for a lifetime but I do want to live together all the time and share thoughts and joys and sorrows and we can't apart as we can together."

It was through these documents and letters, these photographs and ephemera, that George and Ruth began to leap from the page for me. They became very separate from the historical record, separate from who they may have been in their real lives. It's a strange paradox that it was their own words that helped me make the jump to fiction. George and Ruth were no longer simply the tragic hero and his deserted, dedicated wife, the roles in which they had long been cast. Being able to see them as they were, to hear them speak in their own words and in their private moments, gave me the confidence to allow them to be who they needed to be on the page.

Above All Things is a work of fiction, and in writing a novel based on historical figures, you have to make your own rules: you have to decide how faithful to be to the known record and make tough choices about what to keep in and what to leave behind, and what to alter, trim, or expand for dramatic purposes. As such, characters have been conflated, geographies shifted, and timelines altered and compressed for clarity or dramatic effect. There are a few particular deviations from the historical record that I would like to acknowledge.

Mallory's brother, Trafford Leigh-Mallory, was a squadron commander in the RAF. He survived the First World War and died in a plane crash in the French Alps in 1944. I believe the heavy shadow of the war was a galvanizing factor for the men of the earliest Everest expeditions, and, for me, the death of an actual brother alongside the deaths of so many brothers-in-arms became a way to articulate the grievous loss and guilt that George and others of his generation must have felt as a result of simply surviving.

Maurice Wilson did fly a plane to Everest and attempt to meditate his way to the summit. The facts of Wilson's story are much as George describes them to Sandy, with the exception that Wilson's illness and recovery occurred much later, in 1932, and he made his attempt on Everest in 1934.

Although Alfred Wegener proposed his theory of Continental Drift in 1912, it was not widely accepted until the theory of plate tectonics was put forward in the 1960s. The idea of plate tectonics also anachronistically informs Ruth's meditations in the Round Church in Cambridge.

As for the depiction of the technical aspects of the climb, I have followed the general, up-and-down, siege-style mentality—climb high, sleep low—that has characterized Everest attempts since the very beginning.

For many readers, of course, the biggest question will be what happened to George and Sandy. I examined what little factual evidence exists regarding the events of that fateful day and, like everyone who reads about their disappearance, I formed my own opinions as to whether they made the summit and what might have happened on the way up or down. I have tried to keep as much to what is "known" about George and Sandy's final climb as I could, accounting for what we do know and exploring what we don't, which is a great deal. The reader may wish to know that Will Arnold-Forster was a good friend and support to both George and Ruth throughout their lives, and indeed, it was to Will that George first confided his feelings for Ruth Turner. In 1937, some thirteen years after George's disappearance, Ruth and Will were married. She died shortly thereafter, in 1942, of cancer. Will died in 1951.

George's body was discovered on May 1, 1999, by Conrad Anker and the Mallory and Irvine Research Expedition. The discovery made headlines around the world and answered some questions about what might have happened to George and Sandy on June 8, 1924. The position and state of the body made it evident that there had been an accident of some kind high on the slopes of Everest, but it could not answer the greater question: Was George Mallory the first man to reach the summit of Everest?

George did, in fact, carry a photograph of Ruth with him to Everest that he promised he would leave on the summit. Some people point to the fact that the photograph was not found on his body as proof that he did reach the top of Everest. However, the photograph has not been sighted at the summit, either. Professional opinion on the likelihood of George and Sandy reaching the summit is varied, but some researchers still hold out hope that if Sandy's body can be found, and perhaps a camera recovered, a definitive answer to that question may yet be forthcoming. If you would like to learn more about the real George Mallory, there are a number of outstanding nonfiction works available, and I am indebted to too many of them to name them all here. I would like to especially acknowledge *The Wildest Dream: Mallory, His Life and Conflicting Passions* by Peter and Leni Gillman; *Fearless on Everest: The Quest for Sandy Irvine* by Julie Summers; *George Mallory* by David Robertson; *The Irvine Diaries: Andrew Irvine and the Enigma of Everest, 1924* by Herbert Carr; *Lost on Everest: The Search for Mallory & Irvine* by Peter Firstbrook; *The Lost Explorer: Finding Mallory on Mount Everest* by Conrad Anker and David Roberts; and *Ghosts of Everest: The Search for Mallory & Irvine* by Jochen Hemmlab, Larry A. Johnston, and Eric R. Simonson; as well as numerous books about Everest itself, including Jon Krakauer's classic *Into Thin Air: A Personal Account of the Mt. Everest Disaster,* Stephen Venables's *Everest: Summit of Achievement,* and Lincoln Hall's *Dead Lucky: Life After Death on Mount Everest,* which inspired the descriptions of Sandy's final moments on the mountain.

For a complete list of resources as well as a further discussion of fact versus fiction, please visit my website, www.tanisrideout.com.

ACKNOWLEDGMENTS

I cannot thank my editor, Anita Chong, enough for her profound insight, guidance, direction, and commitment to this novel. It really would not be what it is without her. I'm extremely grateful to Amy Einhorn and the team at Amy Einhorn Books/Putnam and Venetia Butterfield of Viking/Penguin UK for their additional insights, suggestions, and support.

For reading early drafts and excerpts, I'd like to thank Simon Racioppa, Jill Barber, Ian Daffern, Stephanie Earp, Britta Gaddes, Sarah Harmer, Sheetal Rawal, Carolyn Smart, and Tate Young.

Thanks to Natalie and Nigel Piper for a place to stay and for showing me some of Mallory's old haunts and around the English countryside.

And to friends and family for their ongoing love and encouragement.

I'm extremely grateful to the staff at the Pepys Library, Magdalene College, Cambridge, and to the Royal Geographical Society, the Alpine Club, the British Film Institute, and the British Library.

Portions of this work could not have been undertaken without the financial support of the Canada Council for the Arts, the Ontario Arts Council's Writers' Reserve, and the Toronto Arts Council.

An early excerpt from the novel appeared in *PRISM International* magazine.

ABOUT THE AUTHOR

Tanis Rideout's work has appeared in numerous publications and has been shortlisted for several prizes, including the Bronwen Wallace Memorial Award and the CBC Literary Awards. Born in Belgium, she grew up in Bermuda and in Kingston, Ontario, and now lives in Toronto, where she received her MFA from the University of Guelph-Humber. *Above All Things* is her first novel. For more, visit www.tanisrideout.com.